THE FACTORY GIRL AND THE FEY

NADINE GALINSKY FELDMAN

Editors: Rosie McCaffrey and Esther White

ISBN: 978-1-7368069-0-6

Ebook ISBN: 978-1-7368069-1-3

Names: Feldman, Nadine, 1958-author.

Title: The Factory Girl and and the Fey

Identifiers: LCCN 2021911827 (print) | LCCN 2021912884 (ebook)

Subjects: Historical Fantasy, World Literature Scotland 19th Century

❀ Created with Vellum

To the 19th century Scottish poet Ellen Johnston, aka the Factory Girl.

To the young women who toiled in adverse conditions in the mills,
whose stories were lost to history.

To the Fair Folk who snuck in uninvited to this manuscript and
charmed me into letting them stay.

To my mother, Lewellyn Stein Pulliam,
who shared stories of her beloved grandfather, Hugh Stein,
a Scottish immigrant who never lost his love for his homeland.

Finally, to the real Jane Thorburn,
my great-great-grandmother. Welcome back to the family.
In this story, you live forever.

CHAPTER 1

Come up here, O dusty feet!
Here is fairy bread to eat.
Here in my retiring room,
Children, you may dine,
On the golden smell of broom
And the shade of pine;
And when you have eaten well,
Fairy stories hear and tell.

Fairy Bread
Robert Louis Stevenson

*T*he newborn shivered in her cradle, eyes closed, trying to make sense of a new reality where she no longer bathed snug in the warm fluid of her mother's womb. Endless space surrounded her. Her arms and legs moved freely now, both intriguing and terrifying her. She lay near enough to the shimmering glow of the firelight to hear its crackles, hisses, and pops, but too far to benefit from its heat.

There were strange smells, too: stale cigar smoke, the sour

stench of the bodies of her father, mother and two boarders who lived packed together in this single room, and the more pleasant scent of the porridge her mother made for breakfast. The infant had no names for these things and understood nothing of her father's long workdays in the coal mine or her birth into poverty. She understood only this: she had entered a strange, new world.

Dim sunlight came through the one window, blocked in part by thick clouds. The woman, her mother, leaned over the cradle and placed a calloused hand on the child's forehead.

"Ye're cold," she said. She removed her shawl and laid it over the bairn, tucking it around her with tender care. "I'm off tae put up some wash. Sleep, lass, an' I'll return soon."

The newborn sighed with satisfaction. Warmer now, she settled in for a nap in the stillness of the now-empty room, safe in the knowledge that the woman would care for all her needs.

"MOVE QUICKLY," said a high-pitched, tinny voice. "Her ma's outside."

The child opened her sleepy eyes to a wondrous sight. Until now, everything in her world overwhelmed her with its size. Yet here were several beings who shared her smallness. She found comfort in this. And unlike the larger beings who cared for her, this group seemed inquisitive, interested—even loving. Of course, she did not know these words yet, but she sensed them, as all children do.

Her visitors had golden wings that cast pinpricks of light across the gloomy room, adding a brightness that the clouds had stolen. Their clothes shimmered in vivid colors, and they all wore snug-fitting red caps.

A couple of them wove silver threads, their fingers moving deftly to create a supportive basket, and, gathering close together like a swarm of bees, they lifted the child from her cradle, suspending her in midair.

"Don't let her fall," one of them said.

Out of nowhere appeared another child exactly her size, shape, and dressed exactly like her, which they placed in the cradle, smoothing a shawl around it as her mother had done for her.

"Ready?" one of them asked, her voice as melodic as the birds that tweeted outside the window.

"Aye," said another.

Then they were outside, and the chilly outdoor air stung the child's cheeks. This is how wee Jane Thorburn found herself soaring through the air on a spring morning, tickled by fairy wings.

While her mother, Elizabeth, hang the washing out to dry, instinct warned her to hurry back to the flat, where she leaned over the cradle to take a look at her daughter. The child turned away as if hiding a secret. Taking her in her arms, Elizabeth inspected her closely. The same hair, lighter than most newborns, with a reddish tinge to it; the same solemn, blue-gray eyes that overwhelmed her wee face; the same tiny body that had slipped out of Elizabeth's womb with no effort...but this wee bairn stared at her with expressionless eyes. Even worse, her scent lost its natural sweetness, replaced by a subtle but unmistakable rot. This child was not her daughter. She was a changeling.

Elizabeth pressed her fist to her mouth in shock. Right behind that feeling, though, was another, one that surprised her: relief.

Ever since her daughter's birth a few weeks before, she had been seized by a deep melancholy. What would she do with a lass? Women were banned from the better-paying jobs in the mines and were limited to working as "pit brow lasses," picking stones from the coal as it came to the surface. A daughter was more trouble than she was worth.

But while Elizabeth's maternal instinct resembled the flicker of a firefly more than a healthy fire, the flame did exist. That fleeting moment of relief dissolved quickly into real panic. How would she explain this to Robert? To her friends?

She ran into the hallway to the next flat, feeling the stone cold on her feet despite wearing heavy socks, and she banged on the door, shouting until her friend Ellen answered.

"What's wrong?" Ellen asked, stifling a yawn and blinking her tired eyes to keep them open. Her dark brown hair, with a premature smattering of gray strands, hung in uncombed strings. Her two young children wailed in the background. "Sorry, we had a bit of a rough night here, an' I feel like I've lost the whole day."

"Fetch Beitris," Elizabeth said. "The fairies have taken Jane."

This news jolted Ellen wide awake. "It canna be. She was baptized." She clutched the cross around her neck. "I... Let me look at her." She followed Elizabeth to her flat, her children following at her heels, their wails now reduced to whimpers as the sense of strange adventure made them forget about their previous complaints.

Leaning over the cradle, Ellen observed nothing that suggested anything amiss, though her senses tingled in warning. She reached to touch Jane, but hesitated. Then, taking a deep breath, she forced herself to tickle the child's wee face. Her fingers met skin as cold as death. The eyes opened: empty, unseeing, doll eyes. Ellen yanked her hand back and brushed it on her skirt.

"How can this be?"

"Go, please," Elizabeth said sharply. "We need tae find her and bring her back before it's too late."

"I'll hurry." Ellen ran back to her flat, where she threw jackets on her children and clutched their hands in hers. In their confusion they began to cry loudly again. "Shh, shh," Ellen said to them. "We'll be right back." Running down the hall to the outside steps, she was almost a comical sight as she dragged her weans along, but Elizabeth did not laugh.

Dazed, Elizabeth picked up the stranger in hopes she, or it, was really her Jane, who simply needed warmth. She held it close to her, rubbing it to move its circulation, her heart lurching at every sound that might signal Ellen's return. Everything about the child repulsed her. It wasn't hers, it couldn't be; it had to be a changeling. Still, her mind had played tricks on her ever since the birth. Every few seconds she looked at the babe again in disbelief, but the child just stared at her with those cold eyes. A clock ticked in the background, reminding her of the passing of time. With each minute that passed, she grew more frantic.

Robert would never forgive her for allowing this to happen. He had loved his daughter from the moment he held her in his arms. Her own father loved her like that. Yet she had left him, run away to live with Robert. Her parents warned her about life as a miner's wife, but she was young and foolish then.

Had she only listened.

Though time slowed and dragged, Beitris arrived in less than ten minutes, with Ellen and her children following breathlessly behind.

Beitris had delivered all the babies in the area since the beginning of time, and she moved with the grace and speed of youth despite her wrinkled face and stooped back. Rolling up her sleeves to reveal arms muscled from hard work, she took the bairn from Elizabeth and moved her fingers with the deft motions of experience across its still form.

"Will she be all right?" Elizabeth asked.

"Aye, but we hinna a moment tae lose. Ellen, gather supper. We canna let Robert think there's anything wrong. But leave a spare pot for me an' boil some water. I'll need Elizabeth tae help me."

Ellen nodded and set about doing her assigned task. First she filled the pot for Beitris, then gathered bread and cheese and made a thin soup with the last of the week's vegetables, which she put onto the fire to heat.

Handing the changeling to Elizabeth, Beitris took a bag from her skirt and shook its contents, a variety of herbs, into the boiling water. They popped and sizzled, their sweet scent filling the room. She waved her hands over them, chanting ancient words passed down through the generations of her family as she did so.

Next, she stuck a poker into the fire and held it there until it glowed with orange-red heat. That's when the reality of what they were doing hit Elizabeth.

"Whit are you doin'?" She asked Beitris, holding the stranger ever more tightly, doubting herself now. There were no such things as fairies or changelings, only superstitious tales.

Beitris continued to heat the poker. In the calm voice of one who spent many, many years calming nervous young mothers, she said, "This is nae yer bairn. This is a changeling. What ye'll see will look strange, cruel even, but you must trust me. Set it in the cradle noo."

Still doubtful, Elizabeth placed the changeling in Jane's cradle with the same care she would have given her own child. Stepping away from her to give the old howdiewife room was one of the hardest things she'd ever done.

Beitris grabbed the now-hot poker in both hands, wielding it like a sword between her weathered arms as she moved toward the cradle.

"Dinna hurt her!" Elizabeth cried.

Ellen grabbed hold of Elizabeth. "This isnae Jane, remember. Beitris will bring the real Jane back."

As she held on to Elizabeth, Ellen squeezed her eyes shut in anticipation of disaster. This was all her fault. She had caused this to happen, back on the day of the baptism. Until now she had managed to shut away the memories, but now they rushed forward to taunt her.

That day dawned bright with sun and promise. Ellen arrived early to help. They dressed wee Jane in a white lace gown that had once been Elizabeth's. Jane, tiny as a doll, swam in the dress, her head nearly disappearing amidst the layers of fabric. Ellen wished for more time to alter it, as Elizabeth was too fatigued and sad to do it herself. This would have to do, though. The town would likely gossip about the child's ill-fitting gown, but that mattered less than giving her God's protection as soon as possible.

Tradition called for someone to offer a gift of bread and cheese to the first person she met on the path to the church. Ellen volunteered, honored to play a role in this special ritual. Carrying Jane in one arm, light as a cloud, and the basket with the food offerings in the other, Ellen headed toward the kirk, with Elizabeth and Robert to follow a few minutes later.

Ellen didn't have to wait long before an old man, listing to the right and hunched over a too-short walking stick, ambled toward her. His clothes were rumpled and torn, and they hung on his gaunt frame. *Poor man*, she thought. Apoplexy had robbed him of his dignity. As she neared him, his face twisted in a grimace. Perhaps the news of a new, precious babe would help to cheer him.

Holding the basket out toward him she said, "Good sir, we offer ye a gift from this new bairn."

He stopped without speaking, looked at her, then at the baby, his face twisting even further into a sneer. "Pah!" He spat on the ground and walked away, leaving her standing with the basket still outstretched. Jane started to whimper and squirm.

"Sir?" Ellen pleaded to his back. "Please, sir, dinna curse the bairn this way."

Yet he kept moving, ignoring her completely.

"What shall we do?" she asked Jane, her knees shaking from the encounter. Jane responded only with sleepy sucking sounds. "Well, I see ye dinna want tae help me. I'll have tae fix this myself."

Normally the streets bustled with activity as townspeople prepared for morning service, but today they were oddly empty. Ellen continued to murmur loving words to Jane as they walked, praying for someone else to cross their path. She walked to within a block of the kirk when a young couple appeared. The woman, not more than eighteen, was ripe with her own child.

Ellen nearly dropped to her knees in gratitude and relief. Holding out the food offering with trembling hands, she said, "Good folks, this is a gift from a new bairn that we offer ye." She hoped she didn't look too desperate.

"Aye, of course," the young woman said, patting her own belly. "May I see the lass?"

Ellen held Jane up and the woman drew in a sharp breath, her eyes alight with the sight of the young beauty. Her mouth twisted and turned, not in bitterness, but rather in protection. To express a child's beauty aloud would invite evil influences.

"Thank ye," the woman said. "We would be honored."

Her husband, who stood next to his wife, silent until now, accepted the basket of food, then tipped his hat and bowed to Jane. "Welcome tae the world, lass," he said. Then the young couple continued on their way.

The baptism occurred as planned, and Ellen breathed easier, telling herself that no harm would come from tucking away the unfortunate details of the first encounter. Surely the goodwill of the young couple would counter the old man's bitterness and bring good fortune to the child. They would put the incident behind them, and no one needed to know.

Yet the scene unfolding in front of Ellen in the tiny flat, with a new mother numb with fright and a howdiewife wielding a hot poker, was no mere bad dream. She moved her mouth in prayer, begging for forgiveness and hoping Beitris could bring Jane back home. Then she remembered her children were present, stunned silent but wide-eyed and open-mouthed. "Go back tae the flat," she said. "We will protect wee Jane."

They didn't have to be told twice. In an instant they were gone.

Beitris said, "I will burn the sign of the cross on the bairn's brow." She edged closer to the end of the cradle and began to lower the end of the poker toward the bairn's new, perfect forehead.

"No!" Elizabeth tried to wrestle away from Ellen, but Ellen held her tightly. "I was wrong. I'm sairie. There's naethin' wrong wi' the bairn. She's sleeping, that's all. Please stop!"

"Trust me, Elizabeth. Hold on tae yer faith." Beitris stood before the changeling in the cradle and edged the poker slowly, slowly toward her smooth, pale forehead. Ellen kept her face turned away while Elizabeth clutched her heart with one hand. The changeling's eyes flew open, and it glared at Beitris, daring her to do it.

The poker reached the changeling's brow, making a soft hissing sound. All at once, the bundle sprang up, letting out a wild, unearthly cry. Beitris fell backward and the poker clattered on the floor, the flat filling with smoke and the smell of brimstone as the changeling disappeared.

Beitris, stunned, sat on the floor with her hands over her face. All three women were coughing, and Ellen opened the door to let out the smoke.

"Are ye awricht?" Elizabeth whispered to Beitris. She extended a hand to the old woman, who took it and staggered to her feet. Her face grew pale, and every wrinkle deepened.

"Aye," Beitris said. "I'll be fine." To prove the point, she stood tall and placed her hands on her hips.

"Ye're sure?"

Beitris nodded toward the cradle. "Look at the bairn. She's back, and that's what matters."

Sure enough, Jane lay sleeping peacefully, her chest rising and falling with each tiny breath. Elizabeth reached for her daughter but pulled her hand back. The deathlike, icy sensation of the changeling and its final cry still haunted her.

Beitris, understanding Elizabeth's hesitation, said, "Go on, then. Touch her. Make sure she's real."

Biting her lip, Elizabeth reached out again, this time cradling Jane's head in her hand, feeling the soft down of her hair. The baby sighed, and her mouth moved in mysterious baby dreams. Her cheeks were rosy, her skin warm and soft. This looked and felt like her daughter. The brow remained smooth and white, with no sign of burns from the poker. Elizabeth kissed the child's forehead and drank in her scent, now sweet and new.

And yet. Was this really her child? She would never be sure.

A darkness descended, surrounding her like smoke. She wished she had let the fairies take the child. Robert's wrath now seemed easier to endure than years ahead with this strange being.

Beitris retreated to a corner and chanted quietly, eyes closed. "Protect this bairn from the Fey," she said. "Surround her for the rest of her life with yer light and care." Then she said more in the ancient language.

"What are ye sayin'?" Ellen asked.

"Words tae bind our prayers. I spoke in the language of the Fair Folk tae add further protection, an' I will watch over wee Jane as she grows sae they canna take her again."

CHAPTER 2

Baloo loo, lammy, now baloo, my dear;
Now, baloo loo, lammy, ain minnie is here;
What ails my sweet bairnie? What ails it this nicht?
What ails my wee lammy? Is bairnie no richt?

The Laird O' Cockpen
Caroline Oliphant (Lady Nairne)

"*W*hat is it? Where is she?" Queen Donella paced the floor, wringing her hands.

The queen's maids of honor had entered the queen's chambers empty handed, Flora trembling, Coira sulking. One moment the child was theirs, and they had even landed right outside the palace, then *poof!* Jane disappeared from their grasp.

Like all the Fair Folk, the queen was a small woman, but her erect posture and penetrating eyes the color of night gave her an imposing air. She trembled with smoldering, silent anger. Her mood even transformed the room: the walls turned from dazzling white to a deep red. Faces in the precious tapestries, which told tales of the timeless history of the Fair Folk that long predated human existence, held Coira and Flora with contempt.

"Well? I'm waiting."

"The howdiewife…" Flora began, then paused and looked at Coira for help.

"Coira? What happened?"

"Somebody—" Coira cast a pointed glance at Flora "—didn't cast a protective shield around the bairn, and the humans took her back." She spat out the words.

"I did protect her," Flora insisted, "but the lass is baptized, which limits what we can do, and the howdiewife is powerful. I'm certain she will be watching the bairn closely from now on."

"I told you we needed to take her before the baptism," Coira said. "But no, everyone told me we had to wait an extra week for the new moon, that our magic would overpower the kirk's blessings. I said it would be too late, but no one listens to me."

Flora lightly stepped on one of Coira's feet to remind her sister to back off. By "everyone" Coira meant the queen, and so had overstepped her authority—not an unusual occurrence.

"Coira," the queen said, "may I remind you that we have traditions that must be followed. We determined that harnessing the power of the new moon would be the most effective way of capturing Jane. We sent the old man to create the curse that would keep her vulnerable, even after baptism. We did not, however, factor in the strength of Beitris." She said nothing more to rebuke Coira. Despite her anger, Queen Donella had always been patient with her rebellious Maid of Honor, as Coira's passion came from caring too much.

"I can handle that old howdiewife," Coira said. "It would give me great pleasure to do so."

Queen Donella shook her head. "We will consult the Wise Women," she said. "They will review the prophecy to determine how to proceed. And Coira?"

"My queen?"

"Do not take matters into your own hands. Impulsive actions are not royal actions."

"Aye." Though she said the word the queen expected to hear, Coira bit her lip, and someone looking carefully might have noticed the crossed fingers behind her back.

When they left the room, Flora took Coira's hand in hers. "We couldn't have done more. The lass is lost to us."

"Not if I have anything to say about it," Coira said.

"You never wanted to do this task anyway. What was it you said? Oh, yes. 'The queen's obsession with bringing a human to save us is insane.' As usual, I never reported this to her, though I should have."

Shrugging, Coira said, "Tell her what you will. The queen has never expected us to agree with her, but she did give us a job to do. To think we lost the bairn to that crazy old woman..." Her voice trailed off as she replayed the events in her mind. "You know how I hate to fail. I'll bring her back myself."

"Promise me you'll do what the queen says. Please let the Wise Women sort this."

Coira merely grunted. Flora said a silent prayer that Coira would behave herself.

Back at the Thorburn flat, Robert strode in through the open door, his face darkened with a heavy layer of coal dust.

"Whit's goin' on?" he asked. "Where did all this smoke come fae?"

"Nothing, I...I burned the soup," Elizabeth said. "Dinna worry, I started again." She handed him a whisky, which he downed in a gulp.

"Ye wasted food? Just when we're gettin' out from under things?"

"It's my fault," Ellen said. She and Beitris were headed

towards the door, but Ellen turned back around. "And the next batch is almost ready. I'm sure ye're hungry, so come sit."

Elizabeth, still trying to compose herself, gathered bowls for their soup and plates for the bread and cheese.

Robert trained his eyes, dark with fury, on his wife.

"Go ahead and go," she said firmly to the other women. Turning to Robert she said, "I'm sairie. It willnae happen again. Sit and eat. Supper is ready."

Once Ellen and Beitris left, Robert took his seat at the table and accepted the food Elizabeth placed before him, saying nothing. She didn't make herself a plate; the events of the day had worn her thin, and she lost her appetite. He didn't acknowledge the hearty soup or the bread she'd made earlier in the day, so chewy inside with its rich, brown crust. He held out his glass for Elizabeth to pour him another whisky, silent as he worked up a hefty rage.

After the drink caused a florid glow to cross his face, he spoke.

"I work hard all week, an' I canna have ye wastin' food like this. We'll have naethin' by Friday if we're nae careful, an' I canna go tae work on an empty stomach."

"Aye, my husband."

She wanted to tell him the truth, but a story of changelings and magic would anger him much more than a burned dinner. Robert refused to allow any mention of fairies in his presence. She never quite knew why, but then, until today she never understood why people feared the fairies. Now she did. But more than that she feared her husband, whose anger often rose from nowhere.

He came toward her and lifted a hand. She flinched, covering her face with her apron, waiting for the blow.

Jane let out a cry. The sound snapped Robert out of his rage, and he went to her, gathering her in his arms as if he knew about the earlier danger. As he cooed sweetly to her in a soft voice, his anger dissipated in an instant. Elizabeth sat quietly, holding the cheek that escaped unscathed.

ONE MIGHT THINK the child's ability to calm her father would endear her to Elizabeth, but this was not the case. As the days and weeks passed, she forced herself to hold Jane, to touch her soft hair, already lightening in color to a sweet reddish-blonde, to drink in the child's beauty—but it did not move her. Guilt gnawed. What kind of mother didn't love her child? Beitris said some women struggled after birth, but all Elizabeth saw in Jane's eyes was a stranger.

Each night she lay awake, unable to sleep more than a few hours. Jane never screamed for her food; her cries were more like whimpering apologies that were easy to ignore, and so Elizabeth would rise only when Robert nudged her. The flat, once spotless and cared for, fell into disarray. Robert came home to uncooked dinners and dried porridge on uncleaned breakfast dishes, his wife seldom dressed for the day.

They argued. She cried and promised to do better, but months passed with no change. The boarders left for more peaceful lodgings, adding to money woes. Elizabeth rebuffed Ellen's offers to help, and soon she no longer welcomed Beitris, who expressed concern for the child's well-being. Jane wasn't growing as well as she should.

As Elizabeth's mind grew increasingly clouded, the seed of a thought grew each day to the size of an ancient oak within her, weighty and thick. It greeted her upon rising each day, and whispered to her as she fell asleep. She would give this child, this being, back to the fairies. That was the only solution that made sense.

When Jane was about six months old, Elizabeth woke knowing she could not wait another minute. She would take her life back this day. With new purpose, she rose quickly and gave Jane more care than usual, feeding her, cleaning her, and dressing her in plenty of warm clothes. Then she took her daughter into the morning, nearly running to the edge of town, ignoring the curious glances of other mothers who were out and about. She didn't stop until she got to the nearest woods, where she called out for the fairies to come. Only silence answered.

Never having attempted to contact fairies before, she assumed it would be easy. They wanted Jane. There had to be a way to reach them. She tried calling out again. Still, only a soft wind responded.

By now, her heart started pounding. She couldn't imagine taking Jane back home. The feeding, the bathing, the changing, day after day after day, with no rest, no escape, no free time. Not for one more minute.

Perhaps they will come for her when I leave.

She lowered Jane to rest on a pile of leaves and adjusted a blanket around her. She felt a pang in her heart at seeing her daughter lying helpless on the ground. Images of wild animals regarding Jane as a tasty morsel caused her to hesitate. But then the cloud fell again over the remainder of her sanity. Turning her back on her daughter, she forced herself to walk away.

"Elizabeth?"

Elizabeth ignored the voice, thinking it was some sort of fairy trick. She heard a rustle nearby but did not look back.

"Elizabeth!" The voice grew sharper now, and this time Elizabeth stopped. She hadn't noticed Ellen running up behind her, but now her friend bent over to catch her breath.

"Ellen? What are ye doin' here? Where are the bairns?"

Ellen picked Jane up and smothered her with kisses. The bairn appeared unharmed. "I followed ye," she said. "Left the weans at home, which I'm sick about, but I'm glad I did, from what I can tell." She walked toward Elizabeth, who slowly backed away. "Dinna run from me. I'll tell no one what I saw."

"I canna take care o' her," Elizabeth said. Her lower lip trembled. "She's...different."

"Dinna worry," Ellen said in a singsong, lullaby voice. "It gets tae be too much sometimes. Let me take her for a while. When ye're ready, we'll bring her home."

"No, no, I canna," Elizabeth said. "She belongs to them. They want her, an' she's too much for me. Please."

Ellen tucked Jane into the crook of one arm and put the other around Elizabeth. "Ye're just havin' a hard time."

The comforting words made their way somehow past Elizabeth's panic, and she began to calm down. Maybe there was another way. "But ye have two bairns already, an' I canna ask you to take mine, too." She nestled her head on Ellen's shoulder as the import of what she had tried to do revealed itself to her. "I left her," she said. "I'll be in hell for that for sure."

"Mebbe not," Ellen said. "God told me tae follow ye. Let's figure out what tae do together." She continued to hold Elizabeth. Jane slept, unaware of the fate that had nearly befallen her. "How about this? Do ye have a family member who can take her for a while, until you feel better?"

"I've felt sae alone," Elizabeth said, tears dropping from her eyes as she shared the weight of her burden. "Mebbe my brother Ewan would take her. They have waited a long time for a bairn, and they love Jane." But there was another problem. "What about Robert? What will we tell him?"

"I have an idea." Ellen cooed and smiled at Jane as the two women concocted a plan. Robert was the only potential problem, and Ellen assured Elizabeth that he would understand what needed to be done. "He's seen yer troubles," Ellen said. "I dinna think it will be sae hard, nae if he loves Jane like I think he does."

They returned to the flat. "I can keep Jane for a few days," Ellen repeated. "The lass is nae trouble at all."

"Naw, ye've done sae much already. I can keep her a bit longer, knowin' I have a place for her."

Ellen rubbed Elizabeth's back while Jane made soft cooing noises. "I'll look in on ye from time tae time," she said. "We'll get through this, I promise."

ELIZABETH INVITED her elder brother Ewan and his wife Kirstin to Sunday dinner. Ewan lived in nearby Menstrie, where he worked at a mill. The couple had inherited a modest sum of money from Kirstin's parents, which they used to buy themselves a small home. To Elizabeth it might as well have been a palace with its two bedrooms.

One thing they lacked, however, was a child. Kirstin delighted in Elizabeth's pregnancy as if it were her own, but after three years of marriage, there was no sign of such a blessing for them.

Kirstin wasted no time scooping Jane up into her arms. "Look at ye!" she exclaimed. "Sae big already."

"Big? She's nae much bigger than my two hands," Ewan said with a laugh, and he tickled Jane under the chin. She watched him with interest, her eyes thoughtful and grave. "But she looks like a wee wise person, sae serious." Ewan exchanged a longing glance with his wife, which Elizabeth noticed. His heartbreak lived just below the surface of his skin.

Robert said little and sat with arms crossed and eyes narrowed. He and Elizabeth seldom had company, even family, and he wasn't happy about others holding his daughter.

Elizabeth fed them all a simple meal of potatoes and cabbage, apologizing for the meager fare. Kirstin brought short-bread for dessert. As they sat at the table, Ewan held Jane in his arms, and she brought a tiny fist to his beard in fascination. Everyone at the table wore a smile, even Elizabeth, though she dreaded Robert's response to her plan. She hoped the presence of others would dull his reaction.

"She likes ye," Elizabeth said.

"Aye," Ewan said. Then to Jane he added, "We love ye too, lass."

"Will ye have another soon?" Kirstin asked, her voice forlorn.

"I hope sae," Robert said.

"I hope nae," Elizabeth said.

Robert and Elizabeth turned away from each other after the awkward exchange. Kirstin raised her eyebrows and grabbed another piece of shortbread to have something to do.

Elizabeth tightened her fists at her side and said, "A bairn is a lot o' work, and a lass canna help sae much wi' the money when she's older. Unless, of course, she can learn a trade." The perfect moment had arrived. "I was thinkin', Ewan, mebbe the lass could learn weavin'. Pays better than domestic service, an' from the looks o' her she'll be too tiny tae think about the mines."

"We have lots o' time tae think about that," Robert protested.

Ewan, still unable to take his eyes from his niece, said, "We can take her when she's older," he said. "She can live wi' us, but visit often, an' I can put her in the mill tae learn. I'd be happy tae teach her."

Elizabeth couldn't wait that long. Jane wouldn't be able to work until she turned ten, eight if some rules were bent. She struggled to think of keeping Jane another year, a month, a week. "If she went noo, it would be better for her. Give her time tae adjust tae a new family. When she's older, it would be harder for her tae leave us. Right, Robert?"

Robert didn't answer her, but stared down at his plate, his teeth clenched and jaw pulsing. "Take my daughter?"

"It would be what's best for her." Elizabeth treaded on

uneven ground, but she preferred navigating his volatile nature to keeping Jane around.

Kirstin's eyes were wide with hope, and Ewan took her hand and squeezed it. The two of them seemed to hold a collective breath as they waited for Robert to speak.

Glaring at Elizabeth, he said, "What are ye up to? Ye just had this bairn, an' noo you want tae get rid o' her."

Elizabeth squirmed in her chair. "That's nae true." She wished he wouldn't talk to her in such an angry tone with her brother present, though his response didn't surprise her.

Robert had plenty more to say. "Ye dinna hold her, ye barely feed her, an' until today ye keep yer sairie bahoochie in bed all day. This past week I came home tae nae dinner an' nae fire. I'm workin' all day, an' I get tired an' hungry."

A look came over his face then, a look of realization as his own words sunk in. He covered his face with his hands and stifled a cry. "Oh, God," he said. "Oh, dear God."

Elizabeth tried to put an arm around him, but he pushed her away.

"Should we give ye some time?" Ewan asked. "Mebbe this needs more thought."

"Naw," Robert said. When he pulled his hands away his eyes were rimmed with red. "She's right," he said, his voice cracking, "Mebbe this is for the best. I'd do anythin' for that bairn, an' her ma's likely tae kill her if we dinna find someone tae care for her." Almost to himself, he muttered, "Ye'd be better off in the asylum." His last words echoed as the room fell silent.

Elizabeth sat up straight. She feared getting committed the most, but in hearing the words, she wondered if she didn't deserve that kind of punishment.

Ewan recovered first. "Sister, are ye havin' a hard time?" he asked.

Elizabeth nodded. Hearing the truth out loud, though horrible, was freeing, too. "Please dinna let him put me away," she said in a childlike voice. "I ken it's wrong, but I canna seem tae stop."

"How about this?" Kirstin asked. She paused, the words to follow too difficult to say. "We keep Jane for as long as ye need. It'll give us great joy an' mebbe some good luck. When ye're feelin' better, we'll bring her back. Meantime, Robert, come visit her anytime. Ye'd still be her da."

All eyes were on Robert, who looked as dazed as if someone punched him. He stood and moved toward the door, but then stopped. Outnumbered, and still facing away from the others, he finally said, "Aye," weakly. He turned to take Jane from Kirstin, and the bairn nuzzled against him. "Ye're wise, lass, wiser than me," he whispered to her.

Ewan, Kirstin, and Elizabeth started talking then, making plans, promising visits, imagining the future. Robert and Jane sat quietly, holding on to each other as if they were drowning, alone together in the sea.

CHAPTER 3

The exquisite scent of the lilac,
The buffeting breath of the May,
The fragrance from fields of clover,
Kiss the soul that awakes today.

My Daughter
Mrs. Lindsay Carnegie

No one knew where the Wise Women lived. They had existed before Queen Donella or even her mother, and they were ancient even then. It was said they were present for all the wars with England, for the arrival of the Vikings, and even further back to the occupation of the Romans. Some stories told of their presence in ancient times, when volcanoes erupted and lands collided with each other, though this was treated as rumor and not given much credence.

In any event, their age gave them a depth of perspective and a wisdom that Queen Donella valued, especially now that the prophecy had not come to pass. Surely they had seen that happen in all their centuries of experiences.

The queen seldom left the palace, and her willingness to go to them demonstrated the esteem in which she held the elders. To reach them, she flew to an ancient stone cottage on the south end of Loch Lomond. The Wise Women had rendered it invisible to the human eye with a protective spell. The recent growth and expansion of human territory required them to take extra measures to secure their sacred sites.

The cottage, ancient but kept in neat repair, contained a single room. Dawn had arrived only a few minutes before, and a shaft of sunlight illuminated the room from a window on the east wall. Queen Donella lit candles and spoke prayers to invite them to visit.

Soon the cottage grew warm, even without a fire. After about ten minutes, sparks of light appeared, and in another minute or two the Wise Women revealed themselves. There were seven of them, so old that their true names had disappeared. They were as gnarled and bent as ancient trees that had weathered many winter storms. Those who feared the ravages of age would call them witches and see them as ugly and frightening, but in truth, they glowed with the light of enchantment. Their wrinkles told stories of life and death, of joys and sorrows, of magic and the failures of magic. Only those who understood and appreciated the wisdom of old age appreciated their rich beauty.

The queen bowed before them, in awe as she waited for them to speak. She had faced them only a handful of times during her reign, and in their presence she felt humble and small, even as Queen of Caledonia.

The Wise Women spoke as one, their lips unmoving and their words reaching the queen's ears through the magic of stardust, as age had taken from them the ability to speak.

We have heeded your pleas, they said.

"You're not angry?" she asked. "I have failed you, myself, and my people."

They let out soothing sounds. *We have seen much in our life-times. Even the best seers cannot see every contingency. Prophecies can be amended.*

"They can?" This made no sense to her. What would be the point of a prophecy, then?

We cannot waste energy, they said. *But yes, they can. Trust us.*

She wanted to tell them how she longed for this child, dreamed of her, waited for her ever since her late sister Bridget whispered the prophecy in her dying breaths. More than that, the queendom was deteriorating at an alarming rate, and the child had been promised as their salvation. With her failure, how could she save her people?

But the Wise Women were not there for comfort. They were there to solve problems. So rather than wallowing in her sad story, she asked, "What can we do? Can we take her again? It appears the mother doesn't want the bairn anyway."

The howdiewife is protecting her, they said, *and she knows more of the old ways than many of our own healers.*

"Have I lost her, then? Is it too late to save us?"

There is a way, but it will take some time. The wind rustled outside, chiming in to the answer.

"What do I do, then?"

"She will grow up with human experience that will be valu-able to us. We can better understand their ways."

"So we wait? For how long? And what do I do in the meantime?"

You will prepare her by appearing in her dreams and revealing yourself to her throughout her life to teach her. Worry not, dear Queen. She will still be the bridge between our world and theirs, but at a different time.

With that, they faded from view, leaving the queen alone with more unanswered questions. How long would that be? If Jane lived for eighty human years, would the Fair Folk survive that long?

She retreated to her palace with the knowledge that, for now, she must summon what faith she could, faith that waivered on shaky ground. The prophecy failed once. It could fail again, Wise Women or no.

CHAPTER 4

She stands with her shy lips parted,
And the dew in her star-set eyes,
With her trustful face uplifted
To the arch of the grey-blue skies.

My Daughter
Mrs. Lindsay Carnegie

*J*ane was five when her experiences with the Fey
first embedded themselves as memory. Up until
that time, they visited her regularly, but anything
they told her vanished once she opened her eyes.

Perhaps that first memory stayed with her because of what
happened right afterward. Flora and Coira appeared to her in a
dream as they often did. "You are one of us, Jane, and as such,
you have abilities and powers other humans do not," they
explained. "Your aunt Kirstin has to cook and clean, for example. You, on the other hand, will summon food from the ethers,
richer and more delicious than anything humans make. All you

have to do is imagine cleanliness, cleanliness will show up for you."

Jane thought about how her aunt, though loving, had little time to play with her, and she liked the sound of the idea of offering a gift. But what to do? Then she remembered a friend of her aunt's, who had visited one day with a pumpkin cake, and Jane fell in love with its piping-hot sweetness. The thought of it made her mouth water. Yes, pumpkin cake.

When she woke the next morning after dreaming that night of such a cake, there it was waiting on the table when everyone got out of bed, fresh and hot and exuding the smell of cloves and cinnamon. Jane stood proudly next to it, doing her best to contain her excitement. This would be such a wonderful day!

"What's this?" Aunt Kirstin asked Uncle Ewan.

"I dinna ken," he said. They looked at each other in confusion.

"I made it for ye, Aunt Kirstin," Jane said. "Flora taught me."

"Who is Flora?" Aunt Kirstin asked, an odd expression on her face.

"Flora's my friend," Jane said. "She's one of the Wee Folk."

Kirstin gasped. "Wee Folk? Oh, dear. Ewan? Help?"

Fully expecting praise for her gift, Jane was confused by the less-than-enthusiastic response. Now her aunt and uncle were talking in low tones among themselves, and she waited as the cake cooled off. Her stomach growled, and she hoped they would end their discussion soon. Unable to wait any longer, she reached for it.

"Jane! Stop!"

Uncle Ewan slapped her wee hand. He had never struck her before, and she burst into a wail.

Then Uncle Ewan said, in a gentler voice, "I'm sairie, wee Jane, but we dinna allow fairies in our hame."

"But Uncle, they dinna like tae be called fairies. They told me." And why wasn't her friend welcome in their home?

Aunt Kirstin picked Jane up and held her. "Awricht, Jane, the Wee Folk. But we are faithful tae the teachings of the kirk, and the fair—the Wee Folk worship other gods. We dinna eat their food because it would bind us tae them." She nodded at Uncle Ewan, who took the cake outside and threw it away.

Jane wriggled out of her aunt's arms and went back to her pallet, where she turned her back to her aunt and uncle and cried for her wee pumpkin cake. Worse, they were telling her to send away her friends.

Once her tears were spent, it occurred to her that her aunt and uncle couldn't see the Fey. Flora and Coira were for her and her alone, so she didn't have to send them away if she didn't want to. She had a secret now, a world that belonged only to her. With this new understanding, she went to the table and ate the porridge her aunt prepared. Later on, after her aunt and uncle forgot the incident, she crept outside and found where he had thrown the cake into the garden. Unable to help herself, she took a few crumbs that didn't lay directly in the soil and sampled them. They were divine! How could anything so wonderful cause her harm?

Over time she learned that her aunt and uncle had secrets of their own. One of them concerned a small, burly man who periodically came to the house, begging for Jane. There were shouts and cries and accusations of drunkenness, and Uncle Ewan always sent him away, screaming her name, his intensity lingering as he left. Her questions were met with "Dinna worry about it," and she learned to stop asking.

Secrets. Everyone had them, and she would keep hers.

WHEN SHE GREW a bit older and was allowed to explore in the outdoors, Flora and Coira met her under trees, by streams, or on hillsides. Though Jane attended school by this time, she found the Fair Folk far more enticing to be with. Her school-mates considered her standoffish and strange, but she didn't care.

"What's it like where ye live?" she asked them one day. She was eight by then and about to go to work at the mill, as many young children did. This excited her, for it made her feel grown-up to go to work and earn a wage.

"Getting worse and worse, what with these humans," Coira grumbled.

Jane laughed, even though Coira seemed quite serious about it.

Coira's eyes narrowed. "Nothing funny about losing our way of life," she said.

Jane forced herself to stop laughing. Coira always found something to complain about, but perhaps this time she had a valid reason to do so.

"Coira, we're not telling Jane about our troubles," Flora said. Jane loved Flora's soothing nature, and she always smelled like violets and sunshine. "She wants to know about our people and how we live."

"Are there dragons?" Jane asked. "Because someone in my school said there are dragons." Schoolchildren spoke among themselves about fairies, though they had no real knowledge about them, not like she did. She never argued with them or shared the story of the pumpkin cake.

"Died out a thousand years ago," Coira said. "After the Vikings lay waste to the land, they perished."

"Oh." Jane thought for a moment. "What are Vikings?" she asked.

"More nasty humans."

"Coira!"

They continued like this for a while. Flora spoke of their queendom, ruled by women since the beginning of time. The Fey had many kingdoms and queendoms throughout the world, but theirs was the most special because of Queen Donella, who ruled all of Caledonia—what the humans now called Scotland. Flora painted a picture in Jane's mind of a magical land where no one had to toil for long hours and little pay, and where a little pumpkin cake was merely an enticing glimpse of a magical life.

Coira, on the other hand, told of failing crops, couples unable to children or having them die young. She told of the loss of dragons, gnomes, trolls, mermaids, and more. "Even our animals spoke to us in our past," she said. "But no more. When humans made factories, they stopped believing in magic. And when magic dies, so do we."

"Magic is still alive," Flora protested. "But as you can see, Jane, the Fair Folk are connected to humans in important ways. That's why we are here with you, and why we will be with you for your entire life."

Jane had many questions about what that meant. "I'd like tae visit," she said. An adventure! Even at her young age, she dreamed of a larger world...and she longed to meet those like herself who carried magic inside of them.

"We'll take you when you're older," Flora said. "It would be good for you, and for us."

Coira started to speak, but Flora nudged her in the ribs and gave her head a firm "no" shake. To Jane, Flora said only, "Much later, when the time is right."

"But when will that be?" Jane asked.

"Aw, come on, sister, she wants to go now."

"Coira. Stop."

Jane did not ask again, but she had other things to think about anyway. Uncle Ewan talked to the mill bosses, who agreed to hire Jane as a spinner. He and Kirstin had planned to wait until she was ten, but Jane begged him until he got the proper approvals. School bored her, and she wanted to grow up as soon as possible.

With some help from Flora, as well as women at the mill, she learned quickly how to turn cleaned, carded wool into thread. She found rhythm with her foot, turning the spinning wheel and pulling the fiber with a perfect amount of tension. Each completed spool brought her a sense of delight. Though the supervisors never praised the workers, the looks on their faces told her they were pleased.

The days at the mill were tiring, and sometimes the supervisors were cross, but she loved the work and the bit of pay she received at the end of the week. She gave some of it to her uncle, and he taught her how to save. Aunt Kirstin took Jane to the general store to buy an occasional sweet treat with some of her earnings.

Then one day, one horrible Saturday, Jane woke, ready to go to work, only to find her aunt and uncle engaging in heated whispers. They seldom argued, and Jane was unclear if they were arguing now. But there were gestures and Uncle Ewan's gentle taps on the wall with his fists. He never raised his voice or stomped his feet. No, he allowed only the wee acknowledgement *tap, tap, tap* to display his distress.

They stopped when Jane entered the room.

"What's wrong?" she asked.

Aunt Kirstin, whose face had borne a dreamlike quality for the past few weeks, now looked haggard and aged. "Jane," she said, her tone gentle, "I'll need ye tae stay wi' me today an' go fetch Beitris."

Uncle Ewan drew Aunt Kirstin into his arms, and she wept a little before pushing him away. "I'll be all right," she said. "Go tae work, an' let the women do what needs tae be done."

Jane gave her uncle a worried look. "I dinna want tae get sacked," she said.

"I'll tell them, Jane. Dinna worry." He ruffled her hair, then put on his hat and cloak and walked out into the chilly, dark morning. Aunt Kirstin closed the door behind him. She held on to the doorknob and rested her forehead on the door, and soon her shoulders were shaking.

"Aunt Kirstin. What is it?"

"I was havin' a bairn, or sae I thought." Aunt Kirstin composed herself and turned toward Jane, her eyes red and face blotchy. "Then this mornin', well." She heaved a sigh as she sat at the table, hands flat upon it, and stared straight ahead.

"Oh, Auntie!" Jane reached for her aunt, who waved her away. Yet she wanted, needed to do something. No one had eaten or drunk anything that morning, she realized, so she set about cooking some porridge and making tea. Soon she would go fetch Beitris, but for now this was a way to help.

"I'll never understand…"

"What?" Jane set down a cup of tea, sliding it closer to Kirstin.

"Some people are terrible parents and yet they are blessed with a child, sometimes many. Like yer ma—" Putting a hand over her mouth, Kirstin stopped speaking.

"What about my ma?"

"Naethin', dinna mind me, Jane. I shouldna say such things. Here, let's have our porridge an' pray for better days."

As always, Jane did what she was told, but she would ask Beitris later.

The old howdiewife welcomed Jane with a smothering hug, the kind that makes a person believe in miracles again, the kind that only old women with bodies softened with age can give. Jane wriggled out of it quickly, though, eager to return back to her aunt. She explained the problem.

"Ah, poor lass." Beitris made the herbs for Kirstin to strengthen her body to receive a child, but these efforts had not borne the fruits they'd hoped for. "Well, let's go see about her."

"Will she ever have a bairn, do ye think?" Jane asked. Her aunt had kept a bassinet and toys handy, and every week at the kirk she prayed for a child.

"Perhaps," Beitris said, though she looked uncomfortable. "I do my best, but the Lord decides these things."

They walked together to the house hand in hand. After a few minutes of striding quietly beside Beitris, Jane mentioned the earlier conversation with her aunt. "Do my ma an' da have other bairns?" she asked.

"I think this is somethin' for yer aunt tae tell," Beitris said. "Every family has its own rules, lass, an' I never disrespect them."

Jane continued to push, but the old woman refused to say more, and they arrived at the little house with Jane no wiser. "Run along, Jane," Beitris said as they reached the doorway. "Go play."

"I can help," Jane protested.

Beitris gave Jane a hug and kiss on the cheek. "Ye're a sweet lass, but try not tae grow up sae soon. I'll take good care o' her, I promise. Run along noo, while I do my work."

Jane left the house and found Coira sitting at the side of a stream, watching the water go by. Surrounding her, hovering, were three Fair Folk who would be small enough to fit in a pocket. Coira moved her arms like a conductor of music while her tiny companions sang and danced, their voices tinny and sweet as nectar, their movements fluid like the water below them. Jane stood back, watching the scene, until Coira called out to her.

"No sense hiding, we all know you're here," she said.

Jane arrived cautiously, and the three entertainers bowed to her before flitting away like fireflies. "What were you doing?" she asked.

"Those were the spirits of the stream," Coira said. "Their job is to keep the water flowing, and I helped them along."

"I didna ken ye had power over water," Jane said.

"There's a lot you don't know yet, wee Jane. But what brings you to me today?"

Jane told her what she wanted to know. "Do Ma an' Pa have more bairns?" Then something else dawned on her, something that never occurred to her before now. "A man comes tae the house an' asks tae see me, but Uncle never lets him in. Is that my da?"

Coira held up a blade of grass, inspected it, then flicked it away. She watched the water for a bit longer then said, "You never belonged to them. Your ma never warmed up to you. She wanted a lad tae work in the mines. Besides, you were rightfully ours."

"What do ye mean?"

"We had a right to take you to our world. You know you don't fit in here with humans."

Jane nodded. She loved her aunt and uncle, but this was true. "But ye didna take me, nae ever."

"We tried." Then Coira told the story of how they came for Jane, weaving a basket to hold her, and getting close to the palace before Beitris stole her back. She left out Robert's anguish, Ellen's loving care, and Elizabeth's guilt.

It sounded like a lie but felt like the truth. Deep in her bones, Jane held the memory, even if it left her mind. Her head started to hurt. She probably should have asked Flora for the story, as she likely would have gotten a more accurate version.

"What about my da?" Jane asked after a long pause.

"That's him. He's a drunk, nothing more, and of no use to you."

Yet he came for her, over and over. One of her parents wanted her, even if he was a drunk.

"Your ma and da had more babies to replace you," Coira said. "You have a sister, Mary, and a brother, William, a newborn."

There was some relief in knowing the story, even if it might not be true. A grand battle occurred in which the Fair Folk fought for her, and that made her very proud indeed. But how could her parents abandon her and then have other children?

The question would haunt her for her entire childhood and beyond.

She returned to the house where Aunt Kirstin grieved. Jane wanted more than ever to help her aunt in some way, to repay her for taking her in. Flora and Coira had revealed Jane's magical powers to her, and she had certainly produced as fine a pumpkin cake as the most skilled baker. She never tried to conjure anything else after that, though. The single slap from her uncle scared her that much.

But what if she could help Aunt Kirstin conceive a child? No one needed to know how it happened. There had to be a way to do this, and Jane was determined to figure it out all on her own.

Each day she focused on Kirstin's desire, and sometimes she would wipe her aunt's eyes with a handkerchief and then put it in a jar to keep the tears moist, praying over them.

The first month, her aunt's courses came, and the next, and the next. Undaunted, each month Jane adjusted her prayers a little. Eventually she worked it out that she needed a bit of her aunt's menstrual blood. Though repulsed by the thought, *she knew, she knew, she knew* this would work. Through a bit of stealth and no small amount of gagging, she obtained the desired substance from one of her aunt's used flannel cloths and prayed with it on the full moon. Why the full moon? Something inside prompted her, telling her what to do. She tested her ideas, following the same inner compass that allowed her to produce a perfect pumpkin cake.

Soon after that, Aunt Kirstin found herself with child again. She said nothing to anyone at first, but Jane would catch her aunt rubbing her belly, a dreamy look on her face—a look Jane had seen many times before. Only when her clothes stopped fitting did Kirsten say anything, and even then, she and Uncle Ewan said little. She didn't make baby clothes like she had in the past. At night before falling asleep Jane prayed for her aunt, asking the Fair Folk to surround her aunt with protection and to reduce her fear.

This time, the pregnancy went to term. Heather was a screaming, red-faced wee lass, and Jane fell in love with her immediately. "Ye're good luck, Jane," Uncle Ewan would say, tousling her hair. "After all this time, a wee family for us all, an' ye'll be like a big sister." Jane tended to the new baby with great joy, basking in the knowledge that she likely had something to do with it.

It was also, however, the beginning of the end of her family life. As her aunt and uncle tended to Heather, a winter wind tugged at her, sending a message. *This is not your home or your family*, it said. *There are greater adventures in the world for you.* It resonated with what Coira had told her that day and with what her heart told her. Her aunt and uncle loved her, but she didn't belong in the way Heather did. And though it would take many more years for her to leave this place, her dreams and plans were set in motion that day. A cord had been cut, and one day she would be on her own.

CHAPTER 5

The spring is come at last, my freens, cheer up,
you sons of toil,
Let the seeds of independence be sown in labour's soil,
And tho' the nipping blast of care should blight
your wee bit crop,
Oh dinna let your spirits sink, cling closer aye to hope.

The Working Man
Ellen Johnston

The town of Alva tucked itself into the lowlands of the Ochil Hills like a baby bird under its mother's wing. There Alva Burn rushed down through thick woods toward town, providing a rich water source for its inhabitants. This mighty water also powered Alva's many mills—nine in total, though some had come and gone over the years.

Jane, twenty-one now and restless as young people are, stood on Main Street surveying the scene and carrying a sack of meager belongings. Among them were a spare dress, worn but kept in thoughtful repair; a flannel nightgown; a book of Robert

Burns poetry, a tattered tome given to her by her aunt and uncle; and a special soap that Beitris made for her since childhood, insisting it would keep her safe.

The old howdiewife had looked in on Jane through her years with Uncle Ewan and Aunt Kirstin, much as a grandmother would. Beitris was superstitious but sweet, and oddly overprotective. Jane didn't worry about needing protection. The Fair Folk had caused no harm thus far. But the soap smelled good, with hints of lavender, sage, and rosemary, so what was the harm?

Main Street ran straight and flat from east to west and boasted the kirk, of course, along with a general store, a butcher, a pub, and a shop with lovely dresses in the window. Jane paused to admire the smart, new styles, hoping to buy one or two once she saved some of her pay.

Above the shops were flats where shopkeepers and some millworkers lived. Additional mill housing for families filled the side streets immediately off of Main Street. Young unmarried workers took up residence in boarding-houses with cheap rents. Further up the hill were actual houses, expansive with large front and back gardens for the mill owners, bankers, and other wealthy elite, allowing them to literally look down their noses on the working class.

Before going to the boardinghouse, Jane sought out the woods that surrounded the burn. She followed the sound of the water to a narrow path, clear but wet and edged by melting snow. It snaked alongside the water, which roared louder as she wended her way up the hill and grew closer to the first of its many waterfalls.

Alva shrank smaller and smaller into the distance as she wandered among hardy ferns and mosses. Ash trees were bare for the season, emphasizing their diamond-shaped bark patterns. Without their leaves, the trees left an open invitation for sunlight to make its way through. A smoky haze covered the town, but she could still see its neat, orderly layout.

Jane paused to take in the view, brushing away a stray curl the color of pale gold tinged with a hint of strawberry. Her eyes, a brilliant gray-blue, overwhelmed her tiny, freckled face. Though young, she bore an ethereal, otherworldly bearing that made her seem older.

High above the mill, the brisk air cleansed her spirit. Tomorrow she would take her place as one of Alva's many young female weavers. For today, though, she intended to find the magic that lived in this place, the magic that drew her here and caused her to leave her family behind.

Her decision to part from her aunt and uncle had led to shouts and tears. Ungrateful, they called her.

"We took ye in, took care o' ye all these years," Aunt Kirstin said. "Now I have a house full o' bairns, I need yer help."

"What are young women thinkin' these days?" Uncle Ewan added. "Goin' off tae live away from family."

With all Ewan and Kirstin had done for her, of course Jane found it hard to leave them. But how could she make them understand that despite their love, she remained an outsider in the family, part of it and yet not a fully-fledged daughter? She never regretted her secret decision to use magic to help her aunt bear children, but with each birth she retreated further and further into the background. Magic was a gift and a curse rolled together, and she preferred to avoid it whenever possible.

She found a large, flat rock to sit on in the sunshine and closed her eyes, drawing her cloak around her to keep herself warm. The sun caressed her shoulders, and she took several deep breaths. In a new hometown, with a new job, possibilities opened themselves to her: earning her own money, buying clothes, and making new friends. She could buy herself a little cake or other treat without having to ask permission or worrying that her aunt and uncle would see her as a spendthrift.

Once she stilled herself, soon the familiar buzz of wings surrounded her, filling her with joy. Then they appeared in her field of vision, and she knew instantly they would be friends. These were Fair Folk she had not yet met, residents of this particular wood. There were seven, with a mix of men and women, plump and jolly with ruddy faces and ready smiles. The men sported long beards. These were not the Fair royalty of Flora and Coira, so their clothes were simpler, with men in red overalls and the women in plain brown dresses with printed scarves covering their hair. They tickled her ears, her neck, even her hands in welcome. She once worried she would lose their companionship when she arrived in Alva. Now, knowing she would not be alone, she laughed with relief.

"Welcome, future queen," they said. It was an old joke, one she had heard many times over the years.

She took hold of her worn skirts and shook them. "Does this look like royalty tae ye? Silly Folk."

Someone said, "But the prophecy—" before others shushed him.

Jane cast them a puzzled look. "A prophecy? Ye have a story tae share?"

They exchanged glances with each other, suddenly reluctant to speak.

"What? Tell me."

They all spoke on top of each other: "Naethin,'" "Never mind," and "We were just playing." There was a lot of nervous laughter.

Jane rolled her eyes and decided to let the moment pass. If she was really fairy royalty, she'd have learned about it by now instead of toiling away in factories. Instead, she removed her shoes and stockings and dangled her feet in the cold, damp grasses, then warmed them on the rock.

"So," she said. "What are yer jobs?" Each of the Fair Folk had a special place in the world, and this group likely cared for the woods.

One of them stepped forward. "My name is Bram," he said, "and I'm the leader of this group." He was the tallest of the lot, though that didn't say much, and barrel-chested with a white beard that reached his knees. He pointed at each of his friends, one by one. "Logan protects the trees."

Logan stepped forward and bowed. He looked a bit like a tree himself, with tanned skin resembling the smooth bark of a hazel tree.

"Aklen is in charge of the rocks," Bram continued.

Aklen, the oldest of the group, nodded in acknowledgement, his face bearing the hardened look of the rocks of the glen.

"Hamel keeps the flowers in bloom and the grasses growing. He manages a whole group of the smallest Folk. Ye'll see them buzzin' around an' think they're bees."

Hamel held back, shyer and more delicate-looking than the others.

"And these three—" Bram pointed at the three women "—these are the keepers of the burn, the water sprites: Eisla, Levene, and Nairne."

The three women stepped forward with linked arms. They looked like triplets, as Jane would have been hard-pressed to tell them apart. Same sandy hair, same eyes the color of sapphires. All three sported dimples in their right cheeks. They reminded Jane of the Fey she'd seen with Coira all those years ago.

"Carin' for the burn is a special job," Bram continued, "makin' sure the rain comes from the sky and there's enough water for everything." A shadow crossed his face.

"What's wrong?" Jane asked.

"Well, I shouldna say tae a human…"

Aklen said, "But she's part—"

"Shh," the three women said in unison.

Bram nodded as if the unsaid words were enough for him to

continue. "It takes all three of the water sprites tae keep the water goin', an' it's gettin' harder these days with the mills an' whatnot. We're afraid one day we willnae keep up anymore. Our problems are bad for humans an' all living things, nae just the Fey."

Jane noticed that Bram spoke more like she did, and not in the formal manner of Coira and Flora. She felt instantly more comfortable with this group because of that.

She also noticed the repetition of a familiar theme, the grumbles from the Folk about the changes going on in their world.

"I'm sairie about yer problems," she said, wishing she had something more helpful to offer.

There were shrugs and mumbles among the group in response. "We'll be awricht," Bram said. "There's still plenty o' magic tae keep us goin' for a long time." He seemed to want to say more but stopped himself.

"What else?" Jane asked, hoping to encourage him to tell her the rest.

He waved a hand dismissively. "We came tae welcome ye, lass, not tae tell our troubles. What brought ye here?"

She thought for a moment, wanting to be truthful but not wanting to tell her troubles either. "I want tae be an independent woman," she said. "No one tae tell me what tae do or be. The job came up in Alva and I decided tae take the chance."

"An' what do ye think sae far?"

"It's too soon tae tell," she said with a laugh. "But if everyone is as friendly and welcoming as yer lot, I'm happy."

"Then let's celebrate." One of the Folk brought out a flute, and raucous dancing commenced to Jane's delight. Flora and Coira were at times lively and funny but never danced in front of her. This group of Fair Folk also did not hesitate to sing human songs, and soon they burst into a rousing rendition of "Blue Bonnets Over the Border":

"Come from the hills where your hirsels are grazing,
Come from the glen of the buck and the roe;
Come to the crag where the beacon is blazing,
Come with the buckler, the lance, and the bow..."

"Come, Jane, join in!" they shouted.

She shook her head but clapped along with them, content to watch them while she rested from her journey. They claimed to celebrate in her honor, but she doubted it. The Folk looked for any excuse to sing, dance, and play.

Her heart brimmed over with joy and possibility as she sat for a while in the sun, then said goodbye to her new friends. Carrying her shoes, she treaded down the path in bare feet, enjoying the cool, damp ground.

"SHE DISNA KEN," Bram said after Jane was out of earshot.

"Are we wrong about her?" asked Eisla, twirling a lock of hair.

Aklen, who fashioned the rock specifically for Jane, said, "Naw, she's the one. The rock glowed when she sat on it."

"I wish I could see the rocks glow," Nairne said. "All I ever get tae do is run the burn."

"That's a big job," Aklen said. "I canna do it."

"Well, I hope she figures it out soon," Logan said. "Queen Donella needs her."

"Sae do we. How come we canna take her noo?" Levene asked.

They were all silent for a moment, each with their own thoughts of what had been lost in only a few years. Sometimes the triplets were unable to coax the water to flow. Aklen didn't always see the rocks glow but told no one of this. And Bram, their leader, helplessly watched them with their individual struggles. These woods remained magical and powerful, but for how long?

"A powerful spell of protection surrounds Jane that even the most skilled elder canna break," Bram replied. "Besides, the Wise Women said tae wait."

"There has tae be something we can do," Hamel said, "though I think I will like making flowers for her."

And so, the Fair Folk debated among themselves, as many had for the past twenty-one years, but spoke only in circles, never coming up with a solution for their dilemma.

GETTING around Alva proved easy enough given its small size, and soon Jane stood in front of the boardinghouse, clutching the paper with the address in one hand and her small bag of belongings in the other. Home. She stood for a moment outside, postponing going inside a moment longer. Once she opened that door, she would leave her old life behind for good.

The building was two stories high and made of gray stone. There were four windows along the front of the upper floor, and two windows on either side of the main door downstairs, all framed by dark green shutters, freshly painted. A small picket fence surrounded the house, and there appeared to be the beginnings of a spring garden in the side yard. It was plain and simple but dignified and well kept.

Willing herself to be brave, she marched to the door and knocked.

A woman answered, dressed in black with a crisp white apron and wisps of salt-and-pepper hair escaping from the bun at the nape of her neck. At perhaps forty, maybe forty-five, she had clear dark eyes and the lines of a woman who laughed much. Jane liked her immediately.

"I'm Jane Thorburn," she said. "I'm here for the bed."

"I'm Abi," the woman said, holding out her hand, "short for Abigail. I run the boardinghouse. Please come in. My word, ye're a wee lass."

Just like a fairy. Jane was grateful Abi didn't add the sentence that often came after someone noticed her diminutive stature. "Nice tae meet you, Mistress."

Abi waved an arm dismissively. "Oh, call me Abi. I do have rules, mind ye, but we arenae formal here."

"Aye," Jane said. "Thank ye...Abi."

After living in cramped quarters with her aunt and uncle and their children, a total of six people in two rooms, this house was luxurious. With her eyes wide open in wonder, she took in the downstairs.

"It's beautiful," she said.

"Well, we make do here. Come, I'll show ye around."

They entered a long room. To the left was a fireplace and a long wooden table with benches for sitting and eating. To the right was a parlor with a sofa, old and faded but still elegant, and two stuffed chairs. A couple of young women were quietly engaged in conversation. They glanced up and smiled at Jane, who imagined herself spending many a Sunday afternoon there.

Upstairs were rows of beds with a tall, narrow dresser at the end of each. "This one's yers," Abi said. "Yer bed mate is out for the afternoon. Lots of the girls are out walkin' since it's such a fair day."

"Aye, I took a walk in the glen before I came here." Jane cast an uncertain look toward the narrow bed. Bedmate? At Uncle Ewan's, the children slept together, while Jane had kept the small pallet on the floor she'd used since childhood. But with the paltry pay of a female weaver, the boardinghouse fit her budget, and it was also the only respectable place for a single young woman like Jane to stay.

"Ye'll get used tae it," Abi said, as if reading Jane's mind.

Abi explained the rules and curfew. Each boarder had to

keep her area neat and tidy, and they all took turns cleaning the common areas. On weekday evenings they were expected to return straight home after work. They were allowed to go out on Saturday evenings but had to be back by midnight, and if Abi caught anyone out unaccompanied at night by at least one other woman, she could be asked to leave.

"Some of these lasses leave home and lose their minds," Abi said. "I run a tight ship here. I canna have anyone livin' here gettin' in the family way."

"I am in nae hurry tae have a husband. I want tae work," Jane said.

"That's a noble goal, and I willnae stop ye. Maybe ye'll have some influence on the other lasses. I've got naethin' against wantin' tae find a husband, but these lasses are goin' about it the wrong way."

Jane had heard the stories, the cautionary tales from Uncle Ewan and Aunt Kirstin. "Well, I'm here tae work. I like weavin' and am good at it. But you, Mistress…Abi…did ye nae mairie?"

Abi's eyes misted, and she drew her right hand to her face. "I did, many years ago, when I wisna much older than you. My Brice was a fair man I met in the kirk, and we wed after a year o' courtin'. But the cholera took him a few years later. I was pregnant, but the child died, too. I never had much use for love after that."

"How horrible! I'm sae sairie." Jane wished she hadn't asked the question.

"Aye." Abi's eyes grew soft, but only for a moment. "But I like my work, too, and I like influencin' young women away from home and family. Ye're like my children, I suppose. An' sae many have no family, or the family needs them to work. How about yersel?"

Jane told her about her aunt and uncle.

"They sound lovely. But what about yer ma and pa?"

After having to answer this question for so many years, Jane had a practiced answer. "They sent me away for a better life. Uncle Ewan helped me get my first mill job. Anyway, I'm here because I want tae make somethin' of mysel. Wha kens? Mebbe one day they'll let lasses be supervisors."

Abi chuckled at that. If she had any more curiosity about Jane's home life, she didn't mention it. "I doubt it. They like tae hire lasses for cheap, an' they keep the better jobs for the men because they think women canna run things. They think the lasses will work only until they mairie, an' that the men need the money more."

"Yet *you* have a good job," Jane said, looking around. "They let women do some things, I suppose." If she never made supervisor, maybe she could find a job like Abi's one day.

"Well, men dinna want this kind o' job." She put her hands on her hips and nodded, satisfied she had told Jane everything. "I'll leave ye tae settle in. We'll have supper in an hour." With that, she stepped briskly away and downstairs, skirts swishing.

Jane unpacked her meager wardrobe in the dresser and stretched out on the bed, where the weariness from her journey took over, and she dropped into a deep sleep.

The sound of giggles and high-pitched voices woke her. Opening her eyes, she forgot for a moment where she was. When she sat up, about a dozen young women were gathered around her. They rattled off their names: Maisie, Wynda, Peigi, Elspeth, Grisell, and more. She didn't even try to remember the names right away, but she joined in as best she could as they all talked over each other. She would enjoy the company of these women.

She hadn't known what to expect of her co-workers. After glimpsing the dresses in the shop on Main Street, she expected them all to be better dressed and more refined. Yet she needn't have worried. Like her, they wore simple dresses in plain colors, and styled their hair in simple plaits or pinned in buns at the napes of their necks.

Despite the effervescent nature of youth, these women all showed the effects of long-term poverty. A few had bowed legs from rickets. Some developed a stoop, and many had missing or decayed teeth. Others had weathered, hardened faces and gray in their hair. Jane drew her hands to her curls to reassure herself that they hadn't suddenly turned white or come loose. Though she started working young like the rest of them, she had escaped these fates. Perhaps Beitris's potions had been good for something.

The women peppered Jane with questions so quickly that she couldn't answer one without getting another.

"Where are ye from?"

"What work do ye do?"

"Do ye have a sweetheart?"

Abi poked her head into the room. "Lasses!" She spoke in a stern voice, but her eyes were merry. "Let Jane settled in. Ye'll scare her off otherwise. Come on down for supper."

The young women backed away and headed down the stairs, still giggling as they took their seats at the dining table for supper. Jane followed timidly behind and tried to sort out the multiple conversations going on at once. As she tore off a hunk of bread and smelled the soup, she realized how hungry she was. She tried to eat small, dainty bites, but it all tasted so good she had to fight not to wolf it all down at once and embarrass herself at her first meal.

The chatter stopped as a woman entered the boardinghouse, immediately commanding the room. Jane stared with admiration at the statuesque beauty. She was older than the rest, probably late twenties, and dressed better than all of them in a dazzling white shirt, dark skirt, and tweed jacket. Her skin was clear, her chestnut hair glossy, and her face bright with an inner light, untouched by the effects of mill work. She exuded a not-so-faint scent of whisky.

Jane stayed away from the drink except for special occasions, such as when babes were born, or family friends married. She didn't much like the taste, and her memories of her father calling out for her in a slurred voice kept her from wanting any part of it.

The woman walked over and extended a hand. "I'm Skye," she said, her voice lilting. Uncle Ewan had told Jane many stories about life on the Isle of Skye, and this woman was as beautiful as the images he painted for her of reddish-brown mountains lit up by the setting sun. "You must be Jane."

"Aye. Nice tae meet ye," Jane said, extending her own small hand.

"I hear ye're a fine weaver," Skye said. "We're lucky tae have ye."

"Thank you."

"We have dances on Saturday evenings. Ye should come wi' us, right, lasses? We have a lot o' fun, and who knows?" With a dramatic pause and a mischievous wink, she added, "Mebbe ye'll meet someone." Leaning in, she added with a conspiratorial whisper, "That's how I met my Nathan."

"Oh, I'm nae…" Jane started to explain her desire for independence but thought better of it. *Best tae get acquainted first.* Jane wanted to make a good first impression on Skye, who radiated beauty, confidence, and strength—everything Jane wanted for herself. "I'd like that," she said instead.

As they all settled in with their tea, the warmth of the fire blazing, Jane couldn't be happier.

CHAPTER 6

I would not leave thee, dear beloved place,
A crown, a sceptre, or a throne to grace;
To be a queen—the Nation's flag unfurl—
A thousand times I'd be a Factory Girl!

An Address to Napiers Dockyard
Ellen Johnston

The five a.m. whistle blew, grating and discordant, and the factory girls rose from their beds with stretches and moans as they shook off the night. Skye grabbed the covers and pulled them over her head, and Jane had to shake her a few times.

Jane slept hardly at all, in part due to the excitement about her first day. Also, she never shared a bed with a grown woman, let alone a taller, plumper one like Skye. Jane's neck cramped, and she moved with stiffness from having to lie absolutely still all night; each time she drifted into a light sleep, she was interrupted by an elbow in her ribs.

Tired and hungry, she went downstairs where Abi greeted

her with a hot cup of tea. Food had to wait, though. Work began promptly at five-thirty a.m., with a short breakfast break not until eight-thirty. At mid-day she would have half an hour to walk to the boardinghouse, eat dinner, and return to the mill, where she would continue working until seven. Saturdays were blessedly shorter, when they ended work at four, with Sundays off for rest and church. Many of the factory girls didn't go, preferring to sleep instead after blowing off steam at the local dances on Saturday night.

This was why many of the townspeople looked down on them—going out at night and missing church? These were not young ladies at all, according to local gossips, but the "strumpets" Uncle Ewan warned Jane about. She pointed out to him that she never missed church while living with them, even when she first started working in the mills, but she never convinced him.

"The mill lasses go wild when they're on their own," he said with a knowing look. "Dancin'. Drinkin'. Chasin' after boys, then gettin' ruined by bringin' bairns intae the world wi'oot a proper weddin'."

In Jane's eyes, her co-workers from her years in the mill were hard-working young women who got tired and needed a bit of fun to make the long workdays bearable. Uncle Ewan came from a different generation, and she loved him for his concern even though she didn't agree with him. She promised to protect her virtue, and to not allow herself to be corrupted by "wanton" women.

"Ye raised me right," she said.

He chuckled at that. "Now ye're tryin' tae butter me up."

It took many more promises to convince him she wouldn't be led astray, but finally he agreed. Now, here she was for her first day! She found the office a few blocks from the boardinghouse and presented herself as a new hire, hoping the man at the desk couldn't detect her shaking knees. He peeked over his spectacles and let out a decided "Hrmph." Jane held her ground, standing straight, hands folded in front of her, and maintained eye contact with him as she waited.

He shook his head. "Ye're a wee fairy lass," he said. "I give ye a week."

Used to this type of reaction, Jane smiled. "I might surprise ye."

Another man entered and held out his hand to Jane. "I'm Mr. Stein," he said. "I'm the supervisor, and I'll take ye to the looms." If he held the same doubts about Jane's abilities, he kept them to himself.

He appeared to be about Jane's age, and a fine-looking young man, taller than most and dressed in an elegant navy blue suit and vest that fit his sturdy frame perfectly. His dark hair was thinning, giving him an air of dignity. Though not traditionally handsome, his infectious smile suggested a hint of mischief, not the harshness that most supervisors conveyed to their workers.

First, he commenced a tour of the mill. It was six stories of rubble masonry. The ground floor held offices for the book-keeper, supervisors, superintendent, and designers. On the first floor, there were baskets upon baskets of wool to be cleaned and dried, emitting the distinct odor of the sheep who provided it.

The male weavers worked on the second floor, and Jane poked her head in only briefly. Rows of looms running at once created a cacophonous din, with each man managing multiple looms at a time, scurrying back and forth. Children ran about, bringing spools of thread to the weavers, cleaning up fluff, and whatever else they were told to do.

The third floor would be hers, so they skipped that for the moment, instead checking in on the upper floors, where carders and spinners worked to turn the cleaned, dried wool into usable thread. Wherever she went with Mr. Stein, employees would look up briefly, and, aware of a supervisor in their midst, double their efforts.

Overall, the mill had plenty of windows to let daylight in, but they were covered with old dust and grime. The walls were a dingy yellowish tinge. Bits of fluff in the air resembled a light snow. For Jane, this all looked similar to Menstrie's mill, so the building's stark appearance actually gave her a sense of home-coming and made her more eager to start.

With the tour complete, Mr. Stein led her to her floor and to a closed set of double doors, behind which the looms clacked loudly. The whole building vibrated with the activity.

"This is where ye'll work," he said, raising his voice to be heard over the noise. "We are the best mill in Scotland. We produce high-quality product and hire only the best, so we expect ye to keep up our standards. I'll start ye on one loom tae see how ye do, an' then we'll add more. Shall we go in?"

"Aye, Mr. Stein," Jane answered.

She followed him inside, her eyes scanning the dusty room. The women worked multiple looms as the men did in the floor below and were so intent on their work that they didn't acknowledge Jane or Mr. Stein. Their movements were fluid and industrious, reminding Jane of ants as they went to and fro.

As with the men's floor a group of children darted between the weavers and beneath the looms, sweeping, dusting lint from machines, and bringing new spools of thread from the spinning rooms. One such girl paused to give Jane a dimpled smile. A gamine lass with a riot of blonde curls tied back with a wee bow, she looked like one of the Fair Folk.

Mr. Stein led Jane to her loom. The noise required him to use hand motions to show her how the pattern worked. It was an easy one, a simple plaid.

Touching the loom in front of her reverently, this key to her independence, she signaled her readiness by lightly waving her hand. Then she set about her work, getting the feel of the machine. She took a few deep breaths and willed her legs to relax, softening her knees a bit to add spring to her step. Turning her palms to face the loom, its vibration worked its way into her body, connecting her to it. Something clicked inside of her, and from then on the work became effortless. She forgot about Mr. Stein, who slipped away without her knowledge once convinced she could handle herself.

Even as a child Jane understood how the looms worked, how to move with direction and timing, and how to manage multiple looms with little to no instruction. Now, in a new town and a new mill, she settled into the routine and her new life, smiling and humming as she did so.

The breakfast break came so fast it felt like time had tricked her. She wanted to stay and work, but her growling stomach had a different opinion.

As the looms went silent, a sweet voice said, "I'm Leslie. Will ye teach me tae weave, Miss Jane?"

Jane turned to see the same dimpled lass who'd spoken to her earlier. Even early in the morning, Leslie scampered around the floor, working harder than her peers and never losing her radiant smile. She reminded Jane of a younger version of herself, so eager to learn, so eager to grow up before her time.

"Perhaps when ye're a bit older," she said. "And ye need tae grow a bit taller, too."

"I'll be lookin' ye straight in the eye in another year."

Jane laughed. "So ye will, lass. I like yer spirit. But ye still need tae wait a while. I dinna want Mr. Stein tae sack me on my first day." She placed a hand on Leslie's soft curls. Though Jane didn't want children of her own, the children of the mills always brought out maternal feelings.

Apparently satisfied, Leslie skipped away, presumably to her home, though Jane wondered if the wee lass had food to eat. A minute or so later, a woman came out and called to her to wait. *Ah. Apparently her mother works here as well.*

At the boardinghouse, the women gathered with none of the chatter of the day before when there was no sense of hurry. Jane wolfed down her porridge, not noticing its flavor or texture, and the minute she finished she rinsed out her bowl and ran out the door.

"Jane, wait!" One of the girls, Maisie, left the building right behind her. "We'll walk together."

Not wanting to be rude, Jane held up, reminding herself that she would have no problem getting to the mill on time. She didn't have to wait long for Maisie to hook an arm in hers. Jane's new friend stood a head taller with a much longer stride, and soon enough Jane struggled to keep up.

"What do ye think sae far?" Maisie asked. Light-brown freckles covered her face, and her abundant hair was working its way out of its bun.

"I like it," Jane said. "Mr. Stein was very helpful this mornin', an' I'm ready for more looms."

As they neared the mill, Mr. Stein crossed their path and tipped his hat. The two women slowed down to let him pass, and Maisie gave Jane a light, playful nudge. "Best watch out for Mr. Stein," she said. "He's broken more than a few hearts."

"I'll keep that in mind," Jane said with a laugh.

They talked a bit more as they entered the mill and walked to their floor, Jane happy to have found a friend. She learned that Maisie fled from Glasgow after a failed love affair, but she still considered herself a city lass and hoped to return one day. That was about all Jane knew of her before returning to her loom.

By dinnertime, she was ready to settle in and enjoy a hearty meal. Abi served a bowl of bean soup with kale and thick slabs of fresh bread, simple but filling. The women ate quickly, chatting only on the way back to the mill. As she sat between Maisie and Wynda, Jane learned more about Robert Stein.

Maisie said, "He started as a young lad in the mills, his da is a superintendent. He's very ambitious. Says he's going tae England one day tae work."

"England," Jane repeated, wincing at the word. Uncle Ewan told plenty of stories about the English, none of them good. It seemed almost traitorous for someone to want to work there.

"Mr. Stein has a way wi' the ladies, ye ken," Wynda said. "There are many more women than men here, so the men get their pick. Mr. Stein is a charmer, and the lasses fall over themselves for a simple look from him."

"I'm nae surprised," Jane said. He seemed so sure of himself.

"Oh, he's nice enough," Wynda said. "He's respectful an' all. He's just nae wantin' tae settle down." Chubby with bowed legs, Wynda demonstrated to Jane that she was one of the best weavers in the mill. She produced tartans faster than anyone, and Jane marveled at the young woman's skill.

Despite Jane's stamina, as the day progressed, between the lack of sleep and the excitement, her energy and focus dwindled fast. By mid-afternoon she was yawning and trying not to rub her eyes.

Weavers were required to check the raised metal "tells" on the back of the loom frequently to prevent them from getting stuck in an upward position, which would ruin the weave. In her exhausted state, Jane stayed too long at the front. Wynda appeared from nowhere to fix the tells, returning to her own station undetected, right before Mr. Stein entered the room to check on them.

The error, if not corrected, would have cost Jane her job on her very first day. Worse, it was a beginner's error, something completely unlike her. When they walked back to the boarding-house, Jane caught up with Wynda.

"I would've been sacked," she said. "I dinna ken where my mind went."

"It's naethin'," Wynda said with a wave of her hand.

"I dinna make mistakes like that, though."

Wynda put her arm around Jane. "We all make mistakes, what wi' the long days an' all. I can tell ye're a good weaver. Mebbe try an' rest tonight."

"I guess so," Jane said doubtfully.

"Ye'll be fine, lass. Dinna worry sae much. We look out for each other here. One day ye'll step in for me, I'm sure."

Jane noticed throughout the day how the women helped each other, unlike at her previous mill, where her co-workers tended to keep to themselves. With such a team of women working together, she relaxed a wee bit while she got comfortable in her new surroundings.

By the end of that first week, she could barely hold her head up to eat the toast and tea served for supper. Though a skilled weaver, the pressure to make a good first impression, along with Skye's restlessness in the bed they shared, sapped all of her energy.

On Saturday evening, Maisie and Wynda invited her to a local dance. Jane tried to decline, longing for a quiet evening and an early bedtime, but they insisted, dragging her outside with giggles and teasing. It felt so good to have real girlfriends, young women just like her; maybe she could keep her eyes open for a while longer.

The walk to the hall took only about ten minutes. The fetching sounds of a fiddle reached her ears first. Inside, she saw the entire band, probably in their forties or so, with an accordion, flute, piano, and drums. A group of dancers circled the floor in a lively reel. On one side, a refreshment table offered tea, shortbread, and fruitcake. Other rectangular tables with benches formed a ring around the dance floor. She, Maisie, and Wynda approached the table Skye saved for them all, close enough to the band to make them visible to potential dance partners, but far enough away that they could hear each other talk.

Other lasses entered and waved at the group at Jane's table, and she waved back, happy to feel a sense of belonging. Most of the men were at the pub and would arrive later. Those who arrived early looked more like grandfathers than potential suitors. For now, the women danced with one another. Jane planned to sit and watch, but Maisie grabbed her and pushed her out onto the dance floor. Jane stood still, uncertain about what to do next.

"Ye never danced before?" Maisie asked.

Jane shook her head as she tried to mimic the moves of her friends. Uncle Ewan frowned upon dancing, so she never learned.

Maisie rolled her eyes. "We learned all the dances when I worked in Glasgow. Ye must come from a small place like Alva. Come on, I'll show ye."

A man holding bagpipes joined the band, and they struck up a Highland Fling. Maisie moved into her rendition of the dance, and Jane watched closely as Maisie bent one leg, placing a foot in front of her knee, then to the back, then to the front again. That looked easy enough, so Jane joined in. When she tried to change legs, though, she found herself in a giggling heap on the floor.

"Up ye go," Maisie commanded, holding out a hand for Jane to grab.

"I dinna think I can do it," Jane said, still laughing. "Let me watch a bit more."

"Ye can do it, lass. Come on, give it another go."

And so, they worked together, practicing until Jane got the hang of it. The first time she did it right, she was so startled she tangled her legs up again.

"Ye've got it, lass. Come on, dinna stop noo."

Jane's legs screamed from the effort, and she wondered how she would be able to walk in the morning. However, she accepted Maisie's mission as her own, and did not stop until she accomplished a few minutes of passable, if not error-free, dancing.

Finally, exhausted, she returned to the table and sat next to Skye. So absorbed had Jane been with her dance practice, she hadn't noticed how the room had filled with more people, including younger men.

Skye gave Jane an affectionate shove and offered her a drink from her flask. Jane shook her head, but Skye wouldn't take no for an answer.

"Just a wee beb," she said. "It'll give ye courage."

Not wanting to be rude, Jane took a sip. The whisky was as horrible as she thought it would be, and she made a face.

"Oh, here, have one more. Ye get used tae the taste."

Obediently, Jane took the sip, but it didn't go down any easier. She handed the flask back to an amused Skye.

"So, which man strikes yer fancy?" Skye asked.

Jane nodded toward the oldest of men, more than double her age, plump and square with ruddy, full cheeks. "I'll go for that one," she said.

Skye winked and leaned in toward Jane. "Hmm. Maybe he's a bit young and randy for ye. How about the one over there?"

Jane leaned over toward Skye to look at the man, almost falling backwards in the process. Skye's steadying hand kept her upright.

The man Skye pointed out was as round as he was tall and had a thick, gray moustache. He wore a green tam o' shanter, with coarse, bushy hair sticking out wildly beneath it. Seeing the young women eyeing him, he gave them an appreciative glance. Jane, not wanting to encourage him, turned away with one hand over her mouth to stifle a laugh.

"There's treasure here tonight. I may dance wi' all of them," Jane said. "My uncle thinks I'm a fallen woman anyway."

"It's not as funny as ye think," Skye said. "Pickin's are slim here in Alva, so some o' the lasses go after these men."

"Ye're liein'!" Jane couldn't ever imagine being that desperate.

"I dinna tease about things like that. Even those men get their pick around here. If ye're lookin' for love in Alva, you'd best think again. The mills bring in all these girls, so the men preen around like peacocks. I was lucky tae land my Nathan."

"Ugh." Jane, a bit dizzy from the sips from Skye's flask, decided to stick to water for the rest of the evening. "I'm nae here tae fall in love, anyway. I dinna want a husband, nae yet."

"One of those modern lasses," Skye said, eyes twinkling in amusement.

"Aye." Skye was laughing at her, and most likely the girls would gossip about her the next day, but she didn't care.

"Nae me," Skye said. "I'll be happy tae leave the mill an' raise bairns. I might keep a little bakin' business on the side. Ye'll change yer mind when you're older."

Jane decided not to argue. Meanwhile, Maisie left the dance floor and joined them at the table, interrupting the conversation.

The door opened, and in strutted the young so-called peacocks of the mill, including Mr. Stein, all dressed in the dark suits they could afford because they lived at home with their parents and were paid more on the job.

Maisie rolled her eyes at Jane. "It's nae fair tae be a lass, eh? They have better clothes an' the pick of the women."

Jane watched as a group of factory girls surrounded the young men, preening and flirting, batting their eyelashes and laughing a bit too loudly. She didn't know whether to be disturbed or amused.

Mr. Stein caught her eye and gave her a little wave. She blushed and dropped her gaze. When she dared to look up again, he had one woman on each arm, both gazing at him with rapt attention as if divulging the secrets of life. Her friends were right. Men like him had their pick of anyone.

"Excuse me," she said to her new girlfriends. "I'm tired, I think I'll go back and sleep."

"Are ye awricht?" Skye gave her a worried glance. "Ye look flushed."

"Aye, the long week and the lack o' sleep are comin' together. I'll make my way back tae bed."

"I'll go wi' ye." Wynda had already slid off the bench.

"Are you sure? I dinna wantae stop yer fun."

"Remember the rules, lass. Abi disna ask much from us, but she insists that no lass walks alone at night. Besides, I'm ready for bed, too. Skye's the only one who gets any time wi' the lads anyway."

They walked home in silence, and both crawled into their beds. By the time Skye returned, Jane was sound asleep, dreaming of Fair Folk who teased her about the handsome Mr. Stein.

CHAPTER 7

But friendship's pure and lasting joys,
My heart was form'd to prove;
There, welcome win and wear the prize,
But never talk of love.

Love in the Guise of Friendship
Robert Burns

It didn't take long for Jane to adjust to sharing her bed with Skye, though they fought for possession of the single itchy blanket that barely covered them both. Skye, being the larger of the two women, usually won the battle, so Jane resorted to using her cloak to keep her warm. The other women didn't speak of these problems, so Jane didn't either. Factory girls learned early in their training never to complain.

Normally the Fair Folk came to her in her dreams, but she was too tired from work and bed-sharing to meet with them there. Sometimes, one of them nudged her, but she mumbled for them to leave her alone. But on Sundays, rested and free for the day, she enjoyed chatting with the Woodland Folk in the glen. Her mill friends were nice, especially Maisie and Wynda, but she wanted to get to know Bram and his friends better, and perhaps see Flora and Coira if they were available.

On one such Sunday in late April, Jane ran out of the boardinghouse right after breakfast to head up the glen. The days were growing longer, wildflowers were starting to appear, and the air was pleasantly dry—a perfect day to be outside. Despite the chill that remained, the sun shone brightly on the path and invited her in to share its warmth.

Her rock, bathed in sun, beckoned to her. The gentle breeze whispered soothing sounds to her and caused a few stray hairs to tremble. Surrendering to its reassurance, she lay back on the rock and stared up at the sky, with its wispy clouds. Her breath deepened, and her soul stretched wide to receive the day.

"Miss Thorburn?"

She jumped at the unexpected sound. Sitting up and smoothing her skirt, she found herself face-to-face with Mr. Stein.

"Mr. Stein, I thought I was alone!"

"I'm sorry tae sneak up on ye that way. Ye looked so peaceful, I almost didnae say anything."

Aware that they were alone in the woods without a chaperone, Jane's spine stiffened. He looked so handsome, standing there with his hands in his pockets, a man without a care, hardly someone to fear.

"Perhaps I should go," Jane said.

"Naw, I willnae harm ye. Nor will I tell a soul I saw ye here. Make a place for me on that rock, will ye? This is my favorite spot, too."

"But what if someone sees us?" Only women risked the ruin of their reputations if they were caught alone with a man. Walks in public were fine, but here in the woods? Townspeople would always think the worst.

"I grew up in these woods," he said. "I can disappear" —he

CHAPTER 7   67

snapped his fingers—"as quick as the Wee Folk. Yer virtue is safe wi' me, lass."

His merry eyes were enough for her to scoot over to make room for him. The rock was large enough for her to keep a respectful distance, but close enough for her to catch his scent. It was as if he bathed in morning dew, fresh after a night's rain.

Taking in a deep breath, she willed herself to relax. Even on a nice day like this, she seldom met other explorers in the glen, so a town gossip was unlikely to appear and witness this improper meeting.

"Lovely day," he said. "Almost summer-like."

"Aye." Only in Scotland would such a day be deemed "summer-like" by anyone, but her tongue failed her, rendering her unable to respond to his joke, and she worried he could hear her heart pounding.

He leaned toward her and whispered, "Ye can tae talk tae me, ye ken."

The whisper of his breath on her cheek gave her a thrill, and she put her face in her hands to hide her blush. "I suppose so," she said. Yet words continued to fail her.

Mr. Stein sat in contented silence. He raised his face toward the sun like a flower, his eyes closed, his face serene and untroubled. Jane, on the other hand, frantically tried to come up with small talk, not a natural talent for her.

"Ye lived in Alva yer whole life?" *There. That's a fair question.* Her clenched shoulders let go. *Relax. Ye can have a normal conversation wi' him, lass.* She thought she heard some tittering in the background and prayed Bram and his gang wouldn't show up to tease her.

"Aye. I was born in Tillicoultry, down the road," he said, "but Da and Ma brought me here before I could walk, so I dinna remember anything else."

"Alva is a beautiful place, especially up here." The breeze pulled a lock of fine hair from its bun at the nape of her neck.

She pushed it out of her eyes and behind her ear. He came across as someone who, unlike her, wasn't easily flustered.

"Aye, sae beautiful." He gave her a sly glance. "Makes me want tae sing."

"What?" She hadn't expected that.

He drummed his fingers on the rock as he thought. "Ah. I have it." Then he burst into a lilting baritone:

"Oh! Alva's woods are bonnie, Tillicoultry's hills are fair; But when I think o' the bonnie braes o' Menstrie, It makes my heart aye sair."

"That's lovely," Jane said. His singing voice was as charming as the rest of him. It startled her, and yet his voice belonged in this private wood as much as any birdsong. She forgot to worry about being discovered. "I grew up in Menstrie, but I never heard the song as well as ye sang it. Do ye ken the story that goes wi' it?"

"Tell me," he said.

She closed her eyes and took in a deep breath to remember Uncle Ewan's version of the tale. "The miller o' Menstrie had a beautiful wife, but one day the king of the fairies spirited her away from him. The miller missed her, for he loved her awfie much, and she missed him, too. She would sing the song, and he heard her. One day, by accident, he broke the spell, and she dropped from the air and landed at his feet. They were never separated after that."

"If she fell from too high, she must have been broken?"

"Aye, Mr. Stein," Jane said with a chuckle. "Sometimes the stories lack a few details. Or mebbe I forgot."

He laughed heartily and gave her a light slap on the back as he did so. The imprint of his palm seemed to burn into her. "Call me Rabbie when we're nae at work."

"Rabbie," she said. The name rolled like honey on her tongue.

Rabbie was more serious at work, always friendly and kind

but never too familiar with the workers, so different from the playful lad sitting next to her. She reminded herself, though, that he flirted easily with other women. He had a force about him as strong as the burn, and he could sweep her away like those roaring waters if she wasn't careful.

They sat in a peaceful silence for a while, until Rabbie finally spoke. "I always preferred tae play here. The trees and the burn and the birds were my friends," he said.

"Aye, mine as well. I love my aunt and uncle, but I never belonged in the family," Jane confessed, surprised at how comfortable she felt saying that. "I much preferred the woods." She didn't mention the fairies and would have to know him a good bit better for that. "I'm surprised, though."

"What do ye mean?"

"I see yer family in the kirk on Sundays. They're nice enough." They were the kind of bustling, lively family she longed for. Rabbie had several brothers and a sister who showed up in different combinations each week. The boys would joke and shove each other until their mother gave them a look that made them settle down and take a seat in the pews. His young sister always kept close to her mother. Whenever Mrs. Stein put a protective arm around her daughter, a lump rose in Jane's throat, wishing she had a mother like that.

His father scared her, though, so she never spoke to the family except to say good morning. The elder Mr. Stein was a mill superintendent, her supervisor's boss. If that weren't enough, mill gossip claimed he was once arrested for threatening two other men with a knife. Co-workers also whispered that he left Mrs. Stein for another woman in his younger days. No evidence remained of that wild young man, though he had a deep scar running down the right side of his face and he seldom smiled.

"They're the best," Rabbie said, interrupting her thoughts, "but somethin' about this place is special. An' I'm the only one in my family who comes up here. Ma worries I spend too much time alone, but I like people fine as long as I can come here when I want. But what about you, Miss Thorburn? What tales have ye from hame?"

"Oh, nae much tae tell," she said, demurring. "I stayed wi' my Uncle Ewan and Aunt Kirstin before I came here. My uncle works in mills and he thought I wid like it there, so he took me in tae teach me." She hoped Rabbie wouldn't notice her downcast eyes or the catch in her throat as she told the edited version of her story.

He didn't. Or, if he did, he didn't let on.

"An' what brought ye to the boomin' metropolis of Alva?" he asked.

"There was a job for me." She wished she had a grand story to tell, something a bit more exciting. Then, hoping to impress him a little, she added, "Though I hope one day tae work in Lowell."

"Ah, the holy grail for a mill lass! All the way to Massachusetts!" Rabbie clapped his hands in amusement.

"Dinna laugh, sir," she said, her eyes flashing. "I save what I can. I wid like tae see the world one day. I willnae apologize for havin' big dreams."

"Nor should ye," he said. "I'm sorry. I am nae laughing at ye. I hear good things about Lowell. Me, I'm going tae England. Have ye been?"

"Oh, no." Land of the conqueror. She couldn't imagine why any Scot would go there willingly. Even mild-mannered Uncle Ewan joked about shooting Englishmen for sport.

"Ah, I like it there. They dinna mind us so much these days, as long as we work hard." His laugh was easy and relaxed, and as musical as his singing voice. "I suppose we shall part ways one day then. I'll be a designer in England, and ye'll find yer fortunes in America."

"It seems that way."

"How about we be friends in the meantime?" he asked. "I like ye, Jane. Ye work hard and have a lot o' spirit."

She dropped her head, turning her face from him, too reserved to show her joy lest she tempt the evil eye. "I like ye, too, sir."

"Then that settles it. From here on out, we are officially friends. Let's shake on it."

Still keeping her eyes averted, she held out a small hand, which he took in his larger one, warm to the touch despite the chilly weather. Then, feeling bolder, she allowed herself to look at him. His expression showed what appeared to be surprise, but Jane wasn't sure.

Then he jumped up, removed his hat, and bowed, breaking the spell. "Enjoy yer time in the glen. Rest tonight, for I'll work ye hard tomorrow."

He left before she could think of anything else to say. "Stupid lass," she muttered to herself, hoping he was too far away to hear. When he left, the glen fell silent. Other than the sound of the water, she heard nothing. No birds, no animals skittering in the brush. The glen felt so empty without him.

CHAPTER 8

I go, my loved one, but I leave no token,
I would have done had fortune smiled on me,
The sad remembrance of a heart that's broken
Is all, my loved one, I can leave to thee.

The Last Lay of the Factory Girl
Ellen Johnston

*O*n a clear, cool Saturday night in summer, the fresh air felt good on Jane's cheeks as she walked arm in arm with Maisie and Wynda to the Saturday night dance. She didn't go out with them often, but she hoped to catch a glimpse of Rabbie and maybe get in a dance or two. With Maisie's gentle encouragement, Jane's dancing improved, even if the selection of dancing partners had not.

The hall was less than half full when they arrived. The musicians were doing their best to create a festive atmosphere, but even they struggled with enthusiasm. It would take a lot more people, and much more whisky, to liven things up.

"Where is everyone?" Wynda asked.

Jane shook her head. "I dinna ken." The men who were already there were the men they never wanted to dance with. So far it looked as though going out was a waste of time.

Still, there were several great tables to choose from, and hopefully things would perk up soon.

"Look at these fools," Maisie said with a groan. "I swear, they get older by the week. I'll never find a husband wi' this crop o' men." She launched into her usual tirade about how Glasgow was so much better, but Jane tuned her out.

Wynda made the rounds, happy to dance with anyone. She always insisted they were good men who lacked a woman's influence to smooth their rough edges. A cheerful sort, Wynda no doubt would make the perfect wife for a nice widower, someone who would be grateful for company and not mind her bowed legs.

Despite the efforts of Wynda and a few others, malaise seemed to be catching that night. Several of the younger men entered the room, all looking like they didn't really want to be there. A few walked in, looked around at the lack of action, and walked right back out again. Rabbie was not among them.

"I'm tired," Jane said, suddenly grumpy.

Maisie gave her a knowing glance. "Dinna get yer hopes up about Mr. Stein," she said. "No doubt he's out on a date."

"I'm nae interested in him," Jane protested, though her voice cracked when she said it.

With an eye roll and a giggle, Maisie said, "Aye, ye just want tae work. Or so ye say."

Jane cast a dark glance at her friend. "Maisie, behave yerself."

"He likes ye for sure, no matter what you think." Maisie's eyes danced with mischief. "Mebbe that scares him. The two o' you are alike, so afraid ye might lose somethin' if you fell in love."

Jane started to protest, but Maisie's remark brought out her curiosity. "Like what?"

"Oh, ye ken. All this talk about Lowell, and England. Ye both have stars in yer eyes about work, but everyone knows none o' that matters. Love disna come along every day. I've been at the mill for three years, and I canna remember when I went on my last real date. Ye dinna want tae die a spinster."

Maisie's words cut Jane more deeply than she expected. "Independent woman" was one thing; "spinster" didn't sound good at all.

"I'm going back," she said again. These dances were always the same: old men looking for young flesh, the younger men showing up late, and conversations with her friends about clothes and men and marriage. Tonight, she wanted some sleep.

"I'm sairie, Jane. I teased ye too much. Shall I walk ye back?"

Jane shook her head. "I'm fine. Abi goes tae bed as soon as we leave, ye ken." The factory girls had all figured this out, and few paid attention to the rule about walking alone anymore. Besides, the drunks were either still at the pub or at the dance; it was too early for anyone to be staggering about and looking for trouble.

Once home, she tiptoed through the parlor, empty and silent without the lively presence of young women. A creak of floorboards caused her to hold herself still, heart pounding, wondering if she would be the first to get caught and expelled.

As she walked up the stairs, moving carefully to avoid more creaks in the old wood, she paused. What was that sound? It took her a few more steps to realize someone was sniffling.

She hesitated, not wanting to intrude on a private moment. The women seldom had them, with so many living together in the same room. Yet the desire to help kicked in, so she tiptoed into the dormitory. There, she found Skye sprawled out on their bed, arm draped over her eyes.

"Are ye awricht?" Jane asked, perching on a corner of the bed.

"Oh, Jane," Skye said, sniffles turning to sobs, shoulders shaking.

Jane sat frozen, wondering what to do. She had seen far more displays of emotion in her short time in the boarding-house than in all her years with her aunt and uncle, and she still found this lack of reserve uncomfortable. "I didna mean tae make ye cry. What happened?"

After a few more minutes of sobbing, Skye quieted. "If I tell ye, promise ye willnae say a word."

"Of course not. Ye're my friend."

She handed Skye a handkerchief and felt the night hold its breath, waiting. A full moon shone through the window, casting an eerie light on her friend. Jane thought how even a tearful Skye had extraordinary beauty; her skin didn't turn blotchy, and her eyes were not red. Yet in this state, with confidence having fled, she looked younger and more delicate.

"Shh, shh," Jane said in her most soothing tone, rubbing Skye's back as it shook with a new round of sobs. "Tell me noo, before the other lasses come back."

Skye sat up, blowing her nose and wiping away one last tear. "Awricht," she said, and blew out her breath. "Swear tae me, Jane, ye'll tell no one."

"I swear, Skye. I have naethin' tae gain if I break yer confidence."

"Well, then." Clearing her throat, she said, "I'm in the family way."

"Oh, God."

Pregnant women worked at the mill, often until their babes were born, then returned to work soon afterwards, in pain as their breasts filled with milk, surrendering their children's nourishment to wet nurses or even a cow's milk formula. They were the married women, lucky enough to have mothers, moth-ers-in-law, or older children to help with the infants. Those without husbands went straight to the poorhouse, where they lived out their days in poverty and shame. The kirk, meanwhile, eagerly held the women to public ridicule.

"Ye have tae help me. I canna have a bairn, nae noo."

"Does yer man know?"

"Aye. He was happy tae lie wi' me, but now he says he didna do it."

The injustice brought a bitter, metallic anger to Jane's tongue. A man could walk away, but a woman had to face the consequences. Though Skye had dated most of the eligible bachelors in Alva, she did so one at a time, and Jane believed her to be faithful.

Still, she had to ask the question. "Is he the one?"

"Aye, Jane. I swear. Ye have tae help me."

Help yes, but how? Rubbing her fingers on her temples, Jane tried to think of their options. One idea immediately sprang to mind, giving her hope.

"What about the foundling home?" she asked. "Ye could take the bairn there."

Skye shook her head. "I could never leave it. And I'd still lose my reputation."

"Let me think." The foundling home idea didn't sound as good when she spoke it aloud. "How about this? Is there a man from the dances ye wid consider? Mebbe a widower?" There wasn't a huge selection of men, but they would line up for Skye.

"Ugh. There has tae be something else. What about—"

Skye didn't finish her sentence, and the two women sat in uneasy silence. Jane's heart pounded as she realized what they were really contemplating. Both women grew up in religious homes. Would either be able to show their faces in the kirk ever again? And what if someone found out? Under The Offenses Against the Person Act, ending a pregnancy carried a life sentence. Yet not doing something guaranteed the ruin of Skye's life. She'd lose her job and live in poverty. No man would love her again, no matter how beautiful she was. Surely no God wanted Skye to suffer for loving someone who didn't love her back.

As both young women realized there were no other options to discuss, a kind, wise face from Jane's past emerged in her mind. "I think I ken who might help," she said.

For the first time in this discussion, Skye's face brightened. "Do ye think? Who wid help me who widnae tell?"

"She's a howdiewife, the one who brought me intae the world. I'll go right awa. Will ye cover for me?"

Skye nodded. "When will ye be back?"

"It willnae take long, but I have tae leave noo."

"I dinna want ye to come across any danger sae late at night."

"I'll be fine. Let me take care o' this for ye."

"Oh, Jane, I didna ken what tae do. I'm glad ye're my friend."

Jane kissed the top of Skye's head as if comforting a child, then grabbed her cloak. Almost as an afterthought, she opened a drawer where she kept a nail and a small cross for protection from troublesome fairies who loved to toy with humans. Despite her own positive experiences with the Fey, she didn't want to take any chances of encountering in the dark those who might wish her harm, whether human or fairy. Once armed, she crept down the stairs and out into the night.

She needn't have worried. Flora and Coira arrived with a group of Fair Folk who surrounded Jane, casting light on her path. The bright moon helped as well. They did not speak to each other, as they understood the solemnity of the moment. In their world, with the troubles in the queendom, they welcomed all children. But they understood the toll unwanted babies had on their mothers and did not judge.

The walk took less than an hour, though it seemed much longer. When Jane reached her destination, the Folk guided her to Beitris's home, a modest cottage where a lone candle still glowed in the window. There, they each gave her a kiss on the cheek and went on their way.

EVEN AFTER A BUSY night of delivering a new child into the world, Beitris spent time in the wee hours communing with her God—not the harsh God of her church, though she dutifully attended Sunday services—but the God from nature. It was the God she understood through years of watching the miracle of birth, and the wondrous, mysterious capabilities of a woman's body. Her God loved and admired women. Her God wept when babies died or were born with problems. Her God worked through her hands, humbling her with an ever-present, gentle attentiveness.

In the wee hours of this Sunday morning, she rose stiffly from time on her knees. She was an old woman, though still vigorous. Her hair had lost its color long ago and fell straight and white down her back. Her once-plump flesh now hung on her like an ill-fitting coat. Children in the street called her a witch and ran from her in fear. They didn't see a lot of old women. Their mothers, with bodies spent from bearing children and working in the factories and the mines, often died young. Most did not know their grandmothers. So Beitris, with each passing year, became more of an oddity.

A knock interrupted her thoughts. This did not surprise her, as several young women in town were due to give birth anytime, and babies often preferred to make their debut in the dark. Opening the door, she was shocked to see Jane standing there, shivering a little, whether from the cool night or anxiety.

"Wee Jane? Oh my, let me look at ye." Beitris stepped back to study the young woman whose beginning to life was far more adventurous than most. Jane's hair was disheveled, but her cheeks glowed with health and her eyes sparkled. "Come here, lass." As she took Jane into her wiry arms, Beitris could read the young woman's joys and struggles. Jane possessed a fierceness that belied her delicate appearance.

As they separated, Jane said, "I need yer help right away."

Beitris settled her attention to Jane's belly to assess the situation. Her arrival in the wee hours suggested an urgent problem, one howdiewives knew only too well. "How far along?" she asked.

"Oh my, no," Jane said, reflexively clutching her abdomen. "I have a friend in the boardinghouse in Alva, an' she has run into a spot o' trouble. The man says he willnae care for the babe. He even says it isnae his, but Skye—that's my friend—swears it is."

"Young men nowadays. Wantin' their fun wi' no consequence." Beitris shook her head and added a few *tsk tsks* for good measure. "Ye walked here at night, did you, tae help a friend?"

"Aye. An' we need tae hurry. If Abi catches me out on my own in the night I'll lose my bed."

"I'll help ye stay hidden. But ye shoulda brought the lass."

"Ah." Jane slapped her forehead with her hand. "I didna think o' that."

"Relax, we can go tae her," Beitris said. "We can take my horse. It'll be quicker than walkin', and it willnae strain me none. First, though, I think we should have some tea." She moved to put the kettle on the fire.

"Do we no need tae go noo?" Jane asked.

"We'll go soon enough. We're better off tae handle these situations wi' a calm mind."

Jane looked uncertain but sat at the table, obedient. Beitris put some oat cakes out, and Jane took a nibble. After a few sips of fragrant, calming tea, her shoulders melted, and the tension lifted from her pale face. Despite the circumstances of the evening, soon she chatted away about work at the mill, about Lowell, about her ambitions. She didn't mention a man, but Beitris suspected one. Something in Jane had awakened, something only love brought to light. She didn't ask questions, letting the lass talk about whatever was on her mind. It was always refreshing to have a youngster around, still filled with life's possibilities.

Once finished with food and drink, Beitris gathered some herbs, tapping her chin as she went through the list in her mind. She wept each time a woman chose to end a pregnancy, but life was too harsh for women under the best of circumstances, and raising a child with no husband and no job prospects was too much to ask.

After stocking her bag with all she would need, Beitris saddled the horse, and together they set out on their terrible errand. She had delivered babies in Alva before, mostly as a younger woman. On the main road, with the morning sun now risen to guide them, they made quick progress to the boarding-house. She whispered a spell of protection for herself, Jane, and Skye, that they be left alone to handle their business without question.

By the time they arrived, Abi and most of the women were up and gone, many of them off to the early church service. Jane motioned Beitris to the stairs, which the old woman climbed with some effort. Jane said nothing, though Beitris saw her questioning look and waved it away with a gnarled hand.

Skye lay alone in the bed, with one arm covering her eyes, as though she hadn't moved since Jane left.

"I have our help," Jane said softly.

Skye opened her eyes and sat up, smoothing her hair. "I must look a sight. Ye were gone sae long, I feared somethin' bad happened."

Skye's beauty, a quality that gave women power in the world, at times like this could work against her. Beitris had seen this play out far too many times. "I hear ye have some trouble," she said, standing at a respectful distance. When a lass got into the family way without wanting to, it was best to approach her like one would a strange, skittish animal.

"Aye," Skye said. Her eyes were wary, but her body let go of some of its tension in response to the old woman's gentle caution. "Jane told ye?"

Beitris took a step closer. In a voice designed to soothe, she asked, "How long since yer month?"

"I've only missed one, but I got sick at work the other day at the mill. I fear I'll lose my job if I have tae miss work. Can ye help me?"

"Aye, and ye'll have an easier time since you found me early. But let me ask ye, lass, are you sure this is what ye want?"

Skye stared at the ceiling in silence while Beitris waited patiently.

"It isnae what I want," she said. "I love him, an' I thought he loved me, too. But I canna raise a bairn on my own." Her voice broke, and a fresh round of sobs poured through her. Jane sat next to her and patted her shoulder, then took one of Skye's hands in hers. Skye tightened her grip.

Beitris stood next to the bed now, having crept toward it step-by-step. "Shall we have a look?" she asked.

Skye gave a tearful nod, and Beitris motioned Jane to move away. It took some doing for Jane to extricate her hand from Skye's, as her friend clung to her, so she followed Beitris's example and took her time, gently but firmly coaxing herself from Skye's tight grasp. "I'll be right here while Beitris checks ye," she said.

Beitris examined the young woman between rounds of sobs, making soothing sounds and patting Skye's hand. "Ye were good to call on me early," she said. "We can fix this without any trouble...but ye must be sure of it."

"I dinna have a choice," Skye said. "Oh God, what a stupid lass I am! I swear, if we take care o' this, I'll ne'er lie wi' a man until I'm wed." She looked Beitris full in the face. "Do it," she commanded.

Beitris went downstairs to prepare the herbs, leaving the two young women alone.

"Are ye sure?" Jane asked.

"I dinna understand why you keep asking me that question," Skye snapped. "What wid you do? Have the bairn?"

"I dinna ken," Jane said. "But ye hesitated, an' that worries me. Yer heart keeps sayin' no. Ye must be sure, Skye, else there will be more problems later. I fear ye'll hate me one day for bringin' the very help ye begged for."

Skye took Jane's hands in hers. "I promise, I'll ne'er hold this against ye. I'd found a woman like Beitris soon enough on my own. I didna ken where tae start."

"Okay, then," Jane said. "As long as ye promise."

Beitris returned with the potion and bade Skye drink it. It was foul in odor, and Skye wrinkled her nose.

"Drink it fast, an' get it over with," Beitris said.

Skye closed her eyes and brought the cup to her lips. "I'll pretend I'm drinkin' a whisky." With one last sigh of hesitation, she steeled herself and gulped it down. When she finished it, her whole body shuddered with the effort. "That's the worst whisky I ever tasted."

In spite of the circumstances, the women all laughed a little.

"Now what?" Skye asked.

"The monthly should come in a day or two," Beitris said. "It will be heavy when it comes, so stay off yer feet if ye can. Ye're nae too far along, so it willnae last too long. If anything else happens, let me know right away."

Skye lay back on the bed, her face white. Beitris leaned over to brush some hair from her face.

"I'll say prayers for ye, lass," she said. "Rest noo, an' I'll see ye soon."

"Is she awricht?" Jane asked as she walked Beitris out.

"Aye. It's a shock tae a woman when this is done, a shock tae both body and soul. Let her cry or scream if she needs to. She needs a good friend like she ne'er needed one before."

"Thank you," Jane said as she hugged Beitris, clinging to her a bit too tight.

"Give her some time," Beitris said, "an' come see me if there's any trouble."

As she watched Beitris mount her horse and ride off into the misty morning, Jane wished she felt reassured.

CHAPTER 9

It once was a garden both lovely and green,
And 'Genius' placed there a song-weaving queen;
But the false-hearted gardener, from motives unseen,
Doomed her an outcast in the morning.

The Morning: A Recitation
Ellen Johnston

he next several days were difficult. Skye's monthly came, heavy as predicted, and her moods were as wild as a stallion. Though Beitris warned the two women, both Jane and Skye were unprepared for the onslaught of anger, tears, and depression, and Skye even pushed Jane out of bed one night. When Jane landed on the floor, she covered herself with her cloak and stayed there, shivering on the bare wood.

"It's all yer fault," Skye hissed. "Ye ruined my life."

Yet the next morning she apologized, begging Jane not to leave her side.

Sometimes Jane caught Skye rubbing her belly and looking

off into the distance, tears rolling down her cheeks. At other times, when in a group she showed an exaggerated cheer, laughing too loudly at even the slightest joke. Occasionally she caught Skye staring darkly at her, but she dropped her gaze and focused on the task at hand.

Unable to take time off from the mill lest she lose her job, Skye went to work every day, but snapped at anyone who looked at her sideways. Ordinarily she glided from loom to loom with ease, but now she marched, stomped, pounded the floor. Sometimes she stood still, hands on hips, glaring at the looms and muttering.

At night, she stayed downstairs until she thought Jane was asleep, and in the mornings she jumped out of bed and ran off without a word. As much as Jane wanted to comfort her friend, Skye demanded to be left alone…except for the moments when she ran up to Jane and hold on to her, sobbing and pleading for forgiveness.

"Why is Skye sae mad at ye?" Leslie asked one day.

Jane paused for a moment before answering. The child didn't miss a thing, so there was no point in lying to her and saying nothing was wrong. But Skye had sworn Jane to secrecy, and besides, Leslie was much too young for such details.

"We dinna see eye tae eye on some things," Jane said at last. "Noo, go back tae work before we get in trouble."

Leslie gave Jane a quizzical look, but the words worked like magic. Though one of the mill's most conscientious employees, the wee lass seemed to fear losing her job more than most. She returned to her labors and didn't ask again.

Skye huffed and sighed as she worked her looms. In the days that followed, she started to show up late in the mornings with a shuffling gait. Worse, her breath reeked of whisky, even early in the day, and Jane feared she would one day push the limits too much and lose her job. Despite Skye's skills and reputation as a hard worker, it wouldn't take long for the supervisors to lose their patience.

Nathan kept his distance. Sometimes Jane caught him staring at Skye as they went to meal breaks, eyes narrowed, as if looking for the telltale signs of a progressing pregnancy. It wouldn't be long before he realized there was no baby, but Jane couldn't think about that now.

At the boardinghouse, when Jane talked to the other women at breaks, Skye mumbled insults under her breath: liar, cow, worthless fairy. Jane did her best to ignore the digs, because she sympathized with Skye's predicament, but it was wearing her down.

After a month or so of this, Maisie and Wynda had seen enough.

"Whatever has the two o' ye mopin' around, it has tae stop," Maisie said, addressing them both. "Ye need tae come out wi' us."

Skye, curled up in bed with a book, ignored Maisie's orders.

"I'm tired," Jane protested. She had hoped to have the downstairs sofa to herself for the evening and do some mending.

"Oh, come on." Wynda put an arm around Jane. "Gie it an hour. If ye dinna wantae stay, I'll walk ye home. Skye, how about it?"

"Leave me alone." Skye closed her book and rolled onto her other side, facing away from the other women.

Jane shook her head at Maisie and Wynda so they wouldn't continue to push.

"I'll go," she said reluctantly, casting one more frustrated glance at Skye. Going out had to be better than staying in the same building as her morose friend. "Only for a wee bit, though."

She changed into a frock she had made for herself, a dark green "princess" style and she used tucks and darts to emphasize her slim waist. It had a modest high neckline trimmed with a white ruffle. Though not as fancy as the elegant clothes Skye wore, it brought out the red in her hair. As they headed out into the brisk night air, the thought of an evening out grew more appealing, and Jane was thankful for the nudge from her friends.

Of the young men who came to the dances, only Nathan was there when the women arrived, and Jane glared at him. She would never forgive him for what he did to Skye. What was he doing there, anyway? Was he looking for someone else to sully? Not wanting to watch the goings-on, she motioned to Maisie and Wynda to dance with her. This led to some remarks from the other men.

One of them, who Jane always turned down for a dance because he was old enough to be her father, said, "Ye dinna have a right tae be choosy, lass. Ye're not gettin' any younger."

Jane knew better than to argue with him. "I'll keep that in mind, sir," she said, and then turned her back.

"Ye're too nice, Jane," Maisie said. "I'd set him straight."

"What's the point?" Wynda said. "It widnae do any good."

"Wynda's right. He'd argue more. Best let it go." Jane rubbed the back of her neck with her hand. The muscles were so tense she could barely move it. Her thoughts were neither on dancing nor dealing with a pushy man.

Maisie looked as if she had more to say on the subject, but the heavy double doors of the hall opened, and she gasped. "Look who's here," she whispered.

Skye, dressed in a red tartan dress with a tight bodice that emphasized her perfect, curved figure, stood in the doorway. She had gathered her long chesnut hair in twists that ended with tendrils reaching her shoulders, the elaborate style held in check with a series of combs. Standing tall and tilting her head, she compelled the whole room to turn toward her.

Jane opened her mouth to say something, then closed it. She had left a morose, defeated Skye at the boardinghouse.

Somehow she had transformed herself. Whatever had happened, Jane was glad of it and ran over to her.

"I'm glad ye came," she said. "What changed yer mind?"

Skye's eyes narrowed, and she set her jaw. "Let me be."

Jane stepped back, dropping her eyes to hide the sting of tears, and made her way to her seat. Skye's attendance did not mean all was well. Hopefully her lively spirit would return soon.

Nathan, having seen her entrance, made his way to Skye and took her hand. The two of them stood silently, staring at each other with longing in their eyes.

"Oh, look, they're back together," Wynda said. She had asked Skye repeatedly what had happened between her and Nathan but received only a withering glance in reply.

Maisie snorted. "No doubt they'll be fightin' again soon enough. Ye're too much of a romantic, Wynda. Right, Jane?"

Jane didn't answer. Instead, she tiptoed over to Skye, daring to make one more attempt to reach her friend.

"Remember what he did," she said under her breath.

"I told ye tae let me be," Skye said, but her voice lost its sharp edge.

"Aye, let us be," Nathan added.

Jane stood there, wishing she could think of something else to say. Instead, she mumbled, "I will. Just...be careful."

"I'll nae let him bring me harm again, Jane, I swear." Though she spoke to Jane, Skye directed her words at him, and he gazed back at her, misty-eyed.

"I've missed you," he said in response.

The sparks between the two former lovers were obvious to anyone. A sick feeling settled into Jane's gut. He wanted her back. Would he want to be a father to the baby, too—the baby she no longer carried?

As the charismatic couple took to the dance floor, it was as if the crowd parted for them. The band struck up a waltz, and they glided about, unaware of anyone or anything around them.

Their beauty and graceful movements held the other dancers spellbound, Jane included, and by the end of the song they were the only couple remaining. A round of applause and cheers at the end startled them back to the room.

"They're somethin'."

Jane, startled, turned to see Rabbie standing behind her. "Aye," she said.

He raised an eyebrow. "What is it, Jane? Ye seem a wee bit tense."

"I'm fine. Ye startled me, that's all."

He held out a hand. "Dance wi' me?" he asked.

Skye and Nathan left the dance floor, now filling with other couples, so Jane accepted Rabbie's hand in hers. It was warm and steadying, but she couldn't shake her unease. When the dance ended, he invited her to his table, but she said she needed to go home. He gave her another questioning look but didn't ask further questions.

As she returned to the boardinghouse and took to her bed, she asked herself: *should we have waited?* With Skye and Nathan back together, they could have had the child. And what would he do if he found out what they had done?

WHEN THE FIRST rays of sunlight poured in through the windows the next morning, Skye was still nowhere to be found. Most of the other women were asleep, but Jane stole downstairs quietly to make breakfast. Rubbing her eyes and yawning, she hoped the food and drink would perk her up.

Abi handed her a cup of tea. "What's wrong?" she asked, eyeing Jane's troubled expression.

"Good mornin', Abi," Jane said, hoping her voice didn't shake too much. "There's nae problem."

"Ye sure?" Abi raised one eyebrow.

Jane studied her teacup, avoiding eye contact. "Aye," she said with a little squeak. "I didna sleep well, that's all." She went through the motions of eating her porridge and drinking her tea like nothing was wrong, waiting for the right moment to make her way outdoors.

If Skye spent the night with Nathan, she needed help covering her folly. The other possibility—that Skye had come to some harm—was too frightening to contemplate. Yet all she knew of Nathan came from Skye. What if he was violent? What if she had become ill and he'd left her somewhere? She would find her friend, however long it took.

Abi, likely because of her experience dealing with young women and their moods, made her exit quickly and quietly. Once alone, Jane went outside, pacing back and forth, wondering where to look first. The outside air, with its gentle coolness, contrasted with the storm brewing inside of her.

Soon most of Alva filled the sidewalks en route to the kirk, where the bells rang out to invite worshippers chatting with each other, all enjoying the morning as they walked to services. She longed to be one of those churchgoers today, to sit in a pew without feeling the penetrating eyes of the minister divining her sins. She had stayed away from services since that night with Skye. If anyone discovered what they did, no one would welcome her there.

"Good mornin'."

"Rabbie," she said. Once again he snuck up on her, and she feared all her secrets showed on her face. She dropped her eyes. "How are ye?"

Rabbie ignored her question. "Ye seem distracted."

She realized she had been fidgeting. There was still no sign of Skye. "I'm fine." She pressed her hands against her skirt to stop them from shaking.

Rabbie raised his eyebrows. "Ye're chewin' yer lip, Jane. That's a sure sign ye're nae fine, at least from what I ken o' you."

He knew her well, and in this moment she couldn't decide if this was good or bad. Certainly she would never share this secret with him.

Standing closer to her, he lifted her chin with a gloved hand, forcing her to look at him. The intimacy of his touch and the sheer nearness of him thrilled her, but this wasn't the time, not with Skye missing. She stepped back from him, hoping no one had seen his boldness.

"Something is wrong. I can see it," Rabbie said. "Are ye nae tellin' me because I'm a supervisor?"

"Aye," she said in a tiny voice. "I canna break a confidence."

"What if I promised ye silence if it meant I could help? Remember, I'm yer friend, nae just one of the bosses."

She drew her eyebrows close together as she considered this. "Wid ye swear on our friendship not tae tell, no matter what?"

He frowned. "Aye, wee Jane, I wid do that for you, but my heart is struck wi' worry now. What intrigue do ye ken?"

She hesitated still.

"Ye're shakin', Jane." He reached to embrace her but then, seeing her hesitation, pulled back. "Tell me what's happened."

She decided to tell him the part of the truth he would not judge. "Skye... She didna come hame last night. She went off wi' Nathan. Do ye know where I might find him?"

Rabbie blew out a long, quiet whistle. "I could check for ye. He lives in the men's house close by."

"Wid ye?" She wanted to cry from gratitude.

"Aye, of course." His eyes narrowed. "Is there more ye're nae tellin' me?"

"I already said more than I should."

"I'll see what I can do." He tipped his hat and walked toward the boardinghouse where Nathan lived.

He had just left when the sound of skirts swished behind her.

"There ye be!" Jane cried out in relief as Skye approached. "I was worried sick! Are ye awricht?"

Skye staggered toward Jane, not entirely sober. Her hair, styled so elaborately the night before, fell in tangles down her back. Jane reached out to steady her, but Skye pulled away.

"What's wrong?" Jane asked. "What happened?"

"I shouldna have tae tell ye. Ye're no my friend, Jane Thorburn, no for one second!"

Rabbie reappeared, having still been in earshot when Skye showed up. "Aye, I see ye found the missing person," he said. He didn't comment on Skye's rumpled appearance.

Skye eyed him with suspicion. "What did she tell ye?" she asked. Turning to Jane, she said, "Did ye blab my secret to everyone in town? Why wid ye tell a supervisor about my plight?"

With questioning eyes Rabbie started to speak, but Skye interrupted him. "I suppose ye'll judge me, maybe even take away my job, all because o' her!"

"Skye, shush," Jane said, "ye talk too much."

Rabbie gave Skye a look of utter helplessness. "I was helpin' Jane look for ye."

Jane tried to signal to Skye not to say another word. "Thank you, Mr. Stein, for yer help. We're fine."

"Shall I walk ye to the kirk, then? We might still make it on time."

"I must speak wi' Skye. If I can come late, I will. Otherwise, I'll be there next week." She gave him a friendly smile meant to reassure him. Inside, though, she longed to go with him and to leave Skye behind. When he turned and walked away, she watched until his sturdy figure disappeared around the corner.

Skye's glare bore into Jane like a torch. "What did ye say to him, really?"

The church bells ceased ringing, signaling the commencement of services, and most of the congregants had filed inside the building. Still, Jane kept her voice to a soft whisper.

"Naethin', I swear. But ye didna come home all night. I worried something bad happened, and I was tryin' tae figure out what tae do when Mr. Stein walked by. I dinna want trouble for ye, I wanted tae keep trouble away."

"It's too late for that." Skye glanced around to see if anyone was listening. "Ye got me in a fine mess, lassie."

"Me!"

"Dinna play all innocent. Nathan came to me tae make up last night, an' says he's goin' tae mairie me. What will he think when he finds out I'm nae expectin'?"

Jane began to pace, her head pounding. "We have tae think."

"He'll want naethin' more tae do wi' me. I've half a mind to tell him what ye made me do."

"Ye canna do it, Skye. What if he turns you in?" *Would Nathan do such a thing?* "Ye'd go tae jail for sure."

"But so will you, and since my life is already ruined, I might as well ruin yers, too. It'd serve ye right," Skye said.

"I asked ye many times," Jane said, spitting out the words. "Beitris asked, too. What wid have happened if Nathan hadna come back? Ye'd be on yer own wi' a bairn and no job, livin' on the Poor Laws. Or did ye forget all of that?"

"Naw, but he did come back. Ye didna tell me tae wait, tae give him time."

"This is nae my fault, Skye." Jane wasn't as sure as she tried to sound. Had she really done enough?

"Ye told me about Beitris." Skye put her hands in fists on her hips, and her large eyes flashed with anger. "Ye brought her tae me. If I said ye both forced this fate upon me, everyone wid believe me."

The sky clouded over, and Jane shivered as she gathered her cloak around her, longing to be inside the warm kirk rather than having this argument with Skye that was going nowhere.

"Think, lass, think!" she said, keeping her voice low but firm. "We're no good tae anyone in jail. I saw the look on Nathan's face last night. He loves you. Let's figure this out."

"But there's no bairn! He'll think I tried tae trap him!"

All at once, Jane knew exactly what to do. "Nae if ye lose it."

Skye's face changed then as panic left, replaced by nervous uncertainty mixed with hope.

Jane's mind raced to come up with the details. "Ye dinna say a word for now, but wait until ye have yer next monthly. We tell Nathan the bairn didna survive. He'll love ye all the more for sufferin', I think."

Skye pursed her lips. "I hate liein' tae the lad."

"It isnae liein'," Jane said. "The bairn didna survive. He'll nae ken we had a hand in it."

Skye put her hand to her belly and patted it as if the child still lived within her. "Ye'd better be right. If I lose him, I'll tell the truth tae everyone, an' ye'll not work in all of Scotland after that. Ye bewitched me. I'm goin' tae ask Abi tae change beds."

"Go ahead if ye want, but Abi disna know a thing," Jane said. "Ye want tae draw attention tae the problem?" Another thought came to her a horrible thought, but one that might work. "I swear, Nathan will stay wi' ye. Did ye lie wi' him last night?"

"How dare ye ask such a private question?" Yet Skye's eyes told the truth, so Jane didn't need an answer.

"Then if he starts tae squirm about the bairn, make him think he had somethin' tae do wi' it." She winced as she said it; it sounded even worse out loud to blame him for a miscarriage. The sins and lies were piling up, with one lie leading to another and another and another. She hoped that God understood what a no-win situation they were in.

"That's evil," Skye said with disgust. "Ye're a bad seed, Jane Thorburn."

"Well, bad seed or no, we have a plan to help ye keep yer man. Is that no what ye want?"

Skye studied her fingernails as she considered the choice laid out before her.

"Aye," she said at last. Her shoulders softened a bit, though a scowl remained. "But I dinna want things tae be this way. All the lies."

"Me, neither, but we'll figure it out. I'm sorry I brought Beitris. I shoulda stayed out of it an' let ye handle it yerself."

Skye's face paled as she recalled that horrible night. The set of her jaw and the flame in her eyes disappeared. In a soft voice, she said, "I felt sae alone that night. I think if ye'd left it up tae me I'd have flung mysel in the burn. I didnae want a wean, nae yet."

"We talked about all the options. We asked ye over an' over."

"Aye, ye did." There was resignation in Skye's voice. "I'm scared I'll lose him over this."

"If we'd only waited a while longer," Jane said.

A bit of the old brightness returned to Skye's eyes. "Naw," she said. "I'm no sorry about what we did. If this plan gets me an' Nathan together for good, we'll be better off. We can mairie an' have a family when we have a proper hame." Skye gave a single firm nod, as though to convince herself of her own words.

"We'll make it work," Jane said, though still doubtful. Until Skye and Nathan were safely back together for good, Jane would continue to worry.

"No more prancin' around in my best dresses. I'd be headed to the poorhouse for sure with a bairn tae feed. I'm sorry. I just..."

"Let's be happy the two o' ye are back together," Jane said. "Get mairiet as soon as ye can, though, because we canna do what we did ever again. And I couldna bear it if ye were no longer my friend."

Skye's chin trembled ever so slightly as she took Jane's hand.

Together they walked back to the boardinghouse. For now, at least, their friendship held firm.

Jane said a silent prayer for guidance to do the right thing. She also offered prayers of thanks that she did not have Beitris's job. She respected the role of the howdiewife as a special one, bringing lives into the world and keeping women healthy, but she did not care to keep these kinds of secrets.

CHAPTER 10

I loved thee well; no tongue can tell
The love I cherished up for thee;
I love thee still, despite thine ill,
But Heaven alone my love shall see.

The Parting
Ellen Johnston

*N*athan, with no reason not to believe the woman he loved, accepted Skye's story without question. The two of them wept together over their loss, which helped Skye with her own, private grief. He swore to marry her as soon as possible and promised her a big family.

"It worked," Skye whispered to Jane on the night of his proposal, a week after their reunion. The two women were curled up in the bed, Skye's head resting on Jane's shoulder. No one else was in the room, but they still spoke quietly lest someone surprised them.

"I hope he didna blame himself," Jane said. That was the part of their plan that bothered her the most.

"Nathan? It never occurred tae him tae think it was his fault. That's a man for ye." Skye snorted with laughter, and Jane followed.

"Well, I'm glad," Jane said once they grew quiet again. "Now the two o' ye can have a happy life together. I'm sae happy, Skye."

The two women hugged, now able to move beyond the terrible secret that bound them together.

"I canna wait tae leave this mill," Skye said.

"I hope I dinna lose ye as a friend," Jane said.

"Why wid ye? We'll stay here in Alva. Ye can come visit anytime."

"I'll do that," Jane promised, though she doubted that's what would happen. With long hours at work, single women had little time to socialize except for Saturday nights and Sundays, and married women were busy with children and husbands to tend to. Even the best of friends tended to drift apart.

Like many young couples, Skye and Nathan chose Hogmanay as their wedding day. Though that meant waiting longer than the couple preferred, the mill closed for the holiday, allowing workers some extra rest.

Time passed quickly as life returned to normal. Jane found relief in the long workdays and went to the kirk on Sundays instead of the glen, still feeling the need to atone for her actions. She saw little of Flora and Coira in her dreams these days, sleeping so deeply that she only caught fleeting glimpses of them and remembered nothing.

Skye's wedding day arrived, and all the factory girls pitched in, cleaning and scrubbing the place not only for the wedding, but also to let go of the old year. Jane hoped for a better year to come. With Skye and Nathan getting married, this would be a good start.

In addition to the cleaning, food for the celebration had to be made and sent to the kirk ahead of time. Skye prepared most of the feast herself, with wedding pies of sweet meats and mutton, and splurged on sugar to make a layered sweet cake with white icing.

The wedding guests, mostly fellow mill workers, met at the boardinghouse, filling the downstairs as they waited for the bride. Layers of conversation brought a din to Abi's house that dwarfed the noise of the factory girls during the loudest dinner hour. When Rabbie entered, he jostled his way through the crowd to stand next to Jane. She rarely thought about how small she was until surrounded by a crowd with everyone a head or more taller, and she smiled gratefully when Rabbie made some space for her with his bulky body.

The din fell to silence when a creak of the stairs signaled Skye's entrance, then the crowd erupted in a collective gasp. They were used to Skye making an entrance, but today she had outdone herself.

Always fashion conscious, Skye spent days ahead of the wedding fashioning a silk dress of dark blue that matched her eyes. The factory girls pooled their resources to pay for the fabric. It had a snug bodice to show off her perfect figure and was trimmed with white lace. At the center of the lace she displayed her Luckenbooth, a brooch of silver engraved with entwined hearts, given to her by Nathan as a pledge of his love. The ruched skirt had a bustle in the back.

Nathan, who waited for her at the bottom of the stairs, wore a kilt of deep blues and greens with a fitted deep green jacket and vest. At the sight of his bride he knelt, clasping his hands to his heart, and let out a whistle. Skye descended the stairs like a queen, taking her time as she savored the moment. When she reached him, she dropped down to her kneeling fiancé, and they collapsed in each other's arms.

"Wait 'til after the ceremony!" somebody yelled, and everyone laughed.

The couple rose awkwardly, still laughing, and Maisie

smoothed Skye's gown and tucked a few stray curls back into place.

The procession began as the couple made their way to the kirk, with the guests following behind. Skye and Nathan stood at the entrance where, as was according to custom, they took their vows before going inside. They first spoke this together:

> *Lord help us to remember when*
> *We first met and the strong*
> *love that grew between us.*
> *To work that love into*
> *practical things so that nothing*
> *can divide us.*
> *We ask for words both kind*
> *and loving and hearts always*
> *ready to ask forgiveness*
> *as well as to forgive.*
> *Dear Lord, we put our*
> *marriage into your hands.*

Then they turned and declared their commitment to each other.

"Now, we will go inside," Nathan announced, "where the minister will bless the food."

"I'm sae happy for them," Rabbie said to Jane. Nudging her he said, "I'd like that one day, too."

"Aye." She didn't know why she said that. Marriage was the last thing Jane wanted for her life. But her heart started beating fast, and she brought one hand up to quiet it.

Seeing the happy couple at the doorway, eyes locked, holding hands, affected Jane deeply. Skye would spend the rest of her life atoning for the unspoken sin, but it was more than that. Perhaps God understood the difficulty of her decision, and this marriage was a sign of his forgiveness. Jane, for her part, offered a silent prayer, swearing to never get involved in a situation like that ever again.

A long evening of celebration followed, first with food and cake at the kirk. When Jane complimented Skye on the cake, Skye said, "I'll make yers one day!"

"Hmm," Jane said, rather than argue with her friend.

After everyone ate their fill, they moved to the dance hall. The band was in top form. Whisky and ale flowed, along with punch and tea for those who chose temperance, though few did so on this day.

Jane started out dancing with her friends, but soon enough Rabbie came and whisked her away to join a group doing a reel. For once she didn't care if people noticed his attentions toward her.

When Jane could dance no more, she broke away from the group with a laugh and went to pour herself some punch. With a full cup in hand, she turned to watch the dancers, only to find Rabbie standing next to her. She handed him her untouched drink and poured another for herself. Together they swayed to the beat. The music was loud, so they did not speak.

During a break, Rabbie said, "Shall we walk a bit?"

Jane nodded, and they fetched their coats. As they walked outside, she noticed a few heads turning in their direction. No doubt the gossips would have plenty to say about this.

They walked along the streets of the town, so quiet away from the dance hall. Even the pub looked quiet this evening. A light dusting of snow covered the ground, and the a brisk, soft breeze played with Jane's hair. Away from the revelers, Rabbie reached for her hand, and she gave his a gentle squeeze. The excitement of the wedding, the feeling of new beginnings, and a walk with a man whose company she enjoyed. Yes, perhaps this year already showed promise.

"What a grand party!" he said. "Skye and Nathan seem happy."

"Aye."

He stood silently next to her for a minute or so, as if hoping she would tell him more. When she didn't, he didn't press her. Instead he said, "Jane, I've been thinkin'…"

She wasn't sure she wanted to hear what he had to say. Weddings tended to bring out the romantic in everyone, including her. They'd danced openly with each other, something they'd seldom done before, and walking outside would attract even more attention.

"I should go back," she said. "It's cold out here."

"Wait," he said softly. "One more minute."

She gave a curt nod but didn't look at him.

"What I said earlier… Well, I hope ye didna think I was pushin' for us tae be together."

A nervous giggle bubbled up. Jane couldn't decide if she was relieved or upset.

"Are ye awricht?" he asked.

"Of course." She willed herself to stop laughing. "We're friends, aren't we?"

"Aye." His voice sounded resigned. "Well, then. Let's go back inside, shall we?"

"Aye," she said, relieved.

He held the door open to her, and they re-entered the hall. Without speaking, they went to opposite sides of the room. He joined his friends and she joined hers, and they did not dance again for the rest of the evening.

The next day, after a long evening of celebration, everyone but Skye went back to work, even the groom. There was neither time nor money for a honeymoon. The supervisors, always eager to save money for the mill, spread the responsibility for Skye's looms to the remaining weavers. It took Jane little time to adjust to the extra work, but Skye's absence took more time and effort to accept. At night, Jane had the bed to herself for now, at least. She remembered how sharing a bed with someone bothered her so when she first arrived, and now the wee bed felt empty.

ONE SUNDAY, in the depths of winter and a few weeks after the wedding, Jane went to the glen. She hadn't visited in a while, not since getting wrapped up in all the wedding preparations.

Bram had cleared the path, though fresh powder dusted the trees and lay in drifts all around her. With the trees stark and bare with no leaves obstructing the view, she could see all of Alva from up high in its neat, orderly arrangement of streets and buildings, along with the undulating, snake-like twists, and bends of the River Forth further to the south. *I'd like tae follow it one day*, she thought. She had seen so little of the larger world, and now she longed to explore, to have an adventure.

Brushing a pile of fresh, fluffy snow from her rock, she took a seat. The Woodland Folk were quiet today, and she wondered if they took extra rest in the winter. With trees and plants dormant, they had less to do. Despite the cold, the burn still rushed, though it carried with it chunks of ice, so perhaps the water sprites stayed busy. She imagined the men staying comfortable in a warm bed with quilts piled on top, sleeping through the winter like bears in their dens.

Soon soft footfalls came up the path, and her heart beat faster with anticipation. Since the wedding, she hadn't seen much of Rabbie other than the occasional nod and greeting.

He entered the clearing and gave her a broad grin.

"Good afternoon, Mr. Stein," she said, using her most formal voice, trying not to show how glad she was to see him.

He tipped his hat in that charming way of his. "I hoped to find ye here, Miss Thorburn. I've missed ye at the kirk."

She had stayed away during the wedding preparations. Too much to do. Since then, staying away had turned into a habit.

"I'm awfie tired by Sunday," she said. "I miss it, too." She still wasn't comfortable there, but with Skye properly wed, the kirk walls would cease to emanate disapproval and judgment.

"Aye. I'd like tae think a just God wid give us a bit more free time an' rest. Anyway, I wanted tae talk tae you about something."

She raised her eyebrows. "Nothing serious, I hope."

"Nae bad news. I dinna think so, at least." Pointing to the rock, he asked, "May I?"

She nodded and he sat next to her, his back straight and tall, his whiskers trimmed neatly on his face. Everything was in its perfect place on him, and she worried the wind had disheveled her.

"Well, then, what is it?" she asked.

"Do ye remember when we first met up here?"

"They say time passes faster as we age," she said. "I dinna feel old yet, but we talked, what, eight, nine months ago?"

"Aye. And do ye remember our conversation?"

"As I recall, we talked about many things." Of course she remembered every detail. She treasured that first meeting and had gone over their conversation many times since. Doing so helped her through long days at the mill. "Was there something in particular?"

"We talked about our dreams. I said I wanted tae work in England, and ye spoke of goin' tae Lowell. How are ye doing on that front?"

"Nae sae well, I'm afraid. I save what I can, but I've cut back on things." Though she tried to save and scrimp everywhere she could, putting money away was no easy task. She felt like a princess in the green dress she had splurged on, but the cost of the fabric had set her back more than she planned.

"Are ye sure ye dinna want tae go tae England, at least for a while? "

"My uncle wid have a heart attack if I left Scotland for England." She cringed at this reaction. He was asking her to go with him to a different country. That had to mean something, and her immediate response had been to invoke her uncle? She needed to know more. "Why do ye ask? Is there opportunity for me?"

"I think so." He stood clasped his hands behind his back in a thoughtful pose. "I'm goin' soon. I have a position in Leeds."

Her chest tightened with the news.

"Ye're lookin' for good help tae hire?" she asked, keeping her voice casual.

"Aye, that, but I've thought about this a lot and, well, I wid miss ye. I ken we dinna want the same life, but we are friends. I'm sure ye could make a good wage." He wore a searching, hopeful look on his face.

On one hand, he had a point. Life in Alva had gone about as far as it would, and any way of saving more to go overseas was worth looking into. On the other, she liked the mill, and Maisie and Wynda became good friends. Plus, she was getting to know the Fair Folk of the woods better, and she could visit her aunt and uncle easily from Alva.

And yet, if she went to Lowell, wouldn't she have the same problems? Yes, England lay distant from all that was familiar to her, but she had contemplated going even farther for years. She gave a quick shake of her head to dispel the confused thoughts. It seemed that every choice in life required some sacrifice she wasn't willing to make.

Another sensation rose within her as well, one that mattered even more with Rabbie's proposal: disappointment. Love and marriage never factored into her plans, but still, the fact that he just wanted a good worker and a close friend was, well, less than flattering.

"My life is here, at least until I leave for Lowell," she said. "I'd best stay, unless ye have some better argument for me goin'.'"

She swallowed hard after the last part, surprised by her own boldness.

He took his hat off and held it in his hands. "I like ye, Jane. A lot. Ye're pretty and smart, and ye're the only lass who likes tae walk in the glen like I do. I suppose I hoped ye wid like it there."

"I ken where I'm goin' in this life, Mr. Stein, and I'd thank ye to not try to talk me out o' it." Her anger came swiftly and took her by surprise, and she regretted her words as soon as she spoke them. But he wanted her to change her plans for him, and that irked her.

He looked mortified. "Oh, Jane, I'm sairie. I was out o' line. I know ye have yer heart set on America, and I never wanted tae talk ye out of yer dreams, but I had to ask. As I said, I will miss ye."

The ache in his voice dulled her anger. He seemed genuinely distressed by her response. He wanted to be with her. Of all the beautiful factory girls in town, he chose her, the one he never dated, his good friend from the woods.

And she was telling him no.

"I will miss ye, too," she said in a whisper. "I dinna mean tae speak ill o' ye. It flatters me ye wid ask."

He sat back down on the rock next to her. "Will ye write me at least?" he asked.

She looked at him, with his face so close that his breath caressed her face. His eyes were so blue and earnest, she thought she might faint. Here he sat, so near, so handsome, so sweet.

"Rabbie," she said, right before he kissed her.

"Look, our Jane is falling in love." Flora had tears in her eyes. She had watched Jane grow from newborn to young woman, and this new development excited her.

On this day, she and Coira were watching Jane through a special mirror at the palace. They were discreet about it, giving Jane plenty of privacy, but it allowed them to follow her life and to connect with Jane through her dreams, where they continued to teach her the ways of the Fair Folk.

"I don't know how this is going to help anything," Coira said. "While she plays kissy with a lad, our world gets worse by the day. Some heir."

Coira had a point. Neither Flora nor Coira understood what the weaver from Alva could do for them. If Coira had her way, they'd be figuring out something else to do to save the queendom.

Flora, on the other hand, had faith to live with the unknown. "The Wise Women say all is as it should be. I trust them to know more than we do."

"Hmph. We'll see about that." But Coira said no more, and Flora hoped her more volatile sister would remain patient. Only the queen and the Wise Women understood Jane's role, and they kept that information to themselves.

CHAPTER 11

Ah! What am I? – A hapless child of song,
Musing upon thy matchless beauty bright,
Tracing thy footsteps through the mazy throng,
And gazing on thee with love-born delight.

Lines to a Young Gentleman of Surpassing Beauty
Ellen Johnston

The next day, Rabbie was gone. He'd left out one important detail when talking to Jane about Leeds: he'd already given his notice. Their kiss was their goodbye. Her feelings were like a jumbled ball of yarn, twisted and knotted. By not telling her the full truth, he betrayed her, and yet he saved her from the heartache of waiting for him to leave. The sensation of his lips on hers remained fresh, and wasn't that a sweeter memory? She didn't know whether to be angry with him or care for him even more.

After Rabbie's exit, the mill buzzed with activity and noise as it always did, but without him it felt empty and dull. Jane managed her looms, grateful for the work, but joyless. The walls of the mill, though always dingy, looked even more dreary. Her feet and back hurt at the end of the day. The supervisors weren't more demanding than usual, but she took their criticisms to heart. She began to doubt her abilities, no matter how much she reminded herself of her skill.

"How come I didna go?" she asked Maisie and Wynda.

"Because it's nae proper," Maisie said. They were drinking tea in the boardinghouse on a quiet Sunday afternoon. Most of the women were out visiting family or taking the fresh air. She was about to say more when a voice trilled, "Hey, lasses, I come bearing tablet!"

"Skye!" The young women all rose to greet their friend, who indeed carried a plate of the sugary confection. Her cheeks were rosy from the cold, but her vibrant, confident energy brought its own warmth to the room.

"Ye're just in time," Wynda said. "Rabbie Stein has left for England, an' Jane is wonderin' why she didna go wi' him."

Skye handed Maisie the plate of tablet and removed her cloak and scarf. "Did he ask for yer hand?" she asked.

Jane, who immediately grabbed a mouthful of the rich candy, shook her head.

Waving a hand dismissively, Skye asked, "How could he ask ye tae move wi'oot some sort of promise? I thought he was a better gentleman than that."

"Ladies, let's nae waste a visit from Skye on this nonsense," Jane said. "We've nae been all together since the wedding. Skye, marriage suits ye."

Indeed, Skye, though always beautiful, had a special glow about her. "He's a good man. I was lucky tae find him."

"Lucky," Wynda said with a laugh. "Ye were the prettiest lass in the mill."

There was a momentary silence. Wynda wanted to marry, and though she never let on that it pained her to not find a husband, her friends knew.

"Well," Maisie said, clearing her throat. "This tablet is the best. I always loved yer treats, Skye."

"I agree," Jane said, grateful to her friend for changing the subject. "But everything you make is tasty." The whole town hadn't stopped talking about Skye's wedding feast.

"Ye should start a business," Maisie said.

Grinning, Skye said, "I am! I've started sellin' sweets and pastries in the general store." She was starting small, she said, but had plenty of plans for the future, maybe even trying to handle special occasions for mill owners. This announcement brought cheers from all the women.

After they finished the sweets, Skye said, "How are things at the mill?"

"Ye mean about the fire?" Maisie asked.

All the women groaned. There had been a small fire in the spinning room, but the smoke had spread throughout the building, forcing a temporary shutdown. It caused enough damage to keep the mill closed for a week, costing everyone much-needed pay.

"Nathan said it was lucky someone wisna hurt or killed," Skye said. "Thank God for that."

"Aye," Jane said. "Everyone ran out o' the building at once." She closed her eyes as she remembered the scene. The men tumbled out first, while the women made sure the frightened children got out in an orderly way.

Sudden anger at Rabbie knifed through her. It would have been nice to lean on him on such a difficult day. But as a child she learned that, sooner or later, people left her life, including Rabbie. Might as well put a good face on it and go on.

They continued, then, each sharing her story of what she saw that day. Most days they never thought about the dangers of mill work. They were there to do a job, and if they worked in fear they'd never meet their daily quotas.

After that thread of conversation ran its course, Skye turned back to Jane. "Tell me more about what happened wi' Mr. Stein," she said.

Jane shook her head, but the other women were having none of that. "Mr. Stein didna act like a gentleman," Wynda said. "Who asks a single lass tae move tae a different country wi'oot gettin' mairiet?"

"I told him I didna want tae mairie," Jane said after a pause. On the one hand she didn't want to talk about it. On the other, she cherished this rare gathering. They cared and wanted to know. "We never were more than good friends. He says he'll write, so we'll see." She hadn't told them about his kiss that day, how right, how sweet, how...natural. There was no point in sharing that information. What did it matter now? She would never see him again.

"Ye fancy him," Maisie said.

"Aye. But most o' the mill lasses do, I suppose."

"That's a fact," Wynda said. "I took a shine tae him for about a year, but he never looked twice at me. He always had a lass on his arm when he wanted one. He never was the type tae settle down. Best he's gone, I say."

"Well, enough o' that, lasses," Skye said with a wave of her hand. "Let's talk about happy things. I have one more piece o' news tae share."

The other women all turned to her, and Jane guessed before Skye could say another word. "Ye're havin' a bairn?" she asked.

"Aye."

"An' ye waited all this time tae tell us?" Maisie asked. "Come around, everyone, it's time for hugs!"

They gathered around, laughing, shrieking, hugging. Jane felt a tugging inside as she let go of whatever guilt and shame remained. As the women stepped back from each other, Jane's eyes met with Skye's, and Skye gave a small nod and expression of pain mixed with hope. They had come full circle. In late autumn the happy couple would bring a child into the world that they were ready to care for.

SOON ENOUGH, Rabbie's letters arrived, brightening Jane's world again.

Dear Jane,

I hope this letter finds you well. Though I enjoy my work, I miss my bonnie Scotland and the sweet lass I left behind. Every day I think of things I want to tell you, but you're not here.

They have made me a tweed designer. I like designing better than supervising. I swear, I have more energy at the end of the day than in the morning. I wish you were here to weave the designs for me, though. There is no one who brings them to life the way you do.

If you see my parents in the kirk, give them my love. I will write to them soon. For now, I remain your humble friend,

Rabbie

Jane wished she could say so much in so few words. When she tried to write him back, she struggled to express herself. He wrote with a precise, perfect script, with not a single blotch on the page. Though he'd had no more schooling than she, his spelling and grammar was impeccable.

As a child she learned to read, write, and do basic arithmetic, but hadn't practiced her skills in a long time, leaving her rusty and uncertain about writing letters. It never mattered to her before, knowing at a young age of her future as a weaver. Her lack of schooling hadn't embarrassed her until now.

Taking a deep breath, she pulled a sheet of paper from the drawer, along with a special pen she purchased for these letters. It was a relatively new invention, a fountain pen where she fed ink to it via an eyedropper.

Dear Rabbie,

I am so happy you enjoy England. Yer work sounds exciting

enough. Here, there is nothing new to tell. Six days a week I go to the mill, and I come home and try to eat something before sleep takes over. My joy is going to the glen, but there is less of that because the glen is empty without you. The fairies send their best.

She looked up from the letter, wondering why she wrote that last sentence.

The last is a joke, of course (even though it wasn't). *If I were to see fairies, though, they would sing and cry out for you to visit. Perhaps you can come home to see your family soon?*

She crumpled the paper, then smoothed it out, chiding herself for wasting it. She didn't want to sound as though she was begging for him to come back, even though she wanted him to.

Rabbie was flighty, flirtatious, and overly optimistic. And yet, the longer he was away the more she missed his finer qualities: his intelligence, his humor, his liveliness. She missed the cut of his suit, his erect posture, his clear blue eyes that welled up when they parted. Touching her fingertips to her lips, she recalled the sensation of his kiss. Since his absence, she understood something she tried to deny: she loved him.

She. Loved. Him.

The notion was both delicious and frightening. She'd never loved a man before. There had been crushes, but nothing like this. But what to do? He lived so far away. In a sense, though, his absence made it easier for her to entertain these new sensations. Freed from having to choose between a man or her independence, she could imagine conversations and kisses from a safe distance. But she would have to rely on the letters, and she vowed to overcome her writing struggles. If she didn't write back, he'd stop writing her, and she didn't want that.

She took another sheet of paper and tried again, rewriting the same letter but without the Fair Folk. Then she added:

Skye and Nathan seem happy together. I see her more than I thought. Skye says she'll have a bairn in the autumn.

She almost wrote "another bairn," but stopped herself in time.

Maisie and Wynda say hello, too. I'd like to share your letter with them. Working in England seems strange and exotic tae all of us.

Nothing has happened about going to Lowell, not yet. We had a shutdown last week after a fire in one of the rooms. No one was hurt, but it was scary. They had to make sure the building was stable before they brought us back in, and they rearranged some of the machines until they fixed the damage. So, I got no pay for the week, and that put me behind again.

I will give your parents my best, as I always do. They are kind people.

She wasn't totally sure about the last sentence. The Steins were reserved. The elder Mr. Stein knew her from the mill, and they seemed to understand that Jane and Rabbie were friends, but when she greeted them at the kirk, they said little beyond a polite "hello." But if they were Rabbie's parents, they had to be kind, didn't they? How could they be otherwise to raise such a son? She decided to leave it.

She sat for a moment, pen poised over the paper, wanting to say something more about what her feelings. Instead, she kept it simple:

Your friend,
Jane

CHAPTER 12

Oh, wert thou in the cauld blast,
On yonder lea, on yonder lea,
My plaidie to the angry airt,
I'd shelter thee, I'd shelter thee.

O, Wert Thou in the Cauld Blast
Robert Burns

*S*pring brought with it the promise of future warmth through tiny shoots of snow drops, white with tears of dew, and crocuses providing lavender contrast. Jane always loved the slow, gentle changes that would soon accelerate. This year, though, she didn't stop to notice as she usually did. Days passed one into the next as she burrowed deeply into her work, waiting for Rabbie's next letter.

Her routine ended abruptly one day with the arrival of her young cousin, Heather, who stood at the doorway of the boardinghouse when Jane came home from work.

Ten-year-old Heather, who Jane held in her arms as a newborn, had experienced an impressive growth spurt and now stood as tall as Jane. Heather's new height provided evidence of how quickly time passed...and how long it had been since Jane last visited her family.

Yet Heather's presence, with no notice, signaled something amiss, and Jane's stomach churned. "Heather? Whit are ye doin' here?" Jane asked as they hugged.

Heather drew back from the embrace. She was a lass on a mission. "Ma is ill an' Da is askin' for ye."

"Whit's wrong? How bad is it?" Jane asked.

"She's burnin' up wi' fever. Last night she didna recognize me. The doctor is checking her today. She needs someone tae care for her, and Da says ye're the only one who'll do sae we can stay in school." The words tumbled out of Heather in one breath.

"Oh, no," Jane said. Other than the fertility issues, her aunt had always been healthy and strong.

"Aye." In a calmer, shyer tone Heather said, "Will ye come? Please?"

Of course she would go. She and Uncle Ewan had given her a home, and Jane loved them both.

Still, this news brought Jane other worries. Would she have a job to come back to? If Aunt Kirstin was ill for a long time, the mill might not hold her job, making it hard to obtain a reference for Lowell. *Stop it, lass. This is family. Somehow things will work out.* The crimson shame of her selfishness bloomed on her cheeks.

"How sick is she?" Jane asked. She didn't want to ask Heather if her mother was going to die.

"She's nae good," Heather said, her lower lip trembling, "but the doctor thinks she'll be awricht wi' some extra care."

"Ah." So, death did not appear to be imminent. That gave Jane enough information to make a decision about timing, at least. "I'll come, of course," she said. "But I need tae work tomorrow an' tell my bosses. Ye go on home an' tell yer folks I'll be there the mornin' after."

"Da wanted me tae bring ye back wi' me. If I come back alone, I'll be in trouble."

"I have tae tell my bosses at the mill, or I'll be out o' work. I'll write a note tae send back wi' ye, an' I promise tae come. My word is good." She took out her pen and paper and wrote a few lines in her careful, uncomfortable script. At least her letters to Rabbie had given her some practice. "Here. Take this. If he's harsh wi' ye, I'll straighten things out when I arrive. Yer da is a stern man but not unfair. I expect the letter will suffice."

Heather looked doubtful, but agreed, then disappeared toward home. Jane skipped supper and went upstairs, where she sat on her bed and hugged herself, rocking back and forth. Part of her wanted to run after Heather and go immediately to her aunt's side. What if Kirstin died before Jane got to her? But a doctor was caring for her, Jane reminded herself.

Maisie and Wynda, having heard the exchange, came and sat with her. "Dinna fret," Maisie said. "Ye'll be back soon."

"I hope so. I dinna want tae lose the job."

"It willnae happen," Wynda said firmly. "Ye're the best weaver we have."

Neither of them could truly make that promise. Too many absences had ended the careers of many skilled weavers. Still, her friends' assurances helped calm her.

She put her few belongings in the same sack she used to bring them to Alva, deciding to leave the book of Robert Burns poetry as a promise to return. She wanted to write to Rabbie once more to tell him, but she couldn't think of what to say. Anything that came to mind sounded like a plea for help, and she had no intention of being beholden to Rabbie in any way. After several attempts, she gave up. She needed to collect herself and to help her aunt. She would write to him when she was calmer.

At the morning bell, she reported to work as usual. During the breakfast break, she told her supervisor the news but promised to finish out the day. Wanting to keep a good reputation at the mill, there were some things not available for compromise. Promising to return as soon as possible, she left tired but optimistic that a job waited for her upon her return.

The next morning, she set out for Menstrie. She tucked her savings, which now looked so meager, into a pocket of her skirt. Without glancing back, she climbed into a coach with two horses that had seen better days, and said her goodbyes to Alva.

The ride was short but bumpy. A hard rain had begun early that day, and the wheels struggled as they encountered deepening ruts in the road. *I coulda walked sooner*, she thought, but at least she would stay dry.

When she reached her uncle's home, she was struck by how small and plain it was. In her memories, the house was larger and grander. How different it looked now, even though she hadn't been away that long.

It was one thing to learn about her aunt's illness from Heather. It was quite another to be confronted with direct evidence. Aunt Kirstin's flowers were tangled and brown from the winter. By now she would have cleared out the old dead plants, making space for new shoots to poke up through the ground.

Apparently she had been ill for a while. The reality of the situation filled Jane with fear. What would happen if Kirstin died? The children were too young to care for themselves. Heather could help, certainly, but Jane would never leave Heather with the burden of full responsibility for the others.. No, if her aunt died, Jane would be their caregiver, ending her freedom.

As selfish as she felt in that moment, she also grew determined for her aunt to recover.

She knocked softly on the front door but let herself in, a sickening fear rising in her belly.

Uncle Ewan came out of the bedroom, where he'd been at his wife's side, and gave Jane a brief hug. "I'm sorry tae take ye from yer work," he said. He sounded sincere. "But ye'll see why I called."

She followed him to the small bedroom and opened the drapes to let daylight in. Aunt Kirstin lay listless in the bed, her face flushed with fever, her cheeks hollowed out. Jane put her bag down in a corner and went to her aunt, feeling her forehead and checking her pulse. Kirstin's forehead burned Jane's cool fingers, with the pulse as fast and fluttery as bird wings. She didn't respond to Jane's touch.

"What does the doctor say?" Jane asked, turning to her uncle.

"He says it's ague, but he dinna ken the cause," Uncle Ewan said. "She's been sick for two weeks." He tapped the wall absent-mindedly with his fist. *Tap, tap, tap.*

"Did he give her any medicine?"

"Quinine pills, but they dinna help. He says he may have tae bleed her."

Jane frowned at this. Lately, bloodletting had fallen out of favor, but some doctors still tried it when they didn't know what else to do. "Does she eat?" Jane asked.

"She'll take broth, but only when I'm home an' she's awake, which isnae often. The weans have missed their schooling, taking turns wi' her. I sent them back today. I'm glad ye're here." He gave her a look of utter helplessness.

Jane perched on a small, hard chair next to the bed. It wobbled on the uneven floor. She leaned over and kissed her aunt's burning forehead. Aunt Kirstin remained still, eyes closed, seemingly unaware of anyone in the room. As Jane watched her aunt's fitful breathing, she thought about what to do. As usual, a familiar face appeared in her mind. Beitris. The old howdiewife understood much that doctors did not.

In the meantime, there were things she could do. Rising from her seat, she grabbed a bucket. "I'll be back," she said to her uncle, and left the house before he responded.

When she stepped outside, the rain had slowed to a light drizzle. As she filled the bucket with water, Jane let the spitting rain wash her fears from her, and by the time she returned to the house, she felt refreshed and ready to deal with the situation.

Once inside, she poured her uncle a dram of whisky and gave it to him.

"I dinna need care," he insisted. "Please tend tae yer aunt."

"Nonsense. I can tell ye're worn out. Drink up, Uncle, or I'll throw ye in the bed next to Auntie and turn both o' you into patients." She managed a sly smile.

"Aye, lassie, I see ye've gained a smart mouth. Too much time wi' mill people." He gave her a wink, though, and then drank the whisky. "There. I'm a good lad."

Jane lay a hand on his cheek in comfort, holding his gaze for a moment. Then she set about her task, gathering cloths and soaking them in the water, then putting them on her aunt's forehead and chest. "I need ye tae fetch Beitris," she said.

The combination of whisky and a specific assignment rescued Ewan from his stupor. "I'll go." He quickly rose and left the house, giving Jane a few minutes alone with her aunt.

She massaged Kirstin's arms, then uncovered her feet and worked to bring the heat down. "Come back tae us, Auntie," she coaxed. "I dinna want tae raise yer bairns, much as I love them."

Soon Beitris entered the house with Uncle Ewan at her heels.

Jane hesitated, remembering their last meeting. Beitris gave her the slightest nod as if to say *yer secret is safe*, and then enfolded Jane in her arms.

"Wee Jane, ye're come back tae us."

"For a while, at least." Jane ignored the look Uncle Ewan

gave her. No doubt they'd discuss her future before her visit ended.

Beitris leaned over and removed the cloths, already hot. "Ye did good work here," she said. "Heat some water so I can make some infusions for the poor lady." She turned to Ewan and asked, "Is there someplace the bairns can stay for a few days?"

Uncle Ewan was a proud man, unused to asking for help. Most likely they had come for Jane only at the doctor's insistence. "Naw," he said, then, "Well, mebbe...my sister."

"Ma an' Da? Really?" Jane asked. This was new. She'd never seen them, not in all the years of living with her aunt and uncle.

"Aye, Jane," Uncle Ewan said. "Yer da goes tae temperance meetings these days, an' yer ma, well, she's changed. I trust them noo."

She recalled the day she realized her parents had other children, and the hurt that they never brought her back to be part of the family. Now they could be counted on to care for other children? In her busy life she buried the pain and abandonment, and now it rushed to the surface. But there was no time to indulge those emotions now. She gulped them down to save them for another time. "Let me take them."

"Are ye sure, Jane?"

"Aye." She wasn't, not really, but she had to see them. Who were these people? What did they even look like? More importantly, she wanted them to see her, and to make them stand face to face with the child they left for others to raise.

She'd managed to keep her parents in a separate compartment of her mind all these years, and she did that again now. Stoking the fire and heating the water as instructed, her focus returned. As little bubbles started to form, Beitris opened her bag and tossed in a mix of fragrant herbs, filling the room with cinnamon, mint, and other less familiar scents.

"What can I do?" Uncle Ewan asked. With his shaking voice

and wringing of hands, he didn't look like someone capable of doing much, even with the whisky to help.

"Go tae the kirk," Beitris said. "Say some prayers."

He brightened a bit at that idea, relieved to leave the house.

"How is she, really?" Jane asked once he left.

"That doctor," Beitris scoffed. "He didna even try rhubarb or calomel. Imagine that!"

Jane gave Beitris a blank look, knowing nothing of the effectiveness of rhubarb, and she'd never even heard of calomel.

Seeing Jane's confusion, Beitris added, "They shoulda come tae me sooner. I'll do all I can, but I canna lie, lass, she's in a bad way. It will take a miracle or two for her tae pull through."

Jane caught her breath. Her determination, her certainty about her aunt's recovery dissipated like smoke, leaving her as helpless as Uncle Ewan.

"I have things well in hand here," Beitris said. "I'd best work alone for a bit. Go on out tae the garden and rest." Jane opened her mouth to protest, but Beitris patted her hand. "Ye'll need yer strength for the days ahead."

Beitris's soothing touch quieted Jane enough to obey. Once in the garden, she bent down and began pulling weeds and trimming away dead plants from what could be salvaged, which calmed her further. Aunt Kirstin had always taken such pride in her garden, and bringing it back from its sorry state helped Jane feel useful.

After a while, she sensed a soft buzzing around her ears.

"Who's there?" she asked softly.

"Flora. Are you all right, lass?"

Jane turned her head to face the fairy. She glanced around before replying, lest someone think she was talking to empty air. Satisfied they were alone, she said, "I'm fine, but my aunt isnae doin' sae well."

"I'm sorry to hear," Flora said. She lit on the bench and

patted it to invite Jane to join her. "How long do you think you'll have to stay?"

"Too long," Jane said bitterly. Somehow Flora always managed to pull the truth of Jane's feelings from her, and once again she scolded herself for her selfishness. "I'm sairie, I should keep a mind o' what's important."

"Maybe we can help."

"Could ye?" With another option beyond Beitris, a glimmer of hope returned. "That wid mean the world."

"We can. We can make her well again. We have potions Beitris can only dream of."

Jane's spine stiffened as distrust mixed with that slim thread of hope. She had never observed the Fey do anything untrustworthy. They had always been her dearest friends. Still, people told stories of people getting snared in a fairy trap, and she'd never been in the position of needing anything from them before. What if they wanted to take advantage of her need for them? "What's the price?" she asked.

Flora kept her tone bright, though Jane noticed a slight squirm. "Saving her life? Can you put a price on that?"

"No doubt ye will," Jane said. "Name the price first, and then I'll decide."

"All right, yes, we have a price, but one we think you'll like."

Jane raised an eyebrow and waited.

"Remember years ago when you asked to come see where we live?" Flora asked.

"Aye, I remember." Jane hadn't thought about that day in the years that passed, until now.

"This would be a good time for that visit," Flora said. "Only for a week in human time. After yer aunt gets well, visit the queen and meet our people."

It sounded wonderful, though perhaps a wonderful trap. She definitely needed more information before saying yes. "If I come, do I go hame after the week?"

"Aye," Flora said. "I swear."

Jane studied Flora's eyes. She didn't trust Coira, but Flora didn't seem like the type to lie. So, when Flora avoided looking directly at Jane, she knew she needed more information.

"What haven't ye told me?" she asked. "Tell me everything I need tae know, or the answer is no."

Flora flitted back and forth, her rosy cheeks growing even redder. "I cannot."

"Ye can and ye will." Years of working in the mill had toughened Jane. The Fey clearly wanted something from her, and she wouldn't say yes until she understood their terms. The fear of her aunt's possible death left her uneasy, but her gut told her to stay strong. She turned her back on Flora and returned to pulling weeds. Her back ached from the angle of the work, but it gave her a sense of being in charge of the strange conversation.

Flora landed on the ground next to Jane. "I will send you back safely as I promised. If you're worried about me tricking you, I think you know me better than that by now."

"I thought I did. But ye're leavin' out details." She raised an eyebrow.

Flora slouched as she sat on the ground, and a cloud of weariness covered her face. "All right then. I'll tell you."

Jane brushed herself off and sat back on the bench, suspecting this might take a while.

"There's a prophecy," Flora began.

Jane stifled a laugh, lest anyone hear her sounding too cheerful in the presence of serious illness. "That again," she said. "I've heard that word here an' there my whole life. As if a simple factory girl wid be part of any prophecy."

But if Flora was teasing her, it didn't show on her face. Jane needed to know the truth, though she wasn't sure she wanted to hear it.

"Would you like to hear it?" Flora asked.

Jane cast one more uncertain glance toward the house. "Beitris may need me."

"I promise you have time for the tale. You'll like it."

Flora perched on the armrest of the bench. As she began to speak, her voice like that of a mother telling a bedtime story, Jane grew drowsy. She tried to fight the sense of enchantment, but Flora's voice soothed her deep into her bones, and she fell deeply into the story.

CHAPTER 13

You were the bountiful well of healing,
You were the loch that cannot be emptied,
You were Ben Nevis over every summit,
The crag that can't be descended...

Sheila MacDonald
Alisdair of Glengarry

*O*nce upon a time, there was a seaman named John who washed ashore on the west coast of Scotland, his boat and spirit broken, his crew dead. He dragged himself onto the rocky beach, spitting out salt water and shivering in the brutal wind. For days, he drifted in and out of consciousness, unable to separate day from night.

Each day his hunger grew with no food to fill him. Each day he thirsted with nothing to satisfy the dryness in his mouth. Wild winds and heavy rains battered his body. As he grew weaker, he saw visions all around him: people coming and going, whispering, poking him to see if he was dead. He tried to speak, to hold on to something or someone, to ask for help, but as soon as he did, the beings vanished.

John had weathered life on the sea, and thus had the strength and resilience found in only the bravest of men. He had stared down storms that tossed and turned his boat like a child's toy; endured scurvy; had his skin burned and blistered from the sun; buried loyal men who served under him; rejoiced when the sea yielded bounty and suffered pangs of hunger when it did not. Every success, every struggle, shaped him into a sturdy man of certainty who could solve any problem.

But the time came when the cold grew too much for him, and he had no fight left inside. His body gave way to fever as his mind gave way to despair, and he prayed for death, accepting the punishing winds as atonement for surviving while his men did not. He closed his eyes and gave himself to it. Now he prayed not to suffer, to not have to wait too long. He drifted into the silent sleep of the dying, a show of mercy from above.

Yet he did not die.

One day, he opened his eyes to find he was no longer on the beach, but in some kind of cave, where a warm fire crackled and cast flickering light. His clothes were dry, his mouth parched. Every muscle, bone, and sinew ached, but he was alive.

A face leaned over him, a tiny, angelic face with a turned-up nose and a sprinkling of freckles. Her eyes were like the sea near the shore, more green than blue, with flecks of gold in them. Hair the color of hay kissed with strawberries fell in tendrils that tickled his neck.

"My hair," Jane murmured, more puzzled than ever.

Flora nodded, then continued.

"Aye, ye're awake," she said, and disappeared into the darkness, then re-appeared with a cup of water. "Take this."

He swallowed as best he could, with most of the water running out the sides of his mouth. The drink did not soothe the scratchiness of his throat, though it did help to rouse him. He tried to sit up, but dizziness forced him back down.

"Don't exert yourself," the angel said, her voice as melodic as a choir. "Rest, sir. You need time to heal."

He closed his eyes. He had so many questions, but his throat remained burned and raw, and every time he tried to speak he could barely whisper. Any attempt at more brought searing pain.

He did not know how many days passed. It could have been two or ten or thirty. He came to the surface of waking, ready to learn his fate, only to succumb again to the depths, as if he were plunging over and over again back into the sea.

When he finally opened his eyes and could keep them open, he was back on the beach. This time the warm breezes and the sun on his body caressed him and gave him strength. When he tried to sit up, he could do so. He was weak and tired, but alert and no longer in pain. He looked around for his angel, and she sat nearby, sunning herself on a rock. When he struggled to stand, she said, "Do not get up. I'll come to you."

This woman resembled a half-sized human but moved with regal bearing, and her dress shimmered and danced with their own life, changing as she moved: magenta, shimmering greens, and golds.

She had to be one of the Fair Folk. All his life he had heard about them, but had never seen one before. How had he not noticed this about her? Was he too ill to see her, or had she used her magic to hide the truth?

"How is your throat?" she asked. She covered his forehead with her hand as she checked for fever.

He swallowed. "Much better." This time words came out without strain, his throat healed. "What happened?"

She checked his pulse with a no-nonsense look on her face. "The sea spit you out. My people said I should leave you to die, but that is not my way."

"How did I get back here to the beach?"

"You are a man of the sea," she said. "I can heal your body with herbs, but for the soul I needed special help. Water is your magic." She spoke with care, the formal speech of someone of the upper classes.

"Who are you?" he asked.

"I am Bridget," she said. "Princess Bridget, daughter of the fair Queen Catriona. Do you know who you are?"

"*My name is John Thorburn, though I canna say how I ken.*"

"John Thorburn?" Jane asked.

"Aye," Flora said. "Your father's father."

"I never met him," Jane said. "He died right after I was born, I think." Though her aunt and uncle told her little of her family, she vaguely remembered that much. The hairs on her arms stood up now.

Flora continued:

He recalled a vague memory of his mother's comforting touch and soft voice. Perhaps the kind ministrations of his caregiver allowed him to connect with that small glimpse into his former life. He remembered that his ship wrecked and he lost his crew, but no details came to him, just the knowledge in his bones. He started at the realization, but her hands on his shoulders brought him instant calm.

"*You have a new life now,*" *she said, her voice soft, like gentle waves lapping at the shore.* "*The sea sent you to me.*"

"*What if I have a wife?*" *he asked, because he knew, deep down, that a woman waited for him somewhere, though he couldn't picture her or recall her name.*

"*That life is gone.*"

He should be afraid now as she dismissed his previous life with a wave of her hand. Was he a prisoner? His past erased? He wondered if she put a spell on him. Yet in spite of that, he trusted her. With each passing day, he let the past die as he should have died on that beach, were it not for Bridget's intervention.

He learned that she was the second child of the queen and a sister to Donella, the future queen. Bridget explained that, though not destined for the throne, she had a special role in the royal family because she possessed a gift for prophecy that the others did not.

"*I thought all the Fey had magical powers,*" *John said.*

"*Aye, but like humans, we have strengths and weaknesses. I can see the future better than anyone else, even my mother, the queen. That's how I found you on the beach that day. I came to find you because I knew you would be there, and you were mine to love.*"

Neither had spoken of it until now, but love is the greatest magic in life. When she leaned down to kiss him for the first time, he surrendered to her.

"Humans and Fair Folk?" Jane asked. "That isnae forbidden?"

"There are some exceptions," Flora said softly.

Jane knew she had no choice but to let Flora tell the story in her way, in her time. With a sigh she said, "Fine. Go ahead."

"Where was I?" Closing her eyes, Flora took a few deep breaths. "Ah, yes. I remember."

They settled on the windswept Isle of Islay, for John would always need the sight and the smell of the sea to hold him steady. Queen Catriona joined them in marriage, a quiet ceremony on the beach, and soon Bridget grew pregnant with their child.

"That canna be," Jane said.

"What do you mean?" Flora asked.

"My grandmother's name was Sarah, not Bridget."

"I'll explain. Trust me."

Jane folded her arms, her impatience growing. She'd be better off tending to her aunt than listening to this drivel.

As if reading Jane's thoughts, Flora added, "There will be plenty of time to care for your aunt. I promise you, Jane, you need to hear all of this. It will make sense in the end."

Jane glowered but said nothing more.

Flora began again:

Theirs was a simple existence. He fished, while she kept a garden. They lived in a fairy knoll, but the ceilings were high enough for a human to fit, and she kept a spotless home. Her body grew round, her cheeks rosy. Together they touched her growing belly and talked of what the future might hold.

Alas, their happiness was not meant to be.

Bridget woke screaming in the night from nightmares, and John calmed her by whispering words of love to her. She curled herself up into a ball to protect the child. In the mornings she rose, exhausted, and reminded herself it was only a dream. Yet the nightmares

*returned, night after night, until fatigue nearly blinded her. She began
to lose her magic, no longer recognizing the herbs she'd used so deftly
with John.*

*One night, wild-eyed, she grabbed him by the collar and pulled
him to her. In his ear she hissed, "You must promise to care for our son.
Promise me."*

*The child in her womb kicked angrily. She stroked her belly, and
soon enough he quieted.*

*John smoothed her curls and kissed her on the forehead. "We will
both raise the bairn," he said. "It might be a lass, ye ken."*

*"It's a lad," she insisted. "And I know something else, too." She
furrowed her brow, wrestling with her inner knowledge.*

"What is it? Bridget, ye're scarin' me."

*She turned away from him then. "Promise me," she said, "promise
me you will shield the lad from whatever comes and raise him to be a
brave, strong man."*

*"I promise," he said. "But dinna fret. There is too much love here
for us tae be parted." He wrapped his arms around her and held her
tight to protect her from all harm. She didn't argue with him but cried
quietly until she fell into a deep sleep.*

*Bridget spoke no more of her dreams to her family, but she
confided her cares to the howdiewife, who prepared tinctures to help
her rest. The dreams settled down, but the dread did not.*

*On a cold winter evening, Bridget went into a labor that lasted
for two full days. The child, half human, was larger than the typical
Fey babies, and her tiny body strained with the effort. Queen
Catriona and Princess Donella stayed with Bridget, singing to her
and helping her breathe through each contraction. Eventually the
child—a lad, as she foresaw—came forth screaming and angry. She
held him and cooed to him, but he wouldn't stop crying. The
howdiewife used chants and herbs to encourage him to feed, but he
fought her, this half-human, half-Fey child who would never fit in
either world.*

Jane brought a hand to her heart as it pulsed with warmth

and compassion toward the angry drunk who had pleaded for her when she was a child.

Flora, sensing this wave of emotion, waited until it passed, and then she continued.

Soon, a fever engulfed Bridget, and the palace physicians said she would not survive. Donella bade John leave the two sisters alone. He left reluctantly, for he wanted to spend every moment with her, but he also respected their royalty.

Bridget drifted in and out of consciousness but found enough strength to speak to Donella. "I need to tell you what to do with Robert."

"Of course, I will raise him as my own," Donella said. "He will be my heir."

Bridget shook her head. "That, my sister, is not what is meant to be."

"Why not? He is one of us." She had fallen in love with him, and he nestled in her arms, calm and quiet. "He would be happy with us. We love John, but he will not give the bairn a good life. We can raise Robert in comfort. He can learn our ways."

Bridget nodded. "That is true, but there is a prophecy, one you need to know." She gazed at him tenderly. "He will grow up with John. Would that it were different for him, but it is not."

"Life in the human world? Why do that to your son? My nephew?"

Bridget reached out her hand to touch Donella's cheek. "My sister, so brilliant in so many ways, but you live without the Sight. I wish he could grow up with our people, because his life will be very hard. And yet, he will marry, and his wife will bear a wee lass who will be the bridge to heal the divide between Good Folk and humans. She will have the disposition we need. The Fey blood in our line has been weakened, and human blood is stronger. It will help us gain strength to survive. We need one more generation to get enough of it to matter."

Donella was repulsed by the idea. An heir with only one-quarter Fey blood? The thought of explaining this to the people caused her temples to pulse. They wouldn't relish that idea. With Robert still an infant, though, she had a generation to prepare them. Surely she could do that.

"So, what do we do when the lass is born?" she asked.

"You take her as soon as you can, before she is baptized."

The words came out so casually they took Donella by surprise. "Kidnap her? As a bairn? And from the poor wee lad you just birthed? You would add even more suffering to his life?" She didn't add that infant kidnapping had been outlawed by Queen Catriona in an attempt to reduce human fear of the Folk.

"Aye," Bridget said. Her voice grew weaker with each word. "I know it sounds horrible. Do you think I would sentence my son to such a painful fate if I didn't have to? But this is necessary, Sister, to save our people."

And with that, Bridget closed her eyes for the last time.

"So that means..."

Jane struggled to breathe. Coira had told the truth of her beginnings, at least to some extent. Had the kidnapping been successful, her life would have been erased and replaced with something unimaginable. There would be no Alva, no Rabbie, no life with her aunt and uncle. It was staggering for someone as independent as Jane to consider. Did life hold so little choice? Was she a slave to destiny? She didn't want to think so.

And since the story didn't go as planned, what next?

As if reading her thoughts, Flora said, "I'll tell the rest of the tale, and then you can ask questions."

"But—"

"I know I'm asking a lot, but please, let me finish." And Flora proceeded with the tale.

John wept so many tears that they formed a small saltwater pond outside their little home. The wind heaved and swirled as Bridget's spirit struggled to hold on, and wee Robert matched its intensity with his cries.

Weary and spent, both John and Robert dropped into a sleep so deep the pain and grief could not find them, a sleep cast upon them by

Donella to bring relief. She then added one more bit of magic: to send them to a new life. Or, in John's case, an old life.

The next day, John woke in a place both familiar and strange.

"Robert," he cried out. A small sound came from near the fire, as if the child understood. That's when he saw the cradle. His son was safe.

A woman came into the room and hovered over him. She was care-worn, tired, and thinner than she should be, but her face reminded him of someone he loved long ago.

"Sarah?" he asked. The name floated up from deep in the recesses of his memory. "How did I get here?"

"Ye came back tae me like a miracle, my love. I have waited years. Ye look exactly the same."

He studied her face. Yes, he remembered her, but she had aged with time and worry.

He glanced over to the cradle. His memory of his other life with Bridget dimmed in his mind. The Fair Folk were kind that way.

Sarah followed his gaze over to the child and went to pick him up. All she said was, "Ye brought me back a gift, I see."

"Do ye like it?" he asked.

"Aye." Sarah asked no questions, delighting in having a bairn of her own, something the good Lord had not granted them before now.

"Goodness," Jane said. "She accepted the child wi'oot question?"

"Aye." Flora said wistfully. "We helped a bit, of course, but Sarah Thorburn was a special woman. The Fair Folk owe her a huge debt for the way she cared for a wee lad as her own. It wasn't easy."

Together they lived out their days. John remained a faithful, loving husband who set about farming a wee plot of land for them, finding a perfect spot not too far from his beloved sea. They adored their son, though Robert remained difficult and sullen. Often he sat outside scanning the horizon, waiting for someone who never came. Then, once, without provocation, he slapped Sarah and said, "Ye're not my mammy."

His parents, both tender-hearted, discussed what to do with him, and decided to send him to the mines to work. There he worked harder than others his age because of his small stature, but he grew tough and proved his worth. Life in the mines suited him, and he turned his rage into heavy toil, gaining the respect of the other men.

When he met the beautiful Elizabeth and married her, his parents breathed a sigh of relief. She smoothed his roughest edges and make him laugh when no one else could. They rejoiced further when Elizabeth gave birth to a beautiful lass. They knew nothing of prophecies, but something in Robert shifted when his daughter was born.

When Flora grew silent, Jane realized they had come to the end of the tale. "I dinna ken what tae say," she said. "It all seems too fantastic, but in my heart it feels real." She didn't tell Flora how unsettled she still felt, how unsure.

"You are one of us, Jane," Flora said. "You may be mostly human, but you see us when others do not. You have used your powers to become a great weaver. And then there's that business with your aunt and her children." Seeing Jane's startled look, she added, "Aye, we know about that. You gave her an incredible gift of love."

All of that was true. Yet the prophecy troubled Jane. "No one helped my da," she said. "The Folk were around me my whole life, helpin' me, playin' like we were friends. Why nae do the same for him?"

"I assure you, we did reach out to him. But he had enough magic in him to know his mother had died at his birth, and we could never reach past his anger. He never allowed us into his life."

This didn't satisfy Jane one bit. "It still feels like he was a means tae an end. He deserved tae learn the truth, too."

"We should have done more," Flora said quietly. "We make mistakes, Jane. No amount of magic can prevent that."

"It's still unfair." Though Jane didn't know her father, the story brought out feelings of protectiveness she didn't know she had. The drunken lout her uncle turned away had lived with an abandonment even she couldn't comprehend. Yet what could anyone do now? Flora admitted regrets, and at least that was something.

Another issue bothered her as well. "The Fair Folk widnae want a human tae lead them. Yer ways are a mystery tae me. Besides, what about the prophecy? I wisna taken as a bairn." She didn't add that running a fairy queendom wouldn't fit well into her already busy schedule.

"Aye, the prophecy." A hint of bitterness infused Flora's melodious voice. "The queen has suffered from our failure to take you as an infant. We have a council of Wise Women who examined the prophecy and decreed it can still be fulfilled. Come, visit our world so you can learn more about our way of life. I promise to return you unharmed. I can guarantee that."

The wind shifted, and Jane brought a scarf up to her face to block the chill. Thick, dark clouds darkened the landscape. This was a lot to take in. But after hearing the story, she believed Flora. Well, perhaps not the notion of a man's tears creating a pond. Like all fairy tales, though, the details were fantastical, but the elements of the story rang true.

Flora wasn't demanding anything permanent from her, she reasoned. And if Aunt Kirstin died, Jane would blame herself for not doing everything in her power to save her. This way she could potentially return to her life, the one where she was independent and free. If Flora was really telling the truth, that is.

She held out her hand to reach for Flora's. It felt like a doll's hand, so tiny and soft. "Well, then. It canna hurt tae visit. Heal my aunt, and ye have my word."

"It is done. We will return soon." Flora gave Jane a kiss on the cheek and floated away.

CHAPTER 14

She took me up in her milk-white han,
An she's strokd me three times oer her knee,
She chang'd me again to my ain proper shape,
An I nae mair maun toddle about the tree.

Allison Gross
Anna Gordon (Mrs. Brown of Falkland)

*A*s Flora left, the clouds parted and the sun came out. Jane stood in the garden, trying to comprehend what had happened. She never met her grandfather, so the legend remained untold in her family. She wished she'd known sooner. She wished her father knew, too.

She turned to go indoors, then heard the shriek of children's voices.

"Aunt Jane! Aunt Jane!"

She turned to see them running toward her. Was school over for the day? Flora's story had taken even longer than she thought, and she needed to relieve Beitris right away. Reaching out her arms, she gathered the children to her. First Heather, then Ewan, Jr., and Andrew. Andrew was the youngest, so she crouched down to look him in the eye. They had changed so much. Ewan Jr. had a gap in one tooth, while Andrew now ran around on chubby legs, a wee lad now instead of a baby.

"How is Ma?" Heather asked.

Jane stood, though she kept hold of Andrew's hand. "She is vera ill, but we will do our best. Beitris is helpin'. Let's go inside an' check on her." As they went inside, she told them they needed to stay with Aunt Elizabeth and Uncle Robert.

"Yay!" Andrew yelled. "I want tae play wi' Robina an' Thomas!"

Robina and Thomas. She'd never even heard of these siblings, let alone met them, and didn't even know how many there were. She felt the familiar tug of abandonment in her heart.

Her attempts to help the children pack were met with some resistance, as they all wanted to see their mother before leaving. She couldn't blame them, impatient though she was to get the visit to her parents over with. Soon all three children were huddled at Kirstin's bedside.

Uncle Ewan poked his head in. "Let Beitris do her work," he said.

"Dinna worry." Beitris rubbed Kirstin's feet with oil infused with pungent garlic. "They're good medicine for her. I'll work around them."

They chattered about their day at school as if Kirstin were wide awake. Occasionally she stirred, and once she made a noise to try to speak, but then fell deep into the private world of her illness. Beitris continued to work, lips pursed and brow furrowed, muttering quiet prayers. Once their conversation was spent, the children grew silent and watchful, occasionally sniffing back tears. It was time to move them along.

"Come, children," she called. When they didn't move, she added, "We'll bring ye back tae visit." And though she had no right to make promises, she added, "She'll be well soon, and then ye'll be back tae stay." She cringed at her own words, but she needed the hope as much as they did.

There were groans and general protests, but they obeyed. Heather took the longest to pack, stopping every few minutes to listen for any sounds from her mother's room.

Uncle Ewan gave Jane directions on how to find her parents' home. They were simple enough. The wee group said little on the way, the heaviness of worry surrounding them all like a thick blanket. Jane tried to think of things to say to cheer them up, but her few feeble attempts fell flat. She carried Andrew most of the time, as his chubby wee legs struggled to keep up with the others.

The walk was shorter than she expected. It was hard to believe she lived so close to them without any contact all those years. But they came upon a small tenement, a few stories high, that looked thrown together carelessly in an attempt to provide quick housing for a growing population.

They made their way through a darkened hallway to the flat. Jane stood before the door, quivering inside, and gave a light knock as if hoping no one would hear her.

The door opened, and there stood a woman taller than Jane, but with similar features. As the children, suddenly energized by the prospect of seeing their cousins, burst in through the door, the woman's eyes widened as they settled on Jane.

There were shrieks and hugs all around, but none of the young Thorburn children even noticed Jane. All the children rushed into a bedroom and closed the door, completely ignoring the woman their older sister. They had to be Robina and Thomas, both much younger than she, but she never even got a good look at them.

That left the two women, strangers, to stare warily at each other.

"Hello, Ma," Jane said in a whisper. She had dreamed about

what she would say in this moment, but standing in front of her mother now, no words came to mind. This person gave birth to her but nothing more. Rather than extend an awkward silence, she decided to get right to the point. "Aunt Kirstin is ill. We need ye tae take her weans while she recovers."

Elizabeth gave a curt nod. "Will ye come in?" she asked. She did not reach out to hold Jane. In fact, she shrank away from her.

Jane entered the flat, crowded with beds and schoolbooks, giving it a cluttered look.

Elizabeth put a pot of water on the fire to boil and motioned for Jane to sit. She looked tired and worn, but Jane recognized their resemblance in the shape of her eyes and her high cheekbones. No doubt Elizabeth had once been a beauty.

As they waited for the water to heat, Jane filled Elizabeth in on Kirstin's illness. "I'll stay until she's better," she said.

"She may nae get better, ye ken." Elizabeth focused on the fire, not looking into Jane's eyes.

Jane was about to respond when the door to the flat opened, and in came her father. She stood and faced him, a stranger with whom she shared the strange bond of their Fey ancestry. She had not forgiven him for letting her go and likely would not, not ever. Yet the pull of their connection was more powerful than her anger. She *knew* him from a place deep inside.

"Da," she said softly.

He didn't respond at first. His face was layered with too many lines for his years, and his eyes searched hers. Then he broke into a broad grin that revealed several missing and rotted teeth. "Jane!"

The two of them were in each other's arms, she trying not to cry.

"Let me look at ye," he said. "It feels like you just left, and here you are, all grown up."

She wanted to say that she hadn't "left," she was sent away. In the corner of her eye she noticed Elizabeth watching them, arms folded. She pulled away from his embrace, but he held her hands in his. They were dry and rough, but soothing somehow. He was shorter than Elizabeth, barely taller than Jane, but burly and strong. He reminded her of a slightly larger version of Bram.

"What brings ye here?"

Elizabeth told him of Aunt Kirstin's illness. "Jane's here tae take care o' her, an' we'll keep the bairns."

Robert raised his eyebrows. "We may have tae stand up tae sleep."

"It willnae be for long," Jane promised. "But I should go back tae her."

"Stay for supper, Jane. Please."

She took her hands back from him and shook her head, unable to speak.

"She needs tae leave, Robert. Let her go." Elizabeth spoke sharply.

His eyes darkened, but he said nothing.

Jane hugged him again, but Elizabeth kept her distance, still eyeing Jane with suspicion, giving her the briefest of nods. *She's still afraid o' me,* Jane thought. *My own ma.* It didn't hurt as much as she thought. After all this time, she barely recognized the woman.

She said her goodbyes to the children, with a promise of bringing them back home soon. Robina and Thomas gave her a curious glance, but Jane decided not to introduce herself.

She hadn't walked along the street for more than a minute when she heard footsteps rushing up behind her. She turned to see her father running to catch up, his cheeks flushed and his breath heavy.

"Da? What is it?"

He stopped and leaned over with his hands on his thighs to

catch his breath. "I needed tae say more tae ye, that's all. Say I'm sairie."

"It's awricht," she said, even though it wasn't.

He looked back toward the flat, afraid Elizabeth was listening. "It wisna right o' me. When ye left I felt like I lost an arm or a leg."

"Why did ye send me away, then?"

Shaking his head, he said, "Yer ma couldna tend tae you. Over time she got better, but by then I lost control of the drink. Ye wisna safe wi' either o' us."

He paused, groping for more words.

"It made no sense after the other bairns came along. I swear, though, ye were the only thing that ever felt right in my life. I've been a better da tae the others, at least since I took the temperance pledge, but somethin' about ye made me complete. An' that ended when ye went away." In contrast to the hardness of his face and body, his eyes were soft with emotion.

She wanted to tell him then of a prophecy that left him cast aside. She wanted to explain his anger to him. Yet if she did, he would think she lost her mind. Instead, she took his hand, one abandoned child to another, and squeezed it.

"Let's see each other again," she said.

"Aye." His voice grew husky.

She said her goodbyes one more time and walked away, not looking back. Nothing could ever be fixed, but she replayed the moment often for a very long time.

Back at the house, Kirstin continued to sleep, her forehead hot to the touch. Fairies or no fairies, Jane wasn't going to leave her aunt's recovery to chance. She heated water over the fire to help Beitris make more infusions. She continued to put wet cloths on Kirstin's head and chest, and to massage her icy feet. She forced fluids down Aunt Kirstin's throat, which was no easy task. Kirstin swallowed, though with some effort, but she remained barely conscious and unaware of her surroundings.

"Will she recover?" Jane asked in a whisper.

Beitris wiped her hands on a towel. "She's in the Lord's hands. I'm leavin' noo, but come and fetch me if anything changes." As she looked at Jane, she frowned. "Is there somethin' ye want tae tell me?"

"What do ye mean?"

The old woman searched Jane's face with piercing eyes that missed nothing. "Ye have lots on yer mind. There are long stories in yer eyes, like ye have seen new worlds today."

She had. Flora's story gave Jane a newer, wider view of her life. Then there was the awkward reunion with her parents and seeing siblings who showed no interest in her. She had no desire to share any of it, though, not yet.

"I just want Aunt Kirstin tae recover."

"Well, then." Beitris didn't look convinced, but she didn't force the issue. "Ye can tell me anything."

"Aye." Jane kept her eyes firmly focused on the floor.

"I'll leave ye, but I mean it. Whatever ye need."

The two women hugged, and Jane realized she would be alone to tend to her aunt.

"Dinna go, nae yet."

Beitris pulled away. "Ye'll be fine, lass."

Jane wanted to protest more, but she took a good look at Beitris's face. The lines seemed carved even deeper than when Beitris arrived that morning, and her eyes had the deadened look of someone with nothing left to give. Jane nodded and let her go.

Alone with Aunt Kirstin, Jane worked diligently. The weight of her task kept her up at night, and she sat next to the sickbed, dozing occasionally but never sleeping deeply. Even the slightest of Aunt Kirstin's movements, a change in breath, startled her awake.

As she worked, Jane thought about Rabbie. She filled the hours picturing long conversations with him where he told her about his workday, and she shared stories about life as a care-giver. He always said the right thing. Sometimes he told her how proud he was of her or talk about the importance of family. Other times, he told her not to worry about her job. She wondered if she would find any letters waiting for her upon her return to Alva.

Imagining Rabbie's presence kept her going during the days that followed, but each evening when Uncle Ewan came home, rubbing the back of his neck as he checked on his sleeping wife, saying little, she berated herself for her continued failure to help.

Her one hope lay in the bargain she made with the Fair Folk. Where was Flora?

On the fourth day, Jane stepped outside for some fresh air and movement. Her muscles ached from carrying buckets of water to and fro, grinding herbs with mortar and pestle, washing clothes... The chores were endless. It was all she could do to come up with soup and bread at supper with everything else she had to do. Rarely did she have time to stretch her arms and back, to breathe.

Then she heard the sound of buzzing wings.

"Flora! Coira!" she whispered. "I thought ye wid never come."

Coira held a bottle in her hand, which she waved back and forth. "I think you've been waiting for this."

Jane reached for it, but Coira pulled the bottle back. "We still have an agreement, correct?" she asked.

"Aye." Jane's hands were still reaching.

"Give it to her," Flora said. "Jane promised, and she's been waiting days for this."

"I want to be sure, my sister. Humans aren't known for keeping their word."

"Please, Coira," Jane said. "I've never lied tae you, and I never will. I meant my promise."

Coira didn't look convinced, but handed the bottle to Jane, who opened the cap and let out a cry. It smelled awful, like a dead animal.

"What on earth?"

"It tastes terrible, but it will work," Flora assured her.

Jane looked suspiciously at the potion, and then at Coira, whose face revealed nothing. She wondered briefly if the foul stuff was poison but dismissed the thought. Coira came across as cold, calculating even, but not evil. And Flora showed her sister genuine affection. They had nothing to gain by doing harm to her aunt. Besides, nothing else had worked, and if she didn't try this, she risked losing Kirstin altogether. She gave them a resolute nod.

"We'll be back for you soon," Coira said. "Do not forget." And with that, they flew away.

Jane took the potion to her aunt. Though not fully conscious, the sick woman wrinkled her nose and turned her head to one side. Jane guided Kirstin's head back to center.

"Ye have tae fight for yer bairns, Aunt. This will bring ye back tae us."

Kirstin opened her mouth. She coughed and gagged as the potion went down, then let out a guttural cry.

"Are ye awricht?" Jane's stomach began to flutter. If she needed to fetch Beitris again, how would she explain this?

She needn't have worried. After the single cry her aunt returned to silence, but something shifted. Her breathing grew smoother, her face bore a touch of color.

"I guess the stuff tasted as bad as it smelled, Aunt." Jane kissed her on the forehead before taking her post in the bedside chair. She was prepared to toss and turn as she had all week, but fell into a deep, exhausted sleep, even before Uncle Ewan came home.

The next morning she woke, stiff from sleeping on the hard chair, surprised she slept at all. Shaking off the grogginess, she reached over to touch Aunt Kirstin's forehead, which she did first thing every morning. This time it was cool.

"Jane?" Kirstin spoke in a whisper.

"Auntie? Oh, Auntie Kirstin, ye're back!" She leaned over, curbing her urge to give her aunt a big bear hug. Kirstin had grown thin and brittle in her illness, and Jane didn't want to break her.

She fetched some water and poured her aunt a glass. Kirstin drank it slowly, tentatively.

"Does yer throat hurt?" Jane asked.

"Aye, a wee bit, lass. How long have ye been here?"

"A few days," Jane said. "Can ye sit up a bit if I prop you up?"

Kirstin nodded, and Jane fussed with the pillows.

"Where are the bairns?" she asked.

"They went tae Ma's." Jane poured Kirstin another glass of water, hoping to keep a cheerful note to her voice. "We need tae get some broth in ye. I'll put some on the fire."

Uncle Ewan came home from work that night to find his wife sitting upright, sipping broth and taking small amounts of bread. Even after years of marriage, their eyes lit up with excitement at the sight of each other.

"Oh, my precious Kirstin, my love." He ran a hand along her jaw, and she kissed it. Turning to Jane, his own eyes full of naked emotion, he said, "Ye brought her back. Ye were always good luck for us, Jane. Always."

For Jane, those words always treasured hugged her soul. Though she wanted to treasure that feeling, it was tinged with guilt. The Fey saved Kirstin, not Jane. And soon they would want their payment from her.

CHAPTER 15

How featly they trip it! how happy are they
Who pass all their moments in frolic and play,
Who rove where they list, without sorrows or cares,
And laugh at the fetters mortality wears!

The Fairy Dance
Mrs. G. G. Richardson

ithin a few weeks, Aunt Kirstin returned to her old self, cooking, cleaning, and washing clothes with the zeal of one who came back from the dead to delight in the mundane tasks of life.

It was time for Jane to leave.

Her aunt and uncle, however, weren't so sure. "I'm still weak," Kirstin said. "Wait until the bairns come back, at least."

"What if she relapses?" asked Uncle Ewan.

Jane's stay would never be long enough to suit them. The only way to be free was to set a date.

"I will go tae church with ye on Sunday, an' then I will return tae Alva." *After I visit the Fey*, she thought, though she kept that to herself.

Jane's mind was made up. If Uncle Ewan didn't agree to her terms, she would steal away in the night.

On Sunday, he fetched the children and dressed them in their best clothes. At services, the congregation celebrated Kirstin's recovery with hugs, gushing about how wonderful she looked, how well! Uncle Ewan held on to his wife as if he needed her support, not the other way around. Afterward, Jane prepared a roast for the family, accompanied by potatoes and carrots. They didn't speak of Jane's leaving during dinner, but spoke instead of the lovely service and how good it felt for everyone to be together again.

After the dishes were done, Jane wiped her hands on her apron, then removed it for the last time. Surveying the room, she saw a family reunited, with everyone huddled together around their mother. Always an outsider, the scene touched her but also broke her heart.

They didn't look up when she gathered her belongings. Only when she said, "I'll be goin' noo," did they jump to their feet to say goodbye.

Uncle Ewan embraced her first. "Ye always have a place here," he said. "I truly wish ye wid stay wi' us."

"Ye brought me back, Jane," Kirstin said. "May the Lord bless ye wi' happiness."

Jane hugged her, then each of the children. The hugs and kisses all around were heartfelt, but no one cried when Jane walked out the door.

She stood waiting at the gate, wondering how to find her way to the Folk. Or would they come to her? Five minutes. Ten minutes. What if no one came? How would they know she was free to leave? *Best to head back tae Alva*, she reasoned. *Mebbe they changed their minds*. Part of her hoped so.

Just when she convinced herself to go home, Flora arrived,

dressed in deep olive green, a more subdued color than usual, but still beautiful.

Jane let out a relieved laugh at the sight of her. "I was worried."

"We kept watch," Flora said. "We've been waiting for you. Follow me."

Jane surveyed her familiar world one last time, her heart beating faster with a combination of excitement and nerves. Then she followed Flora into the woods, making her way into the next unknown. The fact that they wanted her there, welcomed her there, was a unique privilege most humans never experienced. The honor of that overcame any apprehension.

Once they found a clearing, Flora said, "Close your eyes."

Jane did so, and a tickle of something made her sneeze.

"Fey dust," Flora explained. "To prepare you for the journey."

Pressure formed at Jane's shoulder blades, a gentle heaviness, uncomfortable but not painful. Then, from the corner of her eyes, she caught a glimpse of two compact wings sprouting from her back, wide as her shoulders. They were a transparent silver and soft to the touch.

"When you have the blood of the Fair Folk, the wings are always there," Flora said. "Follow me." She rose effortlessly a few feet above Jane.

"How do I move them?" Jane asked.

"Focus your attention on the place between your shoulder blades."

Jane did as Flora instructed, but nothing happened.

"Relax, lass." Flora stroked one of Jane's wings, and it trembled softly. "Your face is all scrunched from the effort."

After taking a deep breath and blowing it out, Jane's muscles released and she tried again. This time a little shiver stirred her mid-back as the wings emerged, soft as a butterfly.

"It's workin'," she said with wonder. In response, they moved a little faster, and she let out a giggle. She remained on the ground, though. "What do I do noo?" she asked.

"The wings will guide ye. Keep focusing, keep trusting."

Jane willed herself to stay calm. Soon she found herself rising a few feet into the air. The sensation startled her, causing her to fall back to the ground. After a few tries, though, she grew more comfortable, flying higher and higher, then practicing landing. Up high she was light and free. *So this is what birds see*, she thought. There were the tops of trees below her, the hills to the north that led to the Highlands, and the River Forth snaking along her southern view. In the distance were lochs she had never visited. Her vision grew sharper, like a golden eagle's; not only could she see far off, but also rabbits, foxes, and even field mice.

Flora took Jane's hand. "Are you ready?"

Jane nodded and together they glided through the air. Once she overcame her initial trepidation, flying felt as familiar as the path along Alva Burn or the sweet touch of Robert Stein's lips on hers, as if she had done this many, many times before.

Beneath her the countryside whizzed by: the green glens with their rolling slopes; Stirling Castle, past its glory days but still a majestic sentinel keeping watch; and to the shimmering blueness of Loch Lomond. For Jane, an untraveled weaver, the world cracked open. If all of this bounty was a wee bit of Scotland, what would it be like to cross the ocean? To visit other countries?

There were glimpses in her memory of fairy ancestors calling to her, one after another, welcoming her home. They whispered to her the history and culture of the Fey. She saw queens and workers alike, tending woods and lakes, growing food, having families. Never before had she felt such a sense of belonging to something. Her heart grew heavy as she thought of her father.

They landed at the southern tip of the loch. Jane's legs

wobbled at first, so she paced a bit until her legs worked normally again. Before them stood a simple mound that looked like nothing special.

"Are you ready to go inside?" Flora asked.

"Inside where?"

Flora, seeing Jane's confusion, said, "Oh, sorry. Your human side can't see yet." She placed her tiny hands on Jane's head and mumbled a few words that sounded foreign to Jane. "There. That should help."

Blinking, Jane found herself standing at a tiny red door at the mound that came only to her knees, something so vivid she couldn't believe she hadn't seen it before. She shook her head and blinked again, but it was still there.

Flora opened the door and motioned Jane to enter. "We live under the ground," she said. "Hold on to me."

"How will we fit in that?" Jane asked.

"Watch." Flora waved an arm and the door grew to Jane's full height.

The sprouting of wings had been strange enough, but she hadn't actually seen them grow from her back. The expanding door was quite another matter, shifting as it did so right in front of her. As Jane grew lightheaded from the shock, Flora steadied her, waiting patiently for the sensation to subside.

"Are you ready?" Flora asked. "I promise our travels will not be unpleasant."

"I doubt it, but let's go."

Flora reached out for Jane's hand. They entered a dark tunnel and dropped swiftly downward, sweeping this way and that, and Jane felt like she'd left her stomach at the door. Yet Flora navigated the curves in the darkness with ease. Unable to see a thing, Jane clutched Flora's hand tightly, closing her eyes and praying not to crash.

Finally they slowed and landed, Jane's feet coming to the

ground without a sound, giving her a chance to catch her breath.

"Nae unpleasant?" she asked. Her knees were still shaking.

"Aye, maybe I went a wee bit fast for your first time."

Though they were far beneath the earth, the room remained bright with what seemed like sunlight. Jane gaped in wonder at its elegance. The walls were lined with shimmering peach-colored fabric, and the high ceiling was white with gilded trim and frescoes of dancing Folk.

"This is Douglas," Flora said. "Douglas, this is Jane, the heir."

A handsome young man with sandy hair and a turquoise suit with long tails bowed to them. "Welcome." When he stood, he smiled with twinkling eyes that matched his suit.

Jane couldn't help but smile back. She didn't know what she expected from life in a palace, but now she realized being treated like a special guest might be fun.

Coira entered the room and greeted them with a grunt. Without so much as a welcome, she said, "Follow me."

The group scurried to keep up with her as they headed down a wide corridor that twisted and turned, with endless numbers of wooden doors on either side leading to who knows where. She wondered how anyone found their way.

"This is huge!" she said.

"This is the home of the queen," Coira said with a sniff. "What else would you expect?"

"She is also very ill," Flora said. "You should be prepared for that."

"How ill?" What else hadn't they told her?

"We need your help." Flora put an arm around Jane, and only then did Jane realize her wings had retracted. With no wings and no way of knowing how to leave the palace, she was truly at the mercy of the Fair Folk.

"Your presence will give the queen strength until you come to us for good," Coira said. "If it were up to me, I'd keep you here for her sake, but we made a bargain, and I'm stuck with it. You'll go back to your precious mill and your human life, though why anyone wants that is a mystery to me."

"We healed your aunt," Flora reminded Jane. "Now we need you to heal our Queen. I'm sorry I didn't tell you, but I promise, we'll send you back home."

Another sick woman needing her attention. Jane shook her head in disbelief. "There must be some mistake," she said. "I couldna heal my aunt wi'oot yer help. I am a weaver, a factory girl."

"Trust us." Flora nudged Jane to walk. "This is a job only you can do."

With no choice in the matter, all she could do was put one foot in front of the other and try to quell the nervous swirling of her stomach.

"These are the queen's private quarters," Flora said as Douglas tugged on the ring of a heavy wooden door with both hands. As the women entered, he left the room, closing the door behind him.

Jane gasped as the room beyond came into view. So much space for one person! At one end two plush sofas faced each other, separated by a small white marble table. A dining table with place settings for ten graced the center of the room. The walls were dressed with tapestries and fine paintings of Fair Folk as warriors, farmers, and sages. When she walked in, the walls were a soft mauve, but then they shifted to a bright, sunny yellow. All of this beneath a small fairy knoll!

At the far end of the room a tiny, pale woman lay propped against pillows on a bed that her aunt and uncle and their three children could fit in with room to spare. Jane had imagined Queen Donella as strong and powerful, not a weak woman wasting away. The queen beckoned to Jane, who moved forward but not too close. Unsure of how to approach, she did her best to make an awkward curtsy.

"Rise, lass," the queen said.

Queen Donella was as beautiful and fragile as a fine glass vase, with delicate, translucent skin that stretched over her high cheekbones. Though ill, she wore a fine finest gossamer gown, the blue of a summer sky, rich and deep and warm. Jane could almost see the clouds shifting with the breeze. The queen's black, wavy hair was freshly brushed and lay in soft tendrils that reached her waist. A small crown of gold with diamonds shimmered when she turned her head.

"My daughter," she said, holding out a withered hand. "Come closer. Here, sit on the edge of the bed."

From across the room, Queen Donella looked as young as Jane. Close up, though, the queen's face displayed deep lines across the forehead, and lighter lines crisscrossing each other on the cheeks and neck. She reminded Jane of Beitris, both youthful and ancient.

"I am here, M—" She stopped, realizing she had almost called her "Mother." Had someone put a spell on her? If the prophecy was even true Queen Donella was her grandmother's sister. Yet the queen radiated love the way the fireplace radiated its warmth, and in her presence Jane wanted to love her back as much as she ever wanted anything. It was all so confusing.

The queen said, "We will do our best to help you to understand and what's happening. First, there is something I must tell you right away so you don't worry. I know you aren't sure about our motives, and you may see this as one more reason not to trust us."

What now? Jane jumped up from the bed and backed away toward the doorway, but then stopped. No wings. Trapped.

"It's all right to take space from me. I can't blame you." The queen pulled herself higher on the pillows, and it took great effort for her to do so. "Our time is different from human time. We bend and stretch it back and forth to suit our needs. I promise you, you will be gone only a week in your time, but it may seem like years here. You have trusted us to keep our word, and we will."

"Years?" Stunned, Jane put both hands to her face and let out a little sob. *What have I done?* Her work, her friends, Rabbie, all gone in an instant, and replaced by what? She couldn't imagine being gone that long, even if their promises were true.

"Oh, dear, I have distressed you. I'm afraid we did a poor job of preparing you for this visit."

"I have a job, and friends. I canna just disappear. Please, send me back."

The queen began to cough, and servants appeared from nowhere. One propped Donella to a full sitting position, and the other fed her an amber liquid. Within a minute or two the queen settled down, and the servants disappeared as quickly as they came.

Calmer now, the queen said, "I swear to you on the soul of your grandmother, my sister, it will only be a week in human time."

Jane shifted from one foot to the other, still fighting the urge to flee. "I... I dinna understand what is happenin', an' all this talk about time—well, I never heard o' such a thing."

"We are asking a lot, I know. I promise, Jane, I will never deceive you. I will not take you from your life, because I know how hard you've worked for it."

"Thank you, Your Highness," Jane said, not knowing what else to call her.

"Please call me 'Mother,'" the queen said. "I have longed for us to be together for many years."

"I canna," Jane said, despite the continuing urge to do so. "I mean no disrespect, but mebbe I can call you somethin' else?"

"Why not 'Aunt Donella'? That would be the truth."

Though still unsure, this appealed to Jane. She had experience with aunts, at least. "Aye. I like it."

The queen held out her hand again. "Will you let me hold you a moment?"

Jane leaned over as the queen wrapped tiny arms around her. They felt forceful in spite of the queen's weakened state. Giving in to the hug, Jane decided to surrender to the strange magic of this place.

The hug invigorated the queen. She sat up straighter, and a hint of rosy color brightened her gaunt cheeks. Snapping her fingers toward Flora, she said, "Bring us some food."

"Is there anything in particular you desire?" Flora asked, her face filled with hope.

With a childlike grin, Queen Donella said, "I'm hungry. Surprise me."

Now everyone smiled as Coira and Flora exited the room. *Apparently*, Jane thought, *when the queen wants to eat it's a cause for celebration.* No wonder the Fair Folk were so concerned.

Soon a stream of servants entered, all women. The first two covered the dining table with an elegant white cloth. A third trailed behind with a basket of silverware and red cloth napkins. A half dozen servants then brought in large silver trays filled with the most beautiful, colorful food Jane had ever seen. This was nothing like the simple fare of her life in Alva. Juicy beef, cooked rare, steaming hot, and smelling of cooked onions filled one large tray. There was a lamb shoulder roast and next to it, salmon that looked freshly caught. There were vegetables of the richest reds, greens, oranges, and purples piled high. Another tray was filled with fresh fruit: blue-red plums bursting with juice, along with an assortment of large, juicy berries. And the sweets! *Oh, my.* One servant, a young woman about Jane's age, stepped forward. Pointing to each item, she named them: apple butterscotch pie, chocolate fudge, honey and whisky cake, and, oh, yes, a pumpkin cake. At the sight of it all, Jane's stomach started to growl.

Two servants helped bring the queen to the table, with Jane

following behind. IThey moved slowly, as Donella's legs threatened to collapse beneath her. Finally, they were seated, with the queen at the head of the table and Jane to her right.

At Donella's urging, Jane took a bite of fudge and tried not to devour it. The sweetness exploded in her mouth, and she wanted nothing more than to dive into the whole tray.

"Go ahead, enjoy all you want," the queen said, smiling. "There's plenty." She took a toffee pastry in her hands and bit into it. "This is my favorite."

"The Fair Folk eat what humans do?" Jane asked. She had never thought to ask any of them over the years.

"Our food looks like yours, but it's different," the queen replied. "We use magic to grow our vegetables so we have them even in the cold of winter."

With all the bounty before her, Jane struggled to reconcile the problems described by both Coira and Bram. "Coira says the Fey are losin' magic," she said. "It disna look like it here."

"Coira is correct," the queen said. "We haven't lost all of it, but some years are better than others, just as they are with humans and their crops. Now, our animals..." Her voice trailed off.

"What?" Now Jane wanted to know everything.

"We do not slaughter animals," she said. "They provide us with the part we desire, and then we assist them in growing that part back."

"Does it hurt them?" Jane asked.

"No. We provide a spell so they do not experience pain."

They sat in silence as Jane processed this information. This world was so different from hers, and there was much to like about it. The queen matched Jane for hunger, and by the time they finished, they had eaten most of the food, both giggling at the sight of the once-piled platters now exposed, with only a few slivers of meat and bits of vegetables remaining. Drowsy from the feast, Jane closed her eyes right there at the table.

"So, what do you think of our home now?" Queen Donella asked.

Jane jerked awake, startled and embarrassed at having dozed off in front of a queen. Recovering quickly, she said, "It's lovely. Vera different from whit I'm used to."

"Perhaps you will learn to love it."

Who wouldn't want a life like this? Fine clothes, never a shortage of food or struggling to pay the rent. But what the boardinghouse fare lacked in variety and elegance, it made up for with the friendship of the women who lived there. And the mill, despite the long hours and low pay, gave her a sense of purpose. This world, no matter how lavish and amazing, was not hers.

"I am grateful for the kind hospitality," she said, "but I am a mill lass. If I ate like this every day, I'd never get any work done."

"We have use for weavers here," the queen mused. "Perhaps we will provide you a loom. Our threads, as you have seen, are unique, and you might enjoy working with them. I want you to feel at home."

"That's kind o' ye," Jane said, "But no, Alva is hame."

Queen Donella would give Jane anything she wanted, but she wanted nothing more than to return to Alva once she fulfilled her obligation.

If the queen was troubled by Jane's declaration, she didn't show it. "Let's show you your room so you can rest."

"Before we do that, may I ask, Qu—Aunt Donella, what is expected o' me here?"

Waving a dismissive hand, the queen said, "I'll introduce you to some people. There will be some dances and celebrations." As Jane's eyes widened in response, she added, "Don't worry about it. We'll show you our ways a little at a time. You'll be given clothes and instructions as they are needed."

"This disna sound sae simple tae me," Jane said. "Remember, I'm a weaver. I never saw a palace before."

The queen patted her on the arm. "You'll be fine," she said. "Now, off to your room. This has been a big day for both of us."

Two silent, stealthy servants were standing next to Jane, startling her yet again. Did they move without sound, or had they appeared out of thin air? She had no idea, but she said her goodbyes and let them escort her to her room.

What a room it was! She expected something much smaller and less ornate than the queen's quarters, but it was as large as the entire dormitory at the boardinghouse, and all for her. Quilts piled high on the spacious bed, with a rose-colored canopy draped over its top. A dresser and matching armoire, stained the color of honey to bring out the knots, smelled delicately of Scots pine. A silver tray on top of the dresser contained a matching silver mirror, hairbrush, and comb. A sitting area provided a sofa, gold wool with soft green leaves woven throughout. Jane ran her hand along it, smiling as it reminded her of home.

As with the queen's room, a fireplace brought warmth and extra light, and a cast iron tub sat next to it. The tapestries in this room showed scenes from—could it be?—the glen. Even Jane's rock was represented there, and she could almost hear the rushing sound of the burn. Had they made this room just for her?

The queen had promised Jane safe return; she might as well enjoy these comforts while while they lasted.

CHAPTER 16

Though richer vales, and balmier gales,
May tempt the wanderer's stay,
His heart will long to be among
Some scenes far, far away!

The Home-Sick Heart
John Imlah

The next morning, Jane woke to the bustling of servants. They set out a tray of pastries, fruit, and tea for her, but she was still full from the day before.

A fresh fire glowed and snapped, while a servant filled the tub with buckets of water. Another entered with an armload of clothes and hung them in the armoire. She then motioned to Jane to get in the tub.

"I… Could ye turn away?" Even in the cramped quarters of the boardinghouse, no one had seen her body, let alone a stranger.

"Of course. We will give you some privacy, Your Highness. Ring the bell when you are finished."

Your Highness? "Please, call me Jane."

"As you wish, milady."

Jane stepped into the tub, reveling in the luxury of hot water for bathing. A faint scent of honeysuckle wafted from the water, with plump blooms floating on top. She soaked until her skin began to pucker and then washed her hair. When she sponged off at the boardinghouse, she could never quite remove all the mill grime. Never had she felt so clean.

When she finished, she wrapped herself in a towel and rang the bell. It gave the slightest tinkling sound, and she wondered if they would hear her, but she needn't have worried. They entered the room silently, and each went to work.

She endured a few minutes of discomfort as they helped her dress. Yet the servants averted their eyes, respecting Jane's modesty. The gown they brought for her was a deep green with a touch of blue like a forest of fir trees, which enhanced her fair skin. They pinned and styled her hair to lift the sides and leave ringlets down her back, *oohing* and *aahing* over the thick curls. She refused the crown they offered, reminding them she was merely on a visit and not official royalty.

When they showed Jane how she looked, she gasped. She turned from side to side to see herself in the mirror. *If only Rabbie could see me!* The thought brought her both joy and pain. The two of them no longer lived in the same world. She tried to imagine describing her new experiences in a letter to him. *He'd think I was daft for sure. He'd probably want me locked up somewhere.*

Once her appearance met with their approval, they brought her to the queen. This time Donella sat on her sofa. Her eyes were bright, and her cheeks retained their new, rosy hue. She looked markedly different from the frail, wan woman of the day before.

"My beautiful daughter," she said. "You're a fine princess."

Jane blushed. Raised never to call attention to herself, her impulse was to change the subject.

"Ye look sae much better than yesterday," she said. "Like a different person." She gave a quick curtsy. "I hope that's nae something I shouldna say."

"Perhaps I have been sicker at heart than in body," Queen Donella said. "Having you here with me has given me new life. Now, my child, you must meet your kinsmen and women."

They headed down an unfamiliar hallway, and she decided to prod the queen yet again. "What am I doing?" she asked. "What is expected?"

"I really wish you wouldn't worry," Donella replied. "You have royal blood in you, so you will know what to do and say. The words will come."

"Words? What words?" Every time Jane found her footing in this strange world, some new expectation was thrust upon her.

The queen shrugged. "You'll greet the council. Say whatever is on your mind."

"But what if I say something wrong?"

They stopped and faced each other, and the queen's eyes bored into Jane. "Listen to me," she said, her tone now commanding. "We have watched you your whole life. You're careful with your words and deeds. Even when Skye had her troubles, you were kind and patient with her."

"Skye? How do ye ken about that?"

It had taken Jane a long time to let go of the trauma of those days, and having it brought up when she already felt nervous didn't help. Nor did she like the idea of them knowing all her secrets. Once again, she sensed that her life was not her own.

"Your troubles are imprinted upon you, my daughter, because it brought you so much pain. But do not fret; the Folk you meet today won't see it. Only those with access to the Wise Women know, and we do not judge."

Pressure formed in Jane's temples. Did they read all of her

thoughts, and observe all her experiences? She had guarded all her secrets so carefully, all for naught, leaving her feeling exposed and raw.

"I've overloaded you," the queen said, her eyes filled with sympathy. "You have much to learn, but we have time. Would it help you if I gave you a small spell to calm you?"

"Aye," Jane said in a small voice. She didn't know how she to get through this day without help.

Donella pressed her forehead against Jane's and stayed there for a few seconds. All at once Jane's head cleared and lightened, giving her a sense of peace.

"I didn't take it all away," the queen explained. "If I did, you wouldn't feel like yourself. But that should be enough to help. Now, let's proceed."

They entered a large banquet room filled with finely dressed Fair Folk. Queen Donella introduced everyone, though Jane doubted she would remember any of their names except for Douglas. The queen's calming spell, as promised, didn't entirely calm her nerves. She took the hands of the council members, accepting their welcomes. Most were warm and jovial, but a few showed contempt in their eyes that belied their attempts to look friendly.

When she came to Douglas, he gave her an encouraging smile as she took his hand. It was firm and warm.

"You're doing fine," he said with a whisper that forced her to move in closer to hear. He was also taller than most of the Folk she'd seen so far, about as tall as she.

"Thank you," she said, then looked away, suddenly shy.

"Jane, why don't you tell everyone about yourself," Queen Donella said.

Thirty pairs of expectant eyes faced her, and she wanted nothing more than to crawl away and hide. Then the words came to her, as the queen promised.

"I am but a visitor to yer land. I am a simple weaver from

Alva, and I am happy tae meet ye." She noticed the exchanged glances and wondered what they were thinking. Ignoring the flutter in her belly and returning to Douglas's friendly face, she plowed on. "I ken humans have different ways from the Fair Folk, an' I wid understand if ye see me wi' suspicion. But mebbe I can learn an' take some understanding home wi' me."

There were murmurs and expressions of surprise before the gathering broke into polite applause. She glanced at Queen Donella, who nodded with approval. She wasn't even sure where her words came from, and a small voice inside warned her of fairy magic at work. And yet...in Alva, as a factory girl, she had no voice at all.

After the introductions, Donella said, "Jane, I have some business to attend to with the council. Douglas, why don't you walk her back to her rooms?"

"Aye." He held out a bent elbow for her to take, and they left the room.

"Did I do awricht?" She didn't understand Douglas's role in the palace, so she hoped he didn't mind the question.

"You did well," he said. "The council will accept your presence soon enough."

"I'm nae sae sure about that. Seems like some wid run me out wi' pitchforks."

He patted the hand that gripped his arm. "No need to be nervous, lass. You're cutting off the circulation."

"I'm sairie." She pulled her hand away.

Laughing, he said, "Don't worry. There's still a bit of blood left in the arm. And the queen won't allow any pitchforks here."

They continued to walk, with Jane grateful to have someone with her to navigate the twists and turns.

"May I ask a question?"

"Aye. What do you want to know?"

"Why am I here? Really?"

"I see you get right to the point of things."

"What's wrong wi' that?" Jane asked.

Rather than answering her questions, Douglas pointed to a door. "That's yours," he said, opening it and waving Jane inside before following her.

They sat at each end of the sofa at a respectful distance, and a servant immediately placed a tray of tea and little cakes in front of them. There was no shortage of food here. No one needed to thin out the soup to make it last through the week.

Once settled, he said, "I haven't forgotten your question. You are aware of some of our problems, and the Folk are getting scared. There have been some rebellions recently, because some of our people are learning about hunger for the first time. There are some who say the queen hasn't done enough to protect us. On the other side, some say we need to learn to be more like the humans to keep our race strong. A small group thinks we need to dispense with royalty altogether."

"I see." She didn't, never having been told of this level of conflict, but she wanted to be polite. "Where do I fit in?"

"The queen has been ill, and without an heir the people are frightened. She brought you here to calm everyone down."

"But I'll go back tae Alva after this visit." Again, didn't entirely trust the promise that the Folk could bend time. "I'll be here a while, but not for good."

"Aye, but it will give them hope. And if you like us, maybe you'll visit us again. I'd like that." He gave her a hopeful glance.

In another life she might have appreciated his attentions. He was handsome, kind, and thoughtful. But he wasn't Rabbie.

"I have someone," she said. As soon as the words tumbled out she wanted to take them back, fearing she misread his intentions. "Well, nae exactly, but my heart is wi' him."

"We won't interfere with your life," he said, giving no indication she had said anything wrong. "I'd best leave, but we will see each other often. Friends?"

"Friends," she said, taking the hand he now offered her.

He squeezed her hand and then disappeared, leaving her to recall the last time she'd sworn friendship with a man. Rabbie seemed so far away from her now.

NEWS TRAVELED QUICKLY beyond the palace of the heir's visit, and that she was humble and kind. Thus began a whirlwind of appearances among the Fair Folk, who marveled at Jane's stature, tiny for a human but a giant among them. Having spent most of her life craning her neck upwards to look at people, the sensation of tallness was new and disorienting. She shook hands, kissed babies, and waved from balconies to excited throngs of people. In each appearance, Jane held on to the comforting presence of the queen beside her, giving her confidence.

Each day, Douglas escorted her to various activities, always cordial but remaining at a respectful distance. One day, about a week into her adventures, he said, "I have a surprise."

"I dinna think I can handle too many more surprises," Jane said with a laugh. "Every day is new. I'm not complainin', but I'm tired."

"I think you'll like this then." He took her to a room around the corner from hers and opened the door with a flourish.

"Oh, my!"

This room, much smaller than Jane's, contained only one item: a floor loom. This type of loom didn't require the power provided by a rushing burn and water wheel. It was an older, slower way of weaving, and the idea appealed to her.

"The queen had it made for you," Douglas said. "And don't be fooled by its simple design. This is a magic loom."

Jane touched it with loving hands, and tears came to her eyes. "I have missed my looms," she confided. "I learned on one of these first as a child." Uncle Ewan had spent hours with her on Sundays when he wasn't working at the mill, and pleasant memories of his undivided attention filled her with nostalgic longing. Eager to work, she asked, "How do I get fiber?"

Douglas pointed to a hole in the ceiling. "You call down moonbeams to make the thread."

Jane burst out laughing. "Moonbeams? Are ye daft?"

Rather than answering, he lifted his hands skyward. A small hole opened in the ceiling and in a few moments, a crack of light came through, bright and thin. Once it entered the room it snaked toward him. He circled one hand clockwise, and the light began to curl around itself. In a few minutes he presented Jane with a bobbin of silvery thread.

"Aye, moonbeams," he said.

She took the thread from him and touched it. It was real, all right, and magnificent, softer than any wool, fragile and light. Taking the end of it, she gave a little tug. Despite its delicate appearance, it held its strength.

"How did ye do that?" she asked.

"Here, I'll show you. Hold out your arm and flex your wrist."

She did so, and he took hold of her wrist. His touch sent belief into her bones that this could be real.

"Look upward and ask the moon to help you."

"That sounds silly," she said.

"Trust me."

"But we're deep underground. How can the moon reach all the way here?"

Douglas let out a hearty laugh that seemed to come from his toes. "This is what happens when you live with humans," he said. "You need logical answers to everything. We have magic because we believe it exists."

She squinted as she looked skyward. "Yet yer magic is disappearing."

"My point exactly. We are losing magic because we are

beginning to lose belief. With each failure doubt sets in, making things worse. Now relax, lass. Don't try so hard."

Closing her eyes, she let the muscles in her face and shoulders relax, taking her time. Once she centered herself, she asked the moon for help, then opened her eyes and waited. At first nothing happened, but Douglas bade her be patient, and soon a thinner, softer light eked its way through to her.

"Now circle your hand like this." He demonstrated the clockwise turn again.

She did so, and within minutes she filled a bobbin of golden thread. "Why is mine different from yers?"

He let go of her wrist, but the sensation of his touch remained. "When you build your skills, you can call up whatever color you want. The moon mixes with other particles in the air, so it can make blues, greens—anything. When you start, though, the color is the color that lives inside of you, the color of your soul."

It all sounded so strange and unreal, but the proof was in her hands.

"Now I'll leave you to it. Enjoy."

He exited before she could thank him. Though eager to start working with the loom, she played first with drawing the thread down from the moon. With some effort and a few false starts, soon she filled several bobbins of thread in many different colors.

With the thread made, now it was time to try the loom. It required her to prepare the warp, the vertical threads, manually. This was the first time since learning to weave all those years ago that she had the time to consider her design and which threads to use, then pull each thread through with a hook.

Though ideas for elaborate designs for clothes were filling her brain, she decided to start with something small, a lap blanket. Soon enough she made a simple blue-green plaid with a red stripe running through. When she finished, she clutched it to her with the same joy as when Aunt Kirstin gave her her first doll many years ago.

No doubt this was a gift to entice Jane to stay, but it was a fine gift, indeed. She spent most of the day there, happy to have time alone to play.

Each night there were dances and parties, with handsome dance partners and beautiful ladies ready for gossip. If anyone there resented her presence, she saw no evidence of it.

More than anything, Jane enjoyed the rich, delicious food. Breakfast always included bacon and eggs, plus beans and toast, with nary a bowl of porridge in sight. Her clothes were let out on a regular basis, and she wondered how she would fit into her regular wardrobe when she returned home. With plenty of food in her and no strain from hours on her feet, Jane blossomed into a beauty. Her cheeks were full and flushed with vitality, her figure more curvaceous.

After multiple fetes, though, the newness wore off. At night she dreamed of running her looms in Alva again, and during the day the various meetings, luncheons, and consultations with the queen interrupted her weaving. She lost count of days and weeks. Despite all the luxuries, she missed Maisie and Wynda. What if Rabbie gave up on her because she wasn't writing back? She even missed her little bed at the boardinghouse and Abi's soothing voice.

"Don't worry," Flora reassured her. "All is as promised."

ONE DAY she refused her dinner. She was sick of rich food, sick of stuffing herself, sick of this life. Instead, she wanted time in her room to toast her feet near the fire. This was not to be, however. A knock on the door disturbed her attempt at peace. Douglas arrived to summon her to appear before the queen. With a sigh, she asked him to wait outside while she changed.

She chose a dress of azure blue with a high neckline and puffed sleeves.

He took her to the throne room, where Queen Donella waited. The throne sat on a dais and was large enough to make her look like a little doll, complete with dangling feet peeking out from under her gown. It was made of rose gold polished to a soft sheen and encrusted with agates. A crown set over two entwined hearts in the Luckenbooth style topped the throne, bringing back memories of the brooch Skye wore at her wedding.

Jane bowed low.

"Rise, child," Queen Donella said, her voice as soft and smooth as rose petals.

"Thank you, Aunt."

"I trust you are treated well here?" the queen asked.

"Aye, I've had a wonderful visit. The Fair Folk have been sae good tae me, and I've wanted for naethin'."

"And my people have welcomed you?"

"Aye, more than I could imagine," Jane said.

"Then I must ask of you: will you stay with us a while longer?"

Jane fidgeted with her gown. "My queen, ye have loved me like a daughter, and I canna lie, I have wanted a mother's love my whole life."

"But?" A shadow crossed Queen Donella's face. The "but" lingered in the mists of the unspoken.

"I am nae ungrateful," Jane said. "I never will forget yer kindness. Being among the Fair Folk, I can feel my Fair blood coursing through me. But I am a factory girl, nae a princess. I make my way wi'oot magic or help from anyone."

Queen Donella raised an eyebrow. "Completely without magic?" she asked.

"Well, these days. I used it at work when I was younger an'

learnin'. And ye ken about my aunt an' her bairns. But I havena used it in a long time. It disna feel right."

"I see integrity is important to you. You have your father's fierceness."

Jane had never thought about that before, but it made sense. Anger, no. But fierceness, pride, and work ethic? All of those ran in her blood. "I always wanted tae make my own way."

"These qualities will serve you well when you join us," the queen continued. "There is much to do here when you take on your duties. Are you sure you won't stay?"

"Join you? My hame is in Alva. I'll be a factory girl until I die."

The queen gave her an indulgent smile. "Of course. We will not interfere with your natural life, but at the end of it, you belong to us. You will live then for hundreds more years." In a conspiratorial whisper, she added, "I'm much older than I look."

Jane bristled at the thought of being beholden to anyone. "I dinna belong tae you or tae anyone. Please let me go." Her fancy gown suddenly seemed gaudy and foolish. She longed to draw her hair back into a simple bun. Mostly, though, she wanted to go back to work. "Please."

"Jane. Come here, child."

Jane stepped forward reluctantly.

Queen Donella reached down and touched Jane's shoulder with her scepter. "I know it's hard for you to understand. Let's not part this way. I promise, I will send you home as soon as we are done, but let's make peace first."

Jane pulled away from the scepter's hard touch. "I always wanted a family. Ye played on that wi' me."

"It was no play, I assure you. Yes, I brought you here because I need you to fulfill the prophecy, but I repeat: we will not interfere with your life. You will not come to us until the end, and no one will accelerate that end in any way. I love you like a daughter. I will never hurt you."

Jane bowed her head. She already was hurt and no longer knew what to believe. But if she really could live the rest of her life unbothered by the Fey...what could be wrong with that? That left one question: "How much time do I have?"

A flicker in the queen's eyes came and went in an instant. "That is best left unsaid, but it will be enough. You'll see, I promise. Until then..."

"Aye." Jane said it softly at first, then reconsidered. "Aye," she said again, this time more forcefully, though she couldn't imagine what "enough" life would feel like. There was so much to see and do and experience. How could it ever be enough?

THE NEXT MORNING, Jane prepared to leave. At her request, the servants let her be, and she put on her old dress. Fortunately, it had fit loosely when she first arrived, because now it strained taut over her body. With any more extra weight she would have burst the seams. She closed the door to her rooms for the last time, touching the dark wood with affection.

Now, how to get back? They hadn't discussed this. She headed down the corridor and barely missed running into Coira.

Dressed head to toe in black, Coira was the only one of the Fey who intimidated Jane, and today was no exception.

"Leaving us so soon?" she asked. "I have to admit, you surprise me."

"Oh? How so?"

"It's not every day a mere factory girl gets to live like a princess. I thought the queen would talk you into staying."

Jane looked around, hoping someone else would enter the corridor. Coira stood a little too close to her, and her breath brought a chill to Jane's face. "I've told the truth. I'm a factory girl. I dinna care about some prophecy. It feels like a big mistake, anyway. Someone else could do the job better."

"Well, we agree on that, at least. Here's the problem, though: your presence has helped the queen get stronger and healthier. When you're gone, she's likely to falter again. The rebels are looking for an excuse to overthrow us."

"I didna ask for this. I appreciate what ye did tae help my aunt, but I need tae go back tae my life." She knew as soon as she said it she had revealed weakness to Coira.

"The queen says you're the one, but she also says she will allow you to live out your days. I'd watch out, though, if I were you. Accidents happen."

"Coira, leave the poor lass alone." Douglas appeared in the way all servants did, from nowhere—something Jane still found disconcerting. To Jane, he said, "I've come to take you back."

Jane happily took his arm. As they walked together, she didn't look back, but she sensed Coira glowering behind her.

"She's all talk," Douglas said. "Her favorite thing to do is to scare everyone, but she means well."

"I'm sure she does. Just the same, I hope I live a long, long life."

"Then I wish that for you as well. Ready?"

"Let me see if I can get my wings going." This time she barely thought about them before they expanded, the sensation tickling her until she giggled. "I'm ready."

Their feet left the ground and they rose upward, going faster and faster. By the time they reached the doorway leading to the outside, she was dizzy and out of breath.

"Are you all right?" Douglas asked as they stopped.

"I need a minute." Though less frightened about flying through the tunnel than before, she still wobbled a wee bit.

"Let's sit. There's plenty of time."

She couldn't wait to return to Alva, but her stomach felt lodged up near her throat, so she obeyed him.

They were next to each other on a rock, much in the way she and Rabbie used to sit together in the glen, enjoying the vastness of the outdoors. Birds were singing, and the nearby trickle of water soothed her.

"I'll miss you," he said. Turning toward her, he added, "I know you're ready to go home, and I know you have someone special there."

She nodded, wary about his next words.

"There will come a time when you return here. It will be hard to say goodbye to your loved ones, but I promise I will be here to help you through that loss."

"Thank you," she said, though she had no desire to continue this line of conversation.

He didn't press for more, but patted her hand. "I'll wait. For hundreds of years if that's what it takes. Now, shall we send you home?"

"Aye."

Once airborne again, she let all her worries go. Soon she would be home, back at work, among her friends again.

As they neared Alva, she Douglas slipped away from her.

"Close your eyes," he said as he left. "Relax and let the wind carry you."

He vanished. After a momentary panic, she followed his instructions. The wind rocked her as if she were in a cradle, and she let herself drift in the breeze.

CHAPTER 17

O there's naught to compare wi' ane's ain fireside.

My Ain Fireside
Elizabeth Hamilton

*J*ane found herself in her bed in the boardinghouse in Alva, dressed in her tattered nightgown. Other than feeling some tightness in her gown, it felt like a long dream.

The other beds were empty and made. What day was it? What time of day? Gloom and rain visible through the windows offered no clues.

She dressed and went downstairs.

"Jane, ye're up!" Abi exclaimed, clapping her hands with joy. "I told everyone ye wid come back tae us. Ye must be so weak, though. Goodness. I'll make tea an' fetch some food for ye. Feelin' better?"

"Ma'am?" she asked, confused.

Abi walked over to Jane and put a hand on her forehead.

"Not even a wee bit of fever left. The doctor said he didna ken if you wid come back. A whole week ye were unconscious."

"I dinna remember." *It wisna a dream. Was it? Was I sick?* She felt a roaring in her head as she tried to make sense of it.

"Ye came back from yer aunt wi' the ague," Abi continued. "We found ye sick in bed. Sit, love, and rest. I'll bring ye some broth tae start, and we'll see how you do. Ye look good, though, like you needed a lot of rest. Oh, and some letters arrived while ye were asleep. That's what I called it, 'asleep.' Sometimes ye opened yer eyes but no one was there. Sort o' scary."

Jane could think of only one explanation for this. The Folk had left an adult changeling in Jane's bed in the "week" between leaving Menstrie and returning to Alva. Jane stifled a laugh at their ingenuity. The Folk knew how to tend to details.

Jane accepted the tea and broth, suddenly starved. The broth went down her throat like nectar. Soon enough, a slice of warm bread with butter appeared as well. Though Donella served the finest food that could be found anywhere, nothing tasted so good to Jane as the simple fare of home. The clothes, the dances, and meeting throngs of Fair Folk were a lark, to be sure, but not real life. The boardinghouse, with its narrow beds, threadbare upholstery, and plain white walls looked beautiful to her. She needed a good, long break from the Fey and intended to fully embrace this life, the life of a factory girl.

It occurred to her that if people thought she'd been unconscious, she could ask questions she thought were stupid. "What day is it?"

Abi paused from drying dishes. "It's Wednesday, just past dinnertime. Too bad ye didna wake up before everyone went back tae the mill."

Jane jumped up. "I should go tae work," she said. "I'll lose my job." Her knees threatened to buckle underneath her. There may have been a changeling in the bed, but she suddenly felt as weak and weary as if it had been her.

"Sit," Abi insisted. "Eat and build yer strength. I've kept the supervisor apprised o' yer health. Take some time tae make sure ye're ready. By the way, ye have the bed tae yerself for now, until you're better."

Grateful, Jane nibbled on the bread. The butter coated the inside of her mouth with its sweet, creamy flavor. "Thank you, Abi. I'm sure wi' some food in me I'll be back tae work in no time. If they'll still have me. But ye said letters came?"

"Aye." Abi took them from her apron and handed them to Jane. "Best ye go lie down an' read them there," she said. "Ye're lookin' a bit green all of a sudden."

"Green" indeed, but not from illness. The bending and twisting of time left her dizzy and disoriented. The lavish gowns, the exquisite food, the dances and merriment—she'd lived months and months in a few weeks of human time, with memories of nursing her aunt more dreamlike than life with the Fey.

Jane finished her meal and went upstairs, thankful to be alone while adjusting to her return home. Perhaps reading her letters would help bring her back to human time. She curled up on the bed and looked at the letters: two from Rabbie. Given how much time had passed in the Fair world, somehow she expected a bigger pile.

She checked the dates at the top to make sure she read them in the right order. Taking a deep breath, she forced herself to move slowly to make the moment last longer. Maybe in doing so, she could extend time, too. Oh, to have that ability! She would have used it to keep Rabbie with her a while longer.

Dear Jane,

I hope this letter finds you well. I've had the oddest dreams lately about you and fairies, and once I swear you begged me to rescue you from a fairy palace. I must have eaten something that didn't agree with me.

Work is exciting. The mill is new and clean. One day I hope to run it, but for now a nice old gentleman is in charge. He has taken me under his wing, so perhaps I will get his job when he retires. I miss my favorite wee weaver, though. You would like it here. I know you don't want to come to England, but if you ever change your mind, there's a place for you here.

Yer friend and admirer,

Rabbie

In her mind she imagined him telling her this in person, with his broad grin and childlike joy. She had missed him when he left, but now his absence threatened to crush her bones. She longed for him in a way she hadn't before.

Mebbe I should go there.

The thought slipped like a single raindrop into her mind. Something inside her had changed, though that something hadn't quite yet taken form. Perhaps she had been too hasty in her dismissal of a life in Leeds. It wasn't Lowell, but why did it have to be?

Smiling and humming to herself, she opened the next letter. This time he wrote about the woods. They were further away in Leeds, but he managed to walk to them every Sunday afternoon, as in the old Alva days. These were her favorite letters from him, the ones written with reverence for the trees and flowers.

It's a paradise for the Good Folk, he wrote, *but there is less of that for them. Sometimes I worry the woods will one day disappear, and when they are gone we will lose life's magic, too.*

As always, he closed with how he missed her: *Take care, my wee pixie, and may the fairies bring us together again one day.*

It seemed ironic for him to write about fairies. If only he knew.

∽

THE NEXT MONDAY, still considered by all to be on the mend, Jane returned to the mill and to her old job. Her time with the fairies started to fade, like a vivid dream that slips from aware-ness when the eyes open in the morning.

"Jane!" As soon as she walked into the weaving room, Leslie nearly knocked Jane over with a big hug. "I missed ye sae much!"

"Aye, me, too," Jane said, returning the hug and kissing the top of Leslie's head. The little girl trembled in her arms. "Are ye awricht, lass?"

Leslie didn't answer, but suddenly broke away and ran across the room to make herself busy. Jane opened her mouth to ask what happened, but an unfamiliar man now stood next to her, far too close for comfort.

"I'm Mr. Lambert, the new supervisor," he said, leering. He was not much taller than Jane, with a slight stoop. He combed his few remaining strands of hair carefully to attempt, without success, to cover the bare spots. It would be a mistake to describe the "whites" of his eyes, as they bore a dull yellow tinge. He smelled of tobacco and flatulence, and Jane's nose wrinkled.

Right away, she could tell he wouldn't be as benevolent as her previous bosses.

"Ye missed a lot o' work," he said. "The men manage tae show up when they're ill, too. If I had my way, I'd hire only men, an' let the women take care o' hearth an' hame."

Of course, he didn't have his way, because the mill owners could pay a woman half of what they paid a man. She decided Mr. Lambert was more bark than bite and set about to impress him.

There would be none of that, though. That first day he wore her to tears. If he couldn't find fault with her work, he criticized her speed.

"Work faster!"

"That's a sloppy weave!"

"Dinna break a thread, or I'll sack ye!"

Having earned respect as a skilled weaver, Jane was unused to someone treating her like a new hire. Each time she started to find a rhythm again, Mr. Lambert appeared behind her, barking some order that made her jump. She began to second-guess everything she did, which put her at risk to make more mistakes. When the women shut the looms down for the day, bringing an echoing silence to the room, Jane's hands continued to tremble. Even the magic passed down to her from her grandmother deserted her as his endless criticisms pummeled her psyche.

It didn't get better the next day, or the next, or the next. At the end of each workday, she returned to the boardinghouse and flopped down on the bed, sleeping without supper as she tried to keep up with Mr. Lambert's demands. Soon the extra pounds she had gained on her adventure disappeared from her frame, and she returned to her lean self.

Even worse, Rabbie's letters dried up, too, though she wrote him back right away. First one week, then another passed with no word. It seemed as though he had vanished. She tried writing to him, but in her growing self-doubt she decided he had tired of her, so she put her letters in her drawer.

Jane's co-workers all grumbled about Mr. Lambert, though they agreed he showed a particular interest in tormenting Jane.

"Mebbe he's got a crush an' disna want tae let it show," Maisie teased.

"Aye, he treats her cruel in hopes she's one o' them women who likes her men tae treat her bad," Wynda added.

"Well, if that's true he must love me a whole lot," Jane said. "He must love all o' us, truth be told. He yelled at Peigi today, so I may have competition. Mebbe he thinks I'll get jealous an' pick a fight wi' her."

They continued in that vein until their giggles left them exhausted. Blowing off steam helped a little. No matter what

Mr. Lambert said or did, she kept coming back with determination to work even harder to win him over.

One day, a few weeks later, a letter finally arrived from Rabbie. It couldn't have come at a better time. Or so she thought. After his usual cheerful greetings and inquiries about life in the mill, he wrote:

You were right not to come to Leeds. It wouldn't have worked out well for you. I still miss you, though.

What did that mean? She wrote back and asked him, but he never answered the question.

More weeks passed. The mill laid off several employees, giving each remaining weaver more looms to tend. Jane tried to keep a cheerful tone in her letters to Rabbie, not wanting to bother him with her troubles. Yet as much as she had longed to come back to her daily life, it didn't quite feel like home anymore. She didn't belong with the Fey, but she didn't belong here, either.

She told herself to stay positive. Difficulties like this happened, and they always passed. Surely this would, too.

One evening, when the whistle blew, Mr. Lambert motioned for Jane to stay. As the looms shut off, the other women headed for the exit, a few casting sympathetic glances toward Jane on their way out.

Then they were alone, the room eerily quiet without the constant clacking of machinery. A bead of sweat trickled down her back as she stared straight ahead, waiting mutely for him to speak.

He took one step closer to her. She curled her body into itself to make it smaller as she retreated from his advance.

"We may have more cuts soon," he said. "There will be competition for the jobs. I need tae see more production from ye."

"Mr. Lambert, wi' respect, we are havin' trouble keepin' up as it is. I canna imagine havin' tae run more looms." Just the thought of this made her weary.

"That's because ye're lazy," he said. "All the mills are goin' this way, an' the other lasses are keepin' up. So far ye have been safe from losin' yer job because Mr. Stein thought highly o' ye, but he's been gone a long time, and I have the say-so noo."

"But I work hard, Mr. Lambert." She fought back tears, unwilling to let him see her pain. A bad reference would ruin her future. "I will work harder, I promise. Ye'll see. Please dinna sack me, sir."

He pulled her close to him, hot breath upon her, tainted by the sour scent of bad whisky. "Ye may want tae think about what you're willin' tae do tae keep yer job." His fingers dug into the flesh of her arm while his free hand ran down her face, the side of her neck, stopping only when it reached her bosom.

She stiffened, imagining every mill lass who had found herself in these circumstances. *No, no, no.* It wouldn't happen to her. Bad reference or no, she wouldn't allow it. Her fists clenched and she waited for the right moment to kick him hard.

Abruptly, he set her free. Confused, she spun around to see why he let her go. There stood Hugh Stein, Rabbie's father, arms folded, glaring at them both.

She didn't hesitate a second before running away from Mr. Lambert toward the doorway. "Good evenin'," she mumbled as she stepped around him, then ran out of the room.

Once outside, she retched. Not much came up, but it took a few minutes for the spasms to cease so she could walk home.

The other women were eating their supper when she arrived numbly back at the boardinghouse.

"Jane, come sit wi' us!" Maisie called.

Jane shook her head and went without a word straight to her room. She lay on the bed, rocking herself, shivering, unable to shake Mr. Lambert's stale, loathsome scent. What would it mean for Rabbie's father to see them together? As a superintendent, he might think Jane offered favors to Mr. Lambert to gain extra privileges. If that were the case, what if word got back to Rabbie? He'd want no more to do with her then.

I gave up being a fairy princess for this? For a fleeting moment she entertained the idea of going back to them. So far her return to human life made her wonder why she ever left. *No, there has tae be another way.* Life with the Fair Folk was just a way of running from her problems.

Determined, she took pen and paper in hand and wrote to Rabbie. Though his silence made her uncertain, she needed to know.

Rabbie, I have given the matter a lot of thought, and maybe it would be good for me to come tae England. I know ye said tae wait, but it's time I left Alva.

She paused, not wanting to tell the whole story, but wanting to let him know the seriousness of the matter.

They have made many cuts here, and Mr. Lambert took me aside to tell me there would be more. They are asking more from us than we should have to give.

She hoped he would read between the lines.

CHAPTER 18

And all day, the iron wheels are droning;
And sometimes we could pray,
'O ye wheels,' (breaking out in a mad moaning)
'Stop ! be silent for to-day ! '

The Cry of the Children
Elizabeth Barrett Browning

*A*fter a rough night of tossing and turning, Jane woke with a deep cough and a head filled with congestion. She didn't dare take a day off, even though she burned with a fever. Putting on her work clothes was a chore as she ached deep into her bones, but she forced herself to prepare for the day.

She dragged herself to the mill, surrounded by the other silent women trudging along, as weary as she. It was as though a collective sense of defeat had settled among them. Scotland acted as weaver to the world, with products in high demand, but the cost to the employees grew, despite soaring profits. The mill owner moved into an even larger house high on the hill, encroaching ever closer to the woods. Jane's fever sharpened her sense of the injustice. She provided a source of profit, and nothing more. If she died tomorrow they would find another factory girl to take her place, with no one knowing the difference.

"Jane, I get tae run one of the looms today!" Leslie was the lone cheerful voice that morning as she tugged on Jane's arm to announce her news. "Maisie's gonnae teach me."

This couldn't be. Leslie was too young for this kind of work, even with only one loom. "Awa' wi' ye," Jane said, extricating her arm. "I need tae work."

"Jane," Leslie said again. This time she grabbed Jane's arm with both hands and jumped up and down in excitement. "I'm old enough! Today!"

As a rule she loved the lass's enthusiasm, but not today. Her body ached, and the prospect of standing for hours over-whelmed her. Yanking her arm back, she snapped, "Well, go on wi' ye!" As soon as the words left her mouth, she regretted them. She started to apologize, but Leslie ran over to Maisie, who glared at Jane and shook her head. Even across the room Jane could see Leslie trembling and trying not to cry.

The day had barely begun, and already she couldn't wait for it to end.

Mr. Lambert started pushing from the moment he walked in the door. "Pay attention!" he yelled to her more than once as she struggled to maintain her concentration. Whatever Mr. Stein might have said to Mr. Lambert the evening before, the super-visor clearly was not going to let up until he found a justifica-tion for sacking her.

Shortly after the noon dinner break, Jane stopped one loom to check the filler thread for breakage. Mr. Lambert, who didn't miss a thing, ran over to her and grabbed her arm.

"Ye ruined it!" he screamed. "That's goin' to cost ye!"

"It's fine," she shouted, more to be heard above the din.

"The pattern willnae be right!" He yanked her away from the loom. She fought him, but he wrapped one arm around her waist and held her throat with the other hand. He tightened its grip, choking her.

No one came to her aid. Everyone kept working like nothing was happening. Time slowed down as she replayed times when she, too, had kept her full focus on a loom while other employees were slapped or punched or screamed at, all in the name of saving her job.

"Let go o' me!" She jabbed an elbow into his ribs.

"Oof!" He staggered back, giving her time to wrestle herself free from his grasp.

She drew a fist back, ready to strike, when other arms wrapped around her, pinning her own.

"Let me go!" she screamed again.

"Jane, love, it's me, Maisie. If ye strike the man, ye'll be sacked. No one else will hire ye."

Mr. Lambert recovered from the blow and reached for Jane again, but Maisie pushed her out of the way.

"Go!" she yelled. "Get outside, and I'll come for ye later."

A high-pitched scream pierced the din of the machines.

Across the room a brutal horror unfolded in slow motion. Leslie's apron caught in the shaft of a loom, which pulled her into it like a wild animal catching its prey. Maisie rushed to turn off the machine, but it was too late. Blood spattered on the nearby looms as the loom mangled Leslie's arm.

The other machines fell silent, too, though their roar still reverberated in Jane's ears. Throughout the room, Leslie's wails echoed off the walls. Mr. Lambert stood there paralyzed.

"Get help!" Jane screamed, her voice hoarse.

Mr. Lambert remained still, his mouth hanging open. She gave him a shove to pull him from his stupor.

"Go noo! Go!"

He snapped to and ran outside, but Jane didn't trust him to

do what needed to be done. A crowd formed around the grue-some sight.

"Fetch the doctor!" she yelled.

"I'll do it!" Maisie ran out the door.

Jane raced over to the child. With the help of a few other women, she managed to extract Leslie from the machine, then tore a piece of her skirt and wrapped it around the top of the arm, or what remained, to try to stop the bleeding. All the while, she murmured to the screaming child. With the machines now stopped, Jane could speak in a soothing whis-per, telling Leslie that help was coming, to hold on a while longer.

"Mammy!" the girl cried, thrashing about like a caught fish.

Jane yelled at Wynda, "Find the child's mother!" Thankfully, she heard Wynda run across the floor, shoes echoing.

Maisie returned with the doctor in tow. He went straight to Leslie to assess the situation.

"Poor wee lass," he said. "She canna be moved right now. We need tae stop the bleeding."

Leslie stopped screaming, and now her body shivered with shock. As the doctor did his work, Jane knelt next to Leslie and laid a hand on the little girl's head.

"Stay calm. Yer ma is comin', I promise." Leslie tried to speak, but Jane shushed her. "Save yer strength, lass. I'll stay wi' ye until she comes."

The response was a slight, weak nod. Her body quivered, and her eyes lost their focus.

The factory girls parted their circle around the child to let Leslie's mother in, and Jane moved aside. A portly woman of about forty, her face white with shock, she pulled her lips into a tight line as she knelt before her daughter. While the doctor dressed Leslie's wounds, her mother removed the bow from the child's hair and stroked the fine, blood-soaked curls. In this room, so unaccustomed to stillness and quiet, there were only the sounds of Leslie's whimpers and the sobs of the factory girls.

"I'm sairie, Mammy," Leslie whispered. Her heart-shaped face paled, and her breathing grew shallow.

"Hush, lass," her mother said. "No one is angry wi' ye." To everyone and no one she added, "She always took on more worry than a child should."

The doctor backed away, leaving Leslie to her mother's loving ministrations. "She'll be gone soon," he said, with a catch in his voice. "Best she be wi' ye in these final moments."

All around Jane were the sounds of sobs and sniffles. Leslie's mother looked up briefly, her gaze lighting on Jane. Jane's guilt lay heavy on the surface on her face. She could never take back her harsh words that upset the child so, and likely distracted her from her work.

Leslie's mother spoke directly to her daughter now. "Rest, and go tae the arms of the Lord. There's no trouble for ye anymore. I send my heart along, daughter, an' I'll be there wi' ye before ye know it." Though she spoke with composure, her body trembled.

The child closed her eyes and neither wept nor cried anymore.

Only when her child died did Leslie's mother let out a deep, guttural wail. The doctor put an arm around her, a tear escaping down his face that he did not try to wipe away.

Jane crept back from the scene. Mill accidents were common, with many young people losing fingers or that kind of thing. Mill work was tough on a body altogether. But never before had Jane seen a death unfold right in front of her. She could not stay there another minute.

As she ran from the room, Mr. Lambert called for a crew of children to clean up the mess, and soon he would yell at the workers for stopping. This was a new level of cruelty.

Once outside, she looked down at the blood on her apron,

her hands, her arms. She went straight to the boardinghouse, where a worried Abi gathered warm water and soap to scrub the blood from Jane's skin, then offered to make some food and a strong drink. Jane refused the food, but she accepted the whisky and drank until she could barely stagger up the stairs.

CHAPTER 19

Farewell to the mountains, high-cover'd with snow,
Farewell to the straths and green vallies below;
Farewell to the forests and wild-hanging woods,
Farewell to the torrents and loud-pouring floods.

My Heart's in the Highlands
Robert Burns

*A*ll of Jane's dreams, which only a day ago defined her
life, now drained away with the blood of a wee lass
taken far too soon. She replayed the events in her mind, and
each time she came up with the same conclusion: she was
responsible for the death of a child. Every time she entered that
room, the sights and sounds reminded her of that fact.

The thought of returning to the mill and reliving Leslie's
gruesome death day after day after day was more than she could
bear. The other option, to live with the Fey, was completely
absurd. She couldn't entertain the thought of living among all
that finery while the people she lived and worked with suffered.
She wasn't worthy to be a factory girl, let alone a princess.

The one solution was what she had fought against her whole adult life. She would return to her aunt and uncle and help them with the children as they wanted, never having to face the mill again.

She would hate it. But it would be her penance.

The morning whistle blew, its fierce sound followed by the rustle of women rising reluctantly for yet another day. Jane rose with them, awake and alert despite drinking so much the day before. The only remaining evidence of too much whisky was a dry, cottony mouth. She dressed quietly and accepted a cup of tea downstairs, one more cup for her final day.

The other women of the boardinghouse surrounded Jane, hugging her. They all knew how much she and Leslie loved each other, and though they were all devastated, they knew Jane took it the hardest. Only Maisie actually spoke about it.

"Ye didnae cause the accident," she said.

"I was sae cross wi' her," Jane said. "And then that business wi' Mr. Lambert..." For he factored into her decision to leave, too. He accomplished what no other boss could: he broke her spirit.

Maisie held her friend tightly. "Jane, poor lass, what happened tae wee Leslie coulda happened tae any o' us. We're all lucky tae make it this far. Look at it this way: Leslie will never have tae work or worry ever again. She's wi' her Lord in Paradise."

"Ye're right," Jane mumbled, but the horrible end to the child's short life was too fresh in her heart. And no matter what Maisie or anyone else said, her mistakes that day weighed heavy as a boulder on her chest.

On the short walk to the mill, Jane's feet tried to stop her many times, but she forced herself to continue. She heard rustling sounds, and once she thought she detected Flora's violet perfume. Yet she saw no one, so she dismissed it as exhaustion playing tricks with her mind.

By the time she arrived at work, Jane resolved to look Mr. Lambert in the eye when she quit and tell him exactly what she thought of him. He wouldn't provide a reference that way, but it didn't matter anymore.

However, Mr. Lambert was nowhere to be found.

Jane set up her looms for the day, repeatedly looking over her shoulder for a sign of him, her palms sweaty and her breath shallow with anticipation, dreading the smell of his sour breath against her neck.

The door opened, and in came Hugh Stein. He motioned for the women to stop their looms, and the room grew silent for the second time in as many days. Jane and her friends cast uneasy glances at one another.

"Ladies, I have an announcement," he said. "I am here tae inform ye that Mr. Lambert has left the mill."

Jane put a hand on her pounding heart.

"What happened yesterday was a tragedy," Mr. Stein said. "We will work together tae make the Alva mill the safest one in Scotland."

There were surprised murmurs among the women. Mill accidents normally were never spoken of. There would be changes, he promised, to keep them safe.

"I was unaware Mr. Lambert had extended the children's hours beyond what the law allows, so we will cut back. We will also review training tae prevent future accidents."

Before Mr. Lambert, the children worked no more than ten hours a day. But no one, not even the children's parents, dared complain about Mr. Lambert's changes, fearing if they said something the whole family would lose their jobs.

"I must caution ye, though," Mr. Stein continued, "we expect all o' ye tae make sure the mill runs smoothly. Ye must focus on work at all times. We hire the best here, so dinna let us down. Now, everyone back tae work." As he looked around the room, his gaze rested on Jane and stayed there, his expression unreadable. Did he blame her for the altercation with Mr. Lambert? Surely not. He would have sacked her for it. But in his eyes she saw her own guilt reflected back. And while Mr. Stein offered at least a crumb of humanity, it wasn't enough. Nothing would change her mind about leaving.

Though she counted down the hours and minutes until she could say goodbye, she wove with the same care of her first day. Jane Thorburn cared too much about the quality of her work.

The walk to and from the boardinghouse for her dinner break felt doubly long, and as she returned to the mill she measured every step. As she stood near the entrance, her legs stopped and her heart began to pound. *One more time*, she told herself. *Go in one more time.* Yet her body fought every inch of forward movement.

"There's my favorite weaver."

The voice, so familiar, seemed from worlds and lifetimes ago. Jane froze, and then slowly turned around.

"Rabbie?" He appeared even more handsome than before, and the eagerness and joy in his eyes brightened her spirit in spite of her sorrow. "My dear friend."

He threw his arms around her. "Wee dove, how careworn you are! I heard about poor Leslie. Ye were her favorite."

All her sorrow lodged in her throat, and she feared losing her composure. Gently pushing him away she said, "I canna talk now, Rabbie. My shift is on, an' I canna be late."

"I'll walk wi' you, and we can talk on the way." He reached for her hand, and she didn't push it away. She was too tired to argue, and too tired to care what others thought.

Her troubles nearly made her forget the obvious question: "When did ye return?"

"A few days ago. I wanted tae tell ye, but I needed tae make sure there I had a place here. Then I thought I'd surprise ye."

At any other time, his words would have made her want to break out in a dance, but not today.

"Ye're replacing Mr. Lambert," she said.

"Aye. Da said a month ago he wished he'd never hired him. If only I'd gotten here one day sooner." His eyes grew misty. "Say, let's have a walk in the glen Saturday after work. I've missed ye, wee dove. We can talk more there."

She opened her mouth to say she wouldn't be here, but the words didn't come out. The thought of meeting him there brought her some comfort, and maybe one more walk with him, to catch up and say goodbye, made it worth staying the rest of the week.

"Aye," she said weakly. Yet the loom where Leslie died remained, even with the blood scrubbed away, leaving an unnatural gleam of the floors and looms. How could she even think about staying a moment longer?

For the rest of that week, each day Jane vowed to quit, and each day Rabbie appeared again, smiling and taking her hand, and at the end of the workday waited to walk her home. They chatted about the weather, about work, about missing each other, but every time Rabbie broached the subject of Leslie she cut him off, and he didn't force her to talk. Instead, he squeezed her hand or rubbed her neck, giving her a look of concern, but let her keep her pain to herself.

The week passed without further incident, but she trembled at every strange noise, every unexpected shout. At night, in her dreams, the accident played itself out over and over and over as she tried desperately to change the outcome. Wynda, who now shared the bed with Jane, tried to soothe her as she flailed about, but she still woke each morning to a pillow moist with tears.

On Saturday afternoon, after the whistle blew for the day, she went straight to the glen to meet Rabbie there. As she climbed to her favorite spot, eager to see him again, she didn't notice the weather or the condition of the path. She didn't hear her own footfalls or the sounds around her. Oh, how she had missed him and these woodland visits!

She took a seat, then closed her eyes and listened to the wind rustling in the trees. Even after a week such as this one, the glen held great power to heal and calm Jane's nerves, and for the first time in days, she began to relax.

The sound of buzzing wings interrupted her thoughts. The fairies were *cluck-cluck-clucking* about her appearance.

"Ye look a sight, wee Jane," Bram said.

The water sprites, Eisla, Levene, and Nairne swirled around her, sprinkling tiny droplets of water from the burn onto Jane's head. They tickled her face as they did so, and a giggle bubbled up from somewhere inside her, some place untouched by sorrow. *How can I laugh at a time like this?* And yet she couldn't help herself.

"Let me be, my pets," Jane said, still laughing. "I canna be seen wi' ye when my friend comes."

"And what a handsome friend he is," said Eisla.

"I think he's nae just a friend anymore," said Levene. "Jane has herself a lover, mebbe even a husband."

"Oh, no, no, no." She laughed so hard her stomach hurt, and she held it, gasping for air.

"Am I that funny tae ye?" Rabbie asked.

She stopped at once, aware that the Fey still swirled around her, now facing him and waiting. Would he think she was mad?

"Naw, I was…thinkin' of a joke," she said, trying to recover.

"And are the Wee Folk yer jokers?"

They moved over to him then, eyeing him curiously. "Aye, I can see ye," he said. "Dinna be lookin' at me that way."

Was he saying what she thought he was saying? "What do ye see?" she asked cautiously.

"The Wee Folk all around ye. They like ye, Jane, and that makes me like ye more."

"Ye see what I see," she said with wonder. Not only did he see them, but he did not judge or shame her for associating with them. In fact, gave off a casual air about it, as if everyone could see them.

The loneliness of all those years rose up: her mother's abandonment, her aunt's frightened glances, all the years of hiding her true nature. When the tears began to flow, they overcame her as the laughter did a few minutes before. Her emotions were flying all over the place like the Fair Folk themselves.

"Jane, wee dove, dinna cry," Rabbie said, looking distressed. To the Fair Folk, he said, "Away wi' ye" and waved an arm to shoo them off. "Jane an' I need some privacy."

They respectfully withdrew, not teasing this time, promising to see Jane again soon.

Once they left, Rabbie put an arm around her, and she rested her head on his shoulder. He held her for a long time, kissing her forehead and murmuring words of comfort until her tears were spent. "Why would ye cry so? Is it wee Leslie?"

She sat up, accepting his handkerchief to wipe her eyes. When she finally looked at him, she saw a face full of love and nearly lost herself again. "I canna bear it wi'oot her there," Jane said. "An' it's my fault."

"Ye're not tae blame, Jane. It was an accident. A horrible, horrible accident. It's nae fair for ye tae take all that on those wee shoulders."

Jane wasn't sure she could believe him, but a great burden washed out with her tears, and she considered the notion that it wasn't her fault. Not entirely, anyway.

Rabbie continued, "Mr. Lambert went too far wi' his cuttin' and skimpin'. Everyone was too tired, and somethin' was bound tae happen. Even the owners figured it out. Da made sure o' that. They like their profits, but news of a pretty wee lass dyin' in such an ugly way is bad for the mill."

Jane let out a chuckle of disbelief. "Yet...yer da saw him wi' me...saw how he treated all o' us. Why did that nae get him sent away?"

Rabbie lifted Jane's chin and studied her face. "Ye didna give in tae him?" The question, rather than a statement, sounded even worse to Jane's ears.

"Is that it? Ye think I'd do such a thing?" She turned away from him and sniffed in scorn. So, his father thought Jane may have encouraged Mr. Lambert? "I didna give myself to him or any other. Ye can tell yer da that."

"Hold on. I believe ye, lass."

A gentle breeze enveloped her in an embrace as she let those words sink in. While her burden did not disappear in that moment, it lightened. Whatever Hugh Stein thought, his son believed she wouldn't do such a thing.

"Ye never said what happened in England," she said. "I wanted tae come when Mr. Lambert started leanin' on me sae hard. Why did ye come back?"

He brushed a hand on her cheek to turn her face toward him in a gentle, uncertain gesture. "I think ye ken the answer tae that, wee dove. When I asked ye tae come wi' me before, that was wrong o' me. I wanted tae ask for yer hand, but I feared you'd say no. Comin' back was the best thing, and that way ye didna have tae give up anything for a man." He studied her, waiting, with an intensity that made her shiver.

"Ye came back for me, even though I canna make any promises?"

"Aye. I swear to ye, I swear on this rock, and tae all the fairy witnesses, I'll not stand in yer way. But let me love ye, Jane Thorburn. Let us know what love is like, for that's a dream we all share. An' if one day ye fly away like the fairies do, I'll remember a wee sprite who loved me in whatever way she could."

Without thinking, she gave him a tender kiss, surprised at her own boldness. His lips were soft and sweet on hers, and as he wrapped his arms around her, a deep longing revealed itself.

When it did, it was more than she could bear, and she pulled away. This was the worst possible time to be in love.

He seemed to understand she needed time to catch her breath. Changing the subject, he asked, "How long have ye seen them? The Fey, I mean."

It took a moment for her heart to stop pounding after the kiss, and she was grateful for his shift in the conversation. "All my life. They carried me off as a newborn. Ma didna want me around much after that. Beitris—she's the old howdiewife who helped birth me—did spells tae bring me back, an' then Ma said I brought bad luck. That's why they sent me away." As soon as the words tumbled out she wished she could take them all back. She had already revealed so much of herself to him.

Letting out a soft whistle, he said, "Bad luck? Someone shoulda told yer ma the Fair Folk take only the best, most precious bairns."

She didn't know what to say to that. No one had ever suggested any such thing. It never occurred to her to think of herself as somehow special, even though the Folk saw her as a princess. Needing time to process this new idea, she turned the conversation back to him.

"And what about you? When did ye start seein' them?"

"For as long as I can remember," Rabbie said. "I'm jealous, though. They never came for me."

She considered telling him about her visit to the palace, of her relationship to Queen Donella. Even with today's revelations, though, she decided against it. Best keep that conversation for another day. Or never.

"Please dinna tell anyone," she said.

"Of course not. If we're mad, we'll be mad together in secret."

They sat in silence for a while, his hand on hers. Then she said, "I want tae leave the mill, Rabbie. Even wi' Mr. Lambert gone, after what happened…"

"I ken ye helped all ye could."

"I'm tae blame." She told him how she snapped at Leslie, and of the scuffle between her and Mr. Lambert. "If I'd kept her wi' me, she might still be workin' today. Her poor ma." Jane started to sob again.

"Shh, shh." He spoke in lullaby tones as he held her in his arms. "Please dinna blame yersel. I'd understand if ye left, an' I'd give you a reference. But I'm selfish, Jane. I came back for ye, and I dinna want you tae go."

"I had it all planned. I thought I would go tae Uncle's house an' help my aunt wi' the bairns like they always wanted me to."

"But?" His eyes were gentle but merry.

"Rabbie Stein, ye messed it all up. I guess I'll try tae stay, for a while at least. My heart's nae in it, though."

"Just try. It's all I ask o' ye. Well, almost all."

"What?" She searched his face for clues.

"Well, since we're together now an' all…"

"Aye? Speak up."

"I want tae take ye for one Sunday dinner wi' my folks. Ye see Da at work, but this way he'll get tae know ye better. An' Ma will love ye, I promise."

Meeting his family? If she said yes, she was committing to staying, at least for a while.

"We can try it, I reckon," she said.

His lips found hers again, and her soul caught fire in spite of her pain and grief. The part of her that wanted to leave remained, but she couldn't deny the comfort of his arms.

They whiled away the afternoon that way, talking and kissing. She loved the softness of his lips, the touch of his hand on her face. Desire swelled deep inside, and she shuddered at the thought of lying with him. It couldn't happen. Her experience with Skye taught her that. But she didn't resist his kisses or embraces, not today.

When she returned to the boardinghouse that evening, she

wore a glow her friends recognized. They gathered around her to hear a story, but Jane preferred to keep the details to herself. All she said was, "I suppose I know what all the fuss is about." And though she still grieved for young Leslie, all thoughts of moving back in with her aunt and uncle left her head.

CHAPTER 20

His brow, like polish'd marble, shines beautiful and fair;
His beaming eyes of azure blue give him a look that's rare;
His cheeks are like the blooming rose that ne'er felt autumn's
blight—
O, who could gaze upon him and not love Johnie White?

Lovely Johnie White
Ellen Johnston

*D*ays passed, one after another, as days do. Little by
little, the nightmares lessened in frequency and
intensity. One night, Jane dreamed of a smiling Leslie handing
her flowers. That morning when Jane woke, her tears came not
from the sadness of Leslie's death, but the feeling of being
forgiven.

At the factory, each finished piece settled her down. Without
Mr. Lambert's daily tongue lashings and threats, Jane began to
remember what she loved about her job. Nothing would ever
fill the emptiness Leslie's death caused, but she learned to weave
her sorrow as but one thread of a larger fabric of her life.

She saw Rabbie twice a week, once after work in mid-week, and on Sundays. In between they wrote to each other, leaving letters in a small box they hid at the entrance of the glen. She saved them all, tucking them away in the same drawer where she kept her savings.

Most Sundays they went to the kirk. Rabbie sat with his parents, while Jane went with Maisie and Wynda. By now Jane had admitted her feelings for him to her friends. They conspired to find seats near Rabbie, where he and Jane stole glances at each other, anticipating their afternoon walk.

They made plans to meet the families. Feeling safer with her own family first, Jane sent a note to her aunt and uncle, and arrangements were made for a Sunday dinner in October. She expected her aunt and uncle to pressure them to marry, but she would manage that somehow.

On the day of their visit, an early morning frost faded, but the air remained crisp. Trees were shedding their brightly colored leaves to fly about in the breeze, filling the air with rich reds, greens, golds, and yellows. Autumn harvests left the fields clean. Elderberries, rose hips, and other hedgerow fruits were picked and turned into jams. Nature let go of the old and dying, to lie in fallow wait for the spring. Jane, though not quite ready to embrace the new, would sweep away that which had died in her and to rest in the knowledge that spring would come again.

Uncle Ewan and Aunt Kirstin received Rabbie with hand-shakes and welcomes. To her relief, they didn't make any jokes about giving up on Jane ever bringing a suitor around.

The house reverberated with the children's energy. Heather chatted away about school and her friends. Ewan, Jr., wanted to impress Jane with his ability to write his name. Andrew crawled all over Jane and Rabbie both, happy to have someone new to lavish attention on him. Rabbie turned himself into a "pony" giving rides to the children, who shrieked with joy and laughter.

When they sat down to eat, their young faces were ruddy from play.

Aunt Kirstin served a roasted hen with boiled potatoes, carrots, and thick pieces of barley bannock. For dessert, she offered Mother Eve's pudding filled with eggs, apples, currants, and breadcrumbs, which she served on special occasions.

Throughout, Rabbie remained completely at ease, bantering with Uncle Ewan about the mill and giving equal attention to the children when they spoke. Jane said little, preferring to watch the goings-on and wishing she shared Rabbie's ability to fit in everywhere he went. Now and then her aunt caught Jane's eye and winked.

"What a wonderful meal!" Rabbie exclaimed once Jane and Kirstin cleared the dishes. "Ye're all Jane said you were, an' more."

"We're happy our Jane has met a nice lad," Kirstin said, smiling. "All her foolish talk about going tae America and whatnot. Now we dinna have tae worry about losin' her."

Couldn't they have left that alone for today? As the blood rushed to her face, Rabbie reached under the table to pat her hand to say *there's no need tae argue. We'll deal with that another time.*

"Jane says ye raised her up," he said. "I know she appreciates all ye did."

Uncle Ewan, who had worn his best protective father look so far, relaxed a little. "Before Jane came, we couldna bear children, an' we feared we widnae ken the joys of family. Jane is good luck for us. I dinna understand these young lasses these days, always wantin' tae run off somewhere away from family."

Rabbie nodded respectfully. "I went away, too," he said. "It's nae good tae go far, an' I'm happy tae be back."

"Where did ye go?" Kirstin asked. She set out tea and the pudding, which caused everyone at the table to groan in an "I'm too full, but that looks so good I must eat it" way.

"England," Rabbie said. "There are many opportunities there, an' they tell me I can come back anytime, but Ma an' Da are in Alva, an' I missed them. Jane, too, of course."

Jane studied her plate in anticipation Uncle Ewan's scorn.

"England." Uncle Ewan put his fork down. "Ye went straight intae the beast, did you?"

"Aye. An' lived tae tell the tale." He proceeded to share stories of incompetent supervisors and lazy workers, all told with bright eyes and an easy, infectious laugh.

Yet as he spun yarns, something in Rabbie's wistful tone caught Jane's attention.

After the final goodbyes, when they made the journey home, Rabbie said, "Ye're awfie quiet, lass. What are ye thinkin'?"

"Naethin'," she said. While that wasn't true, she couldn't quite put words to her unease.

"Jane? What's wrong?"

"Let me think," she said. They continued to walk in silence, Rabbie knowing better than to push. Then, as Alva came into their line of sight, it became clear to her. "Ye want tae go back," she said. It sounded more like an accusation than a statement when the words left her lips.

He didn't say anything, not at first. A hint of color on his cheeks, though, gave her the answer. When he did speak, his words were carefully chosen. "Aye, Jane, ye understand me more than anyone ever has. I do want tae go back one day. I like it there, an' the opportunities are better. But I'll stay here until ye fly away tae America."

Though Jane always planned to leave, hearing that he had made arrangements his future without her stung her in a curious way. She always saw Rabbie as someone who rolled along in life, happy with whatever crossed his path in the moment.

"We gave them false hope," she said. "We let them think we're together for good."

"Lass, we have a different way o' doin' things, that's all. We're headed the same place but going at it on different roads."

"What place is that, exactly?"

"Jane." He pulled her toward him and she collapsed in his arms, filled with both love and frustration. "There's nae point arguin' wi' people when they have expectations. They dinna understand modern ways. Best tae let them have their wee daydreams about what they think our lives should be."

"I'd rather they have the truth," she said. "Aunt Kirstin will be tellin' all her friends tae expect a wedding."

"Let them have their fun," he said. "Besides, we dinna ken what the future holds." He gave her a playful poke in the ribs. "Ye might change yer mind."

She doubted it but thought better of arguing further. As they finished their walk into town, she lapsed into silence, trying to sort out the many, sometimes contradictory feelings he brought out in her. Neither kept their intentions secret from the other. Still, a rush of anger and hurt caused her whole body to tremble, whether or not it was fair.

When they reached the gate to the boardinghouse, she said, "Ye didna want me tae come tae England. Why? Tell me the truth this time."

He took one of her hands in his and brought it to his lips for a kiss. They always parted this way. They kept their passionate kisses for private places, something she usually appreciated about him. Today, though, it felt like a way for him to avoid answering.

There could be only one explanation, at least in her mind. "Ye met someone," she said. "That's why ye told me not tae come."

He shrugged. "I asked ye tae come wi' me, an' you said no."

"I did." She didn't know what else to say. What right did she have to ask him to remain true to her when she offered him no promises? And yet the thought of him with someone else threatened to suck all the air out of her, and she struggled to breathe.

"I'm here, lass. That should say enough." He patted her back, and soon her breath returned to normal. "I came back for ye. That's the truth. I was lonely in Leeds, an' I met a nice lass, but no one could take yer place. I decided I'd rather have what you can give, even if I want more. If I thought ye wid have me, I'd come tae Lowell wi' you when the time comes. I dinna want tae be wi'oot ye."

"What?"

"Ye heard me. I'd go tae Lowell if that's what it took. I dinna ken what else I can say tae convince ye I am in love wi' ye."

For the first time since, Rabbie sounded annoyed with her, even with a declaration of love. Beneath that cheerful disposition was a man with a spine, something she hadn't seen before.

Nothing made sense anymore. One of them needed to compromise, to give up on an ambition, a dream.

"This is why I never wanted tae fall in love, Rabbie Stein. We've made a mess."

"I guess we have," he said. "But it's nice tae ken ye love me, at least."

"What do we do?"

"We love each other until we figure out what's next."

Throwing up her hands, she said, "I suppose that's all we can do."

"So we go my house for Sunday dinner next week?"

She laughed in spite of herself. "Aye."

ANN AND HUGH Stein lived on Main Street. Though they could afford a place higher up the hill, they were frugal. Still, the spacious flat had three bedrooms, a living room, a kitchen with dining room, and plenty of windows to make it cheerful and bright.

Rabbie was their eldest, followed by the twins, David and Hugh Jr., plus Catherine and John. David worked in the mill, so Jane knew him, while young Hugh was an apprentice painter. Catherine was about to start work at the mill, and wee John went to school.

When Jane and Rabbie arrived, the youngest children were chasing each other through the flat, while the twins were having some sort of friendly disagreement. Mr. Stein sat quietly in a corner chair, reading. As Jane walked in, Catherine stopped abruptly and held John close to protect him, while the older boys ended their conversation mid-sentence. Mr. Stein looked up from his book but said nothing. The room took on an eerie stillness, and if Rabbie hadn't wrapped one arm around Jane, she would have bolted right then.

"Ma, we're here!" Rabbie called out. Glancing around at his silent family, he said, "Is there a funeral today?"

"Hi, I'm Catherine." The lass recovered quickly and stepped forward to extend a hand to Jane. She had Rabbie's sea-blue eyes and sturdy frame. "Nice tae meet you. Forgive us. Rabbie's never brought someone tae Sunday dinner afore. We didna think it was true ye were comin'."

With Catherine's reassurance, Jane managed to recover from the awkward atmosphere as the Stein brothers rose as well. Rabbie gave them each a light punch to the shoulder, causing a minor scuffle to break out. Jane took a step back lest she catch a stray fist.

"Lads, dinna scare the lass!" Mr. Stein said, laughing.

Rabbie's mother walked in from the kitchen then, drying her hands on her apron. A head taller than Jane, broad in the shoulder, and more imposing in this smaller space than in the kirk, she gave a curt nod as Rabbie introduced them. The rest of the family fell silent and still yet again. It didn't take an expert to know who headed the household.

"Thank you for havin' me," Jane said shyly. "It's nice tae meet everyone."

Mrs. Stein looked Jane up and down and gave a small "hmmph" of disapproval. "So, our Rabbie says ye dinna live with yer family."

Jane's stomach clenched at Mrs. Stein's hostile tone and immediate leap past small talk. She cast a glance at Rabbie, who stared at his shoes. Apparently he wasn't going to help her out of this.

"No, Mrs. Stein," Jane said in her most polite voice, annoyed with herself for believing Rabbie's promises. "I moved tae Alva for work."

"I widnae dream o' leavin' my parents' home until Mr. Stein married me," Mrs. Stein said with a sigh. "That's no way tae find a proper husband."

Jane and Rabbie cast a glance at each other and tried not to giggle.

"Wi' due respect, I think I'd make a proper husband," he said.

Jane gulped at the thought and dropped her eyes to avoid the curious stares of Rabbie's family.

"Jane is a hard worker," Rabbie added, apparently as eager as Jane to change the subject, "an' the supervisors respect her."

"Except for Mr. Lambert," Mr. Stein said. "As I recall, there was some nasty business between ye." He raised an eyebrow and stared intently at Jane.

Mrs. Stein moved to the table to set out the Sunday dinner— a simple fare of porridge, bread, and tea.

"No roast this week, Ma?" Rabbie asked.

"We save the meat for special occasions," she said with a sniff. "Naethin' special about today."

"Mr. Stein, naethin' happened between Mr. Lambert an' me," Jane said, ignoring Mrs. Stein's comment even though it felt like a slap. "My reputation is unsullied. I live at the boardinghouse, and Mrs. Abi has us keep a curfew. I go tae the kirk every Sunday I can. Ye have seen me there, surely."

"Aye," Mr. Stein said in a grudging tone.

After a few more awkward attempts at conversation, they sat at the dining room table with Rabbie's parents staring into their porridge as though expecting it to tell their fortune. The Stein children glanced at each other and at Jane. At one point, Catherine caught Jane's eye and grinned, and Jane grinned back. At least she had one ally in the family.

"Jane's Uncle Ewan and Aunt Kirstin are fine folk," Rabbie said to break the silence. "They have a lively bunch of children. They tell me Jane was good luck for them, that before she came tae live wi' them they had an empty house."

Mr. Stein smiled politely, but then Mrs. Stein said, "Then why wid they let her come tae Alva tae work? Best the lass stay an' help raise the children. I'm disappointed in ye, Rabbie, bringin' home a lass nae raised proper."

Jane let out an audible gasp. She put her spoon down and rested her hands in her lap, her cheeks burning. How long would she have to endure this humiliation?

This was even too much for Mr. Stein. "Wife, Jane is a guest in our home. We may nae approve of her ways, but many young women work in our mills, and Jane is known tae work hard and have excellent skills. She's assured me naethin' happened wi' Mr. Lambert, an' that's good enough for me. Let's accept her at her word and welcome the lass as best we can."

Mrs. Stein let out a hearty "Hmmph," but didn't argue further with him.

Jane gave Mr. Stein a grateful smile, but he did not return it.

"I want tae be a weaver someday," Catherine said. "Mebbe ye can help me learn."

The young lass's simple comment caused a shift in the room. The image of wee Leslie, who so wanted to weave but never would, made it impossible for Jane to offer any sort of encouragement. Still, Catherine managed to delicately change the subject. At that point, the Stein children began to talk over each other, teasing and arguing. Though the awkwardness didn't lift entirely, the Stein children decided to be themselves, which made the rest of the visit tolerable, at least.

Later, when Rabbie finally removed Jane from the disastrous meeting, she said, "Ye told me they'd love me, that I'd be welcome in their home. How could ye let me think that? I coulda handled them if I knew what tae expect, but they took me by surprise."

"I shoulda known better," Rabbie said, putting an arm around her. "I thought since I love ye, they wid, too."

"Ye never prepare for the worst," Jane said glumly. "It's always sunshine wi' ye, even when that's nae the truth."

They reached the boardinghouse. When Rabbie went to kiss her, she turned away.

"Aw, Jane, dinna be vexed," Rabbie said. "Da backed down, and Ma will, too, you'll see."

"I'm nae sure yer promises mean much," Jane said. "At my uncle's table, ye were treated wi' respect. I work hard, Rabbie, an' I'm a good woman. I willnae be put down anymore. I never needed my family, and I sure dinna need yers."

"It was awfie. What can I say? But we'll get through it."

"Leave me be. I'm goin' tae Abi's." She wrenched herself away from his attempted embrace and ran into the boardinghouse. Inside, she threw herself on her bed, letting the tears come. "Silly girl," she muttered. "Silly, stupid factory girl."

Deep down she knew she was overreacting. Lots of couples had problems with parents, and that wasn't Rabbie's fault. But once again, she was an outsider in a happy family, and she didn't know if she could bear opening that wound again.

CHAPTER 21

But who, alas! will cheer my drooping heart?
Ah! Who to me hope's banner will unfurl?
No other smile can e'er a charm impart
To the lone bosom of 'The Factory Girl.'

Lines to a Lovely Youth,
A Boatbuilder Leaving the Town
Ellen Johnston

When she went to work the next day, Jane found a tiny bouquet of winter jasmine next to her loom. She couldn't help but feel flattered at his attentions, though she reminded herself that Rabbie Stein was a charmer, nothing more. Best to ignore him until he gave up. If she ever were to let a man into her life, he would have to be one she could count on. Flowers and flowery words meant nothing to Jane Thorburn. Well, maybe they meant a little. No man gave her flowers before.

As it turned out, he didn't plan to give up at all. At the dinner break he brought her some extra cheese. "Blue cheese, which I know ye like."

"Mr. Stein," she protested, "dinna make yersel a fool."

"Jane Thorburn, I'm no done wi' ye yet." He gave her a loopy grin, then skipped out of the room, leaving her with the urge to laugh at his absurd antics.

She nibbled on the cheese, its texture like butter in her mouth, its flavor less sharp and salty than what she was used to.

When the whistle blew, he appeared by her side to walk her home.

"Mr. Stein, give up."

"Ye're the lass I want," he said. "Jane, I wid mairie ye if ye'd have me. Ma and Da will come around soon enough."

She glared at him. How could he say such a thing? "Ye believe it, I ken, but that's nae enough tae make it true."

"The dinner was worse than I expected," he said. "I'll grant ye that. But Da softened a little while we were there. And Ma's tough, but she has a good heart. She raised me, right?"

She had to admit, he had a point. "Aye, that's true."

"So we give them time tae get used tae us bein' together. And I have an idea that I think will help."

"An' what in the name of God wid that be?" she asked. "Mr. Stein, I think ye may be mad."

"If I am mad, it's for the love o' ye," he said. "Hear me out, if ye ever were my friend. If ye dinna like what I propose, just say so."

"I suppose that's fair." They stood at the doorway of the boardinghouse now. Out of the corner of her eye the other factory girls gathered nearby, casting sly glances, pretending they weren't watching and listening. Crossing her arms, she said, "Fine, I'll listen, but dinna expect me tae change my mind."

Rabbie took both of her hands in his.

"We do a handfast," he said. "We go tae the glen, you and I, and we will make our pledge in front of the Lord an' the fairies.

We stay together for a year and a day. Ma and Da will see we're committed, and you give me a chance tae prove our love is worth the effort. I'll learn tae stand up for ye. If I fail, we go our own ways. If not, we get mairiet."

A handfast? Many couples in rural Scotland still held this ancient ceremony. Like a wedding, it bound them, but only for a year. Certainly it was something to think about, given its temporary nature.

"Still. We canna agree on a simple thing like how tae deal wi' yer parents," Jane said. "How on earth wid we be ready for such a big step?" Not to mention, she never intended for this level of commitment with anyone. Yet Rabbie knew how to dissolve her objections like dew warmed by a bright sun.

"I think the fairies have a hand in this," she said. "It's the kind o' idea they wid come up wi'. But what about yer family? They'd want us tae mairie in the kirk. They'd see it as one more way I led their son astray."

"Look around. Plenty o' country folk still follow the old ways, kirk or no kirk," he said. "They just need time, an' they'll love ye as much as I do."

"Ye said they'd love me right off."

"Aye." He sighed. "I should o' warned ye about Ma. But they'll work it out, Jane, I swear."

Jane threw her hands up in a gesture of helplessness. "I canna think about this today. Leave me be, Rabbie Stein."

"At least ye called me Rabbie again," he said with a grin. "I like it when ye call me that. I'll be back, Jane! We will be happy together, I promise."

He left and Jane walked inside, ignoring the tittering and giggles around her.

Abi had heard the whole thing.

"He's a good catch," she said. "Any lass in this house who wid want that man as her husband. Dinna make him wait too long."

"I like him right enough," Jane said with a sigh. She wasn't ready to confess her love for him to Abi yet. Those feelings were too private, too personal. "I dinna ken what I want."

"No man is perfect, Jane. And dinna say no tae love because ye're scared. Ye need to think about that," Abi said kindly.

"Aye." With his persistence and promise that she wouldn't have to give up on her dreams, was she being too hard on the poor man?

Jane accepted a cup of tea from Abi and went up to her room to think. No matter what he said, she couldn't quite believe he'd go to Lowell with her. He never lied, exactly, but he said what he thought would make her happy, believing his words in the moment and forgetting them later. And yet, without him, the idea of Lowell no longer brought her the same amount of excitement it once did. She tossed and turned that night, wishing to have never gotten involved with him.

All that week, Rabbie continued his campaign. Every morning, there were new flowers on the loom. One day he even brought her a piece of roast.

"Snuck it away from Ma," he said with a wink.

"I thought she only served it for special occasions," Jane said.

"True, she disna make it much, but it was Da's birthday."

She took a bite of it, savoring its moist flavor. It soothed the hunger pangs that built up late in the week, when food offerings grew lighter until Abi collected more rent.

After work, he waited for her to come out from the mill, then pleaded his case again. Every day she called him a fool, but his persistence was wearing her down. He was fighting for her, and no one had ever done that before.

At the end of the week, on Saturday, she headed to Skye's flat. She needed the advice of a trusted friend.

At the sight of Jane, Skye let out a whoop. "About time ye came tae visit!"

She was as radiant as ever, heavy with the late stages of pregnancy. She and Nathan lived in a single end that she kept neat and tidy in spite of its small size. The sweet smell of cakes and pastries filled the room.

"My new business," she said with a wave of her hand. "Brings in some extra money for us, an' I can still keep the house proper. Here, let me clear a space for us, an' I'll make some tea."

Jane sat at the table, awed at Skye's industry. Skye had always generated more energy than most anyone, staying out late to drink and dance, yet working hard during the day with no ill effect. It made sense she wouldn't approach domestic life any differently.

The two women sat together with their tea.

"Tell me everything, Jane. How is the mill? And Rabbie?"

Jane started with the Leslie incident, complete with a scathing indictment of Mr. Lambert and, truth be told, herself.

"She was such a sweet lass," Skye said, tears coming to her eyes, "but ye canna take the blame."

"Aye, but ye shoulda seen her, Skye. Oh, that poor mother!" It hurt to relive those moments, but as Jane spoke she treasured her friend's loving comfort. "I nearly left."

Reaching for Jane's hand, Skye asked, "What made ye stay?" The look in her eyes suggested that other factory girls may have filled her in.

"That's why I'm here, I suppose. I mean, I want tae see ye, but wi' all we went through together, I believe I can confide in you." She went on to tell Skye about Rabbie, his parents, and the handfast.

"Why, that's wonderful news! Here, let's have a bit o' cake tae celebrate!" Skye dished out slices onto plates. Then she gave Jane a knowing look. "Let me guess, ye worry about losin' yer precious independence."

"Aye," Jane said. Why couldn't her friends understand? All they cared about was marriage. Skye understood more than anyone how difficult it was to be a strong woman in this world.

"Well, then, here's how I see it." With a mischievous grin and a gleam in her eye, Skye said, "Ye came tae me because I will tell the truth. He's a good man and you love him. It's that simple. As ye can see here, I am runnin' a business, so I'm nae just a wife an' future mother. Nae that I wid be wrong if I was 'just' that." She placed both hands on her lower back and winced. "This bairn is comin' any minute."

Jane's eyes grew wide. "Do we need the howdiewife?"

"Naw, nae yet," Skye said. "Soon, though. Anyway, we were talkin' about you. Rabbie loves that ye make yer own path. He'll be there for you."

"Do ye really think so?" Jane asked. "He has a way of changin' his tune dependin' on who he spoke wi' last."

"Of course I do. Give him time tae learn tae stand up tae his ma. Stay strong like ye always do." Skye reached over to squeeze Jane's hand. In a softer voice, she said, "Ye were a friend when I needed one the most. I'll never forget it. Ye took charge that night an' took care o' me. Ye're the fiercest friend I have, an' you'll be that woman no matter what course you take."

Skye was right. The two women embraced, Jane grateful their friendship. She thought back to when Nathan initially turned his back on Skye, and yet he became a model husband. If he could grow into that role, surely Rabbie could, too. Somehow, Skye managed to balance both love and work, and her serenity gave Jane hope.

On Sunday, she met Rabbie at the glen. She didn't bother to say hello or ask how he was. Instead she said quite simply, "Ye have made yer case. I'll have ye, Rabbie Stein, and we'll declare our love in the glen at our rock, among the Fair Folk. Apparently ye willnae be quiet 'til this is done."

Rabbie dropped to one knee and looked up at her with the smile that always made her melt. "Ye willnae be sorry, Jane," he said. "I will pledge my love. Today, if ye'll have me."

"Dinna be silly," she said. "We need tae prepare the ceremony and figure out who tae invite. We'll need tae plan a party, too."

"Then when, Jane? Let's do it as soon as we can."

"Next month," she said. "That will give us time to tae sort things."

He rose then and kissed her, a gentle, sweet kiss on the lips, and she let all doubts fall away. She loved him, and nothing could change that fact.

This time, when she went into the boardinghouse, all the women and Abi gathered around to hug her.

"Ye did the right thing," Abi said. "He will bring ye great joy and laughter, and you'll find naethin' better than that. If he loves ye half as much as my husband loved me, ye will know no greater happiness on this earth."

CHAPTER 22

And I will luve thee still, my dear,
Till a` the seas gang dry.
Till a` the seas gang dry, my dear,
And the rocks melt wi` the sun;
And I will luve thee still my dear,
While the sands o` life shall run.

My Luve
Robert Burns

The handfasting ceremony required many preparations. First, the couple needed to find an officiant to perform the ceremony. Jane sent word to Beitris, who accepted with great joy.

Maisie and Wynda conspired to arrange the details of the event in the weeks that followed. Skye went into labor shortly after Jane's visit, but insisted she would still plan the food with help from the other women. Jane and Rabbie wanted a quiet ceremony with a small group of people, but a party afterwards. Skye promised some cakes. Maisie and Wynda chose the ceremonial broom and decorated it with ribbons. They made invitations and delivered them to friends, mostly workers from the mill.

"Jane, what about yer folks?" Maisie asked. "There's no one from yer side on the list."

Jane didn't want to tell them about her parents. Rabbie knew the story, but she avoided sharing it with her friends. And Uncle Ewan and Aunt Kirstin would never approve of a handfasting.

"Let's keep the guest list small," she said.

Rabbie tried to skirt difficulties, as usual. "We'll tell Ma and Da afterward," he said.

Jane let out an exasperated sigh. "Ye always say that, but if they're ever tae approve o' me, it will be because we didna deceive them."

"You want me tae tell my folks but you willnae tell yers?" Rabbie asked.

"My situation is different," Jane said. "Uncle Ewan willnae approve and he'll blame me. But if we dinna tell yer folks, they'll blame me, too, and I'll never get on their good side." She spat out the last words with bitterness. Since Rabbie declared his intentions, she tried hard to win his parents over, but so far she did nothing right. "Remember when I brought fresh vegetables tae Sunday dinner?"

"Aye. Everything was too ripe or nae ripe enough."

"And then," Jane continued, "I offered tae help wi' Catherine and John, and she decided I thought she was a bad mother."

"I guess ye're right. Ma does get carried away sometimes," he said reluctantly. "They'll come around, though. I keep sayin' that, but it's true."

Jane raised one eyebrow. She wished she shared his optimism. Sometimes at night, when she thought about his mother, she wondered what she was getting into. Deep down, did she want his parents to talk Rabbie out of it? Mr. and Mrs. Stein had the power to break them up if they wanted. *Naw,* she told herself, *I want the truth out in the open. If I ever have a chance for them tae like me, we have tae do it that way, even if it means trouble.*

"I hope ye're right," was all she said.

They waited until the next Sunday dinner to tell them. Jane slept little the night before, and when they arrived she fought fatigue as well as nerves.

Rabbie promised his parents a big announcement at Sunday dinner. Mrs. Stein served roast today—a grudging acknowledgement that Jane wasn't going anywhere. No doubt Mr. Stein insisted on it. Of the two of them, Mr. Stein, though gruff, displayed a softer heart. The conversations on this day, even among the children, were more subdued than normal. Everyone seemed on edge.

When everyone finished eating, Rabbie said, "I have somethin' tae say."

Mrs. Stein began clearing the table and picked up a gravy boat. As she held it in midair, her face froze save for one side of her jaw, which pulsed.

"What is it?" Mr. Stein barked the words, causing Jane to jump.

Rabbie, oblivious as always, took Jane's hand. "Jane has agreed tae a handfast," he said. "We will have the ceremony next Sunday, and we'd like ye tae be there."

The other Stein children burst into cheers. Catherine went over to Jane to give her a hug, which Jane accepted with relief.

"Finally, a sister," she said.

The enthusiasm died down quickly, though, as Mrs. Stein put the gravy boat down in a slow, deliberate way. This scared Jane more than anything. Ann Stein was a formidable woman, and Jane preferred her biting criticisms now to the way now drew inside herself, quiet and fierce.

"That's not goin' tae happen," she said. "I'll not have this lass turnin' yer head from the proper upbringing we gave ye."

"Now, let's talk about this," Mr. Stein said. "Sit down, wife of mine."

"I have dishes tae clear," she said.

"Please," he said, his voice soft but firm.

With a huff, she sat, silent and glaring, and Mr. Stein patted her arm in approval. Then he turned to the young couple. "If the two of you plan tae stay together, why nae wed?" he asked. "Handfasting is for country people, not modern factory folk like we are." Mr. Stein was justifiably proud of his achievements at the mill, working his way up the ladder to superintendent, and disliked anything that reminded him of his humble roots.

"Dinna give them ideas," Ann grumbled.

Jane opened her mouth to explain her desire for independence, to make sure Rabbie kept his promises, to carve out her own life—then thought better of it. Mr. and Mrs. Stein wouldn't understand, any more than Uncle Ewan and Aunt Kirstin.

Rabbie, however, started to speak. "We will wed one day, I'm sure," he said. "This is a ceremony tae show our love for one another and our commitment."

"So this is more of a betrothal," Mr. Stein said, scratching his chin.

Jane realized then that Rabbie's willingness to bend the truth to keep everyone happy was an open secret. Mr. Stein had learned to look the other way long ago. So, that was the magic key to the Stein family! Now that she knew the rules of the game, she could play them.

"Aye," Rabbie said.

Mrs. Stein remained silent, but allowed her husband to lead this conversation.

"Well, then, I can give my blessin'," Mr. Stein said, though he looked doubtful. "Nae that we have any choice in the matter.

When we were young, we respected our elders, but I suppose this is the new way."

Later, as Rabbie walked her home, he took Jane's hand and squeezed it. "It's progress, Jane."

Jane wasn't too sure about that, but she did agree that his parents put up less of a fight than she expected. While they still hadn't warmed to the idea of Jane as a daughter-in-law, they seemed to accept that she wasn't going anywhere. They did, however, decline to attend the ceremony. "Have a proper wedding in the kirk," they said, "and we'll come tae that."

Rabbie shrugged it off, as always. For Jane, though, it heralded other difficulties yet to come.

Unbeknownst to Jane, Maisie and Wynda sent invitations to Uncle Ewan and Aunt Kirstin. They came up with the idea together, though Wynda hesitated.

"Are we doin' the right thing?" she asked. "I dinna want her upset on their special day."

"Of course she wants her family there," Maisie said. "Jane's scared they willnae come."

"Jane is sae private about her family." Wynda coughed, a deep cough from her chest.

"Are ye all right?" Maisie asked. "Ye've been coughin' for a while noo." She put a hand on Wynda's forehead. "Warm, too."

"It's just a cold," Wynda said. "That mill is sae damp this time o' year, an' all the dust disna help. But I'm fine. Back tae Jane's family, though. Jane said no, an' that's enough for me."

"Let's invite them," Maisie insisted. "If they dinna want tae come, we'll nae tell Jane."

The reply came promptly. Ewan and Kirstin said they were thrilled and sent their best wishes, though they declined to attend.

"I told ye," Wynda said. "They disapprove."

"Mebbe they had somethin' else tae do." Maisie wasn't giving up yet. "We could have a party on another day."

Wynda let out an annoyed sigh. "I agreed tae send the invitation. They said no. If they want tae do somethin', they'll do it. Leave them be."

Maisie crumpled the letter and tossed it aside. "Fine, you win. I just wish someone in that family wid stand by our Jane."

"We'll have a good group. Nae big, but Jane will prefer it that way. We dinna want tae scare her away from her own party."

Jane, meanwhile, examined her clothes. She would wear her Sunday dress, though deep down she wished she could afford to have something special for the occasion. From time to time, she saw the daughters of mill owners parading around in their wedding finery, and she envied them. She remembered her time with the fairies, always dressed to perfection; her own clothes looked so shabby by comparison. Once upon a time she created thread from moonbeams. But in this world of humans, the church dress would have to do.

That world, with all its wonders, faded like a dream. Having surrendered to her relationship with Rabbie, trying to ingratiate herself to Mrs. Stein, and prepare for the handfast, she hadn't noticed the silence from her Fair friends. Nor had she considered inviting them to the handfast. Human life had taken over, which was not, in her opinion, a bad thing.

The day before the ceremony, after the mill lasses returned from work, Abi answered a knock at the door.

"Hello?" she asked.

A woman stood before her, tall in stature, with long, dark auburn hair streaked with gray and deep-set eyes like the dark interior of pansies. She carried a bag with her.

"I'm here tae see Miss Thorburn," she said. "I believe the lass lives here."

"Aye. Come in." Though this woman stood taller and

broader, she had Jane's high cheekbones, and her eyes were the same shape as Jane's. Even a casual observer would notice the resemblance. Abi bit her lip and checked the impulse to lecture Elizabeth; Jane's silence about her parents told Abi all she needed to know. "I'll fetch her right away."

She went upstairs, where Jane, Maisie, and Wynda were on Jane's bed finalizing plans. "Ye have a visitor, Jane," she said. "An important one, I'd reckon."

Jane raised her eyebrows. "Who is it?" she asked.

"Come see," Abi said. "I invited her in and made tea."

After exchanging a few puzzled glances with her friends, Jane got up off the bed.

"Shall we go, too?" Maisie asked.

"Naw, I'll be right back." Jane followed Abi silently down the stairs.

When she reached the dining room, she saw her, this woman who had greeted her with coldness and distance not so long ago. "Ma," she said softly.

"Come let me look at ye," her mother said.

Elizabeth had been standoffish at their last meeting, so Jane wasn't ready to hug her. Yet Elizabeth had sought her out.

"What brings ye here? Is Da awricht?"

"I come because ye're gettin' mairiet," Elizabeth said. "I thought ye might need a proper dress." She pulled an off-white gown from the bag.

Jane gasped at the sight: a real wedding dress. She touched the fabric with reverence. "Is this yers, Ma?" she asked. She didn't try to explain the difference between handfasting and a kirk wedding.

"From my weddin' day." Elizabeth met Jane's eyes with hers. "I dinna have much from the past tae hold onto, but I kept this in hopes one o' my daughters wid wear it. It's bigger than ye need, but I thought mebbe ye could cut it down tae fit."

"But who told ye?" Jane asked.

"Beitris. She's sae excited tae do the ceremony." Elizabeth cast her eyes downward. "I shoulda come sooner. I'm sairie." She turned to leave.

"Ma, dinna go. I'd be happy tae wear it." Already she was scrutinizing the dress, which required extensive alterations. Perhaps the Fey would help her.

"Really?" Turning back toward Jane, hope glimmered in Elizabeth's eyes.

Once again Jane recalled dreaming of a moment like this, of reconciling with this woman who had rejected her. She imagined a tearful reunion with old resentments evaporating in a happy cloud of joy. In reality, though, she remained guarded, uncertain.

"Why the change, Ma? Ye thought I was bad luck my whole life. I thought ye widnae want tae sully the dress."

Abi brought a tray of tea and toast for the two women. Seeing the intensity of the moment, she put the tray down quietly and slipped up the stairs.

Elizabeth carefully put the dress back in the bag. "I was wrong. All those years. Beitris says a lot of new mothers go mad after their babes are born, an' it takes a while tae feel better. She said I had a worse case than most, an' it wisna fair to blame ye for somethin' goin' on in my own head." She dropped her chin to her chest and added, "Thank God yer da didnae send me away. In those days, the thought of that scared me the most."

Jane nibbled on her toast. She wasn't hungry, but it gave her a moment to think before speaking. "It's been a long time, Ma. A long time o' not havin' parents." There was so much to say. Too much. No mother to go to when she first started working in the mill and came home too exhausted to move. When she chose to set out on her own, to leave her uncle's home, she made that decision herself, without wise counsel. And when she fell hard for Rabbie Stein, no mother celebrated with her and helped plan their ceremony.

Unable to pack all those words into a few sentences, she said, "But I'm an independent woman. I came out all right."

"I see ye did," Elizabeth said. She put a hand on her heart and let out a heavy sigh. "I give thanks to yer aunt and uncle for takin' care o' you. It shoulda been me."

Indeed. It should have. "How is Da?" Jane asked, changing the subject.

"He's well," Elizabeth said. "He goes tae his temperance meetin's and tae kirk wi' us every week. His workin' days are almost over, though. He's stronger than a lot o' the younger men, but he gets mighty stiff nowadays. A lot o' the miners dinna last as long as he has, an' he's still at it." Clearing her throat, she added, "He never stopped missin' ye, lass. He hasna stopped talkin' about yer visit. I think he'd like tae see ye more. And I wid, too."

Jane sipped her tea. It didn't sound at all like the family she had left behind. She'd avoided seeing her father again, even though promising to do so. He was too much of a stranger to her. Still, her mother brought a beautiful dress, a stunning and thoughtful peace offering.

"Can ye forgive us, Jane? Can we make our peace noo, while we're still able?"

Jane set her teacup down and stared out the window, deep in thought. It wasn't enough. It would never be enough. But despite all that had passed between them, they were her parents. No matter what she told herself and others, she hoped they could be in her life in some way.

"Of course, Ma, of course I forgive ye," Jane said softly, and then the two women were holding each other. The pain of years of abandonment would always be there, never to heal completely, but Jane could make peace with it now.

Elizabeth rose from the bench and ran a hand down Jane's cheek. "Ye're a lovely young woman. I canna take credit for how ye turned out, but I am proud, and I am happy ye found a nice young man."

"Will ye stay for supper, then?" Jane asked. After years of hearing nothing from her mother, let alone praise, it was easier to talk about mundane things.

"I must head back. Yer da will worry if I dinna come home."

"Does he know ye're here?"

Elizabeth's eyes were shiny as she looked away. "I decided all of a sudden tae come. I'll tell him tonight. He'll be happy I came. We'll see ye again, Jane, both o' us. And yer brothers and sisters, too."

The two women embraced once more, and Elizabeth left. Jane realized she hadn't asked her parents to come to the ceremony and considered running after her mother. But she hesitated, not quite ready for that.

Her long-held burden lighter now, she put the dress on the bed and studied it, then went right to work on the alterations.

CHAPTER 23

May the best ye've ever seen
Be the worst ye'll ever see,
May a moose ne'er leave yer girnal
Wi' a tear drap in his 'ee,
May ye aye keep hale an' he'erty
Till ye're auld enough tae dee,
May ye aye be juist as happy
As I wish ye aye tae be.

Scottish Toast

The night before the ceremony, Jane, Maisie, and Wynda struggled to finish the dress in time. It seemed an impossible task, given the size difference between the two women. As they cut the dress down, strips of fabric filled the floor.

"We'll have enough fabric tae make a second dress if this one disna work out," Maisie said with a laugh.

At the sound of muffled chatting and laughing, Jane looked around. Her friends were busy with the dress, unaware of the presence of the Fey. Never before had she sensed them inside the boardinghouse while she was awake.

They hovered in the background, whispering things like, "Tuck in more at the waist," or, "The hem's uneven." They offered to transform the dress themselves, but Jane, in the presence of her friends, gave them only a curt shake of the head.

"Is everything all right, Jane?" Wynda noticed the movement.

"Aye, I was… Well, we should look at this hem again."

Her friends gave Jane an odd look, but Jane stayed focused on the dress and the instructions that were coming with some frequency now. The Fey were having lively discussions about the style. Their ideas admittedly were wonderful and would make the dress her own. She shared the suggestions with Maisie and Wynda, who pronounced them inspired, and soon they created a silk brocade gown with a full skirt and a bodice that narrowed into a "V" at the waist. The neck was round and graceful, with the short sleeves beginning at the edge of Jane's shoulders. Wynda added some lace with a rosette at the neckline.

As night gave way to a gray, quiet dawn, they finished.

"It's beautiful, Jane," Flora said. "We'll be back for the ceremony."

Jane smiled in response so her friends would think she was admiring the dress. "No sleep for any of us," Jane said.

"An' nae sleep for Jane tonight, either." Maisie jabbed her in the ribs with an elbow and grinned. Jane gave Maisie a playful shove in return.

"We have a few hours." Wynda stood, stretching and yawning. Then she coughed briefly into her handkerchief. "We'll eat some breakfast and then sleep the rest of the mornin'."

"Are ye awricht?" Jane asked, noticing the cough.

"Aye," Wynda said. "The air in the mill always bothers me, ye ken. Comin' up wi' us?"

"You go ahead." Jane wanted to spend a few quiet moments

alone before the other factory girls came downstairs. She gave her friends a hug and watched as they headed up to their beds.

With the dress completed, Jane's nerves left her. She stroked the dress, now made only for her, imagining Rabbie's surprised face when she wore it for him. Smiling, she curled up on the sofa with her dress still in hand and closed her eyes. She slept through the din of the factory girls as they chatted at the dining table and didn't wake until Maisie and Wynda returned for her.

Maisie put a hand on Jane's shoulder and whispered, "Time tae prepare."

Jane opened her eyes, blinking. "I canna believe I fell asleep," she said.

Abi brought a cup of tea and a bowl of porridge to Jane, who tried to wave it away.

"Nonsense, lass, ye need yer strength."

Though not hungry, Jane took a bite of porridge, and only then did she realize how hungry she was. Her friends waited for her to finish, and then preparations began in earnest. She washed herself thoroughly, studying her thin body. Tonight she would lie with Rabbie, and today she wished she had a few more curves, as when she lived with the Fey.

After sitting by the fire to dry her hair, she let Maisie and Wynda help her into her dress.

"It looks even prettier than it did last night," Maisie remarked, raising one eyebrow.

"We were awfie tired by then," Wynda said. "My eyes were too blurry tae see it."

Jane smoothed the fabric with her hands. It did, indeed, look a bit brighter, almost glittering. Apparently, her Fey friends worked some extra magic while Jane dozed. They hadn't made any obvious changes, little touches too subtle for Maisie and Wynda to detect. When she put it on, it fit perfectly.

They began to style her hair, piling it on top of her head and leaving a few stray ringlets to dangle at her neck. Abi brought out a full-length mirror so Jane could admire the transformation. Then Wynda said, "Surprise!" and brought out a hair wreath made of dried violets and baby's breath.

Jane gasped. "I never expected flowers this time o' year."

"I collected them in bloom," Maisie said. "They were sae pretty this year, I had tae dry them and keep them."

"Well, I'm glad ye did." Jane let them put the wreath on her. "Oh my," she said as she saw herself in the mirror.

"Ye look sae lovely, Jane," Wynda said. "Rabbie willnae ken what tae do."

Jane didn't tell her friends that she didn't know what to do, either, about her first night with Rabbie. She watched her Aunt Kirstin give birth but was unsure about the act of lovemaking itself. Her friends teased her, which didn't quell her nerves. She didn't have the courage to ask Skye. When she and Rabbie kissed, her body responded with heat and moisture between her legs, but the mechanics were unclear to her. She also wanted to make sure she did not get pregnant. For that and her other questions, she would rely on Beitris.

She felt like the Fey had entered her stomach.

Now fully dressed and ready to go, she and her friends began the trek to her special rock. Bram and his crew had done their magic. A bright sun lit the area, like an early spring day. There was no snow to slog through, and the ground was soft but firm as they made their way up the hill.

Of course, there were more visitors on this day than those visible to the humans. Coira, Flora, and all of the woodland Folk were there, waiting to greet Jane on the path. Coira and Flora were dressed in matching silver gowns that sparkled in the sun. The male Folk, who lived far less formal lives, were nonetheless dressed in freshly pressed red overalls and had carefully slicked their hair back, eschewing hats for this day. Their beards were neatly trimmed. The water sprites wore matching pink dresses with flouncy skirts. They stood in a line on either side of the path, giving her bows and curtseys as she walked by. Jane acknowledged their presence with a nod imperceptible to the humans, hoping they'd be on their best behavior today.

Jane, Maisie, and Wynda took their places at a spot on the path just below the view of the rock. Skye stood right behind them, with Nathan and the new baby in tow. In all of Jane's preparations, she hadn't taken the time to visit Skye since the birth of her son. Skye, unaware and unconcerned about Jane's guilt, gave the bairn to Nathan, who headed up the path to the rock ahead of the women. *After the handfast I'll visit*, Jane told herself.

The women's procession moved up the path, with Skye first, then Maisie, then Wynda. Jane followed behind, waiting to make her entrance. Unaccustomed to having the full attention of a crowd of people, for one more second she considered turning and running back down the hill. But Rabbie and her future were waiting. With her head held high, she made the final steps to reveal herself in all her finery. Even as a fairy princess she never felt so beautiful.

Rabbie waited expectantly on one side of the rock facing the path, dressed in his Sunday suit, which flattered his broad shoulders. Beside him were a few of his friends from the mill. Beitris waited uphill from the men. She had gained even more lines in her wizened face and developed a more pronounced stoop, leaning slightly on a walking stick.

At the sight of Jane, Rabbie let out a long whistle. "Wee dove," he said, and then his voice trailed off. He drew one hand to his breast and gave her a low bow.

She gave him the assured smile of a woman who knows she is beautiful and loved. All the nerves and doubts faded into the background as she stood next to her beloved.

"Welcome, everyone," Beitris began. "We are here to join Mr. Robert Stein and Miss Jane Thorburn in the ritual of handfasting. Today, these two young people will commit tae love one another.

"We join today at this rock, where Mr. Stein and Miss Thorburn first spoke tae one another and became close friends. Recently, their feelings deepened into love."

Jane and Rabbie faced each other. He always looked handsome to her, but particularly so today in his black suit, his whiskers trimmed neatly. Her heart pounded with joy and excitement as he gazed at her.

"Ye're beautiful," he whispered. "Always, but especially today."

"Who will support this young couple in their joining together?" Beitris asked.

"We will," Maisie and Wynda answered together.

"And we," said two other, more breathless voices. Jane turned to see Mr. and Mrs. Stein hurrying up the path toward the assemblage.

"Ye came," Rabbie said, his face exploding into a grin.

"It's the right thing tae do," Mr. Stein said, though Mrs. Stein's face didn't convince Jane of any sort of approval. No doubt this was his decision. Still, it showed some level of acceptance Jane hadn't expected, and reached out to hug them. Ann did not hug her back, and her body remained stiff, but Jane didn't care. She appreciated every step of progress.

"She's trouble," Coira whispered. Jane, who hadn't noticed Coira sneaking up on her, tried not to jump.

"Hush," Flora said. "This is Jane's big day."

Jane felt her happy expression freeze, and she wished she could swat them both away. Rabbie raised an eyebrow and caught Jane's eye, and they did their best not to giggle. Coira's opinion of his mother didn't bother him one bit.

"We now turn this space into sacred ground," Beitris said, "in order to bind the love of this young couple...tae tie the knot. As

I make a circle, I ask each of ye tae send prayers for love, joy, happiness, and all good things."

She circled the couple, moving her lips in quiet invocation.

Next, she consecrated the rings—two plain, narrow gold bands.

"These rings are infinite, having neither beginning nor end. Love is like that, too. These two have chosen tae love one another. This love canna be forced or demanded, but is given freely. When two people give each other this gift, the Lord smiles upon us."

Out of the corner of her eye, Jane caught Mrs. Stein wiping away a tear. Perhaps the Steins had finally accepted her into the family. That, or she mourned her son's choice. Flora and Coira were debating each other on the matter, but Jane chose to believe the former.

Beitris held a candle aloft for all to see, then lowered it and set it alight. "This is a candle of unity, symbolizing the joining of two hearts into one light together, tae chase away all darkness."

She bade them look into each other's eyes and hearts. Rabbie placed a ring on Jane's finger.

"I, Robert Stein, swear tae show ye honor and fidelity, and tae share yer hopes and dreams. I promise tae stand by ye through not only the joys, but the sorrows, too."

Jane placed his ring on his finger. Her hands trembled as she did so, but her conviction was firm. "I, Jane Thorburn, swear tae show you honor and fidelity, and tae share yer hopes and dreams. I promise tae stand by ye through not only the joys, but the sorrows, too." As the words left her, her heart opened to receive his love, and she nearly fainted at its intensity.

"Are ye awricht, Jane?" Beitris asked quietly.

"Never better," Jane said.

"Good. Next, we bind yer eternal connection."

Jane and Rabbie each crossed one hand over the other, forming an "X" at their wrists, then took hold of each other's hands. Beitris wrapped a cord around their hands, bound them together, and tied a slim knot.

"Let it be known that the ties formed today are done so by yer vows and pledges, nae the cord itself. Ye may kiss each other noo."

Rabbie leaned over and gave Jane the gentlest, most chaste kiss she could imagine, respecting her modesty in the presence of others. As he pulled his lips away, the love that drew them together and brought them to this place overwhelmed her.

Beitris released the bonds, but they held hands for a few moments longer. It was as though their skin joined, and she sensed the flesh of his hands more deeply than ever before. His engulfed hers, and she did not want to let them go.

Maisie and Wynda held the decorated broom low, parallel to the ground.

"The couple will jump the besem to symbolize their commitment tae working through all their difficulties," Beitris said. "There are trials in all of life, some big, many small, and they will now commit tae work together through all of them."

Jane and Rabbie faced the broom. Holding hands, they jumped it together to the applause of the witnesses. Beitris said some final prayers to end the service.

"Well, now, ye're mine forever," Rabbie said. "Or at least a year an' a day."

"I'm sae happy," Jane said, her eyes shining as she looked into his. Together, they could face whatever life gave to them.

The women put together a feast, complete with leg of lamb, plenty of ale, thick, crusty bread, and cheese, all served at the boardinghouse. At the end, they presented the new couple with a white bride's cake Skye made. Similar to what Skye served at her own wedding, this cake was coming into vogue, having replaced the traditional bride's pie, a stew-like dish, that Mr. and Mrs. Stein ate in their day.

"Marriage should be sweet," Skye advised, and Nathan reached out to take her hand.

Always astounded at Skye's energy, Jane asked, "How did ye do all this wi' a new bairn?"

"I had some help. As ye ken, the lasses here all pitch in when someone needs a hand."

It was true that the ceremony and celebration had flowed flawlessly, largely due to the teamwork of the women of the boardinghouse. Never had Jane known such friendship and support.

As the celebration ended, though, Jane returned to her sense of unease about what came next. Beitris, as if reading her mind, walked over to her.

"I have something for ye," she said. "Put it in a pocket for later." She handed Jane a cloth bag. "I wrote instructions inside, and when ye need more, let me know. This will prevent ye needin' me like..." She cast a glance toward Skye. In a whisper, she added, "I'm glad tae see how her life is turnin' out."

Jane took the bag but didn't meet Beitris's eyes. "Me, too. But I need tae ask ye about how... I never... I dinna understand..." Try as she might, she couldn't stop stammering.

Beitris put a withered hand on Jane's. "It will be awricht. Ye love him, and the love will guide ye. It may hurt at first, but that will pass quickly."

"What wid I do wi'oot ye?" Jane said, looking into Beitris's face. "Ye brought me into the world, and noo I am grown and in love."

"Dinna worry, wee Jane. I will be around for a long time yet tae answer questions. Who can say? Mebbe I'll be deliverin' a bairn for you one day, when ye're ready." Giving Jane's hand an extra squeeze, she added, "If ye're ready."

The two women embraced, with Jane's heart full of love for the older woman and their long history together. When they parted, Jane tucked the bag into a pocket of her dress, less nervous now.

After the meal, the couple made their way to their new flat. When they reached the doorway, Rabbie lifted her from the ground and carried her over the threshold. As he let her down and her feet touched the floor again, a momentary panic seized her. Whisky at the feast had gone to her head, and the room swirled around her, but it wasn't just the drink that made her dizzy. This was her home now. No more would she share her bed with some young lass elbowing her in the ribs at night. Instead, she would sleep next to Rabbie.

He put his arms around her. "Are ye nervous?"

She nodded and tried not to cry. "Give me a minute," she said. "Beitris gave me somethin' tae keep the bairns away." Turning away from him, she pulled the bag from her pocket. Inside it were some herbs, a small cap, and instructions. "Oh, my," she said as she read them. The cap went inside? Beitris wrote that Rabbie could get fitted for a condom if they wanted, but they were thick and cumbersome, affecting their pleasure. She blushed at the old woman's frankness. "Please look the other way, Rabbie."

"Of course," he said, though he let out a wee chuckle.

"It's nae funny. This is all new tae me." But once he turned his back, she inserted the cap, which, once in place, felt comfortable. She hoped she hadn't fumbled too long, lessening the mood.

She needn't have worried.

"I'll take good care," he said. "Come." He reached out his hand and walked her to their bed. They lay down on it, and he held her in a warm, gentle embrace. "Wee dove, there is no rush," he said. "Naethin' tae fret about. We go as fast or as slow as ye need."

"I love you," she said. "Thank ye for yer patience."

As he held her, he ran one hand up and down her spine, and

she shivered. He kissed her face and her neck, and she thought she might swoon. Then with one hand he cupped a small breast, and she was undone. Her passion rose inside of her, eclipsing her fears.

"I'm ready," she said.

"Are ye sure?"

"Aye." Her voice was husky with desire. "Please, Rabbie."

The pain came quickly but faded equally soon, and their shared pleasure made her love him even more. Now she understood why her family and friends wanted this for her. Only the experience of being in his arms made it clear. There was no way to describe the joy of joining with someone. For a year and a day? *No*, she decided. *For life.*

BACK AT THE PALACE, though, Coira was making other plans. "Separate Jane from Rabbie," she said to Flora, "and she'll be back with us in no time."

"We're not to interfere. I've told you this a thousand times, and so has the queen," Flora said. "Besides, she's happy. Don't we want that for her?"

"I'd love to let Jane be and find another heir," Coira said. "But you've seen what's happening."

Flora admitted to herself, Coira was right. Jane's visit energized the Fey as their beloved queen blossomed with new, radiant health. Alas, it didn't last. The dearth of pregnancies and births hurt Flora the most. She longed for her own child and knew the devastation of infertility only too well, and how it affected every aspect of Fair life.

Coira, seemingly unaware of Flora's thoughtful silence, continued, "The queen is far too patient. I'll handle this, and in the end you'll both thank me."

The wind shuddered in the tree branches. The Wise Women

who observed everything surely were aware of Coira's plans. And yet, for all their wisdom, they never interfered in the way of daily life in the land of the Fair Folk. All Flora could do was appeal to the queen, something she hoped to avoid. Donella's patience with the quarrelling sisters had worn thin. But Coira's twisted loyalty, regardless of how pure her motives were, would likely make a bigger mess of things.

CHAPTER 24

Hard toiling for my daily bread
With burning heart and aching head.

An Address to Nature on Its Cruelty
Ellen Johnston

Soon Jane noticed the first challenge of life with a man: away from Abi's care and the shared chores at the boardinghouse, she now needed to prepare every meal and clean their flat. Having cooked meals when living with her aunt and uncle, Jane knew how to prepare food at least, but now she also purchased it and cleaned up afterwards, all while working long hours at the mill.

Such demands were not placed on a man. When he returned from work, Rabbie sat in his chair while she prepared supper, then washed the dishes and tended to any mending that needed to be done. On Saturday afternoons, he wanted to walk in the glen with her, but there were clothes to wash. Her only respite was Sunday dinner with Mr. and Mrs. Stein, but this meant the young couple were seldom alone.

She hoped Rabbie would pitch in and help, but he didn't. For the first few weeks, after cleaning up the evening meal, she fell straight into bed. Often he considered this an invitation for more amorous adventures. Much as she loved and desired him, she hated these overtures. Could he not see how tired she was?

At first she gave in to him out of duty, and often, once he started making love to her, she found a way to respond. One night, though, she pushed him away.

"Are ye angry at me?" he asked. "Did I do somethin' wrong?"

She sighed and sat up in the bed. "No, love. I'm nae used tae workin' all day, then cookin' and cleanin' after. I'm tired."

Looking puzzled, Rabbie said, "But ye make it look sae easy. I didna think about it. Can I help ye, Jane?"

"Mebbe," she said, with a stirring of hope.

Of course, Rabbie being Rabbie, he waited for her to give him an assignment, which she was reluctant to do. When she did give him a task, he peppered her with questions, even if he had done said task before. Once she asked him to chop onions for the soup. "Is this the right size?" he asked.

"Have I put enough in the pot?"

"How much do you want cut?"

"Which knife do ye want me tae use?"

Over time she asked for help less and less.

Their life together as a married couple—albeit informally—suited Rabbie. He woke up humming and possessed energy to spare at the end of the day. Occasionally he convinced her to go to the glen on a Sunday afternoon. The two of them chatted together about the week, and she reconnected to him as her friend.

The Fair Folk kept their distance most of the time, giving the young couple a chance to spend much-needed quiet time together. However, she sensed them mending her, and she always left feeling refreshed and energized.

During the week, though, if Rabbie wasn't around, or at

night in her dreams, Jane spoke frankly with the Fey. "It's nae fair," Jane said to them one evening when he met some of the lads at the pub for dinner. This gave her a rare night off from cooking, and she happily filled herself up with bread and tea. "His life got easier, while mine got harder."

"Leave him," Coira said. "He's not worth it."

"Don't say that." Flora rolled her eyes. "Coira's never been in love."

"Of course I have. With myself, thank you very much. We are quite passionate, if you must know."

Coira seldom revealed a funny side, so it took Jane by surprise every time.

"What about you, Flora? Are you in love?"

Coira and Flora exchanged glances.

"Is it wrong for me tae ask?" Jane asked.

"No, lass, you're allowed," Flora said. "I have a husband. No bairns, though." She turned her face away.

"It's the humans' fault," Coira said. "All the smoke, all the crowded quarters. Makes it harder to conceive."

"That's sae sad," Jane said. It hadn't come up during her visit. Apparently the Fair Folk wanted to display their best at the time. "My aunt had troubles a long time ago, too." Aunt Kirstin's infertility was part of a distant past. Mass infertility? That could be devastating to the Fey.

Flora recovered from her fleeting moment of emotion. "It will be resolved one day," she said. "I'm confident of that." Clearing her throat, she added, "But we're not here to talk about me. You have powers to help you, so use them. They're there for you."

Jane resisted this option. Sure, she used her powers here and there at the mill, but once she developed confidence in her weaving, she relied only on her hard work and skill. It was a source of pride for her.

More than that, using her powers reminded her of the

prophecy and her birthright, neither of which she wanted to think about. She also didn't want any advantage over the other factory girls, who were just as tired at the end of a long day.

As the weeks progressed, though, she found herself giving in on occasion. Winter turned to spring, then to summer, and her resistance lessened. She fell asleep with the flat unswept, and wake to a clean floor. Dishes were spotless, laundry cleaned and folded. Rabbie, who cared little about the details of running a household, didn't seem to notice.

As the daily routine went on, she thought more about Lowell. If she had to work this hard, she reasoned, she could ask for what she wanted. And maybe having something to look forward to would make her endless tasks more bearable. One Saturday, on a lovely summer's evening, she decided it was time.

After a hot day at the mill, a breeze with a slight chill brought relief. She and Rabbie walked home from work, hand in hand as they always did, and she put on a light supper. Afterward, they set out for an evening walk. The summer sun was still high in the sky, something she treasured.

"Rabbie," she said.

"What is it, wee dove?"

She hesitated. They were just getting settled in properly to their home. But still, hadn't they sworn to protect each other's dreams? And if they were to go, it should be while they were young.

"I thought we could talk about Lowell."

"Aye," he said, though it sounded more like a question, and a wary one at that.

"We should decide when tae go."

He didn't answer her at first. They walked along the trail as it rose into the hills. "I dinna think the time is right. I haven't spoken to Ma about it yet, an' she's no feelin' well."

Jane's shoulders stiffened. He would use Mrs. Stein to break his promise. It didn't matter that his mother appeared to be the picture of health.

"Mebbe I could go on ahead an' get settled there, an' you come on later," she said hopefully.

"Ye wid leave me already?" he asked.

She looked over at him in disbelief. "We talked about this, remember? Lots o' times, in fact. I was yer friend first, and you know my heart. I'd never leave ye for lack o' love. It's somethin' I always wanted, and ye promised tae go wi' me." Her voice grew higher in pitch with each word.

"But my ma," he protested. "I canna leave her behind, not noo. And Da is gettin' older, too."

"I see." Her voice grew icy. "So all we said at the rock with Beitris, that wisna true? Ye made false vows?"

"Jane, dinna be like that. I meant every word."

"Ye always mean yer words at the time, but then change yer mind when the next thing comes along. I believed ye when you looked me in the eyes an' said you'd support my dreams."

"But..."

"But what?" Her footfalls turned to stomps.

"I gave ye a home, an' we love one another. Is that no a dream ye wanted, too? I thought women wanted a home an' family more than anythin'."

She stopped, her throat tightening. "Ye...never...listened ...all...this...time. I canna believe it. How dare ye act like it disna matter tae me anymore?"

"I'm sorry. I know ye always talked about it, but you're a wife noo."

"What do ye mean?"

"Well, we have a good life here. Ye made a home wi' me. I suppose I thought ye changed yer mind."

She covered her eyes with her hands as her head started to pound. "I told ye, and you promised..." She sounded like a whiny child, but what else could she do?

"We can have a great life right here. What about when we have bairns? If we're here, Ma can help watch them. We're right down the street. Over there we'd have no family tae help us, makin' even more work for ye."

"I dinna want any bairns," she said. "I want tae work."

"I'm sairie," he said again. They arrived at the rock. "Wid ye like tae sit here a bit an' rest while I walk further?"

"I want tae go back."

"Ye dinna want tae talk tae yer fairies?"

"I've no got anythin' tae say," she muttered. "I'll go back. Dinna hurry." She turned on her heel and left, not caring if he followed or not. She heard him calling her, but he didn't come after her, and she didn't turn back.

Back at the flat, she took out the bag of savings she kept under a loose floorboard, covered by a rug. Counting it out, it wasn't quite enough money yet, but if she scrimped and stretched, it wouldn't take long to be ready.

After a while she calmed down, and that's when a plan crystallized in her brain. She would let Rabbie think she forgave him, that nothing was wrong, and embrace her life with him. She would renounce her plans to leave and promise to be a good woman and to find a way to win over his mother, staying long enough to lull him into trusting her while she saved the rest of what she needed. *Surely*, she thought, *I can be ready by February, six months away*. Her commitment to the handfast fulfilled by then, she would be free to leave. She didn't want to lie to Rabbie, but he had lied to her.

With a way forward, she settled down and dressed for bed. When Rabbie came home, she pretended to be asleep, but long after he started to softly snore, she lay awake staring at the ceiling, praying for strength. Once or twice she heard the rustling of fairy wings, but she brushed them away.

≈

THE NEXT DAY, Jane apologized to Rabbie, who applauded her "decision" to stay. He believed her completely. She wished she possessed his childlike faith in what anyone told him. From now on she would steel her heart.

They visited his parents for Sunday dinner, where Rabbie, relieved to not have to choose between them and Jane, displayed a celebratory mood. He grabbed his mother and whisked her around the floor in a dance while she giggled, protesting.

"Rabbie, let me cook."

Perhaps Rabbie developed his charming ways to coax some cheer out of his stern mother. Jane marveled at the years that disappeared from Mrs. Stein's face when she laughed. It didn't make Jane feel better, but it gave her a greater understanding.

Only Mr. Stein eyed Jane her suspicion. "Is everything awricht?" he asked her after taking her aside.

"Aye. I'm a bit tired, that's all." She gave him a wide smile that failed to reach her eyes.

"Ye seem on edge. Are ye sure?"

"Aye, Mr. Stein."

"If ye're tired, mebbe it's time tae stop workin' at the mill. Let Rabbie take care o' ye."

"I'll think on it," she replied.

"Besides, soon ye'll have bairns tae look after. Ye can live wi' us tae save money, if that's the problem."

"No, sir, we're fine." She studied the scar that travelled from his face down one side of his neck, resisting the temptation to touch it. She had grown fond of him. "Mr. Stein, I swear tae ye, naethin' is wrong. Money's a bit tight, but Rabbie an' I will sort things ourselves, so dinna fret."

"I'd do anything tae help ye."

"I believe ye." He still frightened her a little, but right now she remembered his kindness when his wife had been less than welcoming. When the time came to leave, her disappearance would hurt him, and she hated the thought of her deception... but best to keep up the ruse.

She remained attentive and engaged during dinner, admiring Mrs. Stein's new homemade kitchen curtains.

"I can make some for ye," Mrs. Stein said. "Dress up the place a wee bit."

"I'd like that," Jane said, even though the last thing she wanted was her mother-in-law's interference. No doubt Mrs. Stein wanted to put her stamp on the young couple's flat, and it wouldn't end with curtains. Still, who cared? Soon Jane would be gone.

Rabbie looked pleased that everyone was getting along so well, and after they walked back to their flat he told her so.

"I'm sae glad. I told ye they wid love you."

At times like these her resolve weakened. Rabbie was as excited as a child, and all he ever wanted was for his family to be close to one another. Yet Jane could never comprehend the concept of a close family, and she reminded herself of her plan.

QUEEN DONELLA DEVELOPED a cough that racked her thin frame. Flora and Coira were kept busy caring for her, bringing the finest herbalists from the queendom.

"How long are we going to let this continue?" Coira asked one day. "She's getting worse, and she's aging faster than a human."

Flora shook her head. "Jane's planning to cross the ocean. I don't know what we'll do if she gets out of our reach."

Coira saw her opportunity. "She won't. I know what to do."

"But you promised..."

"Don't worry, dear sister. I won't violate the wishes of the Wise Women, though they don't strike me as wise at all. But they didn't say we couldn't keep Jane close to us."

Flora, exhausted from caring for the queen, who had gradually weakened since Jane's visit, for once didn't argue. "Be careful," was all she said.

TIME SLIPPED AWAY through long hours, hard work, and Jane's scrimping. Weekly walks to the glen continued until January, which brought deep snows and brutal winds. They spent most Sundays at the Steins', and Jane continued to pretend nothing had changed.

Yet change was in the air, and all of it made Jane even more sure that the time neared for her to leave. Wynda, after multiple bouts of what she thought were colds, was diagnosed with tuberculosis. A small breakout of cases at the boardinghouse prohibited any visitors. She sent Jane a note saying goodbye and returned to her family in the Borders.

Jane recalled her beginner's error on that first day, when Wynda jumped in and helped her out. Wynda comforted Jane when Leslie died, and stayed up all night helping Jane with her dress for the handfasting. It was hard to imagine life without her in it, and she prayed for her sick friend's healing. Wynda deserved better. All the factory girls did.

One Sunday afternoon, Jane and Maisie went to visit Skye. With Wynda gone, Jane needed her remaining friends more than ever. As it turned out, though, both women had news of their own.

"I'm goin' back tae Glasgow!" Maisie blurted out her announcement the minute they entered Skye's flat.

Skye, who was bouncing young Charlie on her lap, stopped. "Ye're leavin'? Why?"

"I'm gettin' mairiet," she announced.

Jane knew nothing of any suitor, and she said, "This is quite a secret. Who is he? Where did ye meet?"

"Aye, let's hear all the details," Skye said.

"His name is Gavin, an' he works at the mill."

"Ahh." Jane met Gavin at one of the dances. He was a steady, quiet man, older than Maisie by about ten years, ordinary looking but with fine manners and a reputation as a reliable worker. "But why leave? Ye both have jobs here."

"Our families are in Glasgow," Maisie said. "I've wanted tae go back for sae long, an' we think we can make a good life there together." Maisie spoke of a quiet wedding, after which they would stay with her parents until they found work and their own place. "He's nae the kind o' man I used tae go for, but he makes me laugh, and I can count on him."

There were hugs and cheers at this happy news. Getting married was Maisie's biggest desire, and she'd always preferred Glasgow to Alva. Jane was thrilled that her friend was getting her dream life.

After more discussion of Maisie's plans, Skye cleared her throat. "I have an announcement, too," she said.

"Is it another bairn?" Maisie asked. "That's sae excitin'!"

"Naethin' like that," Skye said. "We're movin'. Tae England."

Unlike Maisie's news, this brought silence. With Wynda gone, and Maisie and Skye moving, they were going to be split apart, likely for good.

"Nathan has work there," Skye said, apologetically, "an' I can set up my business anywhere. He's even found a little shop for me."

Maisie offered her congratulations first. "Looks like we're all havin' our dreams come true. You get yer shop, I go back tae Glasgow, an' Jane has her Rabbie."

And Lowell, Jane thought. They had been through so much together, she and her friends, laughing and crying together, keeping secrets, finding their way. It was a cause for celebration, and yet all she could think of was what she was losing.

"Dinna look sae sad, Jane," Skye said. "We will all write each other, an' we'll stay friends."

So far they had managed, with Skye and Jane both leaving the boardinghouse, but this was a whole new level of change. Until now, she had been so involved making her own plans that saying goodbye to people she loved hadn't occurred to her. Though happy for herself and her friends, this was a bittersweet parting since she hadn't expected it to happen so soon.

A FEW DAYS LATER, the latest snowstorm felt like one too many, leaving one sick for spring. Jane's fingers and toes were numb from cold, and the mill windows were covered with ice.

At eight-thirty the whistle blew for the breakfast break. She bundled up to make the quick trek home so she and Rabbie could wolf down some porridge. As she walked briskly toward the flat, she thought she glimpsed fairy wings casting light amidst the gloom.

"Jane," a plaintive voice called. "Help me."

Alarmed, she squinted to try and locate the voice, but the sun bounced off the snow and blinded her.

"*Jaaane*," the voice called again, and this time it sounded more like a cry.

Intent on finding the source, she didn't see the patch of ice. As she tumbled to the ground, she heard a loud crack. A sharp, searing pain shot through her ankle.

"Jane? Jane, what happened?" Rabbie caught up to her.

"Shh," she said. Fighting through the pain, she wanted to alert Rabbie that someone was in danger. But now she heard nothing.

"Ye're hurt. Let me help." He lifted her before she could protest, and she cried out with the sudden movement.

"Someone was there," she tried to tell him, but the pain

surged straight to her head, making it hard for her to speak or even think.

"Let's get ye home, lass, and then I'll fetch the doctor," he said.

"Just one more minute," she said, and held a finger up to her lips so she could listen for any sounds. Nothing.

Surrendering to her distress, she wrapped her arms around his neck as he carried her. Once inside the flat, he lowered her to the bed. Though he was as tender as could be, the pain seared through her, and she cried out.

"Shh, shh, wee dove, let me take care o' ye."

He brought her a cup of tea and bread with some jam made by his mother, looking very proud of himself as he did so. She wanted to laugh, but feared that letting out even the slightest sound would hurt her more.

"I'll be right back," he said. "We'll get that leg looked at."

Jane didn't know which was worse: the pain of the break, or knowing that once again, her escape was delayed. She lay there calculating the time left on the calendar before her departure. Instead of February, it would be March at the earliest, but more likely April. She groaned, but this time not from pain.

The doctor arrived and set about checking the leg. He cut away her stocking, revealing an ankle swollen to more than double its usual size, with her toes ready to burst. Blue-black bruising covered the entire foot, and it turned at an unnatural angle.

"Ye've gone pale," Rabbie said. "Here, lean back, lass."

She obeyed. Between the pain and the nausea, lying back was her only option. As she did so, her stomach calmed a little, and now that she saw the injury, she had no desire to look further.

"Ye suffered a bad break," the doctor said. "You're a tiny woman, an' yer bones are soft anyway. We'll set it, but it may no heal completely. Ye could have a limp after this."

"Oh, no." She covered her face with her hands. "How will I go for my walks? Will it hurt me all my life?"

"Time will tell. I'll do my best for ye."

Rabbie hovered, leaning over to stroke her hair. "It will heal, you'll see," he said.

"How long before I can go back tae work?" Jane asked.

"We'll see. First, let's set the ankle. Ye'll want laudanum for the procedure, lass, and afterwards, too, while it heals."

"No, no laudanum." Factory girls often obtained Laudanum when they hurt themselves on the job. Some of them, however, were never the same after they took it. Unable to stop, they eventually drifted away from the mill, never to be heard from again.

He offered it again, more insistently, but she continued to refuse.

This time Rabbie spoke up. "Will some whisky do?"

The doctor let out an exasperated sigh. "It'll do the trick, I suppose, but nae as well. I warned you."

"That's what we'll do," Jane said.

Rabbie fetched the whisky, and Jane downed it in one gulp, scrunching her face as she did so. Unused to drinking, the strong stuff hit her right away. "Ready," she said to the doctor.

Despite the whisky, she was not prepared for what followed. The doctor yanked and pulled at the leg. Though swift and efficient in his movements, Jane screamed the entire time. Rabbie held her down, soothing her as best he could.

Once the doctor pulled the ankle back into place, he wrapped it in wool, then set up splints to keep it immobile. Though these movements were far less aggressive, every touch sent pain all the way up Jane's body. When it was finally over, she was left with a throbbing agony.

"I'll deliver crutches," the doctor said to Rabbie. "But dinna let her stand unless absolutely necessary, and then no weight on the ankle." Then, in a lower tone, he added, "She'll want the medicine. Come see me when she's ready for it."

"Aye."

After the doctor left, Rabbie made sure she was settled. "Ma will look in on ye durin' the day. That way if ye need anythin', ye dinna have tae get up."

Jane nodded, unable to protest. For the next several weeks, she would be completely dependent on the Stein family, and unable to work, so she wouldn't be able to save for Lowell. In fact, this misadventure would likely drain the funds so carefully gathered.

The voice that called to her, the glint of fairy wings so strong, so clear, must have been the Fey, but what were they up to? She was too tired and her mind fogged by too much pain to think much about it. She slept a good bit of the day, as though years of exhaustion had saved themselves up. If the Fair Folk tried to speak to her in her dreams, she couldn't hear them.

Mrs. Stein came by to fix meals, and sometimes Mr. Stein came along at supper. The Steins sat at the table while Jane lay on the bed nearby, close enough to hear the conversation, but not part of it. They talked about work, about Mrs. Stein's latest craft project, and how smart young John was. Rabbie laughed and joked, sunny as always. The lively discussions cheered her, and Jane listened until she dropped into the deep sleep of healing.

Even Mrs. Stein showed concern. Being needed inspired the older woman to action, and upon learning of Jane's reticence to take laudanum, took it upon herself to visit Beitris and returned with a variety of herbs: willow bark for pain, thistle to build strength, and heather to calm nerves and promote sleep.

One night, a few weeks after the accident, Jane lay nestled into Rabbie with her head on his shoulder. She had taken her sleep herbs, but wasn't quite ready to drop off. Rather, she enjoyed the peaceful, drowsy feeling of being in his arms. He had been there for her in so many ways in the past weeks, helping to feed and clean her without complaint, and for the first time she believed she could truly count on him.

Rabbie kissed her forehead. "I know yer leg is still healin' an' all..."

"I miss ye, too, Rabbie."

"Are ye sure? Ye seem sae tired still."

"Aye." She did miss him, and she hadn't stopped loving him, despite her plans. If anything, this detour brought them closer together. Leaving him would be the hardest thing she would ever do.

She reached for him with urgency, and their passion that night far exceeded their first night together. She was desperate, drowning. She wanted to savor her remaining time with him.

The next morning, they were giggly and shy as though they had made love for the first time. She fell in love with him all over again. And that was a problem. If she stayed much longer, she would talk herself out of going away, and then resent him for it.

Newly determined, each day she got up out of bed whenever Mrs. Stein wasn't around and practiced using her crutches. At first her whole body shook from the effort, sweat forming on her forehead, and she could only stand for a few minutes at a time. She rested a while and then tried again, sometimes sobbing with fatigue and weakness, though never in front of anyone, lest they try to stop her. Whenever Mrs. Stein showed up, Jane behaved like a model patient, letting herself be tended to.

Over time she grew stronger. She told no one of her efforts until confident she could move around easily on her crutches. Soon enough she would be able to walk unaided again, and she wanted to see that day as soon as possible.

Despite her progress, recovery proceeded slowly. When the doctor gave her permission to put weight on the damaged leg, her first steps on both feet felt strange and awkward, and she rested after each attempt. But she kept at it, and over the next few weeks, the leg grew strong enough to support her again.

One day, Mrs. Stein came over in the morning to find Jane moving about the flat with a reasonable amount of comfort.

"Ye're gettin' sae much better!" she exclaimed. "How do ye feel?"

"It disna hurt near as much these days," Jane said. She poured a cup of tea for herself and Mrs. Stein. As she sat down, though, an odd sensation came over her.

"Are ye awricht?" Mrs. Stein asked.

The feeling passed quickly. "Aye, just a bit lightheaded."

"Ye're up too soon," Mrs. Stein suggested. "Ye need more rest."

"I've probably been in bed too long."

"Mebbe not long enough." Mrs. Stein looked worried. "Lie down, lass, an' I'll take care o' things here."

Meekly, Jane obeyed. She mumbled, "Thank you for all the help," then lay down on the bed.

She passed out right away, with Mrs. Stein still bustling around the flat, and didn't wake up until Rabbie came home. She heard heated whispers between the two. When she couldn't grasp what they were saying, she sat up.

"What are ye plottin'?" she asked.

"I'll go noo," Mrs. Stein said to Rabbie. To Jane, she added, "Feel better, lass," then left.

Rabbie sat next to her on the bed. "I ken ye want tae go back tae work, but ye're pushin' too hard." He paused, taking in a deep breath.

"I got a wee bit dizzy, but that's all." Jane could see there was more he wanted to say. "What?"

He hesitated. "I dinna think ye should go back tae the mill. We'll have tae scrimp a wee bit and nae save as much, but this will be good for us. Ye're nae well."

"Give me a bit more time," she said. "I admit, the leg has taken more out o' me than I thought. But it's gettin' stronger, so I'm sure I'll be fine."

He leaned down and kissed the top of her head. "Let's ask the doctor, at least. Then we decide."

"Awricht." She didn't have the energy to fight him. She also knew something he didn't, but to confirm her suspicions she needed Beitris, not the doctor. For now she would keep the secret. *I'll tell him I think it's the herbs she gave me for pain*, she thought. He'd believe that.

CHAPTER 25

Out then spake her father dear,
And he spake meek and mild,
"And ever alas, sweet Janet," he says,
"I think thou goest with child."

The Ballad of Tam Lin
Old Scottish Ballad

*B*eitris arrived on Monday afternoon, hunched over her cane and carrying a medical bag. She was even more stooped and frail than at the handfasting, exhibiting an accelerating decline that caused a lump to form in Jane's throat.

The two women hugged, and a sturdy spirit still emanated from Beitris, in spite of a weakened physique. "Let's see what we have here. How is the leg?"

"It disna hurt, but I still have a wee limp."

"Show me."

Jane walked the length of the flat. Though stiff at first, after a few steps it loosened up, allowing her to move more easily.

"I'll make ye a potion tae help the bones," Beitris said. "An' somethin' tae help wi' the stiffness. Now, let's check ye for a bairn."

Starting with the leg helped ease Jane's nerves about this visit. Beitris's calming presence made it all bearable. She lay back on the bed to subject herself to the examination.

"I had other plans," Jane said ruefully. She had been so careful, taking her herbs and keeping a watchful eye on the calendar. "How could this have happened?"

"Man plans, God laughs," Beitris said as she palpated Jane's abdomen. "The herbs and cap work well, but naethin' is a guarantee if a bairn is determined tae come into the world." She continued her examination, then stood up and wiped her hands on a towel. "Sit up, lass, we're done. Ye were smart tae call me. It's early days, but a child is definitely on the way."

Jane sat up and righted her skirt. "I'll make tea," she said, without responding to Beitris. Hearing the words came as a shock, even though Beitris spoke the truth.

The act of serving the tea, along with a bit of seed cake, settled her a little. "I dinna ken what tae say or do about this."

"Do ye love Rabbie?"

"Oh, I do." She set her teacup down and folded her hands in her lap.

"I sense hesitation, lass. What is botherin' you?"

Jane didn't bring up Lowell. Once again her life was out of her hands. Instead, she focused on her more mundane complaints. "It seems silly," Jane said. "I have nae right tae complain since he's such a good man. But sometimes he upsets me when he willnae tell anyone the truth if he thinks it will hurt them. Especially his ma."

Beitris chuckled. "Ah, Jane, that happens all the time. If that be the worst o' yer worries, you're a fortunate woman. He disna drink?"

"A wee bit here an' there, naethin' that's a problem."

"An' he be faithful tae ye?"

Jane nodded, feeling at once like a petulant, spoiled child. "Aye. He loves me wi' all his heart. While my ankle healed, he even brought me my meals."

"Ye canna have it all, ye ken," Beitris said. Her eyes were warm and comforting. "The world isna meant for that. I can help ye take care o' the bairn like I did wi' Skye, but yer heart willnae heal as well as the leg. Ye love the man, and you'll love the bairn, mebbe even more."

"But my work…"

"Yer work is just beginnin'," Beitris said. She took a bite of cake, holding up one finger to signal she had something more to add. "That cake is delicious. I'll have tae get the recipe. Anyway, I'm goin' tae say somethin' tae ye in confidence."

"I willnae say a word."

"Awricht." A small tear formed at the edge of one eye, and she wiped it away. "I always thought I failed ye, right from the start. Ye may think I'm mad, but I need tae tell the tale."

Jane's body began to tremble. Right from the start? She remembered the story Coira told her all those years ago. More than likely, this would be a more accurate version. "Go ahead," she said.

Beitris then shared her memories of that dark day when Jane was almost lost to the Fey, a version far different from Coira's. She told of a young mother's panic, a hot poker, and a disappearing changeling. "No matter what we said and did, yer ma couldna trust it was really you. Yer Da thought he had tae give ye up tae keep ye safe. I brought the soaps an' herbs tae keep the Fey at a distance, at least." When she finished speaking she said, "There. Ye can lock me up noo. But I think this is why ye have trouble lettin' love in."

Even with Beitris's confession, Jane struggled to speak the truth. So far she'd trusted only Rabbie with this information. And if Jane hadn't herself flown to the palace, she never would have believed such a far-fetched story.

"I see them," she finally said. "All my life. If ye're mad, so am I." She told Beitris of her visit to the fairy realm, of wearing fine clothes, eating at banquets, and drawing down moonbeams to weave. She left out the part about the prophecy, preferring to keep that to herself. It was difficult enough to share such a strange story with anyone else, even someone she trusted as much as Beitris.

Beitris looked pleased, though not surprised. "Have they been good tae ye?"

"Aye. Many a time they brought comfort when I felt alone, especially when I figured out Ma and Da didna want me." She didn't mention the voice that called to her, causing her to slip on the ice. That had to have been the Fey, but they had been nothing but kind to her. Yet now, as she spoke of them aloud, doubts arose in her throat. They couldn't be that cruel, could they?

"I'm glad they looked out for ye," Beitris said. "I never liked the way Elizabeth treated ye, always keepin' you on the outside, never part o' the family."

"Aye," Jane said, the lump reforming in her throat.

"I shouldna fault yer ma, though I confess I do. Lots o' young women have trouble, but it passes. For yer ma, it never did. She saw ye as the source o' all her woes."

"Mebbe I was," Jane said. "She did fine wi' the other bairns."

The old woman closed her eyes, deep in thought, before she responded. "Ye were an innocent wee being. Her problems were hers, nae yers. Is that why ye never wanted tae marry or give birth? Is this what makes yer work so important that ye wid walk away from true love?"

"I dinna think so," Jane answered, her voice wavered.

Beitris's eyes, small and deep-set, probed into Jane's mind, willing the truth out of her. "I always loved the mill, even as a wee lass. When I came tae Alva, movin' in tae the boarding-house wi' the other lasses felt so good. Marriage, bairns, I wanted none o' that."

Beitris reached out for Jane's hand and took it in hers. "Are ye sure, lass? Or is it somethin' else?"

"What do ye mean?" Jane asked as she squirmed in her chair.

"Hear me out. Yer ma couldna care for ye and sent ye away. Could ye be scared ye'd do the same?"

"I... Mebbe." Jane started to cry, and sobs rose from deep her heart, sobs of acknowledging the truth, the reason she turned her back on love, the reason she decided never to have children. She didn't understand until this moment how deeply her losses had cut into her.

"Go ahead an' cry," Beitris said. She wrapped her arms around Jane and made soothing sounds. "Let it out."

"Am I..." Jane's attempts to speak were disrupted by her sobs. "...hurtin' the bairn noo wi' all these tears?" Rising panic added fuel to the hurt and sadness.

"No, lass, it will help the child if ye release this burden. It's time."

Soothed by Beitris's words, the sobs slowly receded, and she breathed freely again. Letting it all go left her lighter, cleaner, more alive.

"I know ye have these plans for yer life, but what if this is the best plan of all, one come from the Lord an' not that busy head o' yers?"

"But..." Jane still wanted to argue. Part of her still clung to the old dreams.

"But naethin'. Ye have some problems, but Rabbie's a good, sweet man, and you stood in the glen to declare yer love for each other. Ye will love that child with all yer heart an' soul. I know it deep inside."

Jane placed a hand on her belly. Already she knew this mysterious being inside of her. She imagined the look on Rabbie's face when she told him. Who would be a better father? She loved his childlike enthusiasm. No doubt a child of his would feel loved and wanted. Could she love this child, too? Could she be a better mother than her own?

She couldn't shake the feeling, though, that she had somehow failed. The dream she had kept for years was over for good, if she took this path at least.

But what was in Lowell, anyway? Just another mill, and she'd be just another factory girl, alone in the world. Rabbie was right. Here, family would love her child. The Steins weren't perfect, and Mrs. Stein loved to interfere with their lives, but maybe a grandchild would soften her.

Or, Beitris could make the tea, and it would all be over in a day or two. Yet Jane remembered Skye's anguish, even when she believed Nathan had abandoned her. Rabbie would never walk away. No, Rabbie would share his joy with everyone in town.

Still.

"I'll think about it," she said at last.

Frowning, Beitris said, "Ye have a bit of time left, but nae much. Ye're early on, but I widnae wait too much longer if..."

Jane nodded. "I'll decide soon."

When Beitris left, she stretched out on the bed, eyes trained on the ceiling, barely blinking, wondering how it could have all gone so wrong. Or had it? She felt split in two, with one version of her carefree and responsible only for herself, and the other version in a real family. Both versions appealed to her in some ways, frustrated her in others. How could she choose?

Yet Jane was a practical woman. She would figure it out somehow. For now, it was time to prepare Rabbie's supper. Perhaps the simple actions of housework would help her decide what to do.

If only her body would comply. It took her another half hour or so before she pulled herself out of bed. She grabbed a broom and decided to sweep first, but her arms moved as if fighting restraints. *I have tae decide*, she thought. *No more goin' back and forth wi' one foot out the door. I go or I stay.*

Rubbing her abdomen, she knew the answer. Her heart was here, with Rabbie, and with this child.

She moved the rug and lifted the bag of savings from underneath the floorboard. Rabbie didn't know how much she managed to save, but she decided to tell him tonight. After grabbing some coins, she went out to buy food, energized by the thought of a hearty meal. Once she made the decision, the baby was insistent: *feed me soon and feed me well.*

By the time Rabbie came home, fragrant aromas of roast, neeps, and tatties filled the air. They made her queasy, but not enough to throw up.

"Jane?"

Absorbed in her thoughts, jumped at the sound of his voice. "Rabbie, ye startled me!"

He looked at the feast before him, a much larger and more luxurious supper than usual. "I dinna understand," he said.

"Sit down, Rabbie," she said. "I'll pour ye a glass and tell ye my story."

He sat as instructed, but the look on his face was of one whose wife had disappeared, leaving a changeling in her place.

She handed him a whisky, then focused on gathering two heaping plates of food, not ready to meet his gaze.

Once settled, they began to eat, which gave them both something to do before she shared her news, though hunger left her as soon as she sat down. Thankfully, her queasiness had left her for the time being.

He took a bite of roast and moaned. "Delicious," he said. "But why do I feel like ye're fattenin' me up for the kill?"

"There'll be no killin' tonight, I promise."

He dug into his meal then, and she watched as he shoveled

food in his mouth with relish. Nothing got in the way of his appetite.

When he finished, he put his fork down. "Tell me what ye're up to, lass."

"Oh, wait, let me show ye somethin' first," she said. She brought the bag to the table and emptied its contents. "Our savings. I took some from it for the meal."

He stared at the pile of money. "We had all that, all along?"

"Aye, I've saved for a long time. Some money ye gave tae me, but I put back some o' my own earnings, too. This was gonnae be our fund for Lowell."

He picked up some of it, letting it fall through his hands and back onto the table. It wasn't a fortune, but certainly a windfall for a young couple scraping by. Then the look on his face changed.

"Ye always wanted tae go," he said. "I've hurt ye, Jane, by keeping you here when you made all these plans. Ye always told the truth. Are ye leavin' me noo? Is our time done?"

She burst into tears. *Stop it, lass*, she told herself. But today the waterworks flowed like the burn. She imagined the water sprites delighting in the flow. Poor Rabbie sat there, waiting for her, his jaw dropped open and his eyes wide. His expression struck her as comical and she switched from crying to laughing.

"I dinna ken what tae do," he said. He looked so lost and helpless, she wanted to cry again. She knew of pregnant women with emotions that shifted as quickly as the weather, but didn't understand the impossibility of controlling them in her own body.

"I'm sairie," she said when she caught her breath. She gulped, then gulped again. Once calmed, she reached across the table to take his hand, speaking slowly and with resolve. "I'm tellin' ye, there's no need in me tae go anymore. We have a new dream."

"Are ye tellin' me...?"

"Aye."

He sat back, obviously stunned by the news, but then a crooked grin spread across his face. "When?"

"September, we think."

"So this sickness isna from the broken leg?"

"Naw. There's naethin' tae worry about, Rabbie Stein."

He jumped up and ran around the table, grabbing her from behind to hold her, laughing and crying at the same time.

"I thought somethin' big was wrong. I thought ye were dyin'!"

"Just the opposite," she said.

Then he stopped, and a look of concern came over his face. "I dinna want tae hurt ye," he said.

She held her arms out to him. "Holdin' me willnae hurt it."

"We should tell Ma an' Da," he said. "Let's go over there tonight."

"Nae yet," she said, frowning. "It's early days, an' I dinna want tae bring on the evil eye. I want this child tae have a better start in life than I did."

"Of course, of course," he said. "But how long do we have tae wait tae tell them?"

"Another month or two is all."

"I dinna know how I'll keep it quiet for all that time, but if ye say so, that's what I'll do. An' what about...well, ye know. Can we...?"

"Aye, ye can love me like ye always do, for now at least."

With that she rose and took him by the hand, guiding him to the bed. There was something reassuring about being in his arms. Yet afterward, she lay awake for a long, long time.

THE NEXT MORNING Jane rose full of joy but deathly sick to her stomach. Morning sickness brought yet another blow to her plans to return to the mill.

Rabbie, no longer worried about Jane dying of some mysterious ailment, said, "Rest today. I'll send Ma over tae check on ye."

"All right. But dinna tell her!"

He covered his mouth with both hands. "I promise," he said, his voice muffled. Then he took her in his arms and held her tight. "I'm sae happy, wee dove. We will have our own family soon."

She bid him goodbye, then went back to bed to rest, her heart soaring and her mind clear, in spite of the morning sickness. Closing her eyes, she drifted back into a deep sleep, dreaming of the Fey surrounding her, singing and rejoicing.

A knock on the door brought her suddenly back to the waking world. Reluctantly, she went to the door and opened it.

"Mrs. Stein," Jane said. "Please come in."

Rabbie's mother looked Jane up and down. "Rabbie said tae look in on ye. Are ye gettin' a cold?" Ann asked, her eyes appraising Jane with a mother's scrutiny.

"I'm tired." Jane almost said, "It's a woman problem," but Mrs. Stein would be shrewd enough to pick up on what that meant. "And the leg's still fightin' me a bit." Her stomach started to churn, and she eyed a bucket stashed in a corner with longing. The nausea passed quickly, though, and she hoped it wouldn't return while Mrs. Stein remained in the flat.

"Ah." Mrs. Stein looked around and noticed a few crumbs of roast on the table. "That's a bit rich for a weekday supper wi' ye nae back at work."

"Aye. It was...Rabbie's idea," Jane said. "He worried I was gettin' too weak after the broken leg an' all, so he thought I needed some extra meat." *I'm gettin' tae be as good a liar as Rabbie.* He wouldn't mind, though. Ann never faulted Rabbie for anything, so blaming him would keep her out of trouble.

"My son is a good man, but sometimes he has no sense," Ann replied. "Ye need tae stop him from these crazy notions of his."

So much for that, Jane thought with a sigh. Every time she thought she figured Mrs. Stein out, she was wrong. "It was one extravagance. We watch our money well most o' the time."

Ann took a seat at the table as Jane put on a pot of tea. "I wanted tae talk tae ye about Rabbie," she said.

"Oh?" Jane tried to sound casual, but braced herself. *What else did I do wrong?*

"He's been talkin' again about goin' back tae England, an' I figured ye were behind that." She folded her arms and glared at Jane.

"What?" Jane's head started to spin. "Naw. If Rabbie has that idea, he's got it in his head all by himself, and he didna tell me."

Ann's eyes narrowed. "People always said ye talked about goin' tae America."

"I did talk about that for a long time. But I'm not goin' anywhere noo."

"Why not?"

"Because..." Jane involuntarily put a hand on her belly. "I have a nice family, an' I dinna want tae leave that. Ye've been kind tae me, an' the last thing I want is tae trample on that kindness. Mr. Stein, too. I like bein' part o' the family, an' I dinna want tae go away anymore."

"Ye're sure about that? Ye're not tellin' a tale?"

"I swear," Jane said. "And I've never wanted tae go tae England at all. Uncle Ewan wid fall into his grave if I went there. In fact, I'm a bit distressed you told me this instead o' Rabbie."

Jane's stomach started to lurch, and she fetched a piece of bread to calm it.

"The joy o' my life, that Rabbie," Mrs. Stein said. "He's smart an' he works hard, too. But he gets these ideas in his head sometimes. He wanted tae make us proud, he said, and there are opportunities in England he disna have here. For some reason he thought we'd love for him tae leave again, but he's my firstborn, an' when he left us before I cried almost every day."

"He is a wonderful man," Jane said as she sat across the table, enjoying Mrs. Stein's open expression of love for her child. Rabbie brought out her softer side. "He wants us all tae be happy."

"Well, then, I dinna know where this talk o' goin' tae England comes from," Mrs. Stein said. "We're all happy right here in Alva. It's a good place tae raise a family. I hope the two o' ye have that joy one day."

Jane suddenly turned green and ran to the bucket, vomiting into it until she had nothing left.

"Well, I guess that answers that," Ann said with a sigh. "I'll take care o' the mess, lass. Pour a glass o' water and sit. I'll be right back."

Jane took a long drink and sat at the table, dropping her head in her hands. Many women spoke of morning sickness, but she didn't expect such turbulence from deep in her gut.

Mrs. Stein returned with a clean bucket and a big smile. "Now my son canna go. Did he ken this when he talked tae me about England?"

"I told him last night. We wanted tae keep it a secret for a while. Believe me, I'm on yer side about England."

"This is good news, then! Rabbie willnae leave us wi' a bairn on the way. I canna wait tae tell Mr. Stein!"

"Please, nae yet." Jane reached out to touch Ann, who for once didn't flinch. "Can ye keep my confidence for a while?"

Rabbie's mother wrapped her arms around Jane's shoulders and held her tight. Jane had never seen Mrs. Stein so demonstrative, even with her own children.

"Aye, of course. Oh, but how am I goin' tae keep this a secret from my Hugh? I will, though, I promise. I'll go tae the kirk and pray about it. Ye'll name the baby Hugh if it's a boy."

"Aye." Jane hadn't thought that far ahead. So far, what grew in her belly was something abstract. It never occurred to her to think of it as a boy or girl. She tried to imagine what it might be, but nothing came to her. Tradition dictated naming a boy after his paternal grandfather. "Hugh is a good name."

"What will it be if it's a girl?" Mrs. Stein asked. "What be yer grandma's name?"

"Sarah. I think. Wait, mebbe Bridget." Jane looked helplessly at the older woman, knowing full well it wouldn't do to explain her confusion.

"That family o' yers." Mrs. Stein's face returned to its usual hardness. This time, though, Jane didn't mind—her pregnancy awakened Mrs. Stein's protective instincts. "No wonder ye ken naethin' about how tae be in one. I'd love tae sit yer ma down an' tell her a thing or two sometime."

"Beitris says a lot o' women are sad after the birth, but Ma was the worst she ever saw. Took her a long time tae get better." The words slipped out. Yet telling her felt like the most natural thing to do. Could pregnancy help them get closer to one another?

"What a load o' nonsense," Mrs. Stein said. "I took care o' all my bairns, an' we had our own troubles…" Her voice trailed off. "Well, that was a long time ago. Water under the bridge."

Jane recalled the rumors about Mr. Stein's wilder days and didn't ask any questions. She wanted to explain, to justify her mother's behavior, but she was grateful Mrs. Stein saw what others did not. And Ann, though prickly, included her as family, so Jane said only, "Thank you for seein' it that way. I swear, I'd never try tae take Rabbie away from here." That wasn't entirely true, since she had begged Rabbie to go to Lowell…but that conversation was over now. No need to admit it ever happened. She her son to know the love of a close family.

Her son? The thought surprised her. *Mebbe it's the talk o' names*, she told herself, but no, it was more than that, a deep knowing. She couldn't wait to ask Beitris, to help her bring him

into the world. The old woman would be thrilled at Jane's decision to keep the baby.

THERE WAS one matter to settle when Rabbie came home that
night.

"England?" she asked the minute he walked into the flat.
"What is yer ma talkin' about?"

Flinching ever so slightly, he said, "Naethin'," though he
avoided looking at her and stuffed his hands in his pockets. She
expected to see that guilty look on her son many times, but on a
grown man it was infuriating.

"When were ye goin' tae tell me? Is there a job?" She had so
many questions and couldn't get them out soon enough. Pregnancy gave her even more of a fighting spirit.

He slumped in his chair. "Everythin' is changed. I willnae
leave Ma knowin' her grandchild was sae far away."

"If there was nae bairn, what then?"

"Well, we wid talk about it." He gestured helplessly, his eyes
wide and round. "Look, I was just talkin', thinkin' out loud. I got
a letter from my old boss, an' I wanted advice from Da before I
talked tae you about it. I like it here, but there's more opportunity outside Alva. Money's been sae tight." Reaching out and
stroking her cheek with the back of his hand, he added, "I say
things a lot wi'oot thinkin'. Forgive me?"

She hesitated for a moment, then let him hug her. More than
ever, she needed certainty in her life now. "Promise me, nae
more talk about England. We'll raise Hu—the bairn—wi' his
folks around."

"Of course," he said. But, as always, she wondered if he told
the truth.

CHAPTER 26

Welcome, my bonnie, sweet, wee dochter!
Tho' ye came here a wee unsought for.
And tho' your comin I hae fought for
Baith Kirk and Queir,
Yet by my faith, ye're no unwrought for,
That I shall swear.

Welcome to a Bastart Wean
Robert Burns

Jane's belly grew larger and rounder as the months progressed, and her morning sickness abated. Newly energized, she returned to work at the mill, handling the long hours with no problem. In the evenings she cooked, mended, and cleaned until bedtime. On Saturday afternoons, she and Rabbie hurried to the glen, but instead of sitting on her favorite rock, she insisted on hiking further up. Though a slight limp remained, her injured ankle now held strong.

Beitris, as expected, applauded Jane's readiness to have a baby. "Ye have the glow," she said at her latest visit. She visited often to check Jane's progress, each time praising her while pushing her to eat more.

Rabbie rubbed her shoulders and feet at night, making all kinds of plans for when the baby came. "He'll come tae love our glen," he said, "and mebbe we can give him a brother or sister soon."

"Rabbie, one baby at a time," she said, laughing at his enthusiasm. "I'm just startin' tae get food down again." The early months of pregnancy dropped much-needed weight from her bones, and her appetite had only recently returned. Other concerns awaited as well: difficulty moving, swollen feet, struggles to catch her breath.

Mrs. Stein was unable to keep quiet, so the Steins learned of the news before there was any outward evidence of pregnancy. Fortunately, the Steins were all excited about the addition. There were no lectures on the importance of marriage, only joy about the prospect of a future grandchild. Jane suspected they kept quiet because this new development would keep Rabbie nearby.

Uncle Ewan and Aunt Kirstin also offered their congratulations, but with more reserve. In fact, Uncle Ewan showed a gruffer side this time.

"There's been no weddin'," he said, looking at Rabbie. "How can we be sure you'll nae leave my niece wi' a bairn an' no income?"

"I swear tae ye, sir, I'll nae abandon her or the bairn. If I left Jane, my ma wid disown me. She canna wait for a grandchild."

There were a few more remarks about at least making wedding plans, but Jane couldn't think about that now. She trusted Rabbie, and she trusted herself. They would make things right with the kirk later.

They made one more visit, this time to see Robert and Elizabeth. Jane now waddled when she walked. Her limp, though slight, made her gait even more unwieldy, but for the first time, she was eager to see her parents and to introduce them to Rabbie.

The flat was quiet when her father answered the door.

"Jane! Come in!" He gave her a strong, wiry hug. "Ye look good, lass. Fillin' out, I see."

"That's nae fillin' out," Elizabeth said when she got a look at Jane.

Rabbie stood in the doorway behind Jane. In the excitement she nearly forgot him. "Ma, Da, this is Rabbie," she said. "An' this"—she patted her growing belly—"will be yer first grandchild."

Robert responded first with a resounding *whoop*. He embraced Jane, lifting her off the floor in a tight bear hug. Then, realizing what he was doing, he gently set her down. "Did I hurt ye?" he asked, his eyebrows knitting together in worry.

"I'm awricht," Jane said, laughing and a wee bit dizzy. It didn't matter. The hug from her father meant too much.

"Rabbie, nice tae meet ye," Robert said, vigorously shaking Rabbie's hand.

"Dinna break him," Elizabeth said. Far more reserved than Robert upon hearing this news, she gave Jane a stiff hug. "Are ye awricht?" she whispered. "I mean, I hope ye dinna have my troubles."

The whole room grew quiet. Finally, Jane said, "We're celebratin' today. This is a good thing for us."

"Well, then, let's celebrate! I'll fetch the weans." Robert ran out the door in an instant, returning soon with Jane's siblings. "Ye saw Robina an' Thomas before, but I dinna think you met Annie an' Sarah." Realizing the strangeness of the situation, he mumbled, "There's Mary an' William, too, but, ah, they're grown an' gone like you."

There were more of them than Jane realized, siblings she didn't even know existed. Did they know about her? Did they wonder why she wasn't part of the family? Fatigue swept over her like a fog, though she didn't know if it was her nerves or the pregnancy.

Yet, here they were, inspecting each other, as if opening a door that had been stuck closed for more than twenty years. They were all larger than Jane, built more like Elizabeth. At least the older ones were. Thomas was small, but he looked to be only about four or five. The Fey blood touched only Jane, with her siblings showing only human characteristics. Each said hello while their mother set out tea and little cakes. Jane found it hard to follow their conversations as they talked about friends she didn't know or their work at the mines. Mostly she listened politely and kept quiet. Rabbie kept one hand on hers at all times, steadying her, and she caught her father's sympathetic eye.

With everyone now thus informed and swearing to get together again soon, the couple returned to Alva. At least this baby would be surrounded by love, even by those who were unable to love Jane in the same way.

As SHE RAN her hands along Jane's belly, feeling the child's position, Beitris nodded her head in approval. "Ye've done well, lass. I am proud o' ye for followin' all my instructions."

"I've learned from the best," Jane said. "I canna wait tae have ye bring him intae the world. Or her."

Beitris covered Jane with a blanket and pulled a chair next to the bed, her lips pursed. "We need tae talk about that."

"What?" Jane sat up straight, chewing on her bottom lip. "Is there a problem?"

"The bairn is fine," Beitris replied. "But I think it's time tae bringin' Nora in." Nora was Alva's howdiewife.

"I want *you* tae deliver him," Jane said. "I canna imagine goin' through this wi' a stranger."

"It's time." Her chin quivered ever so slightly.

"What's wrong? Why?"

Beitris held out both of her hands, gnarled with time and hard work. "I am too old. I hoped tae make yer delivery my last, but I want tae keep ye safe. Nora will do right by ye. Plus, she's closer by in case the bairn comes fast."

Jane tried to digest this new information. Beitris had been old for as long as Jane knew her, but she remained strong and competent. "Wid ye come anyway? I mean, let Nora do the delivery, but ye'd be there?"

"We'll see, lass. We'll see." With that, Beitris rose abruptly and gathered her things. "I'll be here next week for one last visit, so I suggest ye call on Nora right away. Take care o' yersel." She gave Jane a swift hug and was out the door before Jane uttered more protests.

Jane got out of the bed and dressed, feeling the sting of Beitris's eagerness to leave.

"Did I say somethin' wrong?" she asked aloud.

Now she needed to make arrangements with Nora, and the thought made her want to go back to bed and pull the covers over her head. With a little more than a month to go, she had no desire to break in a new howdiewife.

The next Sunday, Rabbie went to visit his parents while Jane waited for Beitris. When the appointed time passed without the old woman's arrival, Jane didn't worry at first. Emergencies cropped up regularly for howdiewives. "Bairns come on their schedule, not ours," Beitris always said. Jane kept herself busy with mending and cleaning, stopping frequently to peer out the window.

First, Beitris was an hour late, then two, then three. As the evening shadows fell, Jane began to fret.

Rabbie came home, and she half-heartedly put together a light supper for them, still hoping for a knock at the door.

"Mebbe she'll come tomorrow," Rabbie said. "Or mebbe ye mixed up dates?"

Jane shook her head. "Naw, we talked about it as her last visit. She always comes. There must have been a difficult birth. That's all I can think of." Though that might have explained Beitris's absence, it did nothing to comfort Jane.

Rabbie removed his napkin from his lap and put it on the table. "I'll go out and ask around," he said.

"Oh, wid ye?" That would be one less weight for her shoulders.

He went out into the night. She did her best to keep busy. She had started making baby blankets, socks, caps, and tiny gowns—a task that brought her joy. Unable to focus, though, soon she abandoned her efforts.

The hour grew later and later, with no sign of him. Something was definitely wrong. She'd put off contacting Nora because convinced herself that Beitris would still deliver her child. Now she recalled the look on the old woman's face when she left the last time. What were her words again? "We'll see, lass. We'll see." *She tried tae tell me somethin', an' I didna listen,* Jane realized.

She lit an extra candle and placed it on the table. Then she lowered her body carefully to the floor, holding her expanding belly as she did so, and knelt there to pray. Praying was all she could do.

Finally, Rabbie returned, looking spent. Normally they spent Sunday evenings resting for the long workweek ahead, so they were both going to start out tired. She rose and put her arms around him, and she knew before he said a word.

He held her for a long time before he spoke the words she did not want to hear: "She's gone tae live wi' the angels. Died in her sleep, nice an' peaceful."

Beitris, who delivered her, protected her, and guided her, was now gone. This dear mentor and friend, with her reassuring presence, had been more like a grandmother. Now the woman who knew all her secrets, and didn't judge her, would not be there for the most important moment of Jane's life. For Nora, a stranger, this would be just another delivery.

"What will I do?" she asked, tears flowing down her face, knowing Rabbie had no answers.

"I know ye're sad, wee dove," he said. "She was special."

"Aye." She pulled back from him. "She knew me better than anyone besides you. She tried tae tell me, but I didna listen. That sounds silly, I ken."

"Naw, wee dove, it disna sound silly at all. I'm sure her spirit will be wi' ye tae give you guidance. Who knows? Mebbe she wisna strong enough in this life, but in the spirit world she can take better care o' ye."

Jane wiped her tears and blew her nose. "Ye think that's true?"

"Aye, as sure as I'm holdin' ye noo. Mebbe she's wi' us today, helpin' us."

"Mebbe so." Jane's voice was that of a child, with all the echoes of her abandonment. For now, she let Rabbie hold her. Inside, baby Hugh made gentle movements to reassure her.

BEITRIS WAS LAID to rest on the following Sunday. Jane planned to attend, but a night of twinges left her uncertain, and it felt like she a hundred babies were kicking her lower back. What if the bairn came early?

"Stay," Rabbie said. "I'll stand in for ye. Stay here an' rest."

"I should go," she said. "She was the one constant of my life."

"Nora's comin' tomorrow," he said. "Best not tae go before she checks ye. Besides, Beitris wid understand more than anyone."

With Rabbie gone to the funeral, she offered prayers to her

departed friend. This time she decided not to kneel, but sat in a chair, certain that God wouldn't mind a pregnant woman praying in some comfort.

As she rocked, Hugh stirred inside of her, and she felt they were praying together. No doubt a woman such as Beitris would end up in heaven, and for a fleeting moment she sensed the howdiewife's presence. Her sorrow grew, tinged with peace and contentment, and she dropped off into a quiet sleep.

It is no secret, however, that the moods of pregnant women are subject to sudden shifts. In her sleep, the old woman's reassurances were soon replaced by a restless dream. She was on a sailboat that pitched and rolled in a lightning storm. She clung to the mast as it began to crack and splinter. The sailors were thrown into the sea, leaving her alone and adrift until the boat slammed into the shore, throwing her out. She landed on hard ground, out of breath. Her first thought was of Hugh, and she held her belly as she waited for movement.

"He's fine," a voice said.

Jane sat up and dusted sand off her clothing, which had somehow dried. "Who are you?" she asked, though looking at this woman was like looking in a mirror.

The stranger had hair like Jane's, though she let it flow down her back. Though shorter than Jane, her lean physique bordered on too thin. Her large eyes dominated a small, freckled face, and matched the color of the sea at the shore, a mix of blues and greens swirling together.

Bridget nodded. "I died giving birth to your father," she said. "I come to you from another world, and I have stayed young. Flora was to tell you something, but she couldn't bear it, so I came."

As Jane looked into Bridget's eyes, the prophecy came to life within her. She fully experienced the anguish of her father's birth and the devastation of Bridget's death. The prophecy itself, though, troubled her now.

"I dinna understand," she said. "The queen said I wid come tae the palace at the end of my life, so that means I go there when I'm deid. But you're deid and went tae a different world. Why?"

Bridget sat next to Jane on the sand. "All the Fair Folk die, as humans do," she said. The wind captured tendrils of her hair, and she tucked it behind her ears. "Your time with our people will be long, but not forever."

None of this made sense to Jane, but Bridget said nothing more about it. Instead, she said, "I need to give you Flora's message."

"I had forgotten," Jane said. "Someone I loved just slipped away."

"Beitris, yes," Bridget said. "An extraordinary woman."

"Aye."

The sea, which only a few minutes ago chewed up a boat and spat it out, softened now and lapped the shore, its sounds soothing and gentle. The two women gazed at the horizon together while Jane waited. Bridget seemed in no hurry.

When she finally spoke, her tone was sad. "There is trouble in the world of the Fey," she said. "You are aware of that. There is much disagreement in the palace about what to do—about you."

"Me? But what about the Wise Women?"

With a sigh, Bridget said, "Our ways are crumbling and have been for some time. The Wise Women themselves are in danger, and they have been around since the earliest of times."

"But why? Why them?"

"Fear affects us all, even me, even the queen. Our people have lost so much to humans... The fertility of their land and bodies, their magic. Some say bringing a human in as the heir is treason. Others say you need to arrive sooner. And that's what I want to warn you about."

"My leg," Jane said, a faint glimmer of understanding forming in her brain.

"That was Coira," Bridget said. "She tried to hurry things along a bit. And now that Beitris is gone, you have lost your protector."

"What do ye mean?"

"When Beitris stopped us from taking you as an infant, she created powerful spells of protection for you. All your life, she looked out for you. She was not one of us, but she held powerful magic." With a shake of her head, she added, "She can still help you from beyond, but her abilities are limited, so you need to create your own protection."

"From the prophecy? Are ye tellin' me tae not go along wi' yer own story?"

Bridget shook her head. "Oh, no, no. The prophecy will happen, but at the end of your natural life as promised. If Coira or anyone else takes you sooner, there will be disruptions in both human and Fey realms. This is what the Wise Women decreed."

Jane hesitated. This prophecy business was awfully complicated. So many rules and exceptions. "So I need tae protect myself. How do I do that?"

Her grandmother's mouth moved, but no sound emerged, and her image faded. Jane fought to hang on to the dream. "Come back! Tell me! Bridget!"

"Jane, Jane, wake up!" The voice sounded far away at first, and then she realized it was Rabbie. Opening her eyes, she saw a face full of loving concern. "It's a bad dream, wee dove. Here, put yer arms around me."

As she held him, she sobbed partly due to her grief, but also her frustration at not knowing how to use the magic she held inside.

CHAPTER 27

All things, dear child, that were wont to please thee
Are round thee here in beauty bright,
There's music in the cloudless air.
And the earth is teeming with living delight.

Thou'rt Awa
Lydia Falconer Fraser

*N*ora was maybe all of thirty but looked even younger, which didn't endear her to Jane. She wore a smart, crisp black dress that showed off a fine, erect figure. Everything about her oozed professionalism, but Jane preferred Beitris's warmth. The moment the women finished introducing themselves Nora said, "No one is Beitris. She was my first teacher, and my best teacher."

"Ye studied wi' her?" Jane softened a little at this news. Beitris hadn't told her this.

"Aye. And when ye prepare tae give birth, we will say a prayer and ask her tae join us," Nora said. "I dinna have Beitris's way about me, but I have delivered many bairns, and my mothers do well. When the child arrives, I promise ye will feel looked after."

"Thank you," Jane said, "that helps." It did, a little. That and Beitris's endorsement. It wasn't ideal, but it would have to do.

After the examination, Nora said, "It willnae be long, lass. I'll help ye prepare as best I can, but I wish you had contacted me sooner." Her firm tone made Jane take notice. The birth was imminent.

September brought with it heavy rains and strong winds. Jane didn't mind the weather. Her body burned hot with the pregnancy, and while Rabbie bundled up in a heavy coat, she accepted the chill as a gift.

The day came when she could no longer keep up with her work at the mill. Her back hurt, her sleep grew intermittent, and the baby was getting in the way.

"I'll be back," she told her looms, touching one of them affectionately as she prepared to leave, not knowing when she would return.

Her dreams increased in intensity. Sometimes she imagined holding Hugh in her arms, or watching him grow into a young man. Maybe he would have her reddish-blonde hair and Rabbie's eyes, filled with the same merriment and mischief.

Other times, her dreams frightened her. The fairies flew around her, trying to take Hugh. She batted them away and wake herself up in the process, drenched in sweat. Rabbie held her and comforted her, but often she lay awake for the rest of the night.

Bridget did not reappear, leaving Jane unclear about how to protect herself. One night she tried to pull moonbeams down to make fiber, but the moon did not respond. Without Beitris there to guard her, she felt helpless and afraid. Rabbie could help with day-to-day life, but he knew nothing of magic.

∾

As THE TIME for the birth drew near, the couple grew even closer. While she kept busy by making baby clothes, Rabbie built a cradle and a rocking chair, bringing the same love and skill he did to his work at the mill. The joy that came so naturally to him expanded even more, and it soothed her fears.

One night, a new moon kept the flat shrouded in darkness. After supper, Jane snuffed out the candles and curled up in Rabbie's arms.

If she lay still enough, she sensed Beitris hovering near, promising Jane she would never be alone again. She would never be that wee lass with no one to love her.

That's when a curious thing happened. She felt a strange sensation, a cracking inside, a widening in her heart. There was no pain. No, it was love, love streaming in like the flow of the burn down the hillside, leaving her breathless with its intensity. It stunned her that she could feel such depths of love, joy, and gratitude. Beitris was gone, but the love remained to see them through. She fell asleep more peaceful than any night since learning of the old woman's death.

The feeling did not last, however. That night, another dream ended with Rabbie shaking her awake yet again. This time she sensed something new, something she hadn't worried about before.

"They're going to take him, Rabbie. The fairies are goin' tae take our child from us as payment."

"Payment for what? Jane, ye're nae makin' any sense." He rose and lit a candle, giving the room a soft glow. He sat next to her and took her hand. "Ye're still shakin', lass. I'll put on some tea."

"No, please dinna leave me." She clung to him. "They want him. It was supposed tae be me."

He stroked her hair. "No one will take the bairn, I promise." Rabbie spoke in his most soothing voice. "It's the pregnancy talkin'. Ma says this happens."

Jane let out a yelp. "Oh, God!" she cried.

"What is it?" Rabbie asked, looking around. "I dinna see them. Are they here?"

The contraction made her struggle to catch her breath. "The bairn. It's...time. Get...Nora."

Rabbie jumped up. "Are ye sure?"

"Aye." She paused to drink in the tender look on his face, but the next contraction came right on top of the last. Gasping, she said, "Go noo."

Rabbie gave her a swift kiss, then ran out into the night.

Soon Nora entered, brisk and tidy as usual but wearing white and carrying a leather satchel with her supplies. Mrs. Stein followed close behind looking as if she wanted to break out into a dance. As soon as she saw Jane, she rushed over to give her a big, uncharacteristic hug. Rabbie trailed behind, looking lost and scared. Nora gave him instructions in a soft but firm voice. The fire needed feeding, and water and linens gathered. He went straight to work, approaching all of his assignments with a rare seriousness.

While Nora examined Jane, Mrs. Stein set a Bible, bread, and cheese under Jane's pillow. "May the Almighty keep all ill from this woman, an' be about her, an' bless her an' her bairn," she said. Then she lit a fir candle and carried it three times around the bed.

Listening to the prayer, Jane wondered what this was like for her own mother all those years ago. As her contractions built, she connected with the presence of generations of ancestors who'd given birth, who'd known these same pains and fear, encouraging her.

"Can I do this?" she asked aloud.

"Of course, lass," Nora said. "I'll be wi' ye the whole time."

Mrs. Stein, meanwhile, blathered away, telling tales of all her births. She spoke of long labors and profound pain, all with great enthusiasm and a gleam in her eye. "Every time I was sure

I widnae survive. Catherine was the worst. I really thought I was deid."

In spite of Jane's pain and Rabbie's fear, the couple managed a glance and an eyeroll. Rabbie covered his mouth to stifle a laugh.

"Mrs. Stein, wid ye do a favor for me?" Nora asked.

"Aye, whatever the lass needs." Mrs. Stein stood quickly, knocking over a chair in the process.

"I need more towels, more than what Jane has here. Could ye get some from yer hame?"

"Aye. I'll be back in twa shakes o' a lamb's tail." Mrs. Stein ran out the door, obviously eager to handle her task.

"There's no rush." Nora gave Jane a conspiratorial smile and a wink. "We'll be here for a while."

"Thank you," Jane whispered after Mrs. Stein left the flat.

Too soon the door opened again as Jane another contraction washed over her. The last thing she wanted was more of Mrs. Stein's well-meaning "help." This time, though, Jane heard a different voice.

"I'm here," she said.

"Ma." The word left her throat in a rush.

"Mr. Stein sent for me," Elizabeth said as she leaned over to kiss the top of Jane's head. "If ye'll have me, I'd like tae stay."

As a strong contraction came to an end, Jane gave a vigorous nod. "I'd like that."

"Makes me remember the day ye were born," Elizabeth said. "It was a happy day for us. Ye came out quiet like, an' ye looked like a wise old soul. Ye were sae tiny I feared I'd break you."

This was the first time Jane learned anything about her actual birth, and hearing the story now, a story of love rather than abandonment, calmed her anxiety.

"Breathe," Elizabeth said, leaning down again to kiss Jane's forehead. "Ye're in good hands, I hear."

Another contraction came, this one more intense than any

of the others so far. Jane rose from the bed and sat up to scream, only to see Rabbie hovering, shivering, in the corner.

"Go!" she yelled.

"Elizabeth?" Nora asked, motioning toward Rabbie.

"I'll take care o' the lad." To Jane she said, "I willnae be long. Be brave, lass." Then she took Rabbie's arm, guiding him outside. She returned briefly to grab the whisky and two glasses, one each for her and Rabbie. "We'll wet the wean's head," she announced to the other women.

A few minutes later she reappeared, sans Rabbie, but carrying the empty glasses. She returned to her place next to Jane.

"I sent him off tae stay wi' Mr. Stein," she said.

Jane's current contraction softened, and she let out a long, tired sigh. "Ma, what if...?"

"What, lass?" Elizabeth asked.

"What if I have troubles after the babe is born?"

Elizabeth laid a hand on Jane's forehead and stroked it. "I will help ye," she said. "I had no one tae help me when you were born, other than Beitris who understood. Promise me ye'll let me know if it gets hard. I mean, dinna try tae pretend you're awricht if ye're feelin' poorly."

Jane tried to answer, but another contraction came instead. The fire gave the room a toasty warmth, and sweat streamed down Jane's forehead as she exerted herself.

From a distance, Nora coaxed her to stay awake, but she drifted into a kind of delirium, rising above herself to survey the scene. Though the room was dimly lit, she saw everything. Mrs. Stein had returned, and both she and Elizabeth were bustling around, taking orders from Nora, who massaged oil onto Jane's belly. How beautiful she was! Oh, Rabbie told her so often, but she never quite believed him. From that first day in the glen when they spoke for the first time, she had loved him, and he her...but not until now did she see her own beauty.

"Come with us," Coira said. "Let go, Jane. Let go and be with us forever."

"NO!"

She slammed back into her body with a new level of determination. Surrounded by women who cared for her, knowing Rabbie waited nearby, she fought harder to bring wee Hugh into the world.

But yet again she drifted away into a strange vision. Somehow, she had already given birth. She wrapped her arms around her son as the fairies flew them through the air, taking them both away. When they landed they took her son from her arms and replaced him with another child, a fairy child, who was crying from hunger.

"Where's Hugh?" she cried. "Bring him back tae me!"

A voice that came from everywhere and nowhere said, "Feed our child." Jane couldn't tell if it was man or woman. "If our bairn lives, ye can have Hugh back."

Jane looked down at the fairy child and opened its blanket. A dozen snakes poured out. Screaming, she jumped up and shook them away, surrounded by the laughter of unseen fairies. Hugh cried for her, but his cries came from all directions. She called out to Rabbie, to warn him, but they were flying, flying away…

She returned to her body, confused. Was she home or did the Fey deliver her to their lair? She could not tell. The pain rose yet again, overcoming her. From a distance she heard, "One last push, lass!" but her body did not understand.

"I canna do this!" she cried.

"Ye can, I promise." Elizabeth sat on one side of Jane, with Mrs. Stein on the other. "The bairn is almost here," she said. "Soon ye will hold it in yer arms. Ye can do this."

"It might have been nice if ye'd been as good to yer daughter when she was a wee lass as you are noo," Ann sniffed.

"Shh," Nora said. "We're very close."

Then he was slipping out from her, slipping away. An odd

sensation filled her: despair. She had carried him for nine months, feeling his movements, knowing him in a way no one else could. Did other mothers feel as she did, that she was not gaining a child, but losing one?

"Ye're doin' great, lass," Mrs. Stein said, an uncharacteristic quivering fear in her voice.

Supported by these three women, all strong and brave in their own ways, Jane reached deep inside herself, looking for that place of knowing, that place all women who give birth somehow manage to find. And just as it seemed she would never find it, the infant made an "I'm ready" movement and slipped out of her effortlessly.

"Ahh!" Nora cried with pleasure. "Ye have a son, Miss Thorburn." The child let out a lusty cry. "Wi' strong lungs, I might add. Elizabeth, bring me some fresh water and towels."

"Bring him tae me," Jane said. Though exhausted, she couldn't wait a minute longer to meet her son.

"Let me clean him off first." Nora cooed at wee Hugh as she wiped away blood and fluids, revealing perfect, rosy cheeks and his mother's fair complexion.

"Are ye sure ye're ready?" Mrs. Stein asked softly. She peered anxiously over Nora's shoulder, gazing at Hugh. "I can take him for a minute or two while ye rest."

"Let me see him. I've been waitin' nine months," Jane said. "I promise you'll get a turn."

Mrs. Stein took Hugh from Nora and swayed as she held him. "He looks like my Hugh," she said proudly.

Mrs. Stein wasn't going to give the child up without a fight. Holding out her arms, Jane pushed past her exhaustion and spoke with greater authority. "Let me hold my son."

With a bit of a pout, Mrs. Stein handed the babe over to Jane, and all her misgivings dropped away in an instant.

"Well, hello there," she said, as she looked into those strange, wide eyes, so curious and alert. He was perfect. She had never felt so alive.

Elizabeth ran out and returned soon with Rabbie, who rushed to Jane's side. Jane handed the bairn to him, and Rabbie held him clumsily, giddy with joy. He spoke softly to the wee lad, who raised one tiny fist toward him, which he kissed. In the tenderest voice Jane had ever heard from him, he said, "Welcome tae the world, Hugh Robert Stein."

CHAPTER 28

For it is God, and God alone,
That on the judgment-day shall tell
Who shall find in Heaven a home,
And who for sin shall weep in Hell.

To the High Church of Glasgow on the Rash Judgment of Man
Ellen Johnston

*W*hile the new family celebrated the birth of their child, there was one problem. Baptism had to wait until Jane and Rabbie stood before the elders and received their punishment, but the baptism was necessary to keep the bairn safe from the Fey. She pushed for them to go to the kirk within wee Hugh's first week and would have done it the day of his birth if she could.

They wrapped the bairn, his name whispered only between the parents and grandparents, in a warm knitted blanket. The proud grandparents all accompanied the young couple, ready to stand by them. Elizabeth held the basket of offerings. Rather than take chances on encountering any tricksters along the way,

Rabbie arranged for Abi to wait outside the flat to receive the basket.

The kirk elders were assembled when they arrived. Rabbie and Jane sat in the chairs provided to them; the elders were perched on chairs a step above, so they looked down on the couple and the congregation. The minister stood at their level but was an imposing man who towered over Jane. She felt like a wee lass again, about to get in trouble for running out to play when she should have been helping her aunt and uncle. She looked down at the bairn who eyed her with big, trusting eyes.

"I will take care o' ye always," she whispered. "No one will take ye away from me."

The elders, who had been shuffling papers and whispering among themselves, motioned their readiness to begin.

"Miss Jane Thorburn and Mr. Robert Stein, ye are brought to the kirk sessions to address the charge of antemarital fornication," said the first elder, Rabbie's uncle Malcolm. "This sin has resulted in the birth of a bastard, which ye now wish tae baptize in the name of our Lord. What do ye have tae say for yerselves?"

Rabbie stood first. "I accept the lad as mine," he said. "Though we never wed in the kirk, we are committed tae one another."

The elders nodded. One asked, "Do ye understand this is a sin in the eyes of our Lord?"

"Aye," Jane said, standing now and holding Hugh. His trusting gaze gave her courage. "I humbly ask the kirk tae baptize the child, as we are the sinners, nae he. We are sairie for our sins and intend tae wed, but we ask that the child be baptized right away, lest he die wi' sin upon him because of our mistakes."

The Steins joined the young couple, with Jane's parents following closely behind.

"We will help the couple find their way back to the kirk

teachings," Mr. Stein said. "We will help care for the child, as he is much loved, and we will all turn toward the Lord."

"Aye," Elizabeth added. "I didna raise my daughter properly. I relied on my brother an' his wife, an' poor Jane didna have a proper upbringin'. I hold myself responsible, an' I promise tae help guide her in the future."

Robert added, "I turned away from my daughter when she was still a wee lass. Since then I have become a better man."

Only Jane noticed the buzzing of wings outside, but she ignored them. Keeping her eyes focused on the minister, she resolved to make sure Hugh was baptized. Inside, she quietly pleaded for the elders to hurry.

Outside, a group of the Fey, about ten in all, huddled together by one of the windows. "It's too late," Flora said. "I told you to leave it alone."

"Not yet," Coira said. "They haven't agreed to baptize the child. There's still a chance."

"But the Wise Women…"

"Stop it, Flora. What are they but a bunch of bent old trees? They don't understand our problems anymore."

The others mumbled among themselves. They were loyal to Coira, but Flora's disagreement with the plan created some level of confusion. Coira's mind was made up. Flora pressed her face against the glass to watch the proceedings, trying to think of some way to stop her sister's actions.

Inside, the grandparents returned to their seats, leaving Jane and Rabbie to stand in front of the congregation. Jane shivered as the couple's transgressions were outlined in front of everyone. The charges against them were serious in the eyes of the kirk. Yet to her, their lives were not sinful. She and Rabbie loved each other and intended to stay together.

She tuned out as much of the minister's words as possible but the worst of them made their way to her ears: "Sinner." "Whore." "Strumpet." She felt the stares of the congregation on her back. Too many of them loved to judge others in order to feel better about their own sins. They didn't see Rabbie in the same vein, no matter what the minister might say. In fact, he judged Rabbie less harshly as a man, saying things like, "He succumbed to temptation," or "he allowed himself to fall victim to Miss Thorburn's manipulations." Though his face was white with shame, Rabbie remained next to her, taking the punishment with her. His steadying hand found her arm. *Hurry, hurry.* She sensed the presence of the Fey outside, certain they were going to steal wee Hugh in order to force her to go with them.

The lecture eventually came to its overdue end. "Do ye repent o' yer sins?"

"Aye," Jane and Rabbie said in unison.

"An' do ye promise tae bring the lad up wi' the teachings o' the kirk?"

"Aye," they said again.

The elders pronounced the couple contrite and forgiven, allowing for the baptism to occur. "Bring the lad forward," the minister said.

Outside, one of the Fey said, "This is our last chance."

"We need them tae come outside," someone else said.

"He's not the one we want," Flora insisted. "It's still Jane."

"Of course we don't want him. But if we take him, we get her, too," Coira said. "I'm not waiting any longer. Let's lift the veil and put on a show for the congregation."

As Jane and Rabbie stepped forward, she strained to hear the goings-on outside. She handed Hugh to Rabbie, who was more than happy to hold his son for the ceremony. With closed eyes and one hand clutching her throat, she prayed for protection. What if her lies and sins were too much for the God of this kirk? Would He not intervene and allow the fairies to kidnap Hugh?

The minister began. "Baptism is the sacred beginning of a

new life in Christ. Robert Stein and Jane Thorburn, do you promise to nurture the child's faith?"

"We do," they said in unison.

He's an innocent lamb, she told herself. *Fair Folk, begone from this day an' leave us wi' our child.*

The minister was speaking, saying his own prayers for Hugh's health and safety, something about removing the sin of Eve. Jane appeared outwardly to listen, all while praying fervently to the queen who swore to allow her to live her appointed life, to Bridget, Beitris, angels or anyone else who could hear her and help.

"I'm going in," Coira said.

"You can't! We're not allowed in there!" Flora held on to Coira with every ounce of her strength.

"No one tells me what to do." With strong magic, Coira flicked her arm, and the kirk doors blew open. She flew right in and hovered next to Jane, letting the doors slam behind her. There were startled cries among the congregation, which had hitherto been silent.

"Look!" Someone yelled, pointing to the front of the sanctuary, where Coira revealed herself to all of them. She floated, defiant among cries and murmurs at the sight of a fairy, which most of them had never seen, or at least not since childhood.

In a commanding voice, Coira said, "Come now. Both of you, Jane and the bairn. Can't you see? These kirk elders only want to keep you small. The queen will give you a life of comfort." She started to reach toward Hugh.

The elders were stunned, though the minister acted, surprisingly, as if nothing odd was happening. Only Jane and Rabbie noticed the slight tremble of his hands as he sprinkled water on wee Hugh's head.

"Let's set fire to the place," said one of the Fey.

The minister began making a sign of the cross on Hugh's forehead, and the child quieted.

"No, Coira's inside. Let's break the windows and go in. If she can, we can."

The minister began to pray. "In the name of the Father, the Son, and the Holy Spirit…"

Jane concentrated as hard as she could on her prayers, begging, pleading for protection. This was the moment Bridget had warned her about, and she would give it her all.

And then it happened. The kirk flooded with dazzling white light, and Beitris floated before them, a transparent, shimmering apparition. Gone was the stoop and weakness of old age, and her face was that of a much younger woman.

The minister stopped and stared, slack-jawed, at Beitris's ghost.

"Please, hurry," Jane pleaded, this time aloud, not caring who heard. "They want tae take him from me."

Beitris reached forward to surround the minister and wee Hugh with her strong, sturdy arms, then glared defiantly at the queen's maid of honor. "Begone, Coira," she said. "He is not yers."

Coira stepped back as if burned, but she did not leave. "Back off, old woman. This has nothing to do with you."

Jane held her breath. Beitris seemed to hold hers, too, as though she had breath to hold in the afterlife. Rabbie trembled quietly beside her.

With Beitris giving him new strength, the minister said, "I now present Hugh Robert Stein." Taking wee Hugh from his father, he lifted the baby toward the heavens. Beitris rose with him, surrounding Hugh with her entire body.

With a final prayer, Hugh was protected from Coira and any other Fair Folk who deigned to steal him away.

"I'll be back for you," Coira said to Jane, "sooner than you think." With that, she retreated outside…to a waiting and displeased Queen Donella.

"How did you know to find us here?" Flora asked. Then she added, "You never leave the palace. Is it even safe?"

"I heard Jane's prayers and came right away," the queen replied. Turning to Coira, she said, "He is not ours to take."

"But..."

"Hush, child." The queen's anger softened, but only a bit. "I know you're trying to help. I know your actions come from love for me, but if you continue to act against my wishes, you will be banished from the palace and condemned to wander the earth with no magic. You will have to survive as a human. Do you understand?"

Coira opened her mouth to protest, her cheeks aflame with the public shaming, but Flora shushed her. The Fair Folk, mumbling to each other, now turned away from Coira, insisting they never wanted anything to do with her plan.

"Jane belongs to us," the queen continued. "She will come to us at the right time. Let the family have this day and this moment. I want Jane to have as much happiness as possible." She grew misty-eyed, and Flora and Coira gave each other a questioning look.

Inside the kirk, with Hugh baptized and the Fey silenced, Beitris vanished. The minister made his closing statements to end the service, leaving the Stein and Thorburn families to celebrate. Later, each of the congregants remembered fragments of what happened that day, but only enough to make it seem a trick of the mind.

CHAPTER 29

Though the poor man shares no great fame,
Save a toil-worn soul nigh riven;
Still, with the rich man he can claim
Both rest and peace in Heaven.

Lines on Behalf of the Boatbuilders and
Boilermakers of Great Britain and Ireland
Ellen Johnston

With the baptism behind them and the Fey no longer hanging like vultures over wee Hugh, Jane and Rabbie settled into their lives as new parents. Hugh was a chubby, happy baby who seldom cried, and Jane enjoyed each delicious day with her child, melting when he gave her his first smile.

Sometimes, at night, she still feared they would take him, but the queen appeared in her dreams to reassure her. She tried to conjure Beitris again to feel the comfort of her presence, but as time passed with no response, she wondered if the old woman had been allowed only one intervention in human affairs.

Thankfully, another ghost failed to call: the postpartum melancholy that had so affected her mother. Elizabeth visited frequently, giving Jane a questioning look, but Jane always shook her head. They dared not speak of it, but with each visit Elizabeth looked increasingly relieved.

When Rabbie came home from work each day, he happily played with his son. While Jane made supper, Rabbie cooed and kissed and cuddled his wee lad. She never worried that he would spend evenings at the pub, for he preferred spending time with his child.

Those were joyful times, and Jane walked around humming and singing, her heart filled with perpetual joy. She even managed to ignore Mrs. Stein's occasional digs about her parenting skills or housework. None of it mattered. She and Rabbie started to make plans for a kirk wedding.

Money was tight, though. The mill owners said profits were down, though they continued to have plenty of money for their lavish lifestyles while their employees barely scraped by, some succumbing to debt to keep their families fed. Even Rabbie, in such good standing there, was not immune, and his wages were cut. Without her income, Jane's nest egg, tended so carefully over the years, disappeared.

She cut expenses in every way possible that wouldn't sacrifice Hugh's health. Feeding him required her to feed herself, and while she tried to limit meat to Sundays when they ate at the Steins', sometimes she needed it more often. Rabbie never said a word about this, and even encouraged her to do whatever was necessary to keep herself and wee Hugh properly nourished.

"Come live wi' us," Mr. Stein said one Sunday. Since wee Hugh's birth, Mr. Stein took Jane aside during their visits and insist she accept money from him. No doubt Rabbie mentioned their plight. "We have room, and we'd see the bairn every day."

"What do ye think, Jane?" Rabbie looked ready to run straight home to pack. "It wid help a lot."

Mrs. Stein was noticeably silent, absorbed in her mending.

"Thank you for the kind offer, Mr. Stein, but Rabbie and I will figure this out." Two strong women in the same household wouldn't work for long. At night, though, after wee Hugh fell asleep at her breast, she softened, thinking that accepting some help was a good idea. Still, there must be some other way.

Only one way, in fact. She knew exactly what needed to be done.

Touching his fine hair, she said, "I hope ye forgive me, laddie. I dinna want tae leave ye, but we want a good life for you." He had already developed a wee personality, sweet and even-tempered like his da, and his smiles melted her. It would be difficult to return to work, but Hugh would need to learn soon enough that one must be resolute in this life, and sacrifices need to be made.

Later that week, Jane waited for Rabbie to come home from the mill, rehearsing her words. Hugh watched her with interest, babbling along as if having a conversation with her. She grinned at him.

"Ye're a smart lad," she said. "I widnae be surprised if ye understood every word I said." He responded with a giggle.

By now she learned Mrs. Stein's trick of making supper while holding a child. Already she lost the weight gained during pregnancy, and wee Hugh threatened to slide off her slim hips, but she tilted her hip high to make it work. He grew heavy, though, and she wondered how long she could carry him like this.

She made a simple supper, with some cheese, bread, and tea. At the last minute she decided to make a soup from leftover scraps. It wasn't much, but the soup dressed up the meal a little.

"That's my lad!" Rabbie said as he entered the flat. One would never know Rabbie had put in a fourteen-hour day. He always walked in cheerfully, but especially so since Hugh's birth. He took him from Jane, giving her a peck on the cheek as he did so. Then he lifted Hugh high into the air. "Look, Jane, wee Hugh is turned into a bird!"

Hugh shrieked with joy.

"Be careful, Rabbie."

Rabbie lowered Hugh and gave him a wink. "More o' that later, lad."

He sat at the table, keeping Hugh on his lap as Jane served the meal. He didn't say a word, but a rare shadow crossed his face.

"It's nae much," she said. "We're runnin' low for the week."

"It's a grand meal, my lad, because yer ma made it," he said to Hugh. Despite the cheer in his voice, his eyes conveyed stress and worry. To Jane, he said, "Dinna fret, wee dove. We've been through worse, and tomorrow I get my pay."

She gave him a bit more cheese from her own plate, and he frowned at her. "Ye need tae feed the lad. Eat yer share."

"I have enough," Jane said, though she didn't fool him. "But mebbe we should talk about me goin' back tae work. It wid help us, at least for a while."

Rabbie's face reddened with shame. Easygoing as he was, he wanted to provide for his family. "I like our lives the way they are noo," he said. "For ye tae work all day, then come home tae cook an' clean an' care for the bairn…it's too much."

"I have lots of energy, Rabbie. Hugh brings me sae much joy I feel like I can do anythin'. An' yer ma wid love tae take him durin' the day. She says so at least once every time we visit. This way they could help us, but we can keep our own place."

"She'll not raise him up the way ye like."

"He's such a good lad, I dinna think it matters. We could be the worst parents in the world, an' he'd still be awricht."

Rabbie gazed lovingly at Hugh, who slept snuggled into his father's chest, plump face peaceful with baby dreams. "Aye. He's as easy as they come."

"An' we'd have all Saturday evenin' an' Sunday with him as a family. Once he can walk we'll take him tae the glen every Sunday the way we used tae go."

She hadn't been to the glen in a long time, and she missed it. Taking Hugh there would be as much for her as for him, and besides, the child needed to spend time outdoors. No doubt Mrs. Stein worried he would catch his death of cold, but Jane wanted him to be a hardy lad, and to know the love of nature. Maybe Hugh would see the Fey, too. Though still traumatized by the events at Hugh's baptism, she was certain Bram and his lot wouldn't have been part of that.

Rabbie remained quiet, in deep contemplation. Then he sighed deeply and said, "I feel like a failure. There are more opportunities in England, for more money. If we went there, we could still take care o' him oursels. I know ye hate tae depend on my family."

"England shouldna be our first choice. I canna believe I'm saying this, but it wid break Mrs. Stein's heart tae do wi'oot her grandson. Mr. Stein, too, I reckon. Let me try tae work. If it disna work out, we can think about England." Neither of them talked about living with his parents.

After some more haggling, they planned to talk to Rabbie's parents at Sunday dinner, and Jane would return to work the next week. Though she hated the thought of leaving her child behind, Jane missed the clacking sounds of the looms and the feeling of accomplishment she got when she finished each piece.

As soon as they arrived at the Stein flat, Ann scooped wee Hugh into her arms, showering him with kisses. "Come, I have a new toy for ye, lad." Barely acknowledging Rabbie and Jane, she disappeared with the child.

"I dinna think we'll have a problem gettin' her tae keep him," Jane whispered. "Gettin' him back is another matter."

"Aye." Rabbie let out a merry laugh.

"It's good he has a big family," Jane said. That's when she

noticed the odd silence of the flat. "Where is everyone?" she asked.

"Off wi' friends," Rabbie said. "I asked tae see Ma an' Da alone today."

"What's all this?" Mr. Stein entered the room, his eyes narrowing at the whispered conversation.

She waited for Rabbie to say something, but he had grown mute. With a sigh, she said, "We were thinkin'..."

Mrs. Stein returned to the room with wee Hugh clutching a spinning top in his chubby hands and looking quite pleased with it.

"He's a bit young for that, Ma," Rabbie said with a chortle.

"Oh, I know, but he'll be old enough in the blink o' an eye, and I couldna help myself." She and wee Hugh exchanged adoring glances. The lad did love his grandma, and he managed to bring out her softer side. *We are doin' the right thing*, Jane thought.

"Jane and Rabbie have news for us," Mr. Stein said.

"Oh?" Mrs. Stein raised her eyebrows. Then she looked pointedly at Jane's belly. "Already?"

"No, no, no," Jane said with a nervous laugh.

"Then what?" The older woman's countenance grew darker with worry. Mrs. Stein most feared not having easy access to her grandson. "If this is news tae spoil the day, tell it another time."

Jane noticed that Mrs. Stein didn't ask if they were getting married. Or, if she did, she might consider that news to spoil the day. "I dinna think this is bad news," Jane said. "It's about wee Hugh. We were thinkin' mebbe I could go back tae the mill if you cared for him durin' the day." Her words came out in a rush, but it was better that way. Whatever Ann had to say about it, they'd get it over with that much sooner.

Mr. and Mrs. Stein gave each other the look of old married couples who have learned to read each other's thoughts and finish each other's sentences. Jane didn't know what to think, and Rabbie shifted his weight from one foot to the other.

Mrs. Stein's face burst into the biggest grin Jane had seen yet.

"Of course I'd love tae take the bairn! Though I still wish ye'd stay here wi' us. We have room, so there's no need for two rents." Shifting Hugh in her arms a bit, she added, "But either way, we get wee Hugh full-time."

This was the first indication that Mrs. Stein would welcome all of them in their home. Did she say it it because she knew Jane didn't want to move in? Jane shook her head. Any attempts to figure out Mrs. Stein brought on a headache.

Mr. Stein patted his wife's arm. "You wanted tae care for him, ye said so yersel. And this way Jane an' Rabbie have privacy."

"That's true." Mrs. Stein took wee Hugh in her arms and began to dance with him. "Well, let's give it a go."

When Jane and Rabbie returned home, both were jubilant. Only when she tried to go to sleep that night did Jane realize what she had done. *It's only until we get caught up*, she told herself. For the first time in her working life, the idea of going back to work lost some of its appeal. She had focused so much on what needed to be done that she didn't think about the difficulty of leaving her son early in the morning and returning late in the evening, when he would likely be asleep. She crept over to his cradle and watched him, so still and peaceful.

She steeled herself for the task at hand. They would all find a way together, the three of them.

～

THE FIRST MORNING, reality set in. She rose before five to dress wee Hugh. He remained asleep, limp as a doll, and she hated jostling him about. Once ready, Rabbie grabbed him and ran out the door to hurry to his parents', going to the mill from there, while Jane finished dressing herself. This included, per Nora's direction, binding her breasts with cabbage leaves to help dry up the milk. Nora provided a recipe for baby formula, made with cow's milk, water, and some honey. "A wet nurse is best," she said, "but this is less expensive." Jane would miss feeding her son, but was thankful for modern ways to solve the problem.

After reporting to the office, an unsmiling supervisor led her to her work area. He assigned her several looms right way, perhaps to weed her out if she failed to handle the load. There were few familiar faces left, though from across the room Catherine gave her a quick wave.

After the first hour or so, she found her stride. Once again she produced beautiful plaids at astonishing speed. And yet, though she loved seeing her work unfold, soon her back ached from standing so much, and her ankle felt sore and weak.

Mrs. Stein made a meal for their dinner break, and Jane got to hold wee Hugh for a few precious minutes, but not nearly enough. When she prepared to leave again, he clung to her, whimpering. She cried all the way back to the mill.

At the end of the first day, she and Rabbie walked to his parents' flat together, hand in hand. "How did it go?" he asked.

"I'm ready tae fall asleep the minute I get hame," she confessed. "And I miss wee Hugh."

Rabbie stopped and pulled her to him. "Ye dinna have tae do this. We can find another way."

She leaned into his chest. "It's the first day. Give me a week or so, an' I'll manage."

They stood there for a few minutes, holding each other. She could have fallen asleep in his embrace, but she imagined wee Hugh crying for his mother, so she pulled away and gave her head a little shake.

"Let's go play wi' the bairn, Rabbie."

When they got to Hugh's and Ann's, wee Hugh was still

awake, busy with young John as the two played with the spinning top. Neither lad looked up when Jane and Rabbie came through the door.

"Ah, there ye are," Mrs. Stein said, wiping her hands on her apron before hugging them. "He was no trouble at all. Didna cry once after yer break."

"That's...great. I'm glad." Jane wasn't glad at all, but she wanted to be. *What kind of ma wants her bairn tae suffer?* But no matter how hard she tried to convince herself, all she thought was, *couldn't he miss me a little?*

Rabbie squatted down to the floor. "What's this, lads?" he asked.

John handed Rabbie the top. "You do it," he said.

Hugh clapped his hands and made babbling sounds as if to say, "Yer turn, Da."

Jane watched, arms folded, as her rival—the top—wound its way along the floor to the delight and fascination of all three of the lads. Rabbie was as awestruck as John and Hugh.

"They've been like this ever since John came home from school," Mrs. Stein said. "Wee Hugh canna get enough of it. He tries tae do it himself, but he needs help."

"I'm glad he has his uncle tae teach him," Jane said as she gathered Hugh's things, her mind on preparing their supper

"Ye could stay," Mrs. Stein said gently. "We have enough for the lot o' ye tae eat. Come, sit, lass. Ye must be beat tae death, bein' on yer feet all day."

Exhausted and grateful, Jane let Mrs. Stein lead her over to a chair. It was well-cushioned and soft, and she sank into it with relief, overcome with the older woman's compassion. "I canna let ye do this, Mrs. Stein," she said. "I need tae get used tae things again."

"Dinna worry. Rest, an' I'll make supper."

"I should help," Jane said, raising herself up from the chair.

Mrs. Stein set a strong hand on Jane's shoulder. "Nae today. Another time."

Jane sat, though reluctantly. With Ann preparing food and Rabbie playing with the lads, she had nothing to do. Before she knew it, Rabbie was shaking her to wake up so they could eat. Catherine was helping her mother set out the plates. *When did she get here?* Groggy from the nap, Jane gave her cheeks a little slap.

"Where's wee Hugh?"

"He's asleep," Rabbie said. "All worn out from playin' wi' John."

Jane wanted to cry at this news.

"Come, eat." Rabbie took hold of her elbow and pressed her forward to the table, where everyone else sat. She wouldn't meet Mr. Stein's eyes and the disapproval she imagined there. She reminded herself that Mr. Stein had always been the kinder one, but that made her worry even more about what he might think.

As they ate, Jane didn't say a word. She needed food but couldn't swallow more than some soup and tea. *What have I done?*

The week continued, with more of the same. At the end, though, she held her first pay envelope in a long time. It wasn't much, but it made some of the sacrifice worthwhile. That's what she told herself, at least. And though eager for a Sunday off, her body started to adjust to the new schedule. She even found the energy to rock wee Hugh and sing to him at night. She caught Rabbie watching her, and they smiled at each other. Somehow, they would make this work.

CHAPTER 30

I searched the glen for peace and quiet
one bright summer's day with the sun in the sky
and before it moved west, the heavens turned black
and lightning and thunder sheltered the crags.

The Vain Search
Mary MacKellar

Jane looked forward to Saturdays, when the
workday ended at four o'clock, so she could see
wee Hugh before he fell asleep for the night. One
such Saturday, in late July, when she picked Hugh up after work,
he gave her a big, drooling grin. "Hugh, is that what I think
it is?"

He laughed as though she had told a funny joke.

"One tooth in, an' more about tae poke through," Mrs. Stein
said. "He's crawlin' sae fast I can hardly keep up wi' him, an'
even pullin' himself up sometimes."

"Well, aren't ye the big lad?" *Ye did this wi'oot me.* "Let's go

hame, shall we? We'll have lots o' fun!" She winced at the sound
of her forced gaiety.

Wee Hugh was having none of it. As she tried to pick him up,
he started to scream and reached for his grandmother. Mrs.
Stein gathered him in her arms, and he quieted right away.

"Go wi' yer ma," Mrs. Stein said.

He turned his head away, burrowing deeper into his grandmother, and let out a groan.

"Where's Rabbie?" Mrs. Stein asked, as if that would
somehow solve the problem.

Jane let out a frustrated sigh. "He had a meetin' at the mill
after work. He'll meet me at the flat later. Please, Hugh, let's go."

Mrs. Stein whispered a few words into Hugh's ear. He
refused to move at first, but after another minute or so, he went
to Jane with a resigned air. She wanted to hold him tightly
against her and never let him go, but she didn't want to
scare him.

"Thank you," she mouthed, then took him home, shoulders
slumped.

With each passing day, he fought her more. Sometimes she
gave in and left him there. On those nights, she cried herself to
sleep. She waited until she heard Rabbie's soft snores, not
wanting to bother him.

There was an odd irony in all of this. As a child, Jane never
stopped missing her own mother, and she swore to never turn
her back on her child. And yet, Hugh seemed to have turned his
back on her.

It wasn't working. None of it. Though she and Rabbie were
getting caught up financially, they still had little to show for
their efforts.

"Mebbe I was wrong about livin' wi' yer ma an' pa," she told
Rabbie. She still couldn't imagine her and Mrs. Stein living
under the same roof, especially if she quit her job. Besides,
who wanted to live in a home of people she still called Mr. and

Mrs.? But she had no other solutions. As much as she loved her work, she hated feeling constantly ripped away from her child.

"Are ye sure?" Rabbie's face twisted a little, trying to cover his delight with feigned concern.

Jane burst into tears. No, she wasn't sure, but she didn't know what else to do.

"Shh, lass, we dinna want tae upset the bairn. We'll manage. It willnae be as hard as ye think."

"I wish I could be more like you. Ye never worry about a thing."

"Wee dove, life is short. You an' Ma are gettin' along better. And Da loves ye like a daughter."

While all that was true, or as close to true as Rabbie ever got, life would be different under their roof. But once again, practicality won the day. "We'll tell them next Sunday."

The August heat had wrung them out all week at the mill. Wee Hugh bounced up and down with excitement as they walked down the path. Jane could barely carry him as it was, and his constant movement made it impossible.

"Rabbie, wid ye take him?" she asked.

He scooped wee Hugh into his arms and began making faces at the lad, who responded with peals of laughter.

Catherine greeted them at the door and immediately took Hugh from Rabbie's arms. In a few months she had transformed from a little girl into a young woman. Mill work had made her strong.

"I want tae play wi' him!" David yelled.

"I'm older, so I get him first," Catherine replied.

There followed a rather noisy argument. Wee Hugh, sensing they were fighting over him, laughed and clapped his hands. Catherine won this round, and David ran outside.

Mr. Stein looked up from his book, undisturbed by the chaos. He nodded to Jane and Rabbie. "Yer ma's workin' on dinner," he said before he disappeared into the pages of his book again.

Jane entered the kitchen, where Mrs. Stein bustled about. At this time of year there were fresh tomatoes and sweet corn, and Jane's mouth watered.

"I love summer," Mrs. Stein said as she moved from one pot to another, tasting, stirring, and sniffing. "It goes sae fast, though. The pumpkins and chicory are poppin' up, an' the weather will cool off soon."

"Please let me help," Jane said.

"Rest, Jane. Where's that wean? Catherine!"

"What is it?" Catherine came in holding wee Hugh.

"Let me have my grandchild." She whisked Hugh from Catherine's arms and covered him with kisses. "This is all the helper I need."

Mrs. Stein's efficiency made Jane feel completely inadequate. Though Jane had learned to cook and do housework with wee Hugh in tow, she never managed Mrs. Stein's level of finesse. Jane took a seat at the end of the table. Catherine joined her, chatting away about life at the mill. Jane would have loved to have this conversation in another time, but now she responded with little interest. How life had changed with a child of her own! She envied Catherine's energy.

The boys came inside, and everyone gathered at the table to give thanks for the fresh bounty before them. After that, multiple conversations broke out at once, but Jane didn't feel part of any of it. She ached to hold her child, who went from lap to lap, holding his arms out to the next person and pausing only briefly with Jane before moving on to Mr. Stein. There he seemed content to charm the stern old man.

Rabbie leaned over and squeezed her shoulder. "Should we tell them?" he asked.

"Mebbe wait a bit."

"Tell them what?" Ann never missed a thing. Mr. Stein, who

had been absorbed in making various sounds that wee Hugh imitated, looked up in surprise.

Jane gave Rabbie a little kick under the table, but he didn't seem to notice.

"Jane an' I were talkin', an' we've decided tae move in here."

Rabbie's family all burst out with shouts of joy. Even Mrs. Stein looked pleased. Wee Hugh, startled by the sudden noise, started to cry. Jane, herself a bit overwhelmed with the response, grabbed wee Hugh and took him outside to calm him. "Ye're fine, lad," she whispered, and began to sing one of his favorites to him, "Babbity Bowster":

> *Wha learned you to dance,*
> *You to dance, you to dance,*
> *Wha learned you to dance*
> *A country bumpkin brawly?*
> *My mither learned me when I was young,*
> *When I was young, when I was young,*
> *My mither learned me when I was young,*
> *The country bumpkin brawly.*

He quieted immediately with the song, and as she danced with him to the tune, little giggles bubbled up, the upset soon forgotten. *This is why I need tae be wi' him all the time*, she reminded herself.

Wee Hugh tugged at Jane to sing the tune again. She was happy to oblige, repeating it a second, then a third, and a fourth time. As she sang, he nestled his head in the crook of her neck. She longed for this special time with just the two of them when they were both awake. Her difficulties with Mrs. Stein were worth it to have more of these moments with him.

They went back inside, where the conversation had moved on. Rabbie looked at her thoughtfully, and she gave him a resigned smile. Wee Hugh held his arms out for his grandma, who took him from Jane without acknowledging her with even a look. Once again Mrs. Stein's mood had changed. Living with her was going to require some adjustment. No wonder Rabbie worked so hard to try to keep his mother happy.

After the meal came to a merciful end, Rabbie said to Jane, "Let's go walk a bit. No one will mind."

As they stepped outside, she said, "Oh, you'll be missed, but no one wid notice if I wisna there. It's like I dinna exist. My own babe thinks yer ma is his ma, too."

"Ah, it's nae that bad. Ma comes on strong, but she's just tryin' tae help. She knows how hard ye work, an' she wants ye tae rest a bit."

"I wish I could believe that. Some days, Rabbie Stein, I swear she wants me gone." She folded her arms and kicked up a cloud of summer's dust. She regretted being angry with Rabbie's mother, but Mrs. Stein was the easiest target for the big ball of feelings that rolled up in Jane's gut.

"Dinna say that, Jane. She means no harm, I swear. But if ye want, we can fetch Hugh an' head hame." Then Rabbie stopped and snapped his fingers. "Wait, I have another idea. A better idea."

"What's that?"

"Take a walk tae the glen."

"Hugh's too little tae go," Jane said. "We canna carry him all that way, an' I dinna want tae go back an' get the pram."

Rabbie gave her one of his tenderest looks. "Why not take a bit o' time on yer own?"

"What? I havena seen him all week." *What is wrong with Rabbie?*

"When we move in wi' Ma an' Da, ye'll see him all the time again." Rabbie took Jane's hand. "Ye've worked sae hard for him, an' for all of us, an' I see how tired an' sad ye get. A walk in the glen an' a visit tae the rock wid do ye good."

"I guess so." The idea sounded appealing, but still...

"Go for an hour or so, then come back. After, we'll go tae our place, the three of us, our own wee family. Then ye'll hold the wean for the rest o' the evenin'."

She didn't remind him that if they moved in with Ann and Hugh, it would never be just the three of them again. But she was weary deep in her bones, and a visit to the glen would bring her back, give her energy. Soon enough they would be able to take wee Hugh up there.

Putting on a hat to cover her fair complexion, she set out for the glen. She had been a mother for less than a year, but already a walk alone made her feel as though she was forgetting something. Her arms swung too freely, her stride was too light. Still, it was a beautiful afternoon to be out, though hotter than normal.

Along the way she wondered who she would see. Bram? Flora? *Please nae Coira*, she thought. Months after the baptism, she still feared Coira's interference.

That day the water of the burn held its breath, completely still. The waterfalls dwindled to a trickle. Where were the water sprites, whose job it was to keep it flowing? The birds were silent, with no song or rustling in the trees. No breeze relieved the sun's heat. There were no signs of any of the woodland Folk: no laughter, no merriment, no teasing, or chatter. She moved slowly through the silent world, noticing it but still continuing on her way, for she saw no reason not to.

She burst into tears at the sight of the rock, her rock, the sun dazzling it with light, shining like a welcoming beacon. Among the shelter of trees, relief came to her tired bones, and her inner joy returned.

Yet with that joy also came guilt: leaving her son. What kind of mother did that? How many other mothers walked away from their children on the only day they had with them?

One guilty thought led to another. She thought about Uncle Ewan and Aunt Kirstin. Time passed too quickly these days, and they had only seen Hugh once or twice since his birth. They were as besotted with him as his parents, making Jane feel even more guilty about not making regular visits. It would do them good to spend one Sunday away from Grandpa Hugh and Grandma Ann. And then they would visit her parents, whom she hadn't seen since the baptism. Yes, if she left the mill they stood a better chance of staying close to family.

The soft breeze and the trees did their work, slowly calming her jagged thoughts and quieting her mind. Exhaustion gave way to relaxation, her muscles softening as her mind grew more alert. Already she felt life returning to her body.

When the heat grew too intense, she rose and walked over to the burn. An offshoot formed a small pond, more stagnant than usual. She splashed her face in it, feeling the coolness of the water against her warm skin, taking away the beads of sweat that formed on her face. Then she took a good, long drink.

She didn't know the Fey were there, keeping a respectful distance. In the silence they watched her, holding their wings still, standing witness as Jane returned to her rock and ran a hand fondly along its flat surface. She didn't know that all of them were losing their powers, that on this day even the water sprites, with all their skills, couldn't keep the burn moving. She looked around once more, taking in this place, then set down the path for home. And as her tiny figure disappeared into the woods, silent tears fell down their faces.

CHAPTER 31

My God, is it an empty fight
To be eternally scratching truth from the earth?

Rudderless
Catriona Montgomery

*N*ewly resolute, Jane and Rabbie made their plans. She quit at the end of the week, and they would first visit her aunt and uncle, keeping the promise she made herself at the burn. Then she planned to spend a few weeks preparing to move in with Mr. and Mrs. Stein, allowing her to organize the move and sell the belongings they no longer needed, such as their table and dishes. Though she didn't say this out loud, it also allowed her more time with her son, so he would be less confused about who his mother really was.

Mrs. Stein argued for Jane to continue bringing wee Hugh over during the day so she could watch over him while Jane made her preparations. "He needs his routine," she advised.

"We'll be there soon enough," Jane answered, keeping her tone light and cheerful. Though determined to win Mrs. Stein over, she wasn't going to let the older woman have her way, not on this.

This time, she quit her job without ceremony or tears or regrets. The factory girls were cordial but not friendly with a woman who didn't live at Abi's. Their lives were very different, and Jane accepted this. It made it easier to walk away.

On Sunday morning, she rose excited about the prospect of seeing Uncle Ewan and Aunt Kirstin, but oddly groggy as well. She blamed her lack of energy on the mill, assuming she would feel better soon once she was rested.

As they prepared for their journey, Rabbie asked, "Are ye okay, lass? Ye're a bit flushed."

"Aye, just tired," she said, though she brought a hand up to one cheek, and it was hot to the touch.

"We can go another day." He gathered wee Hugh in his arms and whirled him around. Hugh giggled and raised his ruddy face to the sky.

Rabbie was right. With her schedule freer, they could go any Sunday. It didn't have to be today. And yet, something propelled her forward. "It's warm in the flat," she said. "I'll do better once I get outside, an' I've been lookin' forward tae our visit."

Since it was a fair day, they put wee Hugh in a pram and set out for a walk. Normally Jane could walk a couple of miles with ease, but she found herself struggling, with legs that moved like someone had loaded them with lead. She had to stop a few times to rest, with Rabbie continuing to question whether she should continue. Each time she answered with a curt nod.

When they arrived, the little house looked much different than the day Jane arrived to care for her sick aunt. The garden held abundant greens and tomatoes turning deep red. Flowers of all kinds showed off their many shapes, sizes, and colors, and bees were treating themselves to their nectar.

It cheered Jane to recall her aunt's recovery. She offered a prayer of thanks to Beitris and to the Fair Folk, and then, smiling, she accepted the arm Rabbie offered her as they walked into the house.

"Jane!" Uncle Ewan swooped Jane into his arms, giving her a bear hug that surprised her.

Aunt Kirstin went straight for wee Hugh, who was thrilled to let anyone lavish attention on him. The younger children surrounded her, and when she put Hugh down, they rushed him off to play in the front yard.

"I hope ye're hungry," Aunt Kirstin said. She showed no signs of the devastating illness that nearly cost her her life. "Let me look at ye, lass. Still too thin, I see. And ye look tired." She furrowed her brow and put a hand on Jane's forehead. "Ye're a bit warm."

"I'm fine," Jane said, though she had her doubts. "It's awfie hot today."

She helped Kirstin put the meal out: broth with bacon, potatoes, and oat cakes, along with fresh tomatoes from the garden, no doubt picked immediately before their arrival.

"He's smart," Aunt Kirstin observed as she peeked out the window to watch Hugh playing with the other children.

"I'm sorry I've been away sae much. Now that I'm done at the mill, mebbe we can come by more."

"That wid be lovely." Wiping her hands on her apron, Aunt Kirstin called the children in.

Dinner was a cacophony of conversations, with wee Hugh being passed from lap to lap. Uncle Ewan and Rabbie talked about work, and the children shared their hopes for the school year, all at high volume. Jane mostly listened, content to sit back and hear about their lives. She did belong to them; maybe not in the way she wanted, but she was family. They were glad to see her, and she basked in the warmth of that love.

After the two women cleaned up, they sat at the table together while the men sat in the living room. The children, with wee Hugh in tow, returned outdoors to play.

"It's a good life, in't it?" Kirstin asked as they surveyed the scene. "The bairns are growin' up. Wee Hugh will be off tae school before ye can think."

"Aye," Jane said. She squirmed in her chair, a deep fatigue descending into her bones.

"Are ye sure you're all right?" Kirstin asked.

"It's just that I left the mill this week, an' I'm tired."

"Are ye thinkin' o' having another?" Kirstin gave Jane an appraising look. "I get tired like that when I'm expectin'."

Jane trembled at the thought, but then reminded herself her monthlies came routinely since wee Hugh's birth. "Nae yet. Rabbie an' I want tae wait another year or two if we can, so we can save." They had talked about this only recently. Not so long ago she never expected to have one child, let alone two, and still no wedding scheduled. "He's such an easy baby, and Mrs. Stein is a big help."

Kirstin laughed. "I guess the two o' you are learnin' tae get along."

"We'll see what happens when we move in wi' her and Mr. Stein." Jane propped her elbows on the table and leaned her head into her hands. *Sae tired! Probably a summer cold.*

"Well, dinna wait too long. Hugh wid like a brother or sister, I'm sure."

"Aye, an' we want that for him. If he's older, he'll want tae help take care o' it."

As the day progressed, Jane grew too weary to continue, so they cut their visit short and made a promise to visit more often. Rabbie carried Hugh, who fell asleep with his head on his father's shoulder, while Jane leaned on the pram as she pushed it home. They would go back soon, she vowed. Hugh loved his cousins, and she wanted them all to grow up close.

The next morning, she ached all over, and sweat broke out on her forehead.

"I'll take Hugh tae his grandma's today," Rabbie said. "Ye can use some rest."

"That's nonsense," Jane said. "I'm perfectly capable o' carin' for my son. Plus, we're about tae move in wi' them, an' I have a lot tae do." But as she tried to dress, dizziness took over, and she fell back on the bed. Rabbie brought her bread and tea, but she had no desire to eat. After a few aborted attempts to eat and dress she said, "I reckon ye're right."

"We'll be fine," he said, though his stooped posture revealed his worry. "Rest, Jane, and ye'll be better in a few days."

The next day, though, her symptoms worsened. Headaches and abdominal pain joined her other symptoms. Rabbie left Hugh with his grandparents, lest the boy catch her ailment. He went to work at her insistence, but reluctantly.

"I'll fetch the doctor," he said.

"Nae yet. Give it another day or two, an' we'll see." Jane had always been able to shake off her ailments. All her life she worked while sick, and she saw no reason to stop now. Besides, doctors cost money, and they didn't need another expense right now.

By day five, though, delirium set in. Rabbie called for the doctor and fetched Elizabeth, who offered to stay with Jane during the day to help nurse her.

Jane drifted in and out of consciousness, dreaming that Flora came to her side to soothe her. "It's near time," Flora said. "Time to prepare."

"Prepare for what?" In the dream, Jane looked for wee Hugh, but couldn't find him. Panic choked her. "What have ye done wi' my lad?"

Flora now turned into multiple versions of herself, surrounding Jane. "The bairn will have his grandma. She will love and protect him."

"No." Jane tried to push her way through the group of Floras that surrounded her, but with wings extended they held firm.

Turning around and around, she looked for a way out but saw none. "It's a trick! Ye have my lad! Give him back!"

"Remember when we saved yer aunt?" Flora asked in multiple voices. "We saved her when human medicine could not."

Jane stopped her movement, stopped fighting. Her memory, long fuzzy on the details of what happened after Kirstin's illness, grew suddenly sharp. "Oh God. But my Hugh, my Rabbie... I thought we'd have more time. There must be somethin' we can do. I'll do whatever ye want, but nae yet. Please, please, nae yet!"

The dream dissolved, leaving her in that strange state between wakefulness and sleep. Her body burned with fever and every joint ached.

"Hugh?" she asked, her voice raspy.

"Hugh is bein' cared for, love," Elizabeth said. "Dinna fret, child, just get well."

Ma? As she hovered between waking and sleeping, she tried to figure out why she was there. She also tried to understand what Flora told her. *It was a dream,* she told herself. *In a few days I'll be right as rain.*

Once, Flora's hand took hers, and she yanked it away with a cry. They were coming closer, though. There were several of them drawing near, though she could not see them yet. *Why does it have tae be this way? Why?* But no one answered her. *It's nae real,* she told herself.

Jane tried to call out for her mother but the words remained unformed at her lips. There were other voices talking in hushed tones, trying to figure out what to do with her.

Elizabeth put a wet cloth on her forehead. "The doctor is here, lass."

She nodded, or at least thought she did. She heard the words "enteric fever." Typhoid. Maybe it wasn't fairy enchantment. If it had a name, then surely she could get well.

"Keep her comfortable," the doctor said. "Try tae make her eat and drink tae give her strength. If all goes well, the disease will run its course."

"How could this happen?" Rabbie asked. "Our Jane keeps a fine home. It's as clean as could be."

"She ate or drank something bad, I think. If ye ken where she might o' come up wi' it, we could make sure no one else gets sick."

"We both were goin' tae the mill every day, an' no one else is sick. On Sundays we go tae my folks', an' all are well."

Water. The burn that barely trickled. The silent afternoon where no birds sang, where even the Fey stayed away. The long drink on a hot day. Jane tried to say, *the burn got me, the water*, but her words came out in garbled moans, leaving Rabbie to pat her arm and say, "Rest, wee dove. Ye need yer strength."

The doctor treated her symptoms with herbs to settle her digestion and relieve her pain. "She's young, and she's a fighter. We will do our best for her."

Yet Jane withered away even further. With each passing day her tiny frame grew weaker and frailer. The Fey sent her dreams of sunshine and flowers, of sturdy health and life in the palace. She fought them, but the pull toward them grew ever stronger. It would be so lovely to work that loom again, to call down moonbeams and make designs purely for fun. And the food! She remembered the pastries the most—warm and sweet and fresh, the flavors of chocolate and vanilla and cinnamon coating her mouth. How lovely to not have to ration food to make the rent!

But Hugh. And Rabbie. When she thought of them, she pulled herself back into her sickbed, feeling her strength ebb a little more each time she did so. She needed to hold her son in her arms, to touch his fine hair, now dark like Rabbie's.

"Bring the bairn," the doctor advised. "Give her something tae fight for."

"Will he be safe?" Rabbie asked.

"He canna catch it from bein' in the room wi' her. Make sure she disna give him food or drink from her own hands. We need a miracle, Mr. Stein, or the child will never see his ma again."

From her bed Jane heard the conversation. *I'm nae ready tae die,* she tried to say. *Bring me wee Hugh, my best medicine.* Yet she could not reach him, could not make her way through the haze of semi-consciousness. She heard Rabbie cry, an uncharacteristic, whimpering moan. How dare the doctor scare him like that? *Fight harder,* she told herself. *It's nae time. It canna be time, nae yet. I'm too young.*

"Wee Hugh could catch it. I dinna care what the doctor says," Mrs. Stein said. "Rabbie, ye shouldna be here, either. I'll lose all o' ye by the time it's over!"

Let me hold him, Jane mouthed. Someone—she wasn't sure who—held a glass of water to her lips.

"It's time to let go," Flora said. "Your suffering will end once you join us. I promise, you'll watch wee Hugh grow up."

Hold him. Must hold him.

Flora tried to remind Jane of all the finery she would have. The beautiful clothes, the dancing, the comforts of the palace; she brought forth all the sweet memories of Jane's visit. The fabrics, the colors, the soft bed, the hot water...Jane would have a life of ease.

But no Rabbie, and no wee Hugh.

I never had any choices, nae really, Jane thought.

"It's not true," Flora said. "Your whole life was about choices. Alva. Rabbie. Hugh. Even if Coira hadn't kept you here, you would have stayed, because your heart belonged here all along."

But it's nae my choice tae leave sae young. All those times Jane planned to leave, all the adventures she longed for but never found, she never, ever wanted to leave her son. Fighting back yet again, Jane heard wee Hugh's cries. *He's here? Bring him tae me!* Yet the words only echoed in Jane's brain, never reaching her lips. She tried to protest. Mrs. Stein would leave her here alone if she had her way. *For once, Rabbie, stand up tae her.* All that came out of her, though, was a small cry.

"See what trouble ye're causin'?" Mrs. Stein glared at Jane.

Any goodwill between the two women had never been real. Jane understood that in this moment. They shared only a mutual love for Rabbie and wee Hugh.

When I get well, we willnae live wi' them, nae after this.

"Ma, dinna say that. Jane is the woman I love, an' when she gets well, we will spend the rest o' our lives together. Her, me, and wee Hugh. Now, let me have my lad."

"See what I mean? That lass caused ye tae disrespect yer own mother. Well, take the lad, then, kill him if ye must. When ye bury him, that'll be the end o' her, at least."

Rabbie, ignoring his mother, picked up his crying son and soothed him. "Yer ma needs yer special medicine," he said.

He did it! For once Rabbie did not bend to his mother's will. How Jane longed to thank him, to hold him in her arms and smother him with kisses. *I have tae find my way back.*

There were voices talking over each other. *Stop arguin',* she tried to say. *Ye'll upset wee Hugh.* She tried hard to hear, but found herself on a path leading her away. She caught a glimpse of what must be the Wise Women, sending her messages of comfort and peace. *The world of the Fey awaits,* they told her. *It is the fulfillment of the prophecy. We will help you in your sadness, but there is joy for you here.*

Then she knew the truth. There was never a good time to leave the world, but this was her time. *Let me hold him once more,* she said. *Please give me that, and then I will come.* They didn't have to honor her wish. She didn't even know if they had that kind of power. But she showed them all of her motherly love and pleaded for mercy.

"Rabbie," she whispered, and this time her words, though weak, were audible.

He sat on the bed next to her, his eyes filled with tears. "Ye're back."

"Hugh?" she asked, too weak to say more.

Rabbie curled up next to Jane on the bed so Hugh could crawl up and nestle against her. Quiet and solemn, understanding she was unwell, he patted her cheek with a chubby wee hand.

"The best medicine I could have," she said. It hurt to speak. "Water?"

A glass of water appeared, and Rabbie gave her a few sips. "Everyone's here," he said, "even yer da."

She looked around, startled. The arguing stopped. Mr. and Mrs. Stein were at the end of the bed, and next to Mrs. Stein stood Elizabeth. The two women were clutching each other. Then, to her right, she saw him.

There were new lines on his face, and his skin paler than normal. Both of them had lives determined in large part by the Fey. Both of them had experienced a mother's abandonment. Now, today, she would say goodbye to her son, and Robert Thorburn would say goodbye to his daughter. And soon wee Hugh would join her and her father as motherless children—the one thing she never wanted for him.

"Ye did good, lass," he said, nodding at wee Hugh.

"Aye." She wanted to say, "I forgive ye," but she could only look at him. He took her hand in his and gave it a kiss with rough lips. She noticed how stiff his movements were from all those years in the mines, this man whose mother was fairy royalty. How tough he'd had to be to survive!

Wee Hugh squirmed in her arms, and she held him tighter. Out of the corner of her eye she saw Flora waiting for her. Jane held up a finger to say, *just a little longer*.

"Back off," her father barked as he tried to shoo Flora away. "Away wi' ye noo!"

The room went quiet. Even Jane, in her weakened state,

cocked her head to one side in disbelief. Had she heard him right?

"Ye see her, too?" Rabbie asked.

"Aye. The damn Fey were around her from the beginnin'." Jane's father coughed and wiped his mouth with a handkerchief. "Never a moment's peace wi' them. Jane's ma never saw them, but they were always up tae no good."

Jane wanted to laugh, though she lacked the strength to do so. All this time, and didn't know her father saw them. She knew then that she had one more thing to do. As when she birthed wee Hugh, she dug down deeper into herself. "I have tae tell ye..."

"Shh, Jane, rest." Rabbie laid his hand on her shoulder.

"It's a tale. For you. For Da. It's important."

Then, in a halting voice, not much more than a whisper, she told the story of John Thorburn and Bridget. Of a prophecy. Of her visit to the land of the Fair Folk when Aunt Kirstin was ill. Though she struggled with the words, she watched as her father stood a little straighter, a look of astonished understanding crossing his face.

Flora grew closer, close enough to hold out a hand. Jane shivered, cold now as her life force ebbed.

"Say what you need to," Flora said. "We're running out of time."

Jane took Rabbie's hand. "Take good care o' our lad," she said. "I'll look out for him from the land of the Fair Folk, God willin'."

"Dinna go, Jane," he said. "Ye can get well. You're past the worst of it. Hang on a while longer."

"I canna stay, Rabbie. Our lad has a good life ahead. An' ye have a good life ahead, too. I'll miss ye, though, an' I'll love you forever and ever. But ye'll love another one day." She was as certain of this as anything. Perhaps she had gained a bit of Bridget's Sight.

"Never," he said. "I could love only you."

Jane shook her head, impatient now. "Dinna argue wi' me, Rabbie Stein. I was lucky tae love ye. The best gift ye could give me is tae love again. Let wee Hugh forget me. Promise me, though: when ye fall in love again, tell wee Hugh she's his ma so he never feels left behind. And never, ever think my life was a tragedy." She kissed wee Hugh again. "Here's proof. Now, take the lad away before I lose my nerve."

He did so, and Rabbie leaned her back on the bed. "When ye go tae the fairies, promise me ye'll find love there, too. Take all the love we had here an' pass it on. Promise."

She squeezed his hand one more time. *Dear Rabbie. Dear Hugh.*

With a deep sigh of contentment, she closed her eyes. The sensation in her back from long ago returned, forcing her to sit up as the room filled with light. There was a gasp from the people who loved her, who stayed by her side at the end. She saw them all, loving them, forgiving them, seeing them with compassion. Their lives, wounds, difficulties, wrong turns, and hard work were etched on their bodies and spirits. Like all humans, they had done their best but sometimes fell short. Their humanity touched her as she prepared to let go.

Rabbie, smiling through tears, holding wee Hugh. Her son clapped in wonder as her wings unfurled and she rose into the air. She made a few gentle turns as her body grew light and free. Then she blew them all a kiss and was gone.

CHAPTER 32

I am gone, gone far, with the fairies roaming,
  You may ask of me where the herons are
In the open marsh when the snipe are homing,
  Or when no moon lights nor a single star.
On stormy nights when the streams are foaming
  And a hint may come of my haunts afar,
With the reeds my floor and my roof the gloaming,
  But I come no more to Ballynar.

The Fairy Child
Lord Dunsany

ane's vision was blurred, and when rubbing her
eyes didn't help, she blinked until her eyes returned
to sharp focus. She found herself in an unfamiliar
place, with a soft bed colorful quilts to keep her warm. The
fever and pain were gone. *Thank God. I am well.*

"Rabbie? Hugh?"

No one answered.

A sick feeling rose in her throat. She was no longer in the flat in Alva.

"Rabbie?" she called again, this time more frantic.

"Ah, you're awake." Flora entered the room, holding a cup of tea. "Welcome."

Clutching the blankets to her chest to ward off these strange events, Jane turned away from Flora and the waiting tea. "What have ye done? Where am I? Where's Rabbie? And Hugh?"

Flora brought a mirror to Jane. "Go to him," she said.

"But how do I do that?"

"Look inside."

Jane peered into the mirror, skeptical. At first, she saw only her own face, and the healthy skin and bright eyes that made no sense to her after being so ill. After a few moments, her image began to swirl in the glass, disappearing. And then there she was, in wee Hugh's dream. He reached one chubby hand toward her face and grinned, and she cooed and sang to him, rejoicing in the feeling of his plump flesh against hers.

Then he woke, and Jane returned abruptly back to the room with Flora, heart pounding.

"Where did he go? Whit's goin' on?" Flora smiled at her, which infuriated Jane even more. Whatever this game was, it needed to end. "Take me tae him!"

"You live in different worlds now, Jane. You have crossed over and ended yer human life."

"I dinna understand." Her head hurt. *I canna be deid if I hurt, can I?* "You're alive, so I must be."

Flora took a seat at the edge of the bed. Jane shrank back warily, but Flora seemed unfazed. "Humans with Fey blood can live again among us if we catch you in time. We've been watching you for days to make sure we could gather yer spirit at the first possible moment."

"Rabbie could see the fairies. I'm sure wee Hugh can, too. Will they see me?"

"Sadly, no, not in their daily life. But you can visit in your dreams and theirs. Hugh will not remember you as his ma, but he will know you as a guardian angel. You can tell him everything you want him to know. You can guide him as any mother would."

"So ye're sayin' I deid? But I live again as a fairy?"

"Fair Folk," Flora corrected. "Or Fey. Only the humans refer to us with that word. But yes. I know it's not perfect, but your human body could not recover from the fever. Since you carry Fair blood, we could bring you to us. We need you, and this way you can still be part of Hugh's life."

Jane rubbed her arms. Something about Flora's words calmed her, though her brain still struggled to comprehend what had happened. And Hugh was an infant without his mother. How would any of this be all right? Living in another world, able to see him but not touch him? Torturous. It would be better off to have died and not known.

As if hearing her thoughts, Flora said, "We will lighten your heart, I promise. It will take time, but the queen, the Wise Women, and I will help. Rabbie will care for wee Hugh, and Mr. and Mrs. Stein will raise him in their home. Rabbie will mairie one day, and his wife will love wee Hugh as her own. He will be in good hands."

"I'm glad. Still, though." She put her hand to her heart. "How can I do this? How can I watch him from a distance? How can I bear it that he willnae remember me?"

Flora patted Jane's shoulder. "It won't be easy, lass. There will be times you mourn him, even when you enter his dreams —often *because* you enter his dreams. But you must remember, your human time came to its natural end. There was nothing to be done."

"It's nae enough." Jane's shoulders slumped. It felt so odd, to have a strong, healthy body again, to have a whole new life, alongside the emptiness of a life without her son and Rabbie.

"Prophecy is sometimes harsh," Flora said. "But it is time for you to greet your destiny."

"Wait," Jane said. "Coira…"

"She'll not trouble you anymore, lass. The queen has sent her away, and the Wise Women have taken her powers."

"What happened?"

Shaking her head sadly, Flora said, "My sister cared too much. It's best if that's all I say about it."

Even now, with Jane a part of the Fey, she couldn't get all the answers she wanted. At some point she would demand them, but not now. There were too many other aspects of palace life to adjust to. She would miss Coira, though. Anything Coira did, she did from love. Twisted love, perhaps, but love nonetheless.

"She'll be all right, I promise," Flora said. She rose and reached out a hand, and Jane took it reluctantly. Together, they walked toward the queen's reception room.

As they stood at the door, Jane said, "Wait."

"What is it?" Flora asked.

In that moment Jane understood. Yes, she was a factory girl, a proud weaver. A friend to Skye, Maisie, and Wynda. A lover to Rabbie. Mother to wee Hugh. But there was more. She remembered her aunt's struggles to have a child, and she felt this struggle in Flora now. She would help Flora the way she helped Aunt Kirstin and then help the other barren women bear children. This was her magic, and this was why they needed her so much.

Turning to Flora, she reached out and placed a hand on Flora's belly. Flora did not flinch but nodded in encouragement and took Jane's hand. Together they walked into the queen's quarters, where Donella wore her finest white shimmering gown. She looked younger and more vibrant now that her heir had come.

"At last," she said, tears in her eyes. "My daughter is here. And I have a surprise for you."

"A surprise? What?"

A dimpled face with mischievous eyes peeked out from behind Queen Donella's skirts.

"Leslie?" Jane was incredulous. "Does she...? Is she...?"

"One of us?" the queen ran a hand through Leslie's blonde curls. "Aye, she carries Fey blood like you do. Not as much, but enough."

Leslie ran into Jane's arms, her body magically restored. "I'm sae glad tae see ye again," she said. "It's nice here, an' I dinna have tae work anymore. But I'm glad tae have a friend here."

"Aye, me, too."

NEITHER THE FAIR FOLK nor Jane have revealed much about what happened when Jane took her place as the heir to the throne. They have shared some details, however:

Queen Donella lived for many years. With her heir at her side, she recovered from her ailments and continued to lead, teaching Jane all about the culture of the Fey. Jane remained a diligent student and performed her duties flawlessly, accepting Donella as her true mother. The Fey grew to love Jane, and she loved them in return. She often spent part of her day at a hand-loom, joyfully weaving her own designs.

Jane's presence didn't change the problems created by the Industrial Age, but it did remind the Fair Folk to believe in magic again. The water sprites got the burn flowing again, farmers returned to magic to grow crops, and best of all, the women started conceiving and carrying babies to term. That included Flora, who named her first child after Jane.

They were a long way away from the old days, as the animals remain unable to speak to this day, and nary a dragon in sight, but the Fey welcomed the new, positive changes.

One day Jane would produce heirs to the throne, but it

would take her a long time to stop missing Rabbie. Douglas was an attentive and patient friend, but he would have to wait until the worst of her grief passed.

Still, one wound never healed, the wound of leaving her firstborn, her beautiful wee Hugh. She visited his dreams frequently and, as she watched him grow into a lively, intelligent young man, she understood that in life and death, sometimes we must accept what we are given. *At least*, she thought, *I get tae watch over him for the rest of his life.*

The Fey work in their own ways and in their own time. If we believe enough in their magic and respect their ways, perhaps one day they will reveal the rest of the story.

CHAPTER 33

With a love that knows no distance, though shadows intervene,
Leading back the weary wanderer through the meadows fair
and green,
With a love that lifts her rainbow, though the skies be dark
above—
Sunshine from a sphere immortal, born of heaven—
A mother's love.

Alpine Spring
Wallace Bruce

            he steamship *Ethiopia*, built a few years before his birth, entered New York Harbor. Glasgow showed Hugh Stein how the bigness and wildness of a city, but the sight before him now dwarfed any previous experience. The journey took ten days, and he hadn't slept for the last two of them. Steerage was crowded and it stank, but none of that bothered him. All his life he'd felt led somehow to this moment, and he expected a magnificent future. He carried with him a suitcase with his clothes. At the last moment he tucked one more item in there, a book of Robert Burns poetry given to him by his father, battered and worn. "It will bring ye luck," he'd said. "Treasure it always."

The morning light shone on her, Lady Liberty, raising her torch above to welcome all new arrivals. When he saw her, the lady built and delivered by the French thirteen years before, he knew he had made the right decision.

He had grown up wandering the Ochils, playing near a favorite rock in Alva Glen, and no matter how far from his homeland he went, he would never know anything as beautiful.

His parents, Rabbie and Maggie, moved to England for work when wee Hugh was six. He lived with his grandparents from then on, since Alva was his home, but visited his parents often.

Grandma Ann had died five years before, leaving him alone with his aging grandfather. He planned to stay for Grandpa Hugh's sake, but the old man encouraged him to find his way elsewhere. "The mills here are dyin'," he said. "Go noo while ye're young. Life is short, and sometimes dreams die wi' people." When he said the words, he grew misty-eyed, like he'd seen a ghost in the distance.

"What is it?" Hugh asked. "What do ye mean?"

Grandpa Hugh opened his mouth to speak, then thought better of it and gave young Hugh a wink. "Dinna worry about the ramblin's of an old man. Just go an' be happy."

Still, he hesitated to leave. It was the dream that made him decide for sure. He'd had dreams his whole life, where fairies surrounded him in play. One fairy in particular captivated him more than the others, with a special kind of light. He felt as if he knew her. She didn't trick him like the others sometimes did. Instead, she sang lullabies to him in the night and told him about the long and happy life ahead of him. One night she pointed to a ship and said his future was in America. He woke thinking, *why not?*

He made his plans, and the night before he departed, his

favorite fairy visited him and gave him a special message, one he remembered now as the ship docked at Ellis Island.

A job awaited in Maine. Once processed, another long journey lay ahead, but he would be on American soil and off the crowded ship where so many got sick along the way. Blessed with good health and a sunny disposition, he managed the trip with ease, and he fully intended to sail through immigration. Hugh Stein had that kind of confidence.

An imposing building stood before him, the building he had to pass through to be able to stay. He patted his packet of money —more than the amount he needed, just to be sure.

Once in line, they asked him questions. They checked his eyes for infection. They poked and prodded him but found nothing to cause him to be detained. When they asked him his name, he announced it exactly as she had whispered it to him in the dream:

"I am Hugh Thorburn Stein." He didn't know where the name came from, but he liked the ring of it.

AUTHOR'S NOTE

In 2014, I visited Scotland for the first time. Before I went on the trip, I called my mother. "Is there anything you want me to see on your behalf?" I asked.

"I'd like to know where my great-grandfather was buried," she said. She gave me his son Hugh Stein's date and place of birth.

Within a day, through the miracle of ScotlandsPeople and other Internet sites, I found Robert Stein's grave and Hugh Stein's birth record. That's when I discovered something else: Hugh's mother was not Maggie Stein as believed, but someone named Jane Thorburn. I also discovered Jane's death record, dated ten months after Hugh was born. Who was this woman I'd never heard of?

First I thought I got it wrong somehow. Yet the record was clear enough: I knew his birthdate and place of birth, and both his parents had signed it. There were no other Hugh Steins born that day in Alva.

When I called Mom and asked the question, and she paused before she answered. Then she said, "He called himself Hugh Thorburn Stein, but we thought he made it up!" My great-grandfather told tall tales, often playing fast and loose with facts, so this was not an unlikely conclusion. However, it confirmed for me that I had, indeed, found the right person.

Little is known of Jane's actual life. She left her family as a child, she worked as a weaver in Alva, and she died at age twenty-five from typhoid, but that's about all we know. In this story, I have attempted to bring her back into the family lore. Like my great-grandfather, I was willing and happy to embellish the story. I can only hope that somehow, despite the fantastical nature of my tale, there were things I got right. Maybe she guided me in my efforts. I hope one day she tells me what happens next.

A NOTE ABOUT THE POETRY

When I was researching this book, I discovered a 19th-century Scottish poet, Ellen Johnston, who published under the name "Factory Girl." Johnston worked in the mills, had a child out of wedlock, and disappeared at some point, though it's believed she died in a poorhouse. Ellen's life and spirited poetry was part of the inspiration for this story.

One research thread leads to another, and along the way I found many female Scottish poets whose work is excerpted at the beginnings of these chapters. It was stunning to me to find so many! All the poetry included in this book is by Scottish poets, and female poets wherever possible, though I have also included male appropriates where appropriate.

GLOSSARY

- Afore – before
- Awa' - away
- Awfie – awful
- Bahoochie – butt, bottom
- Bairn – baby
- Burn – large stream or small river
- Canna – can't
- Coulda – could have
- Couldna – couldn't
- Deid – dead
- Didna – didn't
- Dinna – don't
- Dinner – the midday meal, lunchtime
- Disna – doesn't
- Dwam – a swoon or a faint
- Fae – from
- Gie – give
- Gonnae – going to
- Hinna – haven't
- Howdiewife – midwife
- Intae – into
- Isnae – isn't
- Mairie – get married
- Mairiet – married
- Nae – not
- Naethin' - nothing

- Naw - no
- Noo – now
- Sae – so
- Sairie – sorry
- Shouldna – should not
- Slippit' awa – slipped away, died
- Supper (or tea) – a light evening meal
- Tae – to
- Wha kens? – who knows?
- Whit – what
- Willnae – will not
- Wisna – wasn't
- Widnae – wouldn't
- Vera - very

ACKNOWLEDGEMENTS

I didn't set out to write a fantasy tale, but my job as a writer is to let the story be what it needs to be. When the Fey crept in and wouldn't leave, I had no choice but to let them stay, and my life is all the richer for it. I now can't imagine my life going forward without them.

Thank you to my mother, Lewellyn Pulliam, for a telephone conversation we had in 2014 that led to this story, which I tell in more detail at the end of this book. It's not the first time a conversation with Mom led to a book (the seed for **When a Grandchild Dies** was also planted this way).

Scotland is a beautiful country, and I have treasured my visits there. I was able to review old kirk sessions records, seeing the handwriting of my ancestors, which was profoundly moving for me. In Glasgow I saw examples of tenements where whole families often squeezed into a single room, and I spoke with a man who grew up in one, without electricity! I am grateful to everyone who was so friendly and kind, who introduced me to haggis and taught me how to drink whisky (and to spell it the Scottish way!).

My incredible developmental editor, Rosie McCaffrey, patiently worked with me on this project through many revisions as I grappled with a difficult story and an unfamiliar genre. I had to shelve this book for a few years, and I'm glad she stuck with me. I chose Rosie in part because she is Scottish. Though I have traveled to Scotland a few times, I am an American, and I did my best to capture Scotland in an authentic way. Any errors in that regard are mine.

Thanks also to Esther White, my copyeditor. When I needed another pair of eyes to look at the manuscript, she jumped at the chance. I am inspired by her warm, sparkly energy. She is, indeed, the "Word Magician" she bills herself to be!

Lynne Hansen: what can I say? She is one of the most ebullient, joyful, and alive people I have ever known. She also happens to be an incredible cover designer. Though she works primarily with horror, I trust Lynne's detailed eye and thoughtful approach implicitly.

And finally, thanks to my husband, Henry Feldman. Our life together is truly magical.

ABOUT THE AUTHOR

Nadine Feldman writes contemporary and historical women's fiction, including *What She Knew, The Foreign Language of Friends*, and *When a Grandchild Dies: What to Do, What to Say, How to Cope*.

When not writing, Nadine enjoys gardening, cooking, knitting, and being a grandma.

Nadine lives in the beautiful Hudson Valley, New York, with her husband Henry, where they spend a great deal of time talking about their imaginary friends.

Member, Women's Fiction Writers Association and
Independent Book Publishers Association

f facebook.com/nfeldmanauthor
𝕐 twitter.com/author_nadine
⊙ instagram.com/nadine.feldman.author
a amazon.com/Nadine-Galinsky-Feldman/e/B002Q75JQA

9 781736 806906